THE WILDER HOUSE

I hope you enjoy the story,

Mark Lamel

THE WEBER HOUSE

MARK LANCE

atmosphere press

© 2022 Mark Lance

Published by Atmosphere Press

Cover design by Kevin Stone and Kevin O'Connell

No part of this book may be reproduced without permission from the author except in brief quotations and in reviews. This is a work of fiction, and any resemblance to real places, persons, or events is entirely coincidental.

atmospherepress.com

For Alissa Nicole

CHAPTER ONE

NOVEMBER 23, 1996

"A haunted house," Nicole Kelly muttered, slowly shaking her head. She stared into the dark forest as it sped past the car's window. "That's just great."

Her mother kept her eyes on the winding road. "You're not superstitious, are you?"

It was Saturday, past dusk. Nicole wasn't superstitious but she was tired. And hungry. They were in Maine, traveling north on Mountain Highway and just a few miles, her mother promised, from someplace called Elk River. After driving all day, they were finally going to reunite with Nicole's father at their new home.

Nicole knew that Elk River was on the shore of the Atlantic Ocean and they were now very close to the coast. Gulls soared overhead and between the mountains, there were glimpses of the sea. Gray clouds hurried east and snow was falling. They drove alongside a rocky, sloping pasture where a black and white cow slowly chewed her cud. A calf looked up and tilted its head. Then a steep grade surrounded by forest. Nicole slumped down behind a veil of brown hair and thought about how much had happened in the last six months.

The trouble began in May, near the end of seventh grade.

Nicole's family was living in New Jersey. She was looking forward to the spring soccer season and her last year in middle school. She thought of her closest friends, Alexandra, Cheryl and Sue, and a couple of cute boys. *Alexandra said that Brian liked me*, Nicole remembered with a tiny smile. *I wonder what they're doing right now?* She glanced at the gloom outside and her frown returned. *Getting ready to go out, probably.*

Then her father accepted a teaching job at some college in Maine. Suddenly, he was gone. He returned most weekends but mainly, Nicole and her mother were left alone to prepare for the move. She had to look at a map to see where Elk River, Maine, was. *It's practically in Canada.*

Instead of a vacation, the summer was a blur of endless cleaning and open houses, with total strangers walking around the house at all hours. One time, Nicole remembered, some little kid started picking up and examining the things on her dresser! She thought back to the start of eighth grade with the move hanging over her head like a dark cloud. Studying became difficult and her grades slipped. *What was the point?*

The soccer season was a success but there was always the knowledge that it would be the last with her friends. Nicole leaned back in her seat and closed her eyes. *Did anybody ask me if I wanted to move?*

The house was sold at the end of October. The dreaded day arrived just as everyone else was preparing for the holidays.

They passed a farmhouse with dark shingles. An old truck without wheels was on cement blocks in the front yard.

The night before last Alexandra threw a going-away party, but it already seemed like a long time ago. She thought of the big stuffed polar bear Sue gave her, the photo scrapbook of parties and school that Cheryl and Alexandra made. There were hugs, tears and promises to write, call and meet online, if possible.

Friday morning, right after the moving van left, Nicole and

her mother headed for the George Washington Bridge. It was the weekend before Thanksgiving but Nicole didn't feel thankful. For one thing, it was cold and she was a summer person. In New Jersey, it was possible to believe that it was still autumn. Just a few weeks ago, the trees were covered with brilliantly colored leaves. But here, it looked as if it was already the dead of winter. Nicole stared into a forest of evergreens, *Do they even have any trees with leaves here?*

Eighth grade is supposed to be fun. A whole year of being in the oldest class with the younger kids looking up to me and my friends. Now I gotta start all over again not even knowing anybody.

Plus, a haunted house. That ought to help.

"We should be there soon," her mother said after ten more minutes of silence. They rounded a bend and, far below, at the bottom of the mountain, Nicole saw the lights of a small town.

"We're here," her mother said cheerfully. "We're in Elk River."

"It doesn't look like much of a city."

"Let's see."

Nicole looked down on the town and saw that it was shaped roughly like a triangle bordered by mountains on the left and water on the others. Huge rocks were piled along most of the shoreline. There were dozens of boats at the docks and out in the dark water.

They came to an intersection. Her mother slowed down and turned right. The road wound back and forth down the side of the mountain before finally leveling off. Gray smoke rose from the chimneys of the few houses they passed. The car bumped over a railroad track and Nicole's eyes followed the rails. They seemed to end at a large dark building near the water. Nicole turned back to the road and saw a red, white and blue sign that read, "Welcome to Elk River—a Town on the Move."

Yeah, right.

"We're on Main Street," her mother said, glancing at a rusted street sign, "in Maine, get it?"

"Good one, Mom."

"Let's see if we can find someplace to eat. We can ask for directions there, too."

They passed houses, stores, a movie theatre with an unlit marquee, an empty park, a gas station, a funeral home, the Morgan Bank and Trust Company and a library. Nicole thought that everything looked old. "I'd say that there's not much to do around here."

"It's not Bar Harbor, I have to admit."

"There's a place called the Harbor Bar," Nicole said as they passed a dingy tavern.

Her mother smiled. "I'm glad you still have your sense of humor."

Nicole didn't answer.

They drove past the Town Hall. The clock on the tower had Roman numerals and said ten minutes after ten. Nicole looked at her watch. It was 5:45.

They passed a faded white church and a cemetery surrounded by a spiky black fence. Many of the tombstones were leaning at odd angles. Most of the stores seemed to be closed and the streets were mostly deserted.

They drove a few more blocks and Main Street ended at another park. This one had a battered bandstand and a statue of a soldier wearing a long coat and a hat with a slanted top. Beyond the park there was nothing. Nicole knew it was the ocean.

"Where to?" Nicole's mother asked.

A sign read "Jacob's Diner" and a man was going in. "That place is open," Nicole said.

"Let's try it," her mother suggested. She pulled into a space next to the park.

Nicole saw that her cat, Ivy, was still asleep in her traveling case in the back seat. She stepped out into the cold damp air, slipped into her coat and closed the car door softly. She stretched, breathed deeply and took in the smell of the ocean. Seagulls circled and cried overhead. Across the park, Nicole heard a dull thump and turned toward the water in time to see a cloud of spray shoot into the air.

"See what it says on the license plate?" Her mother pointed to an old pickup truck. "Maine Vacationland. We're practically going to be living in a resort."

"*Last* resort, *probably.*"

Her mother shook her head and sighed as they reached the entrance to the diner. A sign in the window offered, "Fresh chowder. Homemade doughnuts and biscuits."

Two men, smoking, sat separately at the counter, hunched over cups of coffee. A few more, wearing heavy clothes, sat in the booths. Nicole wondered if they were fishermen. There were nets, a big lobster and colorful wooden floats on the walls. The tile floor was streaked with mud.

"Some booths in the back," a burly cook said, pointing from behind the counter.

Nicole realized that, aside from herself and her mother, there were only men in the diner. Feeling everyone's eyes on them, she followed her mother to a booth and slid onto the red seat. A spoked steering wheel hung on the wall above them. In the next booth, with his back to Nicole and her mother, a nicely dressed older man sat alone, reading a newspaper. *Not everyone in here is a fisherman*, she thought. The man turned slightly and Nicole saw that he had a long scar on the side of his face and neck. He smiled politely.

Nicole and her mother were scanning the plastic-covered menu when the cook arrived at their table. "Care for some supper?"

"Coffee with skim milk, please," Nicole's mother said, "and

a cup of clam chowder."

"I'd like a bowl of clam chowder and some tea, please," Nicole said.

"And some of your homemade biscuits," her mother added.

The cook nodded.

"People up here talk funny," Nicole whispered to her mother. She looked around to see if anyone overheard. He said "Keh foh some suppah?"

Her mother smiled. "Mainers probably think that we sound funny, too."

Nicole stared out the window while her mother studied a map. The cook came back with two steaming mugs and a little basket covered with a checkered napkin. Nicole reached for a biscuit. It was still warm.

"You folks on vacation?"

Nicole wiped some crumbs from her lips with her napkin. "We're going to be living here."

"I thought you might be from away. Where will you be livin'?"

"Well," her mother said, "maybe you can help us. We don't know how to get there exactly but we're looking for a house north of town on Cliff Road. Maybe you've heard of it. My husband says people call it the Weber House."

The cook's eyes narrowed and for several seconds he didn't say anything. Then he shook his head slowly. "Everyone knows about the Weber House."

"Why is that?" Nicole's mother said, putting her coffee cup down.

"Doubt you'd believe me," the cook said, turning away.

"No, wait," Nicole's mother said. "If we're going to live there, I'd like to know what everyone else knows."

"Not for me to say."

"Please," Nicole's mother said with a smile. "We're going to be neighbors."

The cook turned back toward the table and lowered his voice. "Alright then." He wiped his hands on his apron. "Strange things have happened up there."

Nicole stopped chewing her biscuit. The diner was quiet.

"Really?" Nicole's mother said. "For instance?"

The cook bent forward. "Since you asked, some folks believe that house is haunted."

"So we've heard."

"I'm not sayin' I believe all of it but some say a ghost roams those cliffs and caves up there and that house too."

"I hope he's friendly," Nicole's mother answered with a hint of a smile.

The cook didn't smile. "Some say it's the ghost of a pirate dead more than two hundred years making sure that strangers stay out of his house."

"Well, no offense to local legends, but we're not superstitious."

"Neither was Anna Weber," the cook said, glancing at Nicole. "But this much I know for sure: it was Anna's daughter, just about this young lady's age, that found her mother face down in the surf. And right about this time of year."

Nicole was stunned and stared at the cook. She turned toward her mother, who was no longer smiling. "Thank you for the information," she said coolly.

The cook took a step backwards. "You folks have a real nice visit."

They ate in silence. When Nicole was finished, her mother said "Let's go, Honey. I think I've lost my appetite." Raising her voice, she said, "I want to meet the ghost." She put a few dollars on the table and slid out of the booth.

Nicole didn't say a word as she put on her coat. With a quick look around, she scooped up the remaining biscuits, wrapped them in a napkin and put them in her coat pocket. She felt the stares of the men in the restaurant as she and her mother made their way to the door.

It was dark as they walked to their car. The snow was falling faster. "Imagine telling stories like that and trying to frighten us. Just forget it."

Yeah, okay.

When they were close to the car, Nicole saw a stooped woman near the bandstand. Her clothes were ragged and bare fingers stuck out from unmatching gloves. Tangled, gray hair drooped from under a tattered shawl flecked with snow. A few birds pecked at the breadcrumbs she tossed on the ground. An old woman looked at a young girl and Nicole turned away, wishing she had something to offer. She put her hands into her coat pocket and felt warmth. She hesitated and then slowly stepped forward. Some birds flapped into the air.

Nicole held out the little package of biscuits. "Maybe the birds will eat them."

The old woman looked into Nicole's eyes and smiled. She was missing some of her teeth and didn't smell too good. But she took the biscuits and, still smiling, slowly backed away.

Nicole walked back to the car and got in. Ivy was still asleep.

"That was nice of you."

"She looked like she might be hungry," Nicole said, glancing back at the woman and the birds. "What should we do about the directions?"

"We'll figure it out," her mother answered as she started the car. "We'll go back up to Mountain Highway and turn right. Dad says that Cliff Road runs off that, a couple of miles from town."

They didn't talk as they went back up Main Street.

At the edge of town, they crossed the tracks and started uphill, winding back and forth. At Mountain Highway they turned right, heading north. They crossed a steel bridge. Through a blur of falling snow, Nicole looked down at a town and a river that emptied into a small harbor. On an island in the open water to the east, a lighthouse beacon swept the vast Atlantic Ocean.

Snow pelted the windshield as the car picked up speed. Nicole wondered where the old woman would go during the storm. And she knew that no matter what her mother told her, she wouldn't forget what the cook said.

THE WEBER HOUSE

CHAPTER TWO

Mountain Highway meandered between towering rock walls and dramatic vistas of the menacing Atlantic. Eventually, the road straightened out. Evergreen-covered mountains rose above them on the left before disappearing into the darkening sky. To the right, there was a steep drop down to the rocky shore.

Ahead, it seemed that the land veered abruptly out into the water. Between snowy gusts of wind, she could just make out the long white waves advancing toward the shore before crashing onto a narrow, stony beach. A sheer rock wall rose from there. At the top of the cliff, a dense forest faded in and out of view.

Her mother was looking in the same direction. "I think that's where we're going, and it shouldn't be much further. It's a good thing because the snow is starting to stick." The flakes seemed to shoot toward the car's headlights.

They came to a fork in the road. Mountain Highway went off to the left, up into the mountains. A weather-beaten sign showed that Cliff Road followed the coast to the right. Another sign said "Dead End."

Not much of a road. Nicole heard loose stones crunching under the car's tires. "It doesn't look like a lot of people come up here," she said. "Mostly ghosts, I guess."

"You're probably right." Her mother concentrated on the road. "Up here someplace, there's supposed to be an old covered bridge."

Cliff Road sloped upward as it went into the woods. The driving snow and low-lying clouds made it impossible to see very far. To the left, the woods were very dark. To the right, Nicole saw a slight brightening beyond the trees and she knew that the light must mark the edge of the cliff.

They came to the covered bridge. A sign said "Keep Out." The car coasted to a stop. The bridge was very narrow and inside it was dark. Long icicles hung grimly from the arched entrance. "We're supposed to go across *that?*"

"Dad made it, I guess."

Nicole sighed.

The car thumped slowly across the wooden planks. Some of the sideboards were rotted or broken or missing entirely. When they reached the other side, Nicole twisted around to look back and down. The bridge spanned a deep ravine. Far below, jagged black rocks stuck out of the ice and snow. Ahead, there were two driveways. One led to the left, along the edge of the ravine before disappearing in the trees.

"Dad's directions say to go straight after crossing the bridge. We're almost there."

The snow was falling faster as they came into a clearing. Then, between gusts of wind and snow, Nicole glimpsed a large, dark shape.

"I see the house . . . I think."

It vanished and for an instant, Nicole wondered if she had really seen anything. Then the structure came back into view behind huge, swaying evergreens and swirling snow. It looked abandoned. Overgrown bushes and snowy trees blocked much of the ground floor. Dilapidated shutters covered some of the windows, and the others, except for one, showed no light. Thick black vines spread over the dark walls. Across the yard, at the edge of the cliff, a bleak stone tower stood like a sentinel over the house and the ocean.

Nicole's mother drove to the end of the driveway and stopped behind a familiar car. Nicole stared at the house. Partly hidden behind the bushes and trees, a covered porch stretched across the front. But instead of a railing, black chains draped from the battered, wooden posts. The front door was cloaked in shadow but orange sparks shot from the chimney at the end of the house. At the top of the house, a tiled roof looked like a reptile's scales with two round windows that reminded Nicole of dead eyes. Between them, a weather-beaten figure leaned forward, staring grimly. Her left hand

pointed straight ahead.

Nicole gaped at the gloomy house before her. "We're going to live . . . *there*?"

"I think so," her mother answered. "I wonder where your father is."

Nicole shook her head.

Her mother got out of the car and pulled her coat from the back seat. "Let's see."

Nicole grabbed her coat and stepped into the cold. She reached into the back seat for the cat carrier. There was already more than an inch of snow on the ground. They passed between two black cannons pointing toward the ocean. Nicole looked up at the dark tower at the edge of the cliff. "That must be where they shoot the prisoners from."

With an eye on the pointed icicles overhead, Nicole stepped onto the porch. The front door was made of huge planks of some colorless wood. Beneath a small window was a miniature metal anchor.

"It's a knocker," Nicole's mother said.

"Isn't there any electricity?"

Her mother banged the anchor several times. They listened and waited but there was neither answer nor sound from within the house.

Nicole gripped the handle and pushed. The door creaked open and her mother stepped inside.

"Here's our new home," Nicole said to her cat. Ivy's purring turned to a growl. Daughter followed mother inside. The heavy door swung shut and darkness enclosed them.

As her eyes adjusted, Nicole saw that they were in a high-ceilinged hallway. To the left was a large, dark room where she could barely see strange white shapes. They looked like ghosts.

"Old furniture, probably," her mother said, seeing where her daughter was staring. The door on the right was partly open and the room beyond was dark too, except for an eerie, flickering light which reflected off the walls and ceiling. A stairway led to more blackness above. From somewhere in the shadows down the hall, a bell chimed.

"Hello?" Nicole's mother called. "Paul? Are you here?"

There was a faint echo but nothing more. Then something creaked and Nicole spun around. The sound came from the room on the left. Something moved. She peered into the shadows. Then she saw it. One of the strange white shapes was moving toward them.

"Mom?"

"Boo!"

"Paul, stop that!" her mother said. "And take off that sheet before you fall down and hurt yourself."

The "ghost" uncovered his head.

"Hi guys," Nicole's father said. He hugged Nicole and her mother at the same time. "Welcome to Elk River."

Nicole squirmed loose.

"What kind of welcome is that?" her mother said, shaking her head. "Were you trying to frighten us?"

"Did I?"

"Yeah, Dad, we were real scared."

"You looked a little scared."

Nicole looked at her father without saying anything.

"Well, never mind." He stepped into the room on the right and turned on a light. "Come on in here. I've got a fire going to warm you up."

Nicole picked up Ivy's carrier and followed her parents. The flickering lights came from a huge fireplace on the far wall. The mantel was almost the same height as her father. The burning logs crackled and smelled good. Above the mantel, there was a large painting of an old sailing ship.

"There are boxes all over the place but I've got this room sort of fixed up," her father said. "I put the TV over there in the corner, at least for now." He took their coats and draped them on the back of a worn but comfortable-looking chair near the fireplace. "How do you like it, Mary?"

Nicole's mother scanned the room. "I'd say it needs some work but it must have been beautiful once upon a time. What do you think, Nicole?"

She looked around: tattered curtains, dark wood paneling, flaking paint and peeling wallpaper. "I'd say that was a long time ago." Nicole crouched down and opened the door to the carrier. "Come on out, Ivy. It's warm by the fire." The cat poked her head out, slowly emerged and began to explore the room.

"What does the rest of the house look like?" Nicole asked.

"Yes, we want a tour," her mother said.

"You'll get one but don't you want something to eat?"

"Actually, we *are* kind of hungry," Nicole's mother replied. "We stopped at a diner in town but we didn't eat much."

"The food was that bad?"

"No," Nicole's mother said, "it wasn't that . . ."

"The cook said this place is haunted!"

"Well, there are some crazy stories about this house and, as you noticed, it does need some work but that's why the rent is so reasonable."

"What crazy stories?" Nicole asked without smiling.

"Oh, I'll tell you later. But right now, I'll get some water on the stove for pasta. I'll show you the house while we're waiting for it to boil."

Nicole's father led the newcomers on a quick tour of their new home. But they were tired from the long drive and after a big bowl of ravioli and a slice of blueberry pie, Nicole couldn't stop yawning.

"Why don't you turn in?" her father asked. "I know it's not that late but you've had a long day and your bed is all made up with new sheets and a warm down quilt. I think Mom and I are going to bed soon too."

Nicole didn't argue. A few minutes later she was in her pajamas. Her parents came up to her new room to say goodnight. Nicole shut off the light by her bed as they left the room. The wind howled outside and the radiator rattled but soon she was fast asleep.

CHAPTER THREE

NOVEMBER 24

Nicole was in a dark cave and struggled to see. There was a crashing sound every few seconds. Though frightened, she crept forward, feeling cold stone walls on either side. Nicole inched toward a distant light. She glimpsed a silhouette and, despite her fears, was drawn forward. Nicole heard crying and, approaching the light, saw a young girl. Then she was gone. Nicole was at the mouth of the cave. The wind was blowing hard and it was bitter cold. The crashing sounds were waves pounding onto huge black boulders. The ocean. The girl had climbed down the rocks and faced the icy water. Nicole was staring at the waves, white foam hissing between the rocks, when she saw her. Not the girl, but a woman in a white nightgown, her arms extended, floating face down in the black water. Nicole tried to scream but no sound came. Everything went black and there was strange music.

Nicole sat up in bed. She was breathing hard and her heart was pounding. She looked around the dark room. It took her a moment to realize where she was. Maine. Her first night in a creaky old house.

It was Saturday night. Sunday morning, really. The room was cold.

Nicole took a deep breath and lay back down. *It was a dream. Just a bad dream.* Then she heard it again. It *was* music. Or maybe just notes. A piano. It was very soft but it wasn't her imagination. The sound was coming from downstairs.

Maybe Mom or Dad is doing it, she thought. *But what time is it?* She looked at the clock on her nightstand: 2:30. *I thought they were going to bed early.*

More notes. It was definitely a piano and the same as before. *It's like somebody trying to remember an old piece.*

She got out of bed and stamped on the floor. The music stopped. Nicole yawned, opened her door and went into the hall. The floor felt like ice beneath her bare feet. She looked across the stairs to her parents' room and saw that the door was closed. She put her hand on the railing and slowly felt her way in the dark around to the top of the stairs. At the bottom of the steps, it was pitch black. Nicole shivered. She continued around the balcony to her parents' room, opened the door and peeked in.

Suddenly she was wide awake. *Both* of her parents were in bed.

"Mom, Dad!" Nicole whispered, "I think there's someone downstairs. Somebody's playing the piano!"

"What's the matter?" her mother said sleepily. "What time is it?" She looked at the clock. "Nicole, it's the middle of the night!"

"Mom, I heard someone. I thought it was Dad."

Nicole's father was snoring. Her mother shook him. "Paul. Wake up. Nicole says she heard someone downstairs."

"*Really*, Dad! I definitely heard it."

"I guess we'd better go see so we can all get back to sleep," her mother said.

"You mean, *I'd* better go see," her father said groggily. "All right, I'll go look."

Nicole's mother sat up and turned on a light. "Do you think we should call the police?"

"No," Nicole's father said as he pulled on his robe, "I guess I can handle a piano player."

Nicole and her mother followed as her father shuffled out into the hall and turned on a light. Nicole watched as he went down the stairs and disappeared into the room with the "ghosts." A few seconds later she heard someone play a few notes on the piano. In another minute her father appeared back in the hallway carrying Ivy. He trudged back up the stairs.

"I think I found the culprit," he said. "We must have closed the door on her."

"No, Dad," Nicole protested. "It wasn't Ivy. It was a person *playing*. I know I heard it!"

"Maybe you heard *'Hey, Diddle Diddle, a Cat and a Fiddle'*?" Nicole's father said, yawning.

"No, I didn't. I know what I heard."

"Did you check to see if the doors were locked?" Nicole's mother asked.

"They're locked."

Nicole shook her head.

"I think it must have been your imagination," her father said. "Probably because we're in a big old house for the first time and you heard that crazy story from the guy in the diner."

"Let's talk about it in the morning." Nicole's mother said. I'll turn off the light after you're in bed."

"I can turn off my own light."

"You sure?"

"Yes, Mom," Nicole sighed. "I'm not afraid of the dark."

"I know, Sweetheart. Good night."

Nicole peered down the stairs. *Could it have been Ivy?* Nicole switched off the light at the top of the stairs, and her hand on the railing, felt the way to her room. Now somewhat accustomed to the darkness, Nicole closed the door, climbed into bed and wondered if she would fall asleep.

CHAPTER FOUR

Sunday morning. When Nicole woke up, she didn't feel rested. She found her robe and slippers and went downstairs. Her parents were in the kitchen.

"Good morning," Nicole's mother said. "I was just going to call you. We're almost ready to eat."

"How'd you sleep?" her father asked, flipping a pancake on the skillet.

"Not too well," Nicole said, frowning. "First I had this weird dream and then that music thing, whatever it was."

"What was your dream about?" Nicole's mother asked.

"I dreamed I was in this really dark cave. Then I saw a young girl. But when I got outside, I was looking down at the ocean. The girl was right by the water and a woman was floating in it. I think she was dead."

"That sounds like the story that awful cook told us in the diner yesterday," Nicole's mother said.

"That explains it," her father added. "You had a bad dream and then when Ivy walked on the keyboard, you dreamt it was music."

"No, Dad. I was awake when I heard the piano and it wasn't a cat doing it. It was somebody trying to play a piece of music."

"Let's eat," her mother said.

Nicole ate her pancakes in silence. She knew her parents thought she imagined the music. *The trouble is, I can't explain it either. If it wasn't Ivy that I heard, what was it?*

When she finished her breakfast, Nicole put her dishes in the sink and went into the narrow pantry at end of the kitchen. On the right side there was a door with a small round window. Nicole pushed the door open and, down a few steps, saw the back stairs to the second floor. On the right was the door to the backyard. In between was another one.

"Be careful if you're going down to the cellar," her father called. "The stairs are really steep and there aren't any lights."

"I'm going up to my room," Nicole answered. She glanced out the window on the back door to see how much snow had fallen. She noticed the birds' delicate tracks before starting up the steps. Then she stopped. *If somebody came into the house last night, they must have left footprints in the snow.*

Nicole hurried up to her room, dressed quickly, and crept down the front stairs. Her parents were talking in the kitchen. *I'll be back before they notice.* Slowly, she opened the front door and went outside. It was cold and the sky was gray but no snow was falling. Nicole looked at the snow on the porch. No footprints. She hurried down the steps and around the corner to the side of the house. The snow went inside her shoes and stung her ankles.

Nicole went all the way around the house, ducking down as she passed the kitchen windows. No footprints by the back door or anyplace else. The only new tracks in the snow looked like they had been made by birds and small animals. She went back into the house and quietly closed the front door. When she turned around, her father was standing there.

"Find any footprints?"

"How'd you know what I was looking for?"

"Lucky guess. Now do you think that maybe what you

heard last night was the cat and not a cat burglar? Or a ghost?"

"I don't believe in ghosts, Dad. But I don't believe a cat can play the piano, either."

"I have to agree with you there," her father said. "But the next time you go outside, dress a little more warmly, okay?"

"I was just out there for a minute."

"Come on, you've even got snow in your shoes."

Nicole shrugged.

"I just don't want you to get sick. And I don't want you to worry too much about things that have a logical explanation, even if we don't know what it is, okay?"

Another shrug.

"Well anyway, our neighbor called while you were outside and he's coming over. I think you'll like him."

"I'll be upstairs."

CHAPTER FIVE

Nicole was online when she heard the knock on the front door. A few seconds later, her father called from the bottom of the stairs.

Nicole turned back to the computer. "*luv ya talk to you later,*" she typed to Alexandra before logging off.

She started down the stairs and saw her parents greeting a man bundled against the cold. He had a box in his left hand.

"Let me take your coat, John," Nicole's father said, adding, "This is our daughter, Nicole."

"Hi," Mr. Morgan said, extending his hand. Nicole took half a step forward to shake it. He wore very nice clothes and looked younger than her parents.

"I've heard many wonderful things about you. I think you're really going to like Elk River."

"I hope so," Nicole said, looking down.

"I heard you play soccer."

Nicole glanced at her father. "I used to."

Nicole's mother led everyone into the front room on the right and Mr. Morgan offered his package to Nicole: "Jacob's Homemade Doughnuts." She looked at her mother and smiled. Mr. Morgan noticed.

"Best in town. Don't tell me you don't like doughnuts."

"It's not that, John," her father said. "They had a strange welcome at that diner yesterday."

"The cook thought we might not like living here," her mother said, "in this house, I mean."

"He said it's haunted," Nicole added.

"Oh, not *that* already," Mr. Morgan groaned. "Don't pay any attention to that silliness, Nicole. I'm afraid some people are just superstitious. That guy's probably afraid of black cats, too."

"Nicole's not superstitious," her mother said. "But that cook was really something."

"He should stick to making pancakes," Mr. Morgan said, shaking his head.

Nicole smiled weakly.

"John," her mother said, "can I offer you a cup of coffee? Or would you like to see the house?"

"John probably knows the place better than I do," Nicole's father said.

"I do know a bit about the history of the house," Mr. Morgan said, "but I can't remember when I was last inside." He smiled at Nicole. "I'd love to see your new home. How about if we take a quick tour and try some of those haunted doughnuts?"

"Sounds good," Nicole's mother said.

"In that case, let's start right here," her father said. He draped their neighbor's hat, coat and scarf on the back of a chair. "I guess this would be the sitting room."

Nicole looked around the room and saw things she hadn't noticed the previous evening. There were paintings on every wall, mostly with old-fashioned gold frames. "Why is it called the sitting room?"

"It was something like a living room," her mother said. "In more formal times, visitors would come here first to meet their hosts."

Next was the dining room. Mr. Morgan commented on the paintings of birds, flowers and ships. Nicole noticed the cobwebby chandelier above the large table. Ivy jumped onto a windowsill near a hissing radiator and stared at something outside.

"Next we have the kitchen, or perhaps I should say 'the galley,'" her father continued.

"The *galley*"? Nicole asked.

"That's the kitchen on a boat, isn't it?" her mother asked.

"That's right. The last owner of the house was a sailor and I'm trying to get you in the spirit. There are nautical things all over the house. There's even a ship's clock in the hallway."

Nicole led the way past the old-looking refrigerator and sink. While her mother examined the antique stove, Nicole went on to the pantry. Her father followed and pointed to the door with the round window. There was a little swinging opening at the bottom of the door. "The people who used to own this house must have had a cat too."

The next room was dark. "Ta-da!" Nicole's father said as a light came on.

The room looked like it had been part greenhouse and part artist's studio. The large windows on the outside walls were lined with glass shelves filled with empty clay pots. Paintings, sketches and cobweb-covered bookshelves covered the other two walls. A paint-spattered easel stood in one corner.

Nicole looked out a dirty window facing what was once a garden. It was snowing again. Drifts from yesterday's storm had almost covered the broken stalks of long-dead flowers. Beyond the garden was a dark forest.

Her father opened the heavy wooden double doors that led into the next room. He flipped a switch and some of the lights came on. "Check this out."

One entire wall and part of another one were covered with floor-to-ceiling bookshelves. There was another massive fireplace with a giant world map over it. "It's magnificent," Mr. Morgan said.

With the lights on, Nicole could see yesterday's "ghosts" clearly. It was, as her mother said, just old furniture. Nicole looked under one of the sheets and found a brass telescope on a tripod. She plopped onto an overstuffed chair. The furniture in this room looked old too. The chair, however, was comfortable. Then she noticed a "ghost" she hadn't seen the day before. It stood taller than the rest. Nicole lifted up the sheet.

"It's a harp!" She pulled the cover off and plucked a long string. It gave a deep, low sound.

"There's the piano," Nicole's father said, with a glance at his daughter. She uncovered the keyboard and walked her fingers over an octave.

"Look at these lovely old lamps," her mother said as she examined one with an attached piece that looked like a magnifying glass.

"I think that's a whale oil lamp," Mr. Morgan said. "The lens focused the light."

"Ingenious."

Above a large dusty globe in a wooden stand Nicole saw a shuttered mirror with a silver frame inlaid with delicate golden birds and flowers. She opened the little doors and wrote her name in the thick dust on the mirror. "It looks like you've got a lot of cleaning to do around here, Mom."

Her mother smiled. "Me?"

Nicole closed the shutters. "I like it better this way."

"Who owns all these things, Paul?" Nicole's mother asked. "For that matter, who owns this house?"

Nicole's father held up his hand. "All in good time, but let's finish the tour first." He led everyone back into the center hall, pausing at the foot of the stairs. "Ready for the second floor?" The creaky steps rose to a balcony that wrapped around both sides of the stairs to the front of the house. "Our bedrooms face the water."

The front of the upstairs hall was almost all glass. Windows surrounded both sides of a pair of glass-paned doors that opened onto an outdoor balcony. Above the doors, a large semicircle of stained glass depicted an old-fashioned sailing ship on a dark, blue ocean. A pale, silvery light barely shined through the glass sun.

"It's beautiful, isn't it?" Nicole's mother said.

Nicole nodded.

"Wait 'til you see what happens when the sun shines through it," her father said.

"You mean the sun really comes out here sometimes?"

"Well," Mr. Morgan said, "they say if you don't like Maine weather, just wait a minute."

Nicole smiled and took another look at the stained-glass seascape and the real, snow-filled sky.

"It's kind of surprising," her father observed, "that the house hasn't been vandalized, considering all the nice things and all the years it's been unoccupied."

"My guess," Mr. Morgan said, "is that for a long time, the house was protected by its isolation. Later on, I think my grandfather and then my father kept an eye on the place. I've tried to do so as well. I've asked the police to come around once in a while to discourage prowlers."

"This way, folks," Nicole's father announced as he opened a door to a room on the right. "Here is our room."

Nicole's mother went in first. "It's beautiful, Paul. It just needs a little work."

"A *little* work?" Nicole said, noticing the stained wallpaper.

Mr. Morgan smiled and pointed to the corner of the room. "There's even a fireplace."

"That's right," Nicole's father said. "Every room has one. Just like downstairs. And on cold winter nights, we might use them."

"Are you saying the heating doesn't work?" Nicole's mother said.

"It works, it's just old."

"We're going to freeze to death," Nicole said.

Her father shook his head.

The tour continued back into the hall and toward the rear of the house. "Here we have two spare bedrooms," Nicole's father said, opening a door near the top of the stairs. "This could be a guest room."

"You really think we're going to have visitors?" Nicole asked. "Not counting the ghost, I mean."

"This door," her father continued, frowning at his daughter, "leads to the back stairs, down to the pantry and up to the attic. And here's the bathroom."

"It looks old," Nicole's mother said, eyeing the stained bathtub which stood off the floor on little feet.

"Is this the only one?" Nicole asked.

"There's a lavatory downstairs," her father answered, sounding slightly exasperated. He opened a door on the other side of the stairway. "This room over here will be our study." He gestured toward the computer. "I think Nicole has already been online."

"I had a hard time connecting."

Mr. Morgan nodded. "I'm afraid that is a problem here. But I think it's getting better."

Everyone walked toward the front of the house and Nicole's father opened the door of the last room. "And speaking of our daughter, here is Nicole's room."

"Dad, my stuff is all over!"

"Oh, it's all right."

Nicole hurried inside and covered her clothes and pajamas with the bedcovers.

Next to the bed was a night table with a brass lamp covered by a faded fringed shade. There was a large chest of drawers, a rocking chair, a globe, smaller than the one downstairs, and a lovely rolltop desk. The top rattled as Nicole pushed it up, revealing a green felt blotter underneath. Above the desk, in a dusty gold frame, was a painting of a young girl holding her pet. "That cat looks like Ivy."

"You're right," her mother agreed. "It looks just like her. And see, your front windows look out onto the balcony, just like our room. In the spring we can have tea there."

Nicole looked at her mother doubtfully.

"I think you're going to be very happy here," Mr. Morgan said. "It's a wonderful house."

"I think so too, John," Nicole's mother replied. "But right now, let's go back downstairs and have some doughnuts. If you have the time, I'd love to hear all about the history of the house. And Paul, I want to hear how you found it, who owns it and a million other things."

"I want to hear about the ghost," Nicole said.

"Okay, okay," her father said. "One at a time. All questions will be answered. You'll stay, won't you, John? I'm afraid these two might gang up on me."

"It'll be a pleasure."

"I'll make some coffee and hot chocolate," Nicole's mother said as everyone started downstairs.

CHAPTER SIX

Nicole settled next to her mother on the couch in the sitting room. Sipping hot chocolate, she stroked Ivy's back. Mr. Morgan, sitting in an overstuffed chair, stirred his coffee. Nicole's father put a log on the fire, stood up and brushed off his hands. "Let's see, where should I start?" He pulled up a chair and sat with his back to the fire. "Just a few months ago, we were still living in New Jersey."

"Mom and I were still there the day before yesterday."

"Thank you for that clarification."

"Go ahead, Paul," Nicole's mother said.

"Okay. Last spring, I was unexpectedly offered an assistant professorship up here in Maine. We knew that moving would be hard . . ."

Nicole folded her arms.

Her father turned toward Mr. Morgan ". . . but it seemed like the right decision."

"I'm sure that once you're settled in, you'll all agree that it was a good move."

"I sure hope so," Nicole's father said. "Anyway, my first task was to find a place for us to live."

Mr. Morgan nodded.

"A realtor showed me some houses in a few towns near

here but I didn't see anything I thought we'd like. Finally, she suggested that I call a lawyer here in Elk River. The lawyer said he had a house that I might be interested in. Nicole's father spread his arms dramatically. "This is it. The famous Weber House. The lawyer is trying to sell it but until he does, he wanted to rent. I liked the house, even if it does need some work, and I thought you guys might like it too. The view, as you'll see when the weather clears, is spectacular. And the rent is very reasonable."

"The lawyer owns the house?" Nicole's mother asked.

"No, and it's a sad story. The house was owned by an old lady who abandoned it years ago. Apparently, she moved into a rundown cabin out in the woods someplace. But then she disappeared and most likely, passed away. Now the lawyer is trying to settle the estate and sell the property. Meanwhile, the house was put up for rent and that's where we came in."

"What does 'settle the estate' mean?" Nicole asked.

"And what do you mean, 'most likely, passed away'?" her mother added.

"Maybe I can answer those questions," Mr. Morgan offered.

"Please do," Nicole's father said.

"It really *is* a sad tale," Mr. Morgan agreed, "and I'm afraid I have to go back even further for it all to make sense."

Nicole and her mother looked at each other and nodded. "We want to hear the whole story," Nicole's mother said.

"We should probably start with Henry Weber," Mr. Morgan said, resting his coffee mug on the arm of his chair. "He bought this house more than 70 years ago." Their neighbor took another sip of coffee before continuing. "I believe he was born around 1885. They say he went to sea when he was just 15."

Nicole glanced at the picture of a sailing ship above the fireplace.

"He must have loved the ocean because he sailed all over the world. By 1930 or thereabouts, Weber had been at sea for thirty years. And it was around that time that he met a young schoolteacher right here in Elk River. Her name was Anna. I think she was born in Mexico. They married and before long, a baby girl was born. They named her Dolores and this was their home."

"But wasn't the house already here?" Nicole's mother asked.

"That's right," Mr. Morgan replied. "It was built before the American Revolution by a man named William Taggart. He was a seagoing man too, a captain."

"*Two* sailors. No wonder there are so many nautical touches."

"But Taggart wasn't an ordinary captain," Mr. Morgan continued after another sip of coffee. "He was a pirate."

"Is that who's supposed to haunt the house?" Nicole asked.

"Yes. And even though you and I don't believe that kind of stuff, some people do, as you heard yesterday in the diner."

"We certainly did," Nicole's mother said.

"Anybody want a doughnut?" her husband asked with a grin.

"Please go ahead, John," Nicole's mother said, frowning. "This is fascinating."

"Taggart began sailing under the British flag. He was an excellent seaman but also a very cruel master. They say he ruled his ship with the cat."

"A *cat*"? Nicole and her mother said simultaneously.

"Not *a* cat," Mr. Morgan said. "*The* cat. The cat o' nine tails. It was a whip made of nine knotted cords which captains used on their sailors to enforce discipline."

"How awful," Nicole's mother said, shaking her head.

Mr. Morgan nodded. "British warships were not very pleasant places, I'm afraid. Anyway, sometime in the 1750s

Taggart left the Royal Navy and went into business for himself, you might say."

"You mean he became a pirate," Nicole's father said.

"Not right away," Mr. Morgan said. "At first, he was master of a slaver."

"*A slaver?*" Nicole asked, "A ship that carried *slaves?*"

"That's right," Mr. Morgan said. "Taggart was the captain of ships that brought slaves from Africa to America."

"We read about that in school."

Nicole's mother nodded.

"That's how Taggart began to make his fortune," Mr. Morgan continued. "Later, however, he got into a new line of work and that's when he really got rich."

"Piracy?" Nicole's father asked.

"Yes. And if Taggart was brutal in the royal navy, he was even worse as a pirate. He showed his victims no mercy. But as a mariner, they say that Taggart had no equal. His navigational skills were apparently almost magical. No merchant ship, under any flag, was safe anywhere in the Atlantic or the Caribbean and no navy ever caught him. The legends say his ship came out of nowhere and, just as quickly, seemed to disappear into thin air. Taggart named her *Ghost*."

"Another ghost," Nicole said frowning.

The grownups smiled.

"Taggart had a mansion in Charleston, South Carolina, which was a very important port in the slave trade. But when he became a pirate, I guess it was too dangerous for him to stay there so around 1760 he came up here. Elk River wasn't even settled then."

"You mean this house was his hideout?" Nicole said.

"Part hideout and part fortress in my opinion," Mr. Morgan said. "The walls of this house are very thick and I'm sure you noticed the cannons in front of the house. I'm told that those guns could have hit unfriendly ships in the bay."

"That's one way to keep bill collectors away," Nicole's father said.

Nicole rolled her eyes.

"Taggart probably first visited the area when he was still in the royal navy," Mr. Morgan continued. "In those days, the King of England claimed Maine's tallest and straightest pines for masts for British warships. Eventually, Taggart came back. His ship would have been relatively safe in the bay. I imagine that you can see a long way from that tower in front of the house, and the cliffs would have made an attack very difficult. And if Captain Taggart ever had to flee, they say that right underneath us, there are tunnels in the rock that this house is built on."

Nicole looked down at the floor. "Cool."

"I'm sure that's what Taggart thought," Mr. Morgan said, nodding.

"Have you ever been in the caves, Mr. Morgan?"

"No, Nicole. I'm afraid I'm not much of a spelunker."

"Can we go up in the tower, Dad?"

"I don't know. Is it safe, John?"

"I'm afraid I'm not much help there either. I don't even know *how* to get into it. There's no opening as far as I can see."

"John," Nicole's mother said, glancing at her daughter, "how did the stories about a ghost get started?"

Mr. Morgan took another sip of coffee. "Well, according to the legend, Taggart hid a treasure around here someplace. Some say his ghost is guarding it."

"You mean there might *really* be gold and silver buried around here someplace?" Nicole asked.

"Personally, I doubt it. But some people think so."

"Pirates, ghosts, buried treasure," Nicole's father said. "No wonder the story has grown into a legend."

"I suppose it really isn't surprising," Mr. Morgan agreed. "I think people like to believe old tales, especially when they involve buried treasure."

"What finally happened to Taggart?" Nicole's father asked.

"I'm not really sure. But I know that he was never captured. No doubt that contributes to the legend too. His grave is supposed to be around here someplace."

"What happened to the house after Taggart died?" Nicole's mother asked. "It was a long time before the Webers moved in."

"As far as I know, not much of anything happened. As I said, hardly anyone lived in the area back then. No white people, anyhow."

"Except for the ghost," Nicole's father said.

Nicole's mother frowned at her husband.

Mr. Morgan smiled. "By the time people finally did move into the area," he said, "I think the house was pretty much forgotten. It was a long time before Mountain Highway was even built. And it was Henry Weber who built the covered bridge over the ravine."

"Then how did Taggart get up here?" Nicole asked.

"He must have sailed into the bay and come ashore in a small boat," Mr. Morgan said. "How he got up the cliff, let alone how he built the house, is a mystery to me. I guess he had his own way of persuading people to do what he wanted."

"I'm sure he did," Nicole's mother said.

Nicole's father grimaced as he drew his thumb across his throat.

Mr. Morgan nodded grimly. "Of course, over the years, people *did* come around here from time to time looking for treasure. But the cliffs and caves are very dangerous and some people were hurt. A few died. Of course, that only added to the legend."

"People *died?* Nicole asked. "Around *here?*"

"I'm afraid so, Nicole."

"Taggart's ghost at work," Nicole's father said.

"Exactly. Every incident added to the legend. But now, we're back to where we started. Sometime in the 1920s, Henry Weber bought the property and began fixing up the house between his voyages. It had been abandoned for more than 150 years by then and must have been in terrible condition. But for Henry Weber, who loved the sea so much, I guess it was a dream house. As you know, the view of the ocean is magnificent. And the house itself is practically a ship on land. Much of the wood the house is made of, like the floorboards and beams underneath us, came from old ships. They say that many of the stones, like the ones in the fireplace and chimney, were once ballast in Taggart's ships."

"Amazing," Nicole's father said.

"Anyway," Mr. Morgan concluded, "Weber brought his bride here and then a daughter was born."

"How is it that you know all this history, John?" Nicole's mother asked. "I'm very impressed."

"I heard my grandfather tell the story many times," Mr. Morgan said. "He was part of the story too, in a small way. And that part comes next." Looking to Nicole, he asked, "Should I keep going?"

"Yes, please."

"Well, the first thing to remember is that Dolores was born during the Depression."

"Do you know what that means, Nicole?" her father asked.

"We saw a movie about it in school. Lots of people lost their jobs. Families even had to live on the streets or in tents and had to beg for food."

Her mother nodded. "It was a very hard time."

"It still happens," Nicole said. "I saw a homeless lady yesterday morning in the park when we came out of the doughnut place."

"You're right, Nicole," her father said. "It still happens."

"Hard times came to Elk River, too," Mr. Morgan said. "It

was just like you said, Nicole. People wandered the streets looking for jobs and food. Like a lot of other people, sailors had a tough time getting work. Since Anna Weber had a job teaching, the family might have been a little better off than some but I'm sure it was a hard time for them too. Still, my grandfather always said no one ever came to this house looking for food and went away hungry."

"They must have been fine people," Nicole's mother said.

"I'm sure they were, but, like everyone else, they had their problems. My grandfather said that Henry Weber had a little trouble with alcohol."

"I think that's pretty common with sailors," Nicole's father observed.

"I think that's true," Mr. Morgan said. "Anyway, this is where my family comes into the story. As I said, times were tough, and Henry Weber decided to sell some of his land. It was my grandfather who bought it." Mr. Morgan turned to Nicole. "Do you remember when you turned off Mountain Highway onto Cliff Road?"

Nicole looked at her mother and then to Mr. Morgan "Yes."

"After you crossed the covered bridge, there was a driveway going off to the left," Mr. Morgan said. "That's where I live, in a house built by my grandfather on land he bought from Henry Weber way back in the thirties. Henry Weber and my grandfather were friends."

"Now I see why you know the story so well," Nicole's mother said.

Mr. Morgan smiled. "My father told me that Grandpa knew that his neighbors were having a hard time. I think he wanted to help."

"That was kind," Nicole's mother said.

Mr. Morgan took another sip of coffee before continuing. "During World War II, Henry Weber kept sailing. He made it through the war but in 1946, just a year after it ended, he took his last voyage. Weber was lost at sea during a storm."

"His poor family," Nicole's mother said.

"Yes, it was a terrible tragedy. Weber left a young wife and a fourteen-year-old daughter. But it gets worse. Just a few days later, Anna Weber died, too."

"What happened?" Nicole's father asked.

"I don't think they ever really found out. I do know that it occurred right around this time of year. As a matter of fact, Anna Weber died in the early morning hours of December 21, exactly fifty years ago next month. My grandfather said that it was snowing that morning but for some reason Anna Weber went outside when it was still dark and somehow lost her way. Apparently, she stumbled over the cliff and must have been killed in the fall. My grandfather happened to stop by later that morning and found Dolores, in her nightgown, wading in the surf at the bottom of the cliff. Her mother was floating in the water."

"What a horrible discovery for that poor girl," Nicole's mother said.

Nicole remembered her dream. "It's just like the cook said."

"I'm afraid he was right about that," Mr. Morgan said. "Dolores nearly died from pneumonia. She recovered physically, but my grandfather thought that mentally, she was never the same." Mr. Morgan tapped the side of his head with his finger.

"I suppose that's not surprising after all she had been through," Nicole's father said.

Mr. Morgan nodded. "As you might expect, Anna Weber's tragic death, and her husband's too, for that matter, only added to the superstitions."

"What a terrible story," Nicole's father said. "And there's more, isn't there?"

"I'm afraid so."

"What else could have happened to that poor girl?" Nicole's mother asked.

"For a few years," Mr. Morgan said, "Dolores lived here with an aunt but they didn't have much money and they say that the relationship between Dolores and her relative was difficult. Dolores had been an outstanding student but she stopped going to school. By the time Dolores was 18, she lived alone and must have been penniless. More than once, my grandfather offered to buy this property but Dolores always refused to sell. It seems to me that she made a mistake but perhaps she felt that her parents wouldn't have wanted her to sell their beloved home."

"I can understand that," Nicole's mother said.

"She probably didn't want to move," Nicole added.

"I'm sure you're right," Mr. Morgan said. "But Dolores was going to have even more sadness in her life. They say that she, too, started drinking heavily and that she spent a lot of time wandering in the woods. There were rumors that she performed strange rituals with birds and small animals she captured. Whenever somebody's pet disappeared, people suspected that Dolores was responsible." Mr. Morgan paused. "And then there were the dogs."

"*Dogs?*" Nicole's mother said.

"Yes," Mr. Morgan replied. "I think there've always been some wild dogs in the woods. Strays or abandoned pets, I suppose. You hear them barking sometimes. Some of them are pretty big and can take down a deer. I think Dolores fed some of them. Maybe she thought she could turn them into pets but I wouldn't want to run into one of those dogs out there."

"I'll keep that in mind," Nicole's father said, "if I'm wandering around in the woods."

"What happened to Dolores?" Nicole's mother asked.

"After a few years," Mr. Morgan said, "she moved out of

this house. It must have been the early '60s. I think she was basically homeless although some people said she slept in her mother's studio out in the woods. For years, people seldom even saw Dolores but the stories became even more bizarre. Drivers on Mountain Highway reported seeing fires in the woods late at night. The house was vacant by then but sometimes, after dark, you could see flickering lights in the windows. I remember that myself. Of course, all of this only added to the ghost stories. Once there was a report that Dolores tried to grab some small children who were playing in the woods. After that, the police looked for her for a while and people just stayed away. But that's when the worst of the rumors started. You know how cruel people can be when they're frightened."

"What rumors?" Nicole asked.

"I know it sounds ridiculous," Mr. Morgan said, "but some people said that Dolores was a witch, and dangerous. But they were the same people who said that Taggart's ghost haunted the house."

"Who knows? Maybe it's true," Nicole's father said, making a spooky face.

"Funny, Dad."

"Really, Paul," her mother said seriously, "I wish you wouldn't make jokes like that. You might give Nicole nightmares. And me too, for that matter."

"Oh, don't worry. It's a terrible story but it was a long time ago. Like John said, *we* know it's ridiculous." He looked at his wife and daughter. "*Don't* we?"

"Your dad is right," Mr. Morgan said. "And if any of those strange things, like the fires in the woods, really did happen, most likely they had a logical explanation."

"What happened to Dolores?" Nicole said.

"That part, I'm afraid, isn't ancient history."

"What do you mean, John?" Nicole's father asked.

"No one knows for sure what happened," Mr. Morgan said, seeming to choose his words carefully. "But we do know that a few years ago, again at this exact same time of year, there was a fire, a real one, in the studio in the woods. Some people said that one of Dolores' midnight bonfires set it ablaze so it was her own fault. I think it's cruel to say that because nobody really knows. But poor Dolores was never seen again."

"You mean she *died* in the fire?" Nicole asked, horrified.

"Most people think so," Mr. Morgan said, "but her body was never found. In any case, most people assume that, one way or another, Dolores Weber has passed away. Even if the fire didn't take her, the cold or disease could have. The winters here are not kind to anyone living outdoors. And she must have been sixty-something years old."

"What a sorrowful life that poor woman had," Nicole's mother said. "So much tragedy."

"Yes, that's true. In a small way, I tried to help her. Like my grandfather, I offered to buy this property and perhaps the money would have helped Dolores but I guess I didn't try hard enough. I'm sure she must be in heaven now."

"Sometimes it's hard to know what to do," Nicole's mother said.

"What happened to the other people that rented the house?" Nicole's father asked.

"There *were* a few families before you folks," Mr. Morgan said, "but they didn't stay very long. Sometimes people think they're going to like living in an old house in the Maine woods and then they realize that they don't. But, needless to say, some local folks believe that all the renters before you were chased out by Taggart's ghost."

"Well," Nicole's father said, "I hope we last a little longer. I'm pretty sure that we will."

"I'm counting on it," Mr. Morgan said. "After the last family moved out, I promised myself that I would be a better neighbor if I got another chance." He lifted his coffee cup as if making a toast. "So, welcome to the neighborhood."

"Thanks, John," Nicole's father said.

"Yes, thank you, John," his wife added.

"Nicole," Mr. Morgan said, "you asked what it means to settle an estate. It means what happens to a person's property after their death. But since Dolores didn't leave any instructions, this house and land will probably end up being sold by the state. And that will be the end, I'm afraid, of a long and very tragic story."

Nobody said anything for a few moments. Nicole got up from the couch and stared blankly out the window. It was still snowing. Ivy stretched her legs in front of the fire and ambled out toward the hall. Finally, Nicole's father said, "It's almost lunch time. Should I make some sandwiches?"

"Thanks," Mr. Morgan said, standing up, "but I really should be going."

"How about you, Nicole," her mother asked. "Are you hungry?"

"A little, I guess," she said, slowly turning from the window.

"Thanks for stopping by, John," her father said as they all moved into the hallway. He handed Mr. Morgan his coat.

"You're very welcome," their neighbor said. "You're going to like it here, Nicole. I'm sure of it." He crouched down to pet Ivy. "We'll have you over for dinner real soon."

"That would be great," Nicole's father said.

"Maybe sometimes you and your parents would like to go out on my boat."

Nicole looked to her parents. Her mother smiled and nodded. Her father gave a thumbs-up.

"Sure," Nicole said.

"It's easy to see out in the harbor," Mr. Morgan said, "It's all black."

"Does your boat have a name?" Nicole's father asked.

"Corsair."

"It was a pleasure to meet you, John," Nicole's mother said, shaking his hand. "Come again soon. Please give our best to Mrs. Morgan. And thanks for the doughnuts. Right, Nicole?"

She nodded and smiled politely. "Thank you, Mr. Morgan."

"You don't have to eat them," the neighbor said as he put on his coat and hat.

Nicole's father opened the door. A draft of cold air made Nicole shiver. "Be careful on the way home, John," Nicole's mother said.

"I will," he said. "And once again, welcome to Elk River."

"He seems like a nice man," Nicole's mother said after they closed the door.

"I think so too," her husband agreed.

"I'll get lunch started."

"After we eat," Nicole's father said, "let's unpack a few boxes and then take it easy."

Everyone headed for the kitchen.

CHAPTER SEVEN

After lunch, Nicole went to her room, emptied some cartons, then flopped on her bed and wondered what her friends in New Jersey were doing. *Is anyone even thinking about me? Probably not,* she decided. *And I probably won't have any friends in this weird place either.*

Ivy wandered into the room and jumped onto the bed. She snuggled next to Nicole and purred. Nicole noticed the portrait above her desk. The girl in the picture had brown hair and very dark eyes. *She looks like me.* "Ivy," Nicole said aloud, "you have a famous relative." Ivy's eyes were closed.

Nicole shifted her gaze back to the girl in the picture. She was barely smiling and her sad eyes seemed to be staring right into Nicole's. *I wonder if it's Dolores Weber when she was young.*

Nicole got up and wandered to her side window. Snow was still falling. *What a sad life Dolores had.* She looked eastward. Beyond the trees and the cliff, the ocean loomed. Turning toward the back of the house, past the yard, the deep woods stretched up the mountainside as far as Nicole could see.

Something caught her eye. *That's weird. Fresh footprints.* The tracks came out of the woods and circled partway around the edge of the yard. *Doesn't look like they were made by an animal.* The tracks stopped at a big fir tree, halfway across the yard.

Nicole spotted a carton marked "N's bedroom." In a minute, it was open. She grabbed her binoculars, hurried back to the window and focused on the footprints. Now there were more of them and they led to the bushes directly below her. *Whoever made those tracks is right next to the house!*

Nicole ran out of her room and raced down the stairs. "Mom, Dad! Where are you?"

Nicole heard her mother's voice from the sitting room. "I'm here by the fire. What's wrong?"

"There's someone in the yard!"

"You saw someone in the yard? Now?"

"I saw footprints in the snow and then there were more of them. They lead right up to the side of the house." She pointed to the window. "Right there!"

Nicole's mother got up and looked out the window. "Maybe they were already there."

"No, the snow's falling too fast. Whoever made those tracks is outside the house right now." Nicole's father came into the room. "What's up?"

"Nicole says there's someone in the yard."

"We can go look," her father said. "But you can't go out like that."

Nicole hurried to the hall closet and grabbed her coat. "Hurry, Dad!"

By the time he had his coat on, Nicole was pulling the front door open.

"Here," Nicole's father handed her a hat. "I don't want you to get sick."

Nicole stepped outside. A gust of cold wind whistled across the porch.

"Here are your gloves," her father said as he came outside. "Which way should we go?"

"That way," Nicole said, pointing to the left. She moved quickly down the steps and around to the side of the house. The snow on the ground came up past her ankles. More was coming down in big flakes. Nicole looked up at the sitting room window and, behind snow-covered tree branches, saw her mother watching.

"I don't see anybody," her father said, his breath looking like a cloud of steam.

"Look in the bushes, Dad, but be careful." Her heart was pounding.

He crouched down and peered into the overgrown shrubs next to the house.

Nicole shivered as her father slowly worked his way down the length of the house, pushing aside white-blanketed branches. Suddenly, he yelled and Nicole jumped as a bird flapped out of a snow-covered evergreen and into the air.

When he reached the back of the house, Nicole's father emerged from the bushes and walked slowly toward his daughter.

"Nobody there, except for the bird," he said, brushing the snow off his shoulders. "Where exactly did you see this person?"

"I just saw footprints. They came out of the woods and went behind that tree." She pointed to the big fir halfway across the yard. "And then when I looked again, they came right over here."

"You didn't actually see anybody?"

"I didn't say I did."

Another white cloud came out of her father's mouth but he didn't say anything.

"Wait," Nicole said. She trudged through the snow toward the back of the house and saw what she was looking for.

"Here are the footprints," she said, feeling relieved. "And now there's more of them than before."

Nicole's father looked at the tracks. Some were already partly filled in by the wind and fresh accumulation. "It's hard to say when they were made. Maybe an animal left them."

"No, Dad, there was only one set of footprints before. These other ones must have been made when he was leaving."

Father followed daughter to the big fir tree. "See," Nicole said, "whoever it was hid behind this tree on his way to the house and must have gone back the same way before we came outside. Then he went back into the woods."

"I can't make anything out of these tracks," her father said. "There's hardly anything left of them. Maybe we should just go back inside."

"I saw fresh tracks, Dad. I'm not making it up."

"I don't think you're making anything up but you admit that you didn't actually *see* anyone."

Nicole turned toward the woods. She didn't know what to say.

"Let's go back in," he said. "We don't even have boots on and I'm getting cold. We can keep an eye on the yard from inside."

He started toward the front of the house. Nicole followed and then paused. She turned and peered back into the forest. *Who would have come out of the woods in a snowstorm, spied on our house from the bushes and then went back?* Nicole knew her father thought she was, once again, imagining things. *But I didn't make up those footprints and it wasn't an animal.* Back on the porch, she stamped the snow off her feet and went inside.

"See anything?" her mother asked in the hallway.

"Just footprints," Nicole answered as she pulled off her shoes.

"We saw a bird that nearly scared me to death."

"You two better change your clothes," her mother said. "I'm going to unpack a few more boxes before I start dinner."

Nicole went to her room and changed out of her wet pants and socks. Out her side window, the light was fading. The footprints had been nearly erased by the wind and fresh snow. Beyond the yard, the woods were dark. She lay on her bed and closed her eyes.

There was a knock on the door. Nicole had fallen asleep. Her room was dark. "Dinner's ready." It was her mother's voice.

"Okay," she answered as she sat up, rubbing her eyes. "I'll be right down."

At dinner, Nicole sat down across from her father just as her mother appeared with a steaming platter of spaghetti and meatballs. "Did you get some of your things unpacked?" she asked.

"A few boxes."

"See anybody else in the yard?" her father asked, smiling.

"I never said I saw anybody," Nicole replied, not smiling. "I said I saw footprints."

"Your father was just teasing," her mother said with a glance at her husband as she sat down.

"You think I made it up?"

"No, I don't think you made it up," Nicole's father said as he filled his plate. "I was just kidding."

"Well, I don't think it's funny when someone doesn't believe me, or thinks I'm imagining things when I'm not. Like that music last night."

Nicole's father passed the platter to his daughter. "I know you saw some sort of tracks," he said. "I saw them too. But I'm not convinced that they were made by a person or that they were made today, that's all. I'm not attacking you."

"Whatever."

"Tonight," her mother said, "let's get to bed early. Tomorrow's a big day."

"Are you looking forward to seeing your new school and

making new friends?" her father asked.

"It should be great. Starting a new school in the middle of the year and not knowing anybody."

"Maybe it would help," her father said, "if you could be a little bit more positive."

"I was just kidding, Dad."

After dinner, Nicole did the dishes with her father. There wasn't much conversation. Afterward, they went into the sitting room. Her father turned on the TV. Nicole's mother put a kettle on the stove for tea.

"Okay if I use the computer?"

"Sure, go ahead," her father said.

A few of her friends were online. So, for almost an hour, Nicole messaged with her old classmates and former soccer teammates.

"how is it up there?" Brian asked.

"terrible"

It was great to talk with them but when they had to log off, Nicole suddenly felt very lonely. Wandering back to her room, Nicole left the lights off and went to the front window. The snow had stopped and the sky was clear. The stars stood out against the dark sky.

There was a knock on the door and Nicole turned as she heard her father say, "Can I come in?"

"Sure."

"That's east," her father said, silhouetted in the doorway. "When it's clear, you'll see the sun come up in the morning."

Nicole turned back toward the window. "That's nice."

"I know it was hard to leave your friends, Nicole. And I'm sorry about that. Really."

"Don't worry about it, Dad."

"Even though it's a big adjustment for all of us, I'm hoping that, eventually, we'll agree it was the best thing for all of us."

"Okay."

"I'm going to read for a while. I just wanted to say good night."

"G'night."

"Your mother will be up in a minute. I'll see you in the morning."

"Okay."

Nicole continued to stare out the window for a few more minutes before changing into her pajamas. She was sitting on her bed when her mother came in.

"Find anybody online?"

"Yeah, I talked to a few people."

"That's nice," her mother said. "I'm glad."

Nicole pulled the covers back and got into bed.

"I know you miss your friends. Dad and I miss ours too. But we'll all make new ones. It'll just take a little time."

"I know, Mom."

"Do you want to talk?"

"No, I guess I'll just go to sleep."

"Okay," her mother said. She bent down and kissed her daughter's head. "Good night."

Nicole turned away. "Night," she said toward the wall.

The door closed and the room was dark. Nicole felt tears in her eyes and blinked them away. Outside the wind was blowing hard. Pine branches brushed against the windows as the trees swayed. Nicole was thinking about her friends as she fell asleep.

CHAPTER EIGHT

NOVEMBER 25

That night there were no strange dreams and no music. Nicole did wake up a few times but there was only the sound of the wind in the trees.

In the morning, Nicole got up and dressed. Her mother had bought her new jeans and a nice shirt. After breakfast, she hugged Ivy and put on her coat, boots and backpack.

"I hope you'll like your new school," her father said, walking to the front door. "I'll be anxious to hear all about it tonight."

Nicole followed her mother out to the car and climbed in. She was getting a ride since it was the first day but she knew she'd be taking the bus home and it stopped way out where Cliff Road met Mountain Highway. It would be a long walk in the cold. More than half a mile, her mother said.

Nicole didn't feel like talking on the ride into town. She felt queasy and knew it was because she was nervous. Soon they were driving down Main Street almost to the waterfront. They turned left on Atlantic Avenue and stopped a few blocks later in front of a three-story, brick building. A wooden sign said "Joshua L. Chamberlain Junior High School." The sign and the building both looked old, like everything else in the town.

School buses were already unloading their passengers. The kids jostled and crowded into the building, their winter jackets and backpacks with Beanie Babies filling the doorway. Some of the kids looked tiny.

Sixth graders.

The older students all seemed to know each other. They laughed and talked, pushing and bumping as they funneled into the school. A few looked at Nicole but nobody said anything.

She followed her mother inside and found the main office. A woman at a metal desk was talking on the phone. A nameplate said "Mrs. Williams." Two boys slouched on a bench in the corner.

"May I help you?" Mrs. Williams said when she hung up the phone.

"This is my daughter's first day here. Can you tell us whom we should speak with?"

"You should speak with Mrs. Petersen, the principal, but she's not in the office right now." Mrs. Williams pointed to the benches in the corner. "Would you like to wait until she comes back?"

Nicole looked at the boys on the bench. They glanced at her and one whispered something to the other. Then they laughed.

Nicole's mother took a seat. Nicole remained standing with her back to the boys.

A few minutes later a tall woman with gray hair came into the office. "You boys get to class," she said, "and come see me after school."

They slouched out of the office.

"I'm Mrs. Petersen," the tall woman said. "Welcome to Chamberlain."

"I'm Mary Kelly and this is my daughter, Nicole."

Mrs. Petersen shook hands with Nicole and her mother,

and they all went into the principal's office. Mrs. Petersen handed a big envelope to Nicole's mother.

"Here's some information about the school that may be helpful, including a student directory. And for you, Nicole, here is your schedule, your locker number and the combination. I hope that you're going to like it here at Chamberlain."

"I'm sure Nicole will be fine," her mother said. "She's a good student."

Nicole tried to smile.

"But since homeroom is almost over," Mrs. Petersen continued, "you may as well go straight to your first class."

Nicole looked at her schedule. Math, language arts, science, social studies. After lunch, a tangle of gym, home economics, art, music, computers and study period. Every day of the week seemed to be different. Nicole sighed. *Just when I finally had my old schedule figured out.*

"I know it all seems confusing right now," Mrs. Petersen said, "but in a few days you'll feel right at home."

Nicole tried another smile. *I don't even feel at home when I am at home,* she thought.

As a bell rang, Mrs. Petersen escorted Nicole and her mother into a hallway that was rapidly filling with students. "I'll show you where your first class is."

Joining the noisy flow of students, they walked past colorful displays of science, math and art projects. Then up two flights of stairs that echoed with laughter, talking and footsteps. The hallway was dark, compared to her old school, with a high ceiling and wooden floors. Halfway down the hall, on the right, was room 318. The wall outside was decorated with poster boards covered with graphs, formulas and pictures of famous mathematicians including several of Einstein. A young woman stood next to the doorway. "Here's your new math student," the principle said. "This is Nicole Kelly and this is her mother, Mary."

"I'm Lynne McDowell," the teacher said, shaking hands with Nicole's mother. "We're very glad to have you, Nicole," she said, shaking hands again. She had a strong grip. Nicole thought she was pretty.

"I have to go," Mrs. Petersen said, "but I hope you have a great first day with us." She shook hands with Nicole and her mother once more and disappeared down the noisy hall.

"Your locker is over there, Nicole," Ms. McDowell said, pointing. "Right outside your home room. You have time to hang up your coat."

With her mother standing next to her, Nicole fumbled with her locker's combination and thought she heard some kids snickering. She put her coat inside the locker, shut the door and walked back to room 318. Her mother followed her to the classroom. "Have a great day," she said.

"Bye," Nicole said softly, looking down.

From the classroom doorway, Nicole saw that most of the other students were already in their seats. Nearly everyone was staring at her.

"I'll see you at the bus stop after school, okay?"

"Just go, Mom."

"Very nice to meet you," her mother said to Ms. McDowell.

The teacher smiled and touched Nicole's mother's arm. "I'm sure we'll talk again soon."

The classroom was noisy as Nicole and her teacher entered. "Class, someone new is joining us today," Ms. McDowell said as the students quieted down. "Her name is Nicole Kelly and she's just moved here from New Jersey. Let's all make her feel welcome at Chamberlain."

Nicole felt uncomfortable standing in front of the class. In the back, one of the boys was making a stupid face at her and other boys were laughing. She wondered where she was supposed to sit, hoping it wasn't going to be next to the boy making faces.

"Nicole," Ms. McDowell said. "Will you please take a seat next to Billy in the last group of desks?"

Feeling the stares of everyone in the class, Nicole walked to the back of the room and sat at the empty desk. Billy made an exaggerated frown. It seemed like all the kids were watching and laughing. All except one. A girl near the front glanced at Nicole without smiling and then looked back toward Ms. McDowell. She had long, straight, black hair.

"Billy, behave yourself," Ms. McDowell said. "Now class, last week we were discussing circles. Can anyone tell me the formula for the area of a circle?"

A few hands went up.

"Michelle?" Ms. McDowell said.

A pretty blonde girl in the front of the room answered: "Pi times radius squared."

"Very good. Or you could say 'Pi R squared,' for short."

"No," Billy whispered as the teacher turned to write the formula on the blackboard. "Pie are round." The other kids in Nicole's group laughed.

"That's a very old joke, Billy," Ms. McDowell said as she turned toward her students. "You should get some new material."

The morning classes weren't too bad. In language arts, Mrs. Rotelli had everyone working on their daily journals and in science, Mr. Forbes talked about insects. Nicole especially liked Ms. McDowell and Mrs. Thorn in social studies. But it was hard not knowing anyone. She ate lunch alone.

When they finished eating, many students got their jackets and went outside. There were lots of snowballs. Some of the boys played football. Most of the girls watched the game or talked among themselves. *Michelle is the most popular*, Nicole observed.

Nicole stood by herself and started peeling a tangerine. Then a group of boys approached. It looked like Billy was the leader.

"Hey!" Billy said, with a big grin on his face. "I hear you live in the Weber house. Seen any ghosts yet?"

The other boys laughed. One of them started making spooky noises.

"I don't believe in ghosts."

"Do you know that a witch used to live there?" Billy asked.

"I don't believe in witches."

"Maybe *she's* a witch," one of the boys said.

"Are you going to turn me into a frog?" One of the boys made croaking sounds.

Nicole wished they would leave her alone.

"That would be impossible," a girl's voice said from behind the boys. Everyone looked to see who it was. It was the girl with the straight, black hair.

"Oh yeah? How do *you* know it's impossible?"

"Because you're *already* a frog," the girl said without smiling. A few of the kids laughed at Billy and he didn't seem to like it. He gave the girl a nasty look and muttered "weirdo" as he stalked away.

"*She's* the witch," one of the boys said to Billy.

"Nah. It just *sounds* like 'witch.'"

The girl with the straight, black hair walked away too. Nicole hurried to catch up to her.

"Hey," Nicole said.

The girl turned around.

"I'm Nicole."

At first, the girl didn't say anything. She was a little taller than Nicole. Her eyes were dark, as dark as her hair and, Nicole thought, she was very pretty. She wore a plain coat.

"I know," the girl finally said.

"What's your name?"

"Alice."

"Thanks for doing that," Nicole said. "With those boys, I

mean."

"Don't let Billy bother you. He's just picking on you because you're new in school and he figures that you don't have any friends."

"I don't."

Alice didn't respond.

"Well, anyway, thanks."

"No problem." Alice turned and started to walk away.

"How come Billy called you 'weirdo'?" Nicole said to Alice's back.

She stopped and turned around. "I guess he thinks I'm weird."

"You don't seem that weird to me."

"I usually keep to myself. Maybe that's what they mean."

"*They*?"

"Did you have a lot of friends back in New Jersey?"

"I don't know about 'a lot,' but, yeah, I had some friends, I guess."

"That's what I figured. So don't worry. You'll fit in fine here." Alice turned and started to walk away again.

"You want some orange?"

Alice turned and looked at the fruit in Nicole's extended hand "I think that's a tangerine," she said, almost smiling.

"Whatever. You want some?"

Alice took a few steps forward. "Sure. Thanks."

"What do kids do around here?" Nicole asked as she handed Alice half of the tangerine.

"There isn't much *to* do. Some kids go to parties but, like I said, I keep to myself. And I read a lot. What about you?"

"Maybe now I'll be reading a little more."

"I've got lots of books in case you want to borrow one."

"Thanks." Nicole popped a section of tangerine into her mouth. "So, you don't hang out with the other kids too much."

A chuckle and a smile, barely. "No, not too much."

"How come? I mean, if I'm not being too nosy."

"Well, like Billy said, I guess some people think I'm weird."

"Well, like *I* said, you don't seem that weird to me."

Alice looked at Nicole for a few seconds before she spoke. "Sometimes people act friendly and then I find out that they don't mean it. So, I keep to myself, and I guess some people think it's weird."

"Why do you say that they don't mean it?"

It seemed like Alice was deciding how, or whether, to answer. "I'm Abenaki," she finally said.

Nicole was puzzled.

"Abenakis are Native Americans. Indians."

"Oh."

"Lots of times people act like they like me or whatever and then I hear them talking about me or making jokes about my family or Native Americans. So now when somebody acts friendly, I wait a little while before I get too excited."

"I don't blame you."

Alice finished her half of the tangerine. "Do you really live in the Weber House?"

Nicole sighed and nodded. "You've heard about it too?"

"Sure," Alice said, "everybody has. Last year a boy in my math class lived there. But he wasn't in the class for long. Almost as soon as his family moved in, they moved back out."

"What happened?"

"Our teacher just said they had to move. But Billy and his stupid friends said it was the curse. You know, the ghost and all that."

"Like I told Billy, I don't believe in ghosts but that house really *is* pretty weird."

"What do you mean?"

"Well, when I went to bed the first night we got here, I'm sure I heard someone playing the piano in the middle of the night. My parents didn't hear anything so they think I imagined it. Then yesterday, I saw footprints in the snow that led right up to the house. My dad said it was probably an animal but I know it wasn't."

Alice seemed to be taking it all in. "Everyone's going back," she finally said. "We better go too."

The rest of the day was okay. Nicole went to the library and the computer lab. She was glad that Alice was in most of her classes. At the end of the day, Nicole returned to room 308 for a study period in her homeroom with Mrs. Thorn.

At 2:45, a bell rang and Nicole's first day at Joshua L. Chamberlain Junior High School came to an end. Mrs. Thorn showed Nicole which bus to get on. She waved to Alice before she boarded and sat next to one of her classmates, Michelle. As the bus started up Mountain Highway, Michelle suggested that maybe she and Nicole could do their homework together sometime since they didn't live too far apart.

"That'd be great."

The bus struggled up the mountain and Nicole peered out the window looking for Cliff Road. She saw her mother waiting at the bus stop.

"See you tomorrow," Michelle said. "And welcome to Chamberlain."

"Thanks," Nicole answered as she picked up her backpack. "See you tomorrow."

She stepped off the bus and slipped into her backpack. Mother and daughter walked toward the woods.

Maybe Elk River will be okay after all.

CHAPTER NINE

"I'm glad that you like your new school," Nicole's mother said between sips of tea.

Nicole nodded. She finished her yogurt and put the container and spoon into the sink. "I think I'm going to check out the attic."

"Okay, Dad and I will be unpacking. Let us know if you find anything interesting."

Nicole went to her room for a flashlight. The stairway to the attic was cold. At the top of the worn steps, Nicole scanned the area with her light. The round windows she had seen from the outside gave no light. Thick wooden rafters slanted upward into the dark.

Shivering, she saw a dressmaker's dummy, an antique sewing machine and several suitcases and trunks covered with stickers. Nicole lifted the rounded lid of the nearest trunk. It was filled with dolls and stuffed animals. She closed the lid and continued to explore. There was old furniture and cobweb-covered paintings leaned against empty frames. She saw some rolled-up tubes of paper sticking out from wooden shelves. It looked like wrapping paper but when Nicole unrolled one, she saw a yellowed map of the *water* near the Rock of Gibraltar. There were hardly any details on the land but hundreds of little numbers on the water. *Must be the depth of the ocean.*

Feeling cold, Nicole decided to explore the basement. As she descended from the attic, the warmth felt good. She passed the second floor and then the first floor and proceeded to the next landing. Straight ahead was the door to the backyard. To the left was the entrance to the cellar. It had a large sliding lock. Nicole slid the bolt and pulled the door open. *Dad was right. It's dark down here.*

She shined her light on the wall. No light switch. She gripped the thin metal railing and stepped down. At the bottom, she pointed her light into the darkness. No windows. She walked carefully over the uneven stone floor. When Nicole reached a wall, she saw that it was just like the floor. It felt cool, too. *It looks like the whole basement is carved out of solid rock.*

An orange light flickered in one corner of the cellar. It was coming from a huge, weird thing with padded pipes that looked like a giant octopus. *The furnace.* She thought she heard squeaking. *Mice. Great.*

She considered retreating but decided to continue. *Nothing to be afraid of.* Nicole took a step and felt something brush against her face. She waved her hands wildly, the flashlight's beam swinging across the walls and ceiling. *Cobwebs!* Nicole fought off her panic. Holding her free hand up as a shield, she proceeded.

The cellar was one big room. In the center was an upside-down boat, like a rowboat, only bigger. *How did they get that in here?* A ladder lay against the side of the boat. Then she saw a doorway in the back wall. The bolt was rusty but loose. Nicole tugged the door open. Bugs scurried away from her light. "Ew."

A stairway led upward. She closed the door, slid the bolt back into place and brushed off her hands.

At one end of the cellar, there were cobweb-covered

shelves with rusty coffee cans filled with nails and screws. She worked her way around the basement, being careful not to trip. In another corner there was a workbench with old tools. Underneath there were cobwebby boards.

Nicole turned and saw a light pointing right at her. She nearly screamed until she realized she was facing a cracked, full-length mirror and the light was a reflection of her own. She let out a long breath. The mirror had a fancy, old-fashioned gold frame. *This house is crazy.*

She noticed a clunky black switch on the wall next to the mirror. She twisted it but nothing happened. *Naturally,* she thought. *But maybe there's a light down here someplace that does work.*

With her flashlight, she followed the wire from the switch. It went up the wall and divided. One wire disappeared above the mirror. The other one looped through the overhead beams and crossed the room. Nicole followed the wire. On the other side of the cellar, it came down the wall and ended at a switch next to the steps. *I knew there had to be a light down here.*

When she twisted the switch, it broke off in her hand. She shook her head.

Nicole decided she had seen just about everything in the cellar and started up the steps, then she stopped. *That feels like a draft. But how can that be? This cellar is carved out of solid rock.* She shrugged and trudged up the stairs.

CHAPTER TEN

NOVEMBER 26

On Tuesday, Nicole ate lunch with Alice and Becky from Mrs. Thorn's class. When Becky learned that Nicole had played soccer in New Jersey, she suggested that Nicole join the indoor soccer club. "It's today," Becky said. "You can wear your gym clothes and there's a late bus on Tuesdays. The girls are really nice."

Nicole finished her lunch and went to the pay phone. "That sounds great," her mother said. Becky was right. Nicole already knew some of the players but everyone was friendly. It felt good to play again.

By the time soccer was over, it was getting dark. Nicole pushed the handle on the fogged-up gym door and stepped into the cold. A few girls were waiting for rides. "See you tomorrow," a tall girl named Jerry said with a smile.

"See you tomorrow." Nicole climbed into the waiting bus. No one she knew was on it so she plopped down alone next to a window near the back. The ride through town and up Mountain Highway went quickly and the bus soon arrived at Cliff Road. Nicole had told her mother that it wasn't necessary to meet her, so as the bus pulled away, she started to walk. She clumped across the bridge and into the woods. It was cold but not yet completely dark. An owl hooted somewhere and Nicole heard the muffled sound of the surf. She scanned the darkening sky and smiled as the gulls, with bent wings, soared above the trees. Even higher were the hawks. They were beautiful to watch but Nicole knew that as they coasted gracefully in broad circles, they were hunting for an unsuspecting mouse or rabbit.

Recalling the weird piano music on the first night and the mysterious tracks in the snow the next afternoon, she felt a sudden chill. *Maybe the walk from the bus stop is a little scary.* Nicole quickened her pace. As she emerged from the trees, she was happy to see lights on in her house.

Her mother was preparing dinner. The kitchen was warm and smelled good. They chatted while Nicole ate some yogurt before she went up to her room.

After turning on some music and doing some math problems, Nicole heard the front door open. A few minutes later her mother knocked on her door. "Dad's home. We'll eat in a few minutes."

After dinner, Nicole finished her homework. She noticed the notebook with the fake marble cover: the daily journal for Mrs. Rotelli's class. Nicole picked up a pen and flopped onto her bed. She opened the notebook to the first page and thought for a few seconds before she began to write.

Tuesday, November 26, 1996

Mrs. Rotelli said to write something every day so here goes.

School was actually all right today. In math, they were talking about navigating and at first, I had no idea what they were saying. I got called on but it ended up okay. Now I know what a binnacle is. At least I didn't sound like a complete idiot. Or maybe I did. Who knows?

After school, I went to the gym and played soccer for

a while. The girls seem pretty nice. There were guys there too.

At dinner, my dad grilled me about it.

That's it for now.

Nicole slid the journal into her backpack. She walked into the study, went online after a couple of delays, and found some friends from her old school. A few girls were going to sleep over at Dorie's house Friday night. After logging off, Nicole went downstairs, watched part of a movie on TV, had some ice cream and said good night to her parents. Back in her room, she closed the door, climbed into bed and read for a while but soon became sleepy and turned off the light. She listened as the wind swept through the trees. Nicole snuggled under her blankets and soon she was asleep.

But in the middle of the night, she woke up. Nicole had to think for a moment to remember where she was. A branch brushed against the house and it came to her: *Maine*. Nicole thought she heard something downstairs, but what? She looked at her clock. It was 2:27 a.m. She listened. Only the wind.

Then Nicole heard the noise again. It came from the hallway and it sounded like a creaking floorboard. The mysterious piano music flashed in her mind.

Maybe Ivy is trying to get in, Nicole thought, trying to remain calm. She got out of bed, crept to the door and opened it. No Ivy. She looked across the stairway to her parents' room. The door was closed and no light reflected under it. Nicole picked up the flashlight on her desk. Following its beam, she walked around the balcony to the top of the stairs. Her free hand gripped the railing. The house, and especially the floor, were cold.

"Here, Ivy. Come on, girl."

Nicole thought she heard something at the bottom of the

stairs but when she looked there was only darkness. As she tiptoed onto the first step, the ship's clock chimed five times.

"Do you want to come in my room, girl?"

She thought she heard a noise in the library. *It's just Ivy.*

She took a deep breath, continued down the stairs and shined the light into the pitch-black room to her right. Thinking she heard something, maybe a metallic click, Nicole crept into the library. She pointed the light past the "ghosts" and there was her cat. Ivy was standing on her hind legs next to the fireplace, scratching on the wooden molding. Nicole exhaled, crossed the room and crouched next to her pet.

"Ivy, you silly thing," she said, stroking the cat's back, "Why is your fur is standing up? *I'm* the one who was scared. Come on, let's go back to bed."

Cradling Ivy in her arms, Nicole stood up. But as she turned to leave the room, the shuttered silver mirror caught her eye. The doors were open! Nicole aimed her flashlight at the mirror. For a moment she stared blankly at its dusty surface.

Her name was still there in the dust but now a line was drawn through it and "My house" was written underneath.

Suddenly, Nicole was afraid. She dropped Ivy, ran out of the library, raced up the stairs and around the balcony and burst into to her parents' room. "Mom! Dad! Someone's in the house!

Nicole's mother sat up. "What's the matter?"

"Downstairs! There's someone in the house! They wrote on the mirror! Hurry!"

Her father propped himself up on one elbow. He didn't look happy. "Nicole, what are you talking about? Are you trying to give me a heart attack?"

"Look for yourself. I woke up and I heard something. I thought it was Ivy. When I went to look for her, I heard it again, in the library. I found Ivy but then I saw the mirror was open. And someone wrote 'My house.'"

Nicole's mother looked at her husband. "Did you do that?"

"No, I did not." Now he didn't *sound* happy. "But I'll go look."

Nicole listened as her father trudged downstairs and walked around the first floor. She heard him curse when he bumped into something. Soon he was coming back up.

"There's nobody there, and I didn't see anything wrong with the mirror."

Both parents looked at Nicole.

"That's impossible! I just saw it. Do you think I'm making this up?"

"Maybe you just had a dream, dear," her mother said.

"I'm going to look," Nicole said. "You must have looked in the wrong place."

"Fine, we'll all go," her father said.

When they were in the library, Nicole's father stood in front of the mirror. "Is this what you're talking about?"

The mirror's shutters were closed.

Nicole couldn't believe it. "They were open before." She walked up to the mirror, opened the shutters and was stunned. The mirror was clean. She looked from one parent to the other.

"It's all right, dear," her mother said. "I'm sure you *thought* you saw something. You were sleepy and the darkness must have played a trick on you."

"No!" Nicole insisted. "I know what I saw. I didn't imagine it. I saw Ivy over there just where she is now." Everyone looked toward the fireplace where the cat was once again scratching at the woodwork.

"I picked Ivy up and the mirror was open. When we first came in here, I closed the doors because I thought it looked better. Remember, Mom, I wrote my name and said that you needed to dust?"

"I guess so but I don't really remember you writing your name."

"Well, I did. And then I closed the doors. But when I came down here tonight, they were open but my name was crossed out and someone wrote 'My house.' Somebody was in here! That must be what I heard."

"Nicole," her father said slowly, "the front door and the windows are all locked in this room. I'll check the other rooms and I'm guessing they're still locked too. I don't know about the mirror and the dust but I don't think anybody came in here. Maybe you or Mom dusted it."

"That *is* possible," her mother said, yawning. "I did do some cleaning in here."

Nicole was near tears. "Why won't you believe me? Just a minute ago, I saw my 'My house' under my crossed-out name in the same room where I heard the piano."

"I'll go check the back door and the rest of the windows."

Nicole and her mother went upstairs while her father went into each room on the first floor.

"Everything's locked," he said, when he came into his daughter's room a few minutes later. "I'm sorry you were frightened, Nicole. And I know you didn't make anything up. I'm sure you really did hear something. This house is full of noises."

"We'll straighten it out in the morning," her mother said.

"I know what I saw, Dad," Nicole said. Desperately, she looked to her mother but it was no use. *They don't believe me.*

"Let's just try to go back to sleep," her father said.

Nicole lay down on her bed and pulled the covers up to her chin. Her mother stroked her hair but Nicole turned away.

"Good night, Sweetheart," her mother said. She kissed Nicole's head and stood up.

"Mom?"

"What is it, Nicky?"

"Will you stay for a while?"

"Of course I will." She sat down on the bed next to her daughter. Nicole rolled over to face her mother. A few minutes later, just before her mother turned off the light, Nicole glimpsed the portrait hanging over her desk. Even in the darkness, the little girl with the sad eyes seemed to be looking right into her own.

They don't believe me. She felt tears coming into her eyes. It was a while before Nicole fell asleep.

CHAPTER ELEVEN

NOVEMBER 27

As Nicole came downstairs for breakfast, she heard her parents' hushed voices in the kitchen. They stopped when she entered the room and dropped her backpack on the floor.

"Good morning," her mother said, putting a steaming bowl of oatmeal onto the table. "Did you sleep the rest of the night?"

"I guess so."

"I'm glad you just have half a day today."

Her father took a sip from his coffee mug. "Try not to worry about last night. A lot has happened to us lately. We moved. We're in a strange—I mean, a different house. You're at a new school with all new teachers and you've just started to make new friends. It's not surprising that you might have dreams that seem real or that your imagination could play tricks on you. I had a dream the other night that I was back at my old job."

Nicole took a deep breath. "That's great, Dad, but I didn't imagine anything. I wasn't dreaming."

"I know you're not making anything up. But it's easier for me to believe that you *thought* you saw something than it is for me to believe that a pirate or a ghost or somebody came into the house through locked doors in the middle of the night, wrote a message on the mirror and then, a minute later erased it and disappeared."

"I didn't say *who* did it. Who said anything about ghosts and pirates?" She stirred her oatmeal. "I know what I saw," she mumbled into her bowl.

"We can talk about it later," her mother said, "but for now let's try not to worry, okay? If you want, I can meet you at the bus stop after school. Then you won't have to walk home by yourself."

"I don't mind walking through the woods," Nicole said as she put her bowl in the sink. "At least nobody calls me a liar there."

"That's not fair," her father shot back. "Nobody said you were lying."

"Fine," Nicole muttered, picking up her backpack. She walked out of the kitchen and into the hallway. She put on her coat, beret and gloves, pulled on her boots and slung her backpack over her shoulders. Without turning around, she stepped outside.

The morning was clear and cold. The powdery snow crunched under her boots. Her breath came out in big clouds. She trudged through the yard and into the woods barely noticing the trees and birds. As Nicole neared the wooden bridge, she heard a car coming out of Mr. Morgan's driveway. It slowed, then stopped beside her. The driver's dark window came down and her neighbor waved.

"Hi, Nicole. Do you want a ride the rest of the way to the bus stop?"

"No, thanks, Mr. Morgan. I'm almost there."

"How's Chamberlain?"

"It's okay."

"Are you starting to feel at home in your new house?"

Nicole looked down at the snow and nudged a clump with

her boot. "It's okay."

"I'm glad," Mr. Morgan said. "Have a good day."

"Thanks. You too."

The window went up and the car pulled away. Nicole crossed the bridge and walked the rest of the way to the highway. When the bus arrived, she climbed aboard and saw Michelle sitting near the back. She beckoned for Nicole to sit next to her. When she did, Michelle handed her a small envelope.

"What's this?"

"Open it and see for yourself." Michelle said with a smile.

Nicole tore the envelope open. It was an invitation to a party. "Thanks."

"It's going to be a holiday party. It's a week from Saturday. Just about everyone will be there."

"Well, I'll have to ask my parents but I'm pretty sure they'll say it's all right. I'd love to come." Her smile was genuine.

"Great!" Michelle said. "Let me know, okay?"

"I will, don't worry. It's really nice of you to invite me, especially since I just moved here."

"That doesn't matter. We all want you to like it here."

When Nicole got to her locker, the first person she saw was Billy. "What's the matter with you?" he asked with a grin. "You look like you were up all night. Is the ghost keeping you awake?"

Nicole glared at him. She slammed the locker closed and looked across the noisy hall for Alice. Then she weaved through the crowd and met her friend as she spun her combination lock.

"You look tired," Alice said, looking up.

"I know. Billy just told me."

"Sorry."

"That's okay, but I really need to talk to you."

They made their way back across the hall and into room

308. "What about?"

"My house. Weird things have been happening. And scary things. *Real* scary."

But before Nicole could say anything else, Mrs. Thorn told everyone to take their seats.

"We'll talk later, okay?" Alice said.

Since it was a half-day, the last class was social studies. After a quiz, Mrs. Thorn said she had a special assignment. "Between now and New Year, I want each of you to work on a research project." Mrs. Thorn waved away the groans.

"Your subject is going to be our town, Elk River. Your research can be about anything that ever happened here. It can be something that happened last month or 100 years ago. You can look in the town library, in newspapers or talk to people that know about your subject. Ms. Deagan can also help you in our school library." Mrs. Thorn raised her voice over the rising clamor. "A week from Monday, I'd like everyone to tell me what their project is going to be. When you've finished your research, I want you to write a report. Everyone will read his or hers to the class on the first day back after Christmas vacation."

"Great!" Billy said. "They're not due 'til next year."

Everyone in the class laughed.

Mrs. Thorn smiled. "That's true, Billy," she said. "But if I were you, I wouldn't wait until then to get started."

"How long does it have to be?" a boy named Simon asked.

"About like an article in the newspaper," Mrs. Thorn said. "I don't care about the length as much as the quality."

Brian raised his hand. "Can it be about sports?"

"Yes. It can be about anything you like but choose your topic carefully and be ready to share your decision with the whole class a week from Monday." The teacher scanned the classroom for additional questions but there weren't any. "And now," Mrs. Thorn said, "it's almost time to go."

The room was suddenly noisy as the students began getting out of their seats, talking and loading their books and papers into their backpacks.

"I said *'almost'* time to go."

Mrs. Thorn waited for silence. "One more thing. A little assignment while you're eating your turkey."

"Come on, Mrs. Thorn," one of the boys moaned, "it's a holiday."

"Don't worry, Nick, it won't be too painful. Over the weekend, I want each of you to think about what Thanksgiving means to you. I'll ask you to share your thoughts on Monday."

"That's it?" Nick asked. "We don't have to *write* anything? All we have to do is think?"

"That's it," Mrs. Thorn replied. "That won't be too hard for you, will it, Nick?"

"No problem, Mrs. T."

Mrs. Thorn smiled. "Enjoy your holiday and I'll see you next week."

Everyone streamed into the hallway making even more noise than usual. Nicole could hardly wait to talk to Alice. Nicole went to her locker, loaded her backpack and slammed the door.

"Hey," Alice said.

"Hey."

"So, tell me about your house."

The hallway was still crowded and noisy.

"Let's go outside," Nicole said.

The afternoon was gorgeous and everyone seemed happy as the holiday weekend began. Nicole led Alice away from the lines forming for the buses. "I've got to talk to somebody before I go crazy."

"Well, I'm somebody," Alice answered with a faint smile.

Nicole told her friend about the previous night's strange events. "Worst of all," she concluded, "my parents don't believe me. They think I'm imagining everything."

Alice didn't say anything.

"And you don't believe me either, do you?" Nicole said.

Her friend took her time before answering. "Of course I do."

"You don't think I'm imagining it?"

"Nope. I don't think you'd imagine stuff like that. Who would?"

Nicole felt like hugging her. "What do you think is happening then?"

Alice lowered her voice and looked around to see if anyone was listening. "I don't know the answer to that but I do know that weird things happened in your house before you moved in. At least the kids that lived there said so."

"Weird things like what?"

"Strange sounds, things getting moved or disappearing when no one was around. Stuff like that."

"And did their parents believe them?"

"I don't know. Maybe their parents thought *their* kids were going crazy too. But the kids really *were* scared. They weren't making *that* up."

"Well, I'm sure glad that you believe me. I was starting to think that maybe *I* was going totally crazy."

"Maybe you are," Alice said with a grin. "But not because of a ghost."

A school bus started its engine with a big cloud of blue smoke. Nicole picked up her backpack. "I guess I better get going. I'll call you, okay?"

"Okay," Alice said with a smile.

"Oh, are you going to go to Michelle's party?"

Alice's smile disappeared. "Michelle's having a party?" she said. "No, I don't think I will be going. I guess you are, though."

"You're getting invited too," Nicole said. "Michelle said that everyone's coming."

"I sit next to her in math, remember. You really think she forgot to tell me? You probably weren't supposed to say anything about it."

The bus revved its engine, making another cloud of smoke.

"You're going to miss your bus."

Nicole climbed onto the first step then turned. "I'll call you."

Alice was already walking away.

As the bus started to move, Nicole walked slowly down the aisle. The bus passed Alice but she didn't look up.

"Hey, Nicole."

"Oh, hi, Michelle."

"Have a seat."

"Thanks."

"How'd you do on that social studies quiz?" Michelle asked.

"Okay, I guess. How'd you do?"

"Pretty well, I think."

"I was just talking to Alice."

"I know," Michelle said. "I saw you."

"I think she's upset 'cause she didn't get the invitation to your party yet."

"You told her about the party?"

For a few seconds, she stared blankly at her classmate. "Yeah, I guess I did." She glanced out the window before facing Michelle. "Didn't you say that everyone was invited?"

"I said *just about* everyone."

"Alice isn't invited?"

"She's too weird."

"I think she seems nice."

"You haven't known her as long as I have. You should have seen her at Debby's Halloween party last year."

"What happened?"

"Somebody wore an Indian costume. You know, with war

paint and feathers and everything. It was just for fun but all Alice could say was 'Native Americans aren't a joke.' Then she just sat by herself. It kind of spoiled the party."

Nicole didn't know what to say.

"She's always so serious about everything," Michelle continued. "Like her report on Christopher Columbus a few weeks ago. Whether he was good or bad, who really cares? It was like, a thousand years ago."

"She told me she's Native American."

"That's no secret," Michelle said. "But that's not why I didn't invite her. I'm not prejudiced or anything. I just think she's weird and so does everyone else."

"She doesn't seem weird to me," Nicole said softly, once again looking out the window.

"Let's just say that she's not much fun at a party and that's why I didn't invite her."

"I'm sorry I said anything about it to her."

"Yeah, I don't want to hurt her feelings or anything."

Nicole rode the rest of the way home in silence.

"Bye," she said to Michelle when the bus arrived at Cliff Road.

"Happy Thanksgiving."

"You, too," Nicole answered.

She stepped off the bus and trudged into the woods.

CHAPTER TWELVE

NOVEMBER 28

Nicole slept late. When she went downstairs, the kitchen smelled good. "Happy Thanks-giving," her mother said as she mixed chopped onions into a bowl of stuffing.

"Happy Thanksgiving," Nicole mumbled. She opened the refrigerator and decided on some juice and a bagel. She sat at the kitchen table. "Where's Dad?"

"He went into town to pick up some things for dinner. We'll probably eat around five-thirty."

Nicole took a bite of bagel. "I got invited to a party yesterday."

Her mother looked up from the mixing bowl. "That's great. Who invited you?"

"A girl named Michelle. She's in some of my classes."

"When is it?"

"A week from Saturday."

"I think it would be great to do something with your new friends."

"Yeah," Nicole said between bites of bagel. "It *would* be."

Her mother tasted a piece of stuffing, then sprinkled in some spices. "What do you mean?"

"Remember I told you about Alice? She stuck up for me

when some boys were teasing me."

"I remember."

"Well, she's *not* invited to the party. And after I stupidly told her about it, her feelings were hurt and she's probably mad at me. Then I had to admit to Michelle that I told Alice about the party. Now Michelle's probably mad at me for having a big mouth. In half a week of school, I managed to make everyone hate me."

"I'm sure it's not as bad as that," her mother said. "Both girls must know that you didn't mean to upset anyone."

"You don't get it, Mom."

Nicole's mother put the bowl of stuffing in the refrigerator and then sat across the table from her daughter. "You'd like to go to the party but you don't want to hurt Alice's feelings."

"It's not just that. Michelle says she didn't invite Alice because she's weird."

"Do *you* think she's weird?"

"No. She's just quiet."

"Maybe it's just Michelle that doesn't like Alice," Nicole's mother said.

"Alice is Native American."

"Oh. Now I see. You're afraid that Alice might be unpopular because she's Native American."

"Michelle says it's not true. Even Alice didn't say it. All Alice said was that sometimes she hears people saying mean things or making jokes about Native Americans and she doesn't like it."

"Well, you can't blame her for that."

"I know. I'm just trying to figure out what to do. I feel like I'm caught in the middle."

"I'm sorry, Nicole. I agree. It's a tough situation."

"What did we have to come here for? If we were back home, I'd probably be with my friends right now. Instead, I'm stuck up here in the middle of nowhere with no friends. Just people who're mad at me."

Nicole's mother reached across the table and put her hand on her daughter's arm. I'm sorry, Sweetheart, but I think it will get better. It just takes time."

"Whatever you say, Mom."

"Do you want to help me with dinner? I still have some things to do."

Nicole looked at her mother.

"How about if setting the table is your job? We're going to eat in the dining room."

"Okay."

Nicole went upstairs, showered and got dressed. Looking out her front window as she dried her hair, she saw that the sun was out. The blue sky was bright behind the evergreens and snow. When her hair was nearly dry, she went back down to the kitchen.

Nicole's mother was looking at a cookbook.

"I think I'll take a walk, Mom. It looks like it's nice out. I'll help you when I get back, okay?"

"All right. If you see some nice pinecones, pick them up, okay?"

"Okay."

After tugging her boots on, and putting on her coat and hat, Nicole pulled the front door open and stepped onto the porch. The icicles on the edge of the porch weren't dripping and the treetops swayed with the gusty wind.

Pulling her mittens out of her pockets, Nicole stepped down onto the un-shoveled path and followed it to the driveway. In a few minutes she was in the woods and her house disappeared behind the trees.

She crossed the covered bridge. The forest was still dense but after the road curved left, there was a nearly unobstructed view of the water far below. The sun was almost overhead, the sky was cloudless, and the bay was a white-capped, sparkling blue-gray. Across the water, Elk River stood out clearly. Beyond the town, and dominating the entire view, was the ocean. Nicole left the road, made her way down past some stone outcroppings and stood next to a craggy pine near the cliff. The wind coming off the water was stiff but it felt good. Nicole stood for several minutes simply enjoying the view.

Across the bay, a fishing boat struggled toward Elk River and a gust of wind convinced Nicole that it was time to head back to a warm house. She spotted some big pinecones and stooped down for them. But as Nicole stood up, she was startled to see a man in the middle of Cliff Road. He was looking through binoculars and seemed to be staring right at her.

Frightened, Nicole ducked behind the pine. The wind was very cold.

After what seemed like an eternity, she slowly peeked out from behind the tree. The man had turned. He was old, had a gray beard and, under a hunter's cap, silver hair. He wore a long dark coat.

Did he see me?

The man lowered his binoculars and reached into his coat pocket, producing glasses and a small book. He looked at it briefly before returning the book and glasses to his pocket. The man turned toward Nicole and stepped forward. She tried to be invisible behind the tree.

Seconds passed but it seemed much longer. Nicole was shivering. When she dared to look, the man was walking, with a limp, toward Mountain Highway.

Nicole waited until the man disappeared before she climbed up to the road. A car was coming. *I should have stayed where I was.*

But the car was her father's. Nicole ran into the road and waved. The car crunched to a stop and the passenger window came down.

"Nice of you to come out to meet me."

"Did you pass an old man walking toward the highway?"

"*A man? On foot? Out here?*"

"Yes! Wearing a long coat. And limping. Did you see him? He was just here a minute ago."

"I haven't seen anyone on foot since I left town. Who was he?"

"How should I know? I went down near the cliff and when I turned around this old guy was staring at me through binoculars. I can't believe you didn't see him."

"Well, I'm sorry, Nicole, but I didn't. Why don't you get in. We'll drive out to the highway and maybe we'll see him."

She jumped into the car and pulled the door shut. Her father turned the car around. When they arrived at the intersection, he stopped.

"I swear I saw someone. I can't imagine how he disappeared so fast."

"He probably went down a path or something."

"You probably think I'm making it up, like the piano and the mirror."

"I thought no such thing. He was probably taking a walk and slipped past us somehow. Maybe he went into the woods for some reason. Maybe he had to pee."

"Why was he looking at me with binoculars?"

"Maybe he was looking at the ocean, same as you. Why didn't you ask him?"

"You think that's what I should have done? Out here? By myself?"

"I don't know, Nicole. Do you want to ride up or down the highway a little way to see if we see him?"

"Okay."

Her father drove more than a mile north on Mountain Highway. Then he drove back past Cliff Road halfway to Elk River. There were few cars and no pedestrians.

"Forget it, Dad," Nicole said, staring out the side window. "Let's just go home."

CHAPTER THIRTEEN

"Do you want another piece of pie?"

"No thanks, Mom. I'm full."

"That was really great, Mary," Nicole's father said, leaning back in his chair. "How about if Nicole and I take care of the dishes and you relax by the fire?"

When the dishes were done, Nicole and her father went into the sitting room. Nicole's mother was reading.

"Anybody mind if I put on the game?"

"It's okay with me," her mother said from the end of the couch closest to the fireplace. Nicole slumped at the other end. Her father turned on the TV and moved a chair to face it. "I just want to see what the score is."

Nicole stared at the fire and wondered what she would do during the next three days. Frowning, she remembered Mrs. Thorn's homework assignment. As the fire crackled, she thought of her friends in New Jersey and then her classmates at Chamberlain. *Alice. Michelle. The party.*

Nicole stood up. "I'm going upstairs to do my homework."

Her mother looked up from her book. "Really?"

"We're supposed to think about what Thanksgiving means to us. This is probably a good time to do it. Maybe I'll go online too."

In her room, Nicole turned on her CD player and reached into her backpack for her assignment notebook and journal. She took a pen from her desk and flopped onto her bed.

"Thanksgiving," Nicole wrote. She thought for a moment and then jotted "turkey" and "family." She paused and added "friends." Nicole put pen and notebook down beside her. *Friends.*

She got off the bed, walked to the study, and sat in front of the computer.

Only one of her New Jersey friends, Tanya, was online but she had to log off to go to her grandmother's. There was going to be a party at Maria's house on Saturday night.

"We miss you," Tanya wrote.

"I miss you guys too. Say 'hi' for me."

She went back downstairs and into the sitting room.

"Mom, where's that list from school with everybody's phone number?"

"It's in the drawer under the phone."

Nicole rummaged through the drawer until she found the Chamberlain directory. Students were listed by homeroom and there was only one Alice, Alice Attean, under Mrs. Thorn's name. She copied the number onto a notepad and hurried back upstairs. Feeling nervous, she dialed.

After a few rings, Alice answered. "Hello?"

"It's Nicole."

"Hey."

"Happy Thanksgiving."

"Oh, thanks. Same to you."

"You're not still eating dinner or anything are you?" Nicole asked.

"No, we finished a while ago."

"Yeah, we did too. I had to help clean up."

"Oh," Alice said.

"I was trying to work on our social studies assignment.

You know, about Thanksgiving? Have you, like, started working on it yet?"

"We were talking about it at dinner."

"So far, I haven't really thought of anything very good," Nicole said. "Just, you know, turkey and stuff."

"We couldn't think of much good either."

"I was going to look in our history book."

"It doesn't have anything," Alice said.

"Are you doing anything this weekend? Like with relatives or anybody?"

"We're going to visit some relatives in Bangor."

"Oh, that's nice," Nicole said. "I guess I won't be seeing any relatives for a while. Christmas, maybe."

"That'll be nice."

"Yeah, I guess so."

For a moment there was an uncomfortable silence.

"Well," Nicole said, "I just wanted to say 'Happy Thanksgiving.' I'll see you in school on Monday."

"Okay," Alice said. "See you."

"Bye."

"Bye."

Nicole put down the phone and walked back to her room. She got onto her bed and looked at the ceiling. After a few minutes, she got up and shut off the light on her nightstand. She went to her front window and looked toward the ocean. The moon wasn't full but it was bright and the bay shimmered. Lights from Elk River flickered on the far shore. Alone in the open water, the lighthouse beacon swept past every few seconds.

It all looked cold.

Nicole began to turn away from the window when something caught her eye: a glimmer of light. Nicole scanned the dark sky and saw nothing unusual. She was about to turn away a second time when she saw it again. A dim yellow spot but not from the sky. It came from the top of the tower. Nicole stared at the silhouette that blocked a column of stars. The light appeared again. *It's coming from inside! There's someone in the tower!*

Nicole ran to her closet, found the binoculars and hurried back to the window. It took a moment to focus the binoculars but the light was still there. Magnified, it seemed to flicker but otherwise didn't move. *Is it a candle?*

Nicole put the binoculars on the windowsill, hurried out of her room and down the stairs. She paused and took a breath before entering the sitting room. Trying to sound calm, Nicole said "There's a light in the tower. I think someone is up there!"

Nicole's mother closed her book. "Really? Let's go see, Paul."

Without taking his eyes off the TV screen, her father got up from his chair. "What a hit!"

"Come on, Dad!" Nicole called from halfway up the stairs.

"Okay," her father answered from the bottom of the steps.

Nicole hurried to the window. "Close the door," she said as her parents arrived. The room went black. Nicole peered at the tower through the binoculars. It was completely dark. "It's gone," she said, without turning to face her parents. "But I saw it, I swear."

"Of course you did," her mother said. "I wonder what it was."

"Can I take a look?"

Nicole stepped aside and held out the binoculars for her father. He squinted through the glasses and adjusted the focus. "Do you think you might have seen the lighthouse?"

"Dad, you're looking in the wrong direction. It was at the top of the tower. It looked like it might have been a candle or something."

"Pretty far away to see a candle. How about the moon? Or a ship?"

"It wasn't the moon and it didn't come from the ocean, okay? You're not even looking in the right place. Try looking at the top of the tower."

Her father swung the glasses upward.

Nicole walked to her door and switched on the light. "Forget it. I just made it up. Just like the man out by the cliff."

"What man by the cliff?" her mother said.

"When I was coming back from town this afternoon, I met Nicole on the other side of the bridge. Apparently, she saw someone who startled her just before I showed up."

"*Apparently* I imagined it, just like all the other things I made up since we got here."

"I didn't say that," her father answered. "We just didn't see anybody, that's all."

"Oh, right. You said maybe he had to pee or something."

"What do you want me to say, Nicole? I believe you saw someone this afternoon and I believe you saw a light in the tower too. Do you want me to say *I* saw them? Okay, I saw them. Satisfied?"

"Yeah, that's what I want, Dad. Thanks a lot."

"All right, you two," her mother said.

Nicole returned to the window. Her father shook his head.

"I have an idea," Nicole's mother said. "In the morning why don't we go out to the tower? We can go inside and maybe in the daylight we can figure out what made the light. Plus, I'll bet the view is wonderful from the top. What do you think?"

Nicole stared out the window.

"We can go right now," her father said.

"*Now?*" Nicole's mother said. "In the dark?"

"Yes. Right now. If anybody was, or is, in the tower, there should be footprints in the snow." Nicole spun around. "Let's go!"

"*Nobody* should go," her mother said. "Wait until morning. The footprints will still be there. And if someone *is* out there, I don't want to run into him."

"No," Nicole's father insisted. "I want to get to the bottom of this."

Nicole started for the door. "I'm getting my coat."

"If your father wants to run around in the dark and fall off the cliff, I can't stop him. But *you* are definitely *not* going."

"It's my word that's at stake. Besides, there's nothing out there, right?"

"No one has ever doubted your word," her mother said.

"We can all go," Nicole's father stated.

Her mother shook her head. "What if someone dangerous *is* out there?"

"We won't go into the tower," Nicole's father answered. "We'll just look for footprints."

Nicole opened her closet and produced a flashlight. "There's another one downstairs."

"It's a nice night," Nicole's father said. "We can use a little exercise."

"Come on, Mom, let's go."

"Yeah, Mom," Nicole's father added. "Let's go."

"This is insane."

Within minutes, the whole family was outside. It was bitter cold with a stinging wind but the sky was clear. The moon cast crisp shadows from the trees onto the snow. The flashlights' yellow circles danced across the yard. It took several minutes, and a few slips, to get near the base of the tower. Nicole shined her light on the dark stones rising before them. They were covered with a tangle of thick vines whose dead leaves were covered with snow. But the flashlight lacked the power to illuminate the top of the structure, a looming void against the starry sky.

"I didn't realize how tall it was," Nicole's mother said.

Her husband pointed his flashlight upward. "I'll bet it's seventy feet."

Nicole shined her light at the base of the curved wall. "There's no opening on this side and I don't see any footprints."

"Let's work our way around," her father said.

They circled the dark structure to the right until they were almost at the edge of the cliff. There were no footprints other than their own.

"Don't go any closer to the edge," Nicole's mother warned.

Far below, the breaking waves pounded the rocks, leaving momentary wisps of white in the moonlight. "Let's go back to the other side," Nicole's father said. They traced their steps to their starting point and continued until they were, once again, close to the cliff. The flashlights' beams crisscrossed over the snow.

No footprints.

"I didn't even see a door," Nicole said.

"Maybe we missed it underneath all the vines," her father suggested.

Nicole pointed her light down at her boots and let out a big breath that made a cloud in the beam. "Let's go back inside."

They crossed the yard in silence.

"Anybody want some hot chocolate or tea?" Nicole's mother said in the hallway as they took off their coats.

"No thanks, Mom. I think I'll just go up to my room."

"You know," her father said, "it *could* have been the moon. It's real bright tonight. Maybe it reflected off something in the tower and that's what you saw."

"Yeah, maybe you're right, Dad. Anyway, I'm going upstairs. I'll see you tomorrow."

"Okay," her mother said. "Sleep late. Happy Thanksgiving."

"Thanks," Nicole answered as she started up the stairs. "Dinner was great."

Nicole sat blankly on her bed. She didn't feel like going online or reading or even listening to music. She noticed her journal and pen beside her. *Might as well finish the perfect day with some homework.*

Thanksgiving

It's been a horrible day.

Actually, it started out okay. It was beautiful outside so I went for a walk. Then I saw a weird guy with binoculars watching me by the cliff. My father drove up right after that but of course he didn't see anybody and probably thinks I made it up. After dinner, I called just about the only person I've made friends with up here and she basically didn't want to talk to me. Next, I saw a light inside the tower in front of the house. But when I got my parents so they could see it too, the light was gone. So my father, who always has to be right about everything, makes everybody go outside to check it out. Naturally, there's no light and no footprints and I look like an idiot again or a hysterical little kid.

It's been a great day. Happy Thanksgiving.

CHAPTER FOURTEEN

DECEMBER 2

"Good morning, everyone," Mrs. Thorn said in homeroom on Monday morning. "I'm sure you're all delighted to be back in school after your long weekend."

A few students groaned.

"The good news is that we have less than three weeks until Christmas."

Nicole looked around the classroom and felt like a stranger. On the bus, Nicole sat alone. At the lockers, Alice nodded but that was all.

"Have a good morning," Mrs. Thorn said when the bell for first period rang.

Nicole got her books together and headed for math class. Just in front of her, Michelle was talking to another girl, Irene. "How was your Thanksgiving?" Michelle said.

"Boring. How was yours?"

"It was all right, I guess. Did you do your homework for social studies?"

Irene looked puzzled. "What homework?"

"The 'What does Thanksgiving mean to you?' thing."

Nicole realized that she had forgotten about the assignment.

Irene shrugged. "I'll make up something. Turkey or whatever."

Michelle laughed. "I wonder what Alice is going to say."

"What do you mean?"

"You know, Pilgrims, Indians and all that."

Irene chuckled. "Oh, right."

Nicole wanted to say something but couldn't find the words. Michelle and Irene moved on to a different subject. Feeling very alone, she arrived at room 318 and took her seat. In math, language arts and science, she didn't say a word.

Fourth period arrived.

"Who would like to tell us," Mrs. Thorn said once the class quieted down, "their personal thoughts or feelings about Thanksgiving?"

No hands went up.

Nicole opened her notebook and saw "turkey," "family" and "friends."

Mrs. Thorn called on Sarah when she put her hand up. "We went to a neighbor's for dinner. I was thankful for my family and friends."

Nicole crossed out the words in her notebook.

"Thank you, Sarah," Mrs. Thorn looked around the classroom. "How about you, Nick? As I recall, you indicated that the assignment wouldn't be a problem."

"Well," Nick said with a grin, "mainly, I was thankful that I didn't have school."

Everybody laughed, including Mrs. Thorn.

"Anything else, Nick?"

"Definitely. I was thankful that I didn't have any homework."

More laughter.

"Anything *serious*, Nick?"

"Yes. I was thankful for a really good turkey dinner."

Nicole crossed out "turkey." Then a girl in the back of the

room put up her hand.

"Theresa?" Mrs. Thorn said.

"At first I forgot about the assignment," Theresa admitted. "But I was watching the news after we finished eating and there was a story about a homeless shelter in Bangor where people went to get a free turkey dinner. That's when I remembered our assignment and I thought that a lot of us probably forget what we have, like warm houses and food and everything."

"Thank you, Theresa," Mrs. Thorn said. "I think you're right."

Theresa glanced around the room for approval as she sat down. A few boys rolled their eyes.

"Anyone else?"

No response.

"Jerry?"

Jerry was one of Nicole's soccer teammates. "Well," she said slowly, "we had a nice dinner with some relatives, probably like everyone else, but after it was over and everybody went home, I went online. There was a story about a Native American protest at Plymouth Rock. You know, where the Pilgrims landed in Massachusetts. They were saying that Thanksgiving was like, a bad day for them. They called it a "Native American Day of Mourning." She held up a sheet of paper. "I printed it."

"What does that say to you, Jerry?"

"It says that Thanksgiving doesn't mean the same thing to everybody. I never really thought of it before but I can see how it could be a sad day for some people."

Nicole glanced at Alice and saw that several other students did too. Alice stared straight ahead, not changing her expression.

"Thank you, Jerry," Mrs. Thorn said. "Would anyone else care to share their thoughts?"

Once again, Nicole noticed that many of her classmates, more this time, turned toward Alice.

"No one has to speak," Mrs. Thorn said.

A few more students raised their hands and spoke about food or family and even football but Nicole barely paid attention. She was thinking about Alice.

Social studies ended and Nicole walked alone to the cafeteria. She got in line in front of a vending machine to buy a bottle of water. The line moved slowly.

"I thought for sure she was going to say *something*," Nicole heard a familiar voice say from behind her.

"Especially after Jerry did her Plymouth Rock thing."

The voice was Michelle's. She was talking to the boy right behind Nicole.

"What's taking this line so long?" he said.

Nicole stared straight ahead. The girl at the front of the line had dropped her change and had crouched down to pick it up.

"Maybe I should have said I was thankful that she didn't give a speech."

The boy laughed.

Nicole turned around. For an instant, Michelle looked surprised. "Oh, hey, Nicole."

"Hey."

"Why do *you* think Alice didn't say anything?"

"I don't know."

"If you're not gonna buy something," the boy called out, "get out of the line, all right?"

Nicole looked over her shoulder. The girl at the front of the line was on her hands and knees trying to reach something under the machine. A coin, probably.

"We were just wondering why she didn't say anything," Michelle said.

"I don't know," Nicole said, looking down.

"I just thought you might have an idea," Michelle said, smiling. "You're friends, right?"

The line moved slightly. Somebody had decided to quit waiting. Nicole turned toward the front of the line and shuffled forward a few inches. She was second from the front.

"It's no big deal," she heard Michelle say.

Nicole turned and faced her. "Maybe she didn't want people to say she was making a speech."

Michelle's smile froze. Then she shrugged. Nicole turned and faced forward. It was her turn at the vending machine. The coins in her hand were sweaty.

The girl who had dropped her change stood up. It was Alice. She looked at Nicole. Then she looked at Michelle, smiled and walked away.

Nicole stared at Alice's back as she disappeared into the cafeteria.

"Next!" the boy said, pointing to the vending machine.

Nicole turned and saw Michelle looking at her. Nicole returned her stare. Neither spoke.

"Before Christmas?" the boy said.

Nicole got her water and scanned the room for Alice without success. At the far end of the cafeteria there was a table with empty seats. With her back to the room, Nicole ate alone.

Study was the last period of the day. When the bell finally rang, Nicole deliberately took her time getting her books together, hoping the area by the lockers would clear out before she got there. When she finally went into the hall, there were only a few people at their lockers. One of them had her back turned but Nicole knew who it was.

As she dropped her backpack and dialed the combination, Nicole heard a locker door slam.

"Hey," Alice said from across the hall.

Nicole turned around. "Hey."

"Did Mrs. Thorn make you stay after?"

"No," Nicole answered as she reached into her locker. "I'm just sort of in a daze."

"Don't you have to catch a bus?" Alice said, crossing the hall.

Nicole crouched down to put some books into her backpack. "I still have a couple of minutes."

"I heard what Michelle said about me today," Alice said quietly. "You know, at lunch."

Nicole reached into her locker. "I didn't see you at first. I guess you were trying to pick up your change or something. I don't think Michelle saw you either."

"No, I guess not," Alice said with a chuckle.

Nicole looked up.

"I heard what *you* said too."

"Mrs. Thorn said nobody had to talk if they didn't want to. I didn't say anything either."

"Not in class. But you said something in the cafeteria and I just wanted you to know I appreciated it."

Nicole stood up and looked into her friend's dark eyes. Alice was almost smiling. "I'll see you tomorrow," she said, turning away.

Nicole watched her start down the hall. "Hey, Alice?"

Alice stopped and turned.

"Thanks for telling me," Nicole said. "That means a lot."

Alice nodded.

Nicole closed her locker and put on her backpack. "Aren't you going out in front?"

"No. I walk home. It's shorter if I go out the back."

"Okay, I'll see you tomorrow then."

"See ya."

Nicole walked to the stairs and down two flights. In front of the school the last stragglers were climbing aboard the bus. There was an empty seat near the back and she slid into it.

Across the aisle and a few rows up, Michelle and a boy were laughing.

As the bus turned right from Atlantic onto Main St., Nicole noticed the diner where she and her mother stopped for breakfast on their first morning in Elk River.

At the edge of town, she saw the red, white and blue sign that read "Welcome to Elk River—a Town on the Move."

Yeah, right.

But the sign reminded her of the Elk River research assignment. *What should I do?* Nicole wondered as she gazed out the window. *I don't know anything about this place.*

The bus struggled up the hill at the edge of town and turned right onto Mountain Highway. Passengers got off at various stops along the way and Nicole continued to stare out the window. When her gaze shifted, Michelle was sitting alone.

The bus picked up speed. After another look at the ocean, Nicole took a deep breath. She stood up, grabbed her backpack and walked up the aisle. She sat down in the empty seat in front of Michelle and turned to face her classmate.

"Hey," Michelle said. "What's up?"

"I just wanted to tell you that I'm not going to be able to come to your party this weekend."

"Oh, that's too bad."

"Yeah, I'm sorry but I think I'm going to be doing something else."

"Is this really about Alice?"

"Well," Nicole said, "I *am* friends with her and it doesn't feel right for me to go if she's not invited."

"Okay."

"But thanks for asking me."

"Sure," Michelle said.

The bus slowed and Nicole glanced out the window.

"Here's my stop. I'll see you tomorrow."

"See ya," Michelle said.

Nicole got off the bus and started down Cliff Road. She watched the ocean until she got to the edge of the woods. She was smiling.

CHAPTER FIFTEEN

DECEMBER 3

"Nicole, it's almost seven thirty." Her mother called from the bottom of the steps. "You're going to be late."

Nicole took a last look at the mirror over her dresser, grabbed her backpack and hurried out of her room. Downstairs, she slipped into her coat and went into the kitchen where she gulped down some juice and plucked a waffle out of the toaster.

Her father put his coffee mug on the table and shook his head. "What takes you so long in the morning, anyway?"

Nicole shrugged.

"Aren't you going to sit down to eat?" her mother said.

"Don't want to miss the bus."

"Is it okay if Alice comes over Saturday?"

"Is she one of your friends from school?"

"That's right, Dad."

"I think that'd be all right," her mother said.

"Great."

"Do you want to ask Alice if she wants to stay overnight?

"Is that okay?"

"If that's what you girls want to do."

"Okay," Nicole said. "Thanks."

"What about your breakfast?"

"I'll eat on the way to the bus."

Her mother sighed. "I'll see you after school."

It was clear and cold outside with a breeze off the ocean. The sky was blue but powdery snow flew off the trees with each gust of wind. The snow tingled on Nicole's face. Everything looked bright and distinct. The woods were a pleasure.

When Nicole got to school, Alice wasn't at her locker. There wouldn't be a chance to talk until lunch.

At the end of the morning's classes, she found Alice in the cafeteria, eating alone.

"Hey," Nicole said.

"Hey."

Nicole sat down and emptied her lunch bag. She opened her bottle of water and took a swig. "Do you want to come over to my house on Saturday to work on homework or whatever?"

For a moment, Alice stared at Nicole. "Isn't Michelle's party on Saturday?"

"Yeah, but I'm not going." Nicole thought that Alice looked surprised. "Anyway, do you want to come? You can see the famous Weber House."

Alice sipped some juice.

"You're not scared, are you?"

"Yeah, I'm scared. How come you're not going to the party?"

"Too scared."

Alice smiled.

"Well, do you want to come?"

"Yeah, I'd like to," Alice said. "I'll have to ask my parents but it'll probably be okay."

"Do you need directions?"

"Everybody knows where the Weber House is."

"Oh, right. I forgot."

"Anyway, thanks."

"I really hope you can come."

"Me too."

"I'll call you tonight."

The girls had separate classes in the afternoon. They didn't meet again until the end of the day at their lockers.

"Hey," Alice said.

"You going home?"

"Yup. I have to help my father clean his boat. He's a fisherman."

"Out in the ocean?"

"Uh, yes. The Atlantic one."

Nicole smiled sheepishly. "Do you ever go fishing with him?"

"Sometimes. In the summer mostly."

"I've never been fishing."

"Maybe you can go out with us sometime. It's pretty hard work, though."

"I bet."

"*You* going home?"

"No, I've got soccer on Tuesdays."

"Well, have fun."

"Thanks. Have fun cleaning the boat."

Alice frowned. "Thanks. I won't. Talk to you later."

"Okay. Talk to you later."

The girls waved and went in opposite directions.

After soccer practice, Nicole changed her clothes and walked to the waiting bus. She sat by herself. When the bus arrived at Cliff Road, the sun had already dropped behind the mountains. Frowning, Nicole slung her backpack over her shoulder and walked toward the covered bridge. The icicles hanging from the arched entrance looked like sharp teeth. She stepped into the bridge's shadows. When she emerged, Nicole looked down into the ravine she had just crossed. *Jagged ice.* She started into the woods. *No birds at this hour and not much light, either.*

For a moment, she glimpsed the moon but clouds quickly blotted it out. A cold wind blew from the ocean. Surf crashed on the rocks. Nicole pulled her hat over her ears.

She took a few steps, then stopped. *What was that?* Something metallic jingling on the bridge. Nicole spun around. "Who's there?" No answer.

She kept walking. Nicole heard it again. She whirled around a second time, fighting down a rising fear. "Who is that?" But the sound had stopped.

Maybe I'm imagining it. Nicole exhaled. Silence never sounded so good. But then she heard the same metallic sound a third time. Trying not to panic, Nicole shut her eyes and concentrated. Again, it stopped.

Her heart racing and her backpack weighing a ton, Nicole ran. The sound was closer. *Keep running!* She heard growling. An animal, a big animal, a dog. The moon broke through the clouds. Nicole saw an opening in the bushes to her right. She dropped her backpack and plunged into the hedge, the branches whipping her face.

Nicole was on a narrow path. She rushed forward, thorns snagging her pants, icy branches stinging her face. *Faster! Keep running!*

The path twisted and turned. Her chest burned. She stopped to rest—she had to—and listen. Something rustled in the bushes and the growling was close. Nicole fought back a scream and plunged ahead into the darkness.

Running downhill. Faster—too fast! Nicole lost her balance and knew she was falling. She closed her eyes and put her arms over her face—and something grabbed her from behind. Nicole started to scream but a rough hand covered her mouth. She wriggled violently but two strong hands held her tight. The moon broke through the clouds and Nicole saw the face of her captor—an old woman.

With one hand still covering Nicole's mouth, the old woman turned her captive back in the direction she had been running and pointed a bare finger downward. Nicole squinted into the darkness and saw . . . nothing. But she felt wind in her face and heard a crashing sound. Nicole looked straight down. Far below, reflected in a moment of moonlight, there were moving shadows and hissing streaks of white. She tried to focus. The shapes were waves smashing onto jagged rocks. Nicole had nearly run over the cliff!

Something moved in the underbrush—it was close—and Nicole felt another wave of terror: the dog!

The old woman bent down and whispered into Nicole's ear. "Shhh."

Petrified, Nicole obeyed and listened as the animal came near. Nicole stared into the woman's dark eyes, pinpoints of light. *Do I know her?*

Silently, the woman removed her hand from Nicole's mouth. Then she pulled back a branch and pointed to a path. "Go," she whispered.

Nicole struggled to her feet. "Who are . . ." but the old woman put a cold finger over Nicole's lips.

"Go!" she rasped and coughed into her tattered sleeve. "Go!"

Nicole crept a few feet onto the path then turned back. The old woman was gone.

Clouds swept over the moon and Nicole was shrouded in darkness. She took a few steps and heard the growling again. The dog had to be just a few branches away, near the spot where Nicole had stumbled. The old woman had to be nearby as well. Her heart pounding, Nicole tried not to move. The growling stopped and she thought she heard whispering. After a few seconds, Nicole heard the jingling again but fainter. *Is it going away?* She waited.

Something else, something bigger, was coming through

the brush. An animal cried out in pain.

The woods were silent. The only sound was the waves at the bottom of the cliff. Nicole looked at her hands. They were shaking, and not just from the cold. With small steps, she crept up the path the old woman had shown her. It was slippery and the snow was deep. She could barely see where she was going and pictured the cliff and the waves and the rocks far below. When Nicole saw lights from her house filtered through the evergreens, she did her best to run. As she emerged from the woods, Nicole looked over her shoulder, back toward the dark forest.

Stumbling, crying, she ran for her house as fast as she could.

CHAPTER SIXTEEN

"Mom!" Nicole screamed as she burst into the house. "Where are you?"

"In the kitchen."

Nicole raced down the hall and through the pantry. Her mother was chopping onions. When she saw her daughter's scratched face and torn clothes, she dropped her knife. "Nicole, what happened?" Onions spilled onto the floor.

Nicole ran to her mother and hugged her. "I was walking from the bus stop," Nicole began as she pulled away from the embrace. "I heard something behind me so I said 'who's there?' but nobody answered and I kept walking and I heard it again and I got scared so I started running but it kept following me so I went onto a path but I couldn't see and I heard growling and it was getting closer so I tried to go faster but I slipped and started to fall and I almost went over the cliff but an old woman caught me and held me so I couldn't scream or get away . . ."

"It's okay, Sweetheart. You're home now," Nicole's mother said, hugging her daughter again and stroking her hair. "Are you hurt?"

Nicole shook her head "no."

"You're safe. That's all that matters. Everything's going to be all right."

Nicole looked at her mother and saw tears on her cheeks. "I was so scared," she said, wiping her own eyes. "But she showed me a path that led out of the woods and I wanted to ask her who she was but she was gone and I heard the growling a lot closer but then it stopped 'cause I think she was whispering to the dog but someone else came and I think he hit it and I don't know what happened after that and I followed the path out of the woods."

She tried not to sob. "I don't know what's happening here but I want to go back home and, and . . ." Nicole shut her eyes and hugged her mother again.

"Sit here at the table and have some milk," her mother said when Nicole finally pulled away.

Nicole heard the front door open and close. "I'm home," her father called out. "Anybody here?"

"We're in the kitchen," Nicole's mother answered. As soon as her father came into the kitchen, Nicole saw the shock on his face. She struggled to calm herself and repeated the events after she got off the bus.

"You believe me, don't you?" she asked, looking from one parent to the other. "You don't think I'm making this up?"

"Of course we believe you," Nicole's father said.

"Absolutely," her mother agreed. "And I think we should call the police."

"I agree. Wild dogs and whoever is with them don't belong here," Nicole's father said as he put his coat on. "I'll drive out there. Tell the police I'll meet them near the bridge." He got a flashlight from the pantry and tested it. "We'll get to the bottom of this, Nicole. If there's someone around here who's trying to scare you, we'll put a stop to it. I swear."

Nicole picked up Ivy and stroked her soft black fur as her mother asked the operator for the phone number for the Elk River Police Department.

Half an hour later, Nicole heard footsteps and voices on the front porch. She followed her mother into the hall. Her father came in with a policeman. "We found your backpack," Nicole's father said. "But anyone who was out there is long gone."

"I'm Mary Kelly," her mother said, extending her hand to the officer. "This is our daughter, Nicole."

"I'm Officer Baldwin. I heard that someone had occupied the premises." He turned to Nicole. "Can you tell me what happened?"

As calmly as she could, Nicole told the policeman everything that happened after she got off the bus. He jotted notes on a little pad.

"Can you describe the old woman?"

"I didn't get a good look at her," Nicole answered, glancing at her parents. "It was dark."

Officer Baldwin closed his note pad and turned to Nicole's mother. "Like your husband said, we didn't see any sign of her. I'll file a report that there may be a female prowler in the area."

"What about the dog and whoever was with it?" Nicole's mother asked. "If anything, I'm more worried about *him*."

"Your daughter didn't actually *see* them so it's hard to know what to make of that."

"I'm *sure* it was a dog," Nicole said, looking to her mother, "and *somebody* was with it."

"I'll make a note that the little girl *said* she heard a dog and possibly a man," the policeman said as he buttoned his coat.

"Thank you for coming," Nicole's father said as he opened the door. "Please let us know if there are any developments. This was a terrifying experience for our daughter."

"It sounds like it," the policeman said as he stepped outside. "I'll keep you posted."

"Thank you, officer," Nicole's father said before he closed

the door.

"Starting tomorrow," her mother said, "I'll meet you at the bus stop no matter what time you get home. Will that make you feel a little better?"

"A little, I guess."

After dinner, as she helped with the dinner dishes, the phone rang. Nicole's father stepped into the hall to answer it. "That was John Morgan," he said when he came back into the kitchen. "He saw the police car." He looked at his daughter. "I told him what happened today and he said to tell you that if you're ever worried about walking home, you can always go to his house. If he's not there, Mrs. Morgan or their housekeeper will be there. You can call home and we'll come and get you."

"That's nice of him," Nicole's mother said.

Nicole nodded.

That evening, she tried to concentrate on her homework, watched a TV show and got ready for bed. Nicole said good night to her parents and then got under the covers with a book. She read until she was drowsy and turned off the light. At first the frightening events in the woods came rushing back but a few minutes later her mother came in and sat on the bed. Nicole relaxed a bit and eventually closed her eyes.

CHAPTER SEVENTEEN

DECEMBER 4

Alice was late for school on Wednesday morning so the girls didn't have a chance to talk until lunch. "I thought you were going to call last night," Alice said as she unwrapped a sandwich.

"Oh, I'm sorry, Nicole replied. "So much happened, I forgot."

"Tell me."

Before lunch was over, Nicole told her friend everything that had occurred the previous day. Throughout the story, Alice was nearly speechless. When the bell rang, she re-wrapped her untouched sandwich. "I'll eat this later."

"I feel bad talking about *me* all the time," Nicole said. "It's just that all this stuff's been happening and you're the only person I can talk to."

Alice smiled. "Yeah. I forgot to tell you that I live in a haunted house too. Policemen and strange people and vicious dogs are showing up all the time."

"Well anyway, I appreciate it."

Alice nodded.

"By the way," Nicole said as they left the cafeteria, "are you still coming on Saturday?"

"Well," Alice said slowly, "I don't know."

"My mother said we can have a sleepover if you want to."

"I don't want a witch to get me."

"Come on, Alice. We'll have fun."

"I know" Alice said. "I'm just kidding. Actually, I love witches."

"Glad to hear it. So, you're gonna come?"

"I'll have to ask my parents about the sleepover but I'm definitely coming."

"Great!" Nicole said.

"My dad asked me if I was afraid of ghosts."

"What'd you say?"

"I said, 'Yeah, Dad, I'm afraid. That's why I want to go.'"

"Sounds like one of *my* father's jokes."

"The funny thing is," Alice said, "if they knew all the stuff that's been happening at your house, maybe they *wouldn't* let me come."

"I wouldn't blame them," Nicole said. "How come *you're* not afraid?"

"Well, I don't think I'll do any walking around in the woods by myself but if it's daytime and we're together, I don't think it should be *too* scary. It's kind of exciting."

"Right. It'll be way different if you're there. Anyway, I'm glad you're coming."

"Me too."

When Nicole got off the bus that afternoon, her mother was waiting in her car. On the drive back to the house, Nicole pointed to the spot where, the night before, she had plunged into the underbrush.

Her mother stopped the car.

"There's nothing to see, Mom."

Nicole's mother shook her head. They rode the rest of the way to the house without speaking. "How was school?" her mother asked as they took off their coats.

"Okay. Alice is going to come Saturday but she has to ask her parents about sleeping over."

"Good. Did you tell Alice about what happened yesterday?"

"Yeah."

"I probably should call her mother."

"What for?"

"To introduce myself for one thing. But also in case she's worried about Alice coming here."

"You don't have to do that, Mom. Alice tells her parents everything. If they were worried, I'm sure they wouldn't let her come."

Her mother opened the mail on a table in the hall. "Much homework?"

Nicole swung her backpack over her shoulder. "Math, science, social studies," she answered, starting up the stairs.

"I unpacked some pictures from your old room today but I couldn't find any nails."

"I saw some in the basement," Nicole said. "I'll get them later."

She dropped her backpack in her room and went into the study. She dialed onto the Internet and found Alexandra.

Within a few minutes, Nicole was caught up on all the gossip from her old school.

"what's happening up there in maine?"

Nicole stared at the screen. *How can I possibly answer that without taking all night or sounding like a complete idiot?*

"not much," she typed. *"i do have a good friend though her name's alice"*

"that's great," Alexandra responded. *"gotta go luv ya"*

"say hi to everybody for me"

Nicole went back to her room. She picked up one of the pictures that lay on her bed, a pastel from her old art class. She put the drawing down, went to her closet and reached for the flashlight. Then down the back stairs to the pantry. Her mother was in the hall, on the phone.

Nicole looked out the back door window. It was almost dark. She unbolted the cellar door, pulled it open and switched on her light. Slowly, down the steps. At the bottom, she pointed her light into the corner where she remembered seeing a workbench. Holding her hand up as a shield against spider webs, she inched across the cellar. Something rubbed against her leg and she jumped. Frightened, she shined the light downward.

It was her cat.

"Ivy, you scared me to death, girl." Nicole crouched down but Ivy darted away.

Nicole spotted the cans she was looking for and picked out some small nails.

She felt a slight draft on her face and recalled the same sensation the first time she was in the cellar. She shined the light straight ahead. A light shined back.

Startled at first, Nicole remembered the mirror and stood up. She was face to face with a full-length, cracked reflection of herself holding a flashlight. She noticed the light switch next to the mirror and twisted it, knowing it didn't work.

She stared at the switch, then focused on the wires that led to it. She remembered that they went up the wall next to the mirror and divided. One wire went across the ceiling and came down at the broken switch by the steps. The other one disappeared. Nicole aimed her light at the point above the mirror where the wires divided.

It looks like the other wire goes into the wall.

Nicole shined her light at the mirror's gilded frame. A piece was broken off. Underneath the "gold," the frame looked like plaster. She felt the draft again.

Nicole gripped the frame of the mirror and pulled. It swung open. The mirror was a door.

She shined her light into the utter blackness. Somewhere

nearby she heard a faint squeaking.

She glanced at the light switch and turned it again. Fifty feet away, a dim light came on.

"It's a tunnel!"

Nicole stepped inside. Wherever the tunnel led, the end was not in sight.

At that moment, something streaked past her feet. Ivy. "Come back!"

Nicole followed her cat about 50 feet, stopping under the electric light. Nearby, a whale oil lamp, just like the one in the library, was attached to the wall. Up ahead, Ivy was sniffing at something.

Nicole turned around and pointed her light back toward the cellar. There was only darkness.

I should go back and get Mom. She won't believe it. But this time they'll both have to. Then she stopped and turned back toward her cat. "Stay there, girl."

Ivy looked up and promptly disappeared around a bend in the tunnel. Slowly, Nicole followed for what seemed like twenty or thirty feet. *There's another light. After that, it looks like it ends.*

But no Ivy. "Where are you, girl?"

Nicole crept past the second light, pointing her flashlight into the darkness before her. A short distance ahead, on the right, there was an opening. She shined her light into the dark space. Ivy's yellow eyes glowed.

"There you are." Nicole stepped into the room, crouched down and stroked Ivy's back. Then she saw some rusted chains dangling from the wall with metal straps fastened to the ends. *Were people chained here?*

The nails were still in her hand. She put them in her pocket, picked up her cat and walked back into the tunnel. She was almost at the end. After a few dozen more steps Nicole was in a small circular room. A narrow stone stairway with a metal railing circled upward. Nicole walked into the center of the space and pointed her light straight up. The stairs disappeared into the darkness beyond the flashlight's beam. *This must be the bottom of the tower!* She peered upward. "Maybe we can get out this way."

Cradling her flashlight and cat in her arms, Nicole started to climb. She moved up and around the inside of the tower until she was far above its floor. "We've got to be *way* above the ground by now, Ivy," she said.

Nicole was breathing hard. She leaned against the cold stone and shined her light upward. The top was still not in sight. "What do you think we should do now?"

Nicole crouched down and released her cat. Ivy immediately disappeared down the stairs. "Gee, thanks."

Nicole stood and looked upward. She switched her light off. *It looks like there's some light coming in up there.* She turned the light back on and continued upward, each spiral slightly smaller than the one below.

She paused to rest and, looking up, switched her light off and saw light from above. *I'm almost there.* Another thought jolted her. *What if somebody else is up there?*

Nicole concentrated. *If someone is up there, they'd probably have heard me already.* She closed her eyes and listened. Just a faint whistle of wind. Nicole looked up toward the dim glow at the top of the stairs. *About ten more steps.*

She took a deep breath and inched upward until, crouching, her eyes were just above a wooden floor. Another deep breath and Nicole rose up enough to see the room. She was able to make out various shapes but nothing that looked like feet.

Nicole climbed up the last few steps and stood in the room. It was circular with large windows around the entire circumference. She turned her light on, pointing it at the opening in the floor she had just passed through. A trapdoor leaned against the wall.

A strange shape stood in the center of the room. It looked like one of the "ghosts" in her house. Nicole lifted the sheet and saw a wooden stand. The top was covered with glass and underneath was what looked like a big compass. *It's a binnacle!*

She went to a window. The sun was gone but a big crescent moon shone just above the horizon. She could see for miles in every direction. Behind her house, the silhouette of the mountains stood out against a darkening sky streaked with orange. In the opposite direction, across the bay, lights twinkled in Elk River. Far out in the water, to the left of the town, the lighthouse beacon swept past every few seconds. Beyond, the open ocean loomed, endless.

A doorway led outside. Next to it was a light switch. Nicole turned it but nothing happened. She tried the door's handle. It turned easily and she went outside onto a balcony that went all the way around the tower. The air was bitter cold. Clouds of breath were swept away by the stinging wind. Glancing up, Nicole saw a white light shining from the top of a long pole which extended above the tower's roof. She leaned back inside and turned the switch.

The light went off.

Amazing. It works.

On the ocean, dots of light. Boats. *I wouldn't want to be out there tonight.*

She looked down. The tower rose up from the very edge of the cliff. It was a sheer drop to the water. Waves crashed against the rocks, leaving white foam that reflected the moonlight and vanished.

Nicole shivered and turned to go back inside, then stopped. "*What was that?*" She peered into the woods beyond the right side of the house. *A light!* She remembered the light she'd seen in the tower on Thanksgiving. *Maybe it's the same person. Maybe it's the old woman!*

The light began to move. In a moment, it was gone.

Nicole watched for a minute or so to see if the light reappeared. It didn't. She went back inside the tower and rubbed her arms to warm up.

Nicole shined her light at the trap door and stairway and began her descent, gripping the railing tightly with every step. When she reached the bottom, she took a few steps and pointed her light into the dark space with the chains on the wall.

"Ivy? Are you in there?"

Her cat was licking a paw.

"Come on, girl, let's go back." Cradling Ivy in her arms, Nicole quickly walked the length of the tunnel. Back in the cellar, she turned off the lights, swung the mirror back into place and hurried upstairs.

Her mother was washing some dishes. "There you are. I thought you got lost down there."

"I was just looking around."

"Did you find something to hang your pictures with?"

Nicole pulled the nails out of her pocket. "Yeah. They're right here."

She debated whether to tell her mother about the tunnel and the tower.

"Maybe you'd better get started on your homework before dinner."

Nicole went up to her room and sat on her bed. She looked at the painting of the young girl with the cat. When she went to the window, her reflection stared back at her with a quizzical expression. Instinctively, Nicole brushed her hair away from her face but as she did, the reflection of the painting came into view. It was almost as if the girl was watching her from midair, outside. She turned around and looked carefully at the young face. *So sad*, she thought.

Nicole noticed her journal and picked it up. There was a pen marking the place of her last entry. She sat on her bed and began to write.

Wednesday, December 4

A lot of stuff has happened around here since Thanksgiving. Maybe that's why we're supposed to write something every day.

The most important thing is that Alice and I are friends again. I don't know what I'd do if I didn't have her to talk to. She is <u>such</u> a good friend.

Nicole glanced up and saw the young girl, watching, listening.

What if Dolores Weber didn't die? What if she's the woman in the woods? What if it was Dolores Weber who stopped me from running over the cliff and saved me from the dog and whoever was with it?

Nicole looked out the window again before she continued writing.

    But how could anyone live in the Maine woods in the winter?

When Nicole looked up, the moonlight had broken through the clouds and she saw the big pine trees swaying.

    I've got to talk to Alice. But now I've got something to show her.

CHAPTER EIGHTEEN

DECEMBER 5

A brilliant sun outlined the edge of the window shades. Nicole rose and dressed. Walking down the stairs, she stopped on the landing. There was a rainbow on the wall, brilliantly colored light glinting from the stained-glass seascape above the doors. *That must be what Dad was talking about.* She went back up to the second floor and around the balcony to the front of the house. Standing below the window, it looked like the refracted light was coming from the glass sun. Nicole dragged a chair in front of the doors and climbed up. Stretching, she put her hand in front of the sun and saw a tiny rainbow on her palm. The light on the wall was gone. When she moved her hand, the rainbow on the wall reappeared.

It's a prism. She put her finger on the crystal. It protruded slightly. *It's not round, either,* she realized. *I think it's a hexagon.* Nicole climbed off the chair and dragged it back where she found it. With another glance at the rainbow, she continued downstairs.

After a quick breakfast, Nicole rode to Mountain Highway with her father. The bus came a few minutes later. She nodded to Michelle and sat alone by a window. As the bus drove down Mountain Highway, Nicole wondered if she should have told her parents about the tunnel, the tower and the light in the woods.

Once the bus arrived at Chamberlain, she hurried up to the third floor. Alice was at her locker.

"I've got to talk to you," Nicole called over her shoulder as the girls hung up their coats and took the books they needed for morning classes.

"Now what?" Alice said with a smile.

Another girl arrived at a nearby locker.

"I'll tell you at lunch."

Ms. McDowell gave a surprise math quiz. It was persuasive essays in Language Arts, the anatomy of worms in Science. In social studies, Mrs. Thorn continued the lesson about navigation. How centuries ago, sailors used a compass, a sextant and even a clock to know where they were and how to get where they were going. Mrs. Thorn asked if anyone had chosen the topic for his or her research project. Simon said he was going to report on the man the school was named for, Joshua Chamberlain.

"Very good, Simon," Mrs. Thorn said. "Joshua Chamberlain was a great man. Anyone else? How about you, Alice? Have you chosen your topic yet?"

"I haven't decided yet. Maybe something to do with ships or the ocean."

"Excellent!" Mrs. Thorn said. "I'll bet you already know a lot about that subject."

Other students' topics included famous crimes in Elk River, Native Americans in Elk River and celebrities from Elk River.

"Have there been any celebrities in Elk River, Nick?"

"I don't know. I didn't do the research yet."

The class laughed.

"Billy," Mrs. Thorn said, "Did you decide on your topic?"

"Yes, Mrs. Thorn," Billy said, standing up. "My report will

be on the worst disasters in Elk River history. Fires, hurricanes, stuff like that."

"Well," Mrs. Thorn said with a smile. "Good luck."

Alice was shaking her head. *At least he has a topic*, Nicole thought.

At lunch, the girls met at their usual table. Nicole told her friend about her discovery of the tunnel, the tower and the light in the woods she saw from the tower.

"Unbelievable," Alice said. "Weren't you scared? What if somebody was up there?"

"I *did* get scared when I realized there might be," Nicole said. "Luckily, there wasn't."

"What's it like?"

"The view is unbelievable. You can see the mountains, Elk River, the ocean, everything.

You'll see for yourself when you come over. It won't be so scary if we both go. Plus, it'll be daytime."

"And you didn't tell your parents?"

"No. Just you."

"How come?" Alice asked.

"How come I didn't tell them or how come I *did* tell you?"

Alice laughed. "Both."

"I *wanted* to tell you. And I was about to tell my mom and then, I just didn't. I guess it made me mad that they didn't believe me when I told them about all the other stuff that happened."

"What about the old woman that grabbed you by the cliff? They believed *that,* didn't they?"

"Yeah," Nicole admitted. "But I wanted to ask you about that. The old woman."

"What about her?"

"What if she's Dolores Weber?"

Alice twisted the top off her water bottle and took a sip. "They say she died. In a fire. A long time ago."

"I know. But I don't think they ever found her body."

"And that's who you think the old woman might be?"

"Well," Nicole said. "Dolores Weber *could have* been the person in the tower on Thanksgiving *and* the one in the woods I saw from the tower last night."

"If she's Dolores Weber, she'd have to be really old. And living in the woods for all this time?" Alice shook her head. "I don't know."

"Me either," Nicole said. "But you know how people say all these bad things about her? About her being a witch or doing stuff to kids and animals and everything?"

"Yeah. I know people say that stuff. *You* don't believe it though, do you?"

"Not about her being a witch. I'm just saying that whoever that old woman is, even if it *is* Dolores Weber, even if she *is* scary or did stuff, she kept me from going off the cliff when the guy with the dog was following me. And then she showed me how to get away from them."

"Okay, I agree. That was good. So let's say it *was* Dolores Weber."

"Okay."

"Well, what if she was also the one who came in your house those nights. I don't think you liked that too much."

Nicole shook her head slowly. "No, I didn't." She paused. "I don't know what to think about that."

For a minute, Alice didn't say anything. "What are you going to do now?" she finally asked.

Nicole looked at her friend. "I've got it!"

"What?"

"Go to gym."

Alice shook her head, then smiled. "You idiot."

They both laughed.

CHAPTER NINETEEN

Nicole's mother was waiting at the bus stop. "It's such a nice day, I thought we could walk."

Amid the trees, they talked about school until they came to the spot where, two days earlier, Nicole realized that she was being followed. They stopped talking until the house was in sight.

"Much homework?"

"Math. We have a quiz tomorrow."

"Is that it?"

"Some reading for social studies and science."

Nicole wiped some of the snow off her boots and opened the front door. Her backpack thudded to the floor and she took off her coat. "Something smells good."

"I made some soup today," Nicole's mother said.

"What kind?"

"Chicken dumpling. Want some before you start your homework?"

"Sure."

Nicole went into the kitchen, got a spoon and filled a mug with hot soup. "I'm going up to my room."

"I'll be getting dinner ready."

Nicole lugged her backpack up the steps and dropped it in

her room. She went to the side window and stared into the woods while she sipped on her soup. *I wonder where that light was.*

At the edge of the yard, she noticed a space between two pine trees. *That could be a path . . .* Further into the woods, it looked like there was a small clearing among the trees. *I'll bet that's where I saw it.*

Nicole tipped the mug up to finish the soup and used her finger to get a dumpling stuck to the bottom. She looked at the clearing in the woods again. *I'm gonna go out there.* Another look out the window. *It's not that far. Just uphill a little.*

Nicole picked up the flashlight on her desk and quietly walked down the front stairs. She heard water running in the kitchen as she put on her coat and hat. Nicole stuffed the flashlight into her coat pocket, picked up her boots and slipped out the front door.

The sky was clear and it wasn't even that cold. The icicles hanging down from the porch roof were dripping. Nicole pulled on her boots on and mittens, stepped off the porch into the snow. She walked across the side yard to the two pine trees. Nicole glanced back toward the house. *I hope Mom doesn't look out the window.*

She faced the woods. *There is a path. But no tracks.*

Walking slowly uphill, Nicole entered the woods. *The clearing isn't as close as I thought,* she realized after a few minutes of slogging through the snow. She turned around. *But I can still see the house.*

Due to the hill, the snow and fallen branches, it took Nicole ten minutes to reach the clearing. She crouched behind a little fir tree at the edge. No one was there. Nicole walked into the clearing. There were lots of footprints, including some that might have been made by a person.

The forest was lovely. Some of the snowdrifts looked like delicately carved sculptures. Most of the trees were evergreens.

Some were huge, their great branches sagging under the weight of snow. The bright, red berries on a big holly bush stood out against its dark, green leaves. In every direction Nicole saw gigantic gray rocks, some of them bigger than a car. At the far side of the clearing, a huge boulder was cracked in two as if split by a giant's axe.

She crossed the clearing and saw that another path led from the split rock and went further into the woods. The only footprints on that path were definitely made by animals. Nicole followed them. *I'm pretty sure that deer made these,* she thought, looking at one set of tracks. *And raccoon, maybe. Or a rabbit.*

When the animals' paths divided, Nicole stopped. *I think that's far enough.*

She took a few steps back toward the clearing when she heard something. It sounded like cracking wood.

Nicole froze. Something or someone was in the clearing. Fear flooded over her: *A bear. A coyote. The man with the dog.*

She heard another sound. *I've got to go the other way.* Nicole turned and, looking over her shoulder every few seconds, crept deeper into the woods. The path went uphill and before long, she was breathing hard. Now exhaustion mixed with fear. The snow was getting deeper and the top was crusty but not firm enough to walk on. When her boots broke through the crust, it scraped against her shins.

Nicole stopped to catch her breath. She was on a ridge. All around, the woods were completely wild. Many of the trees were snarled with thick vines. The blackened branches of fallen trees stuck up at crazy angles. In the shadows, with snow on their branches, some of the bent-down evergreens took on the shapes of people or animals. Nicole shivered. Up ahead, the ridge got narrower and the sides were very steep. She plowed ahead and upward, occasionally looking back over her shoulder.

To the left, at the bottom of the ridge, a small stream splashed between icy banks matted with leaves and broken branches. Just ahead, a large, fallen tree lay across her path. Nicole gripped a branch, climbed onto the trunk, nearly slipped, and then looked back in the direction she had come from.

I guess no one's chasing me, at least, she thought, letting out a big breath. *But how am I going to go back?* She looked around. *I don't want to go the way I came. But I don't even know where I am.*

Slowly, Nicole climbed off the fallen tree and peered further up the ridge. It looked like it eventually leveled off. She saw some light between the snowy evergreens ahead. *Maybe I can see the house or the ocean or something from up there.*

She trudged toward the light. In a few minutes she was approaching another clearing and looked back. She was near the top of the hill. In the distance Nicole could just make out the tower near her house. "Thank god," she said out loud.

But the light was fading.

Maybe I can find a different way back to the house. Nicole worked her way around the edge of the clearing. Then she stopped. Something moved. She saw it. Just fifty feet away, a deer, two deer, were running into the woods. Nicole squinted at the spot where they disappeared. Nearby was a tiny stone cabin.

Nicole stepped behind a tree. *What if someone's there?*

She remained still. There was no light or sound coming from the little structure. Nicole crept forward, stopping behind another tree. At her feet, some wooden markers stuck out of the ground. She crouched down and saw that the markers had faded writing on them. The only one legible said "baby earthling." Closer to the cabin she saw some burnt wood inside a ring of stones.

Nicole peered at the cabin. Some of the windows were

broken and covered with cardboard. The walls above the windows looked scorched. A tattered blanket hung where a door should have been.

Nicole inched forward. "Is anyone there?"

Silence.

She crept to the blanket-covered "door." Nicole pulled her light from her coat pocket and turned it on. With her heart pounding, she stuck the light past the edge of the hanging blanket and nudged it aside.

Suddenly, just inches from her face, a big black bird sprang through the opening. She screamed and nearly fell into the snow. The bird flapped into the gray sky.

Shaken, Nicole leaned against the doorframe. She tried to calm herself and listened. Hearing nothing but the wind, she stuck her light into the cabin and peeked inside. It was dark. She took a step forward and the blanket fell back into place behind her.

There was only one room. Scraps of wood and paper were stuck in the holes and cracks in the walls. The windows were also covered with tattered blankets. Some stubby candles had dripped wax onto the windowsills. There were newspapers and blankets on the floor that might be a bed.

Someone was living here.

A faded sketch of a black dog was tacked to the wall. At the bottom of the drawing, it said "Lucifer." An oval-shaped photograph with cracked glass hung next to the bed: a woman sitting beside a young girl with a kitten in her lap. Behind them, with his hands resting on their shoulders, a man with a beard. All three were smiling. Nicole thought the girl looked like she was about her own age.

There was something else on the floor. Nicole shifted her light. It was a plate with food on it. An apple, some bread and an open tin can.

Somebody's living here now!

Suddenly very frightened, Nicole leapt past the hanging blanket and was outside again. Looking down, she saw fresh-looking footprints she hadn't noticed before. Nearly panicked, Nicole raced back to the path that had brought her to the clearing. *What if whoever lives in there was inside? What if he's watching me right now? How could I be so stupid?*

At the edge of the clearing, Nicole looked across the trees and saw the top of the tower. *I have to go back the way I came. And I better hurry. It'll be dark soon.* She looked into the woods. *At least I'll be going downhill.*

She was among the trees and back on the ridge, only now she could barely see. Ahead, the forest was nearly black and blocked any view of the tower. Nicole looked back toward the clearing. The evergreens were just jagged silhouettes against the darkening sky. She remembered how steep the ridge was on either side of a path she could barely see.

Nicole pointed the light and followed her own footprints. When she came to the fallen tree, she decided not to climb over it. Too slippery. But the narrow end of the tree stuck out just past the edge of the ridge. With her free hand, Nicole gripped a branch of the dead tree and tried to step around the end of the trunk.

She slipped.

Nicole felt her feet go out from under her and in an instant, she was sliding down the side of the ridge. She put her arms out and grabbed for something, *anything*! She rolled, her face went into the snow and she felt the cold sting on her arms and back. She tumbled and slid before coming to a stop. She opened her eyes and, for a few seconds, just lay there. Black trees loomed over her against a dark sky. She heard water splashing.

Slowly, Nicole got to her feet. She was breathing rapidly and her legs were shaking. Immersed in darkness, she was on the brink of tears. *What am I going to do?*

Slowly, she turned around hoping to find something familiar. To her great relief she saw light reflecting off a flat rock and stumbled toward it. Nicole crouched to pick up her flashlight and saw that something was carved into the stone. She brushed away some snow and saw the worn outline of a skull and crossbones. *It's a tombstone!* Nicole looked down. *This is a grave!* She stepped to the side. There were words carved into the stone. The letters were worn but legible. Underneath the skull and crossbones it said:

> **The Lords call me a pyrate**
> **Newgate's press, 'tis true, I did cheat**
> **But worse there are who ne'er fired a gun**
> **Their lair is Threadneedle Street**
> **William Taggart**
> **1769**

Nicole stared at the tombstone. In the distance, she heard a bird's mournful call and looked up. The trees were barely discernible against the sky. She noticed that her flashlight's beam was getting weak. Even on the snow, the beam wasn't white, or even yellow. It was orange and Nicole knew what that meant: dying batteries.

She banged the flashlight against her other hand. At first, the light got brighter. She shined it on the tombstone but then the light faded before going out. Nicole banged it a few more times but it was no use. *Now what am I going to do? I can barely see and I don't know which way to go. And I'm freezing.*

She took a few small steps, holding her hand in front of her face as a shield. She slipped and her free hand went down. Suddenly, it was wet and ice cold. Nicole regained her balance and stood up. Water splashed at her feet. She took off her mittens and tried to squeeze the water out of the wet one. When she put them back on, both hands were cold. She closed her eyes and felt tears.

After a few seconds, Nicole blinked her eyes open. She thought she saw a light in the distance and wondered if she was imagining it. It was swinging slowly back and forth and not too far ahead. It wasn't a flashlight. It was flickering. *A flame?*

The light was about 25 feet ahead. She took a few steps forward, then a few more. As she went toward the light, it moved away.

"Who's there?"

No answer.

The light kept moving and though the going was difficult, Nicole kept pace. There was no other choice. A few times she stumbled as they went downhill. *Is it the old woman?*

Nicole followed for another ten minutes. It wasn't steep anymore and the light disappeared. She crept forward until she saw a dim glow on a rock. It was a reflection on the inside of the split boulder. Nicole walked between the slabs of rock and saw the light moving away once again. Soon she'd be out of the woods.

"Wait!"

Swinging slightly, the light moved ahead.

Nicole recognized some of the trees she had seen just after entering the forest. The ground was almost level and between the trees she could see the lights from her house. She heard her mother calling.

"Please wait," Nicole called toward the light.

It stopped moving and she walked toward it. She could see it clearly now: a kerosene lantern. But when Nicole got close, no one was there. The lantern was hanging from a tree branch. Its glass was cracked. She heard a rustling in the trees behind her and spun around.

"Wait!" But the sound was fainter.

"Please come back."

There was only a soft breeze at the top of the trees.

"Dolores? Are you Dolores Weber?" Nicole listened and heard a sound like coughing. "Dolores?"

Nicole took a few steps forward and listened. She heard a soft moan. It sounded like an old woman's voice.

"Wait, please," Nicole called. "Come back."

But, apart from the breeze, the woods were silent again.

"Thank you," Nicole said softly.

She took the lantern off the branch and walked a few steps forward. There was a lever on the side of the glass. She moved it and the flame disappeared. Her mother called again. Nicole turned and walked out from the trees and into the yard. "Here I am, Mom."

"Where have you been?" Nicole heard the strain in her mother's voice. "It's almost 5:30 and I've been calling for 15 minutes. I was worried."

"I'm okay, I just took a little walk in the woods."

"Look at your clothes," her mother said when they got close to the house. "Are you alright?"

Nicole saw the ice and leaves and that were stuck to her coat. A little branch was sticking out of one boot.

"I'm okay, Mom. I just slipped in the snow."

"Where did you find that lantern?"

"In the woods."

"You probably should have taken a light with you."

Nicole held up her flashlight. "I did but the batteries died."

"I don't want you walking around out there by yourself in the dark," her mother said as they went into the house. "I don't want you running into any more strangers."

"Me neither. Not strangers."

The kitchen was warm and smelled good. Nicole took off her boots, hat, coat and mittens and stood close to the stove, rubbing her hands together.

"You're awfully quiet," her mother said as she prepared

dinner. "Are you sure you're alright?"

It took Nicole a few seconds to answer. "It gets really cold out there after dark."

Her mother nodded and stirred something on the stove. "Dad is going to be a little late tonight, so we might as well eat now." She handed Nicole another warm mug of soup.

Nicole wrapped her hands around the mug. "Really cold," she whispered.

CHAPTER TWENTY

DECEMBER 6

The third-floor hallway was noisy when classes ended on Friday. Standing at her locker, Nicole ignored the din and slipped into her coat. She slammed the locker shut and dragged her backpack across the hall. Alice was crouched down, loading her bag. "I'll see you tomorrow morning," Nicole said. "Okay?"

Alice looked up and shook her head. "I don't know."

"What do you mean?"

Alice struggled to her feet. "You *do* remember telling me at lunch about what happened in the woods last night?"

"Yeah. So?"

"Too many witches and ghosts hanging around your house."

"Come on, Alice. You're as curious about all this as I am."

"And pirates."

"The *pirate*! I almost forgot."

Alice chuckled. "This oughta be good."

"When I fell down the hill, I dropped my flashlight. When I found it, it was shining right on this old tombstone with a creepy skull on it and under that it said 'Taggart' and some date, seventeen-hundred something."

"I've heard that his grave was supposed to be out in the woods someplace. Do you remember how to get there? I'd like to see it."

"Sure, I remember. You go way out in the woods and go up to this abandoned cabin. You get scared because somebody lives there. Then, when it's getting dark, you start going back down the hill but you fall down an even steeper part. You knock your head and nearly drown in a river and that's where it is. I'll show you tomorrow."

"I can hardly wait."

"By the way," Nicole said, "you're going to sleep over, right?"

"Yeah, my mom said it would be okay."

"I think my mother is going to call your mother," Nicole said.

"How come?"

"To introduce herself, she said. Plus, I think she wants to tell your mother about my getting chased by the dog in case your parents decide it isn't safe."

"What about all the other stuff?" Alice asked. "The tunnel, the tower, the cabin, getting lost, getting found. Am I leaving anything out?"

"Yeah. The pirate's grave."

"Right. Is your mother going to tell my mother about all of *that* stuff?"

"I doubt it. She doesn't know about any of that."

"I won't mention it to my parents either," Alice said, smiling. "It would only upset them."

Nicole laughed. "Right. It's for their own good."

"Definitely," Alice added.

"Okay. So, it's all set. What time are you going to come?"

"What time should I come?"

"How about around eleven? We can have a pizza or something."

"Should I bring anything?"

"I guess we could do some homework together if we felt like it."

Alice raised her eyebrows. "Homework?"

"Just if we feel like it. Did you start your Elk River project yet?"

Alice shook her head. "No, I haven't thought of a topic. What about you?"

"Me either. Maybe we'll think of something tomorrow."

"That'd be good." Alice slammed her locker shut and twirled the combination dial. "I gotta go. I have to babysit my brother." She frowned.

"I didn't know you had a brother."

"If he were your brother, you wouldn't mention him either."

"How old is he?"

"Ten, I think. Yeah, ten. He's in the fifth grade. He's such a pest."

Nicole shrugged sympathetically. "I'll see you tomorrow."

Alice picked up her backpack and slung one strap over her shoulder. She waved and started down the hall toward the stairs and the school's rear exit.

Nicole turned the opposite way. Down the hall, down two flights and onto the bus. She took a seat, alone, near the back.

The ride home was always more enjoyable on Friday. The bus echoed with laughter and chatter. A few seats ahead, Michelle was whispering to another girl. Nicole smiled and turned toward the window. As the bus made its way up Mountain Highway, she stared at the choppy ocean and the graying sky.

Her mother was waiting at the bus stop. With a stiff breeze coming off the water, and snow beginning to fall, the walk home was good.

Inside the house, Nicole went straight to the kitchen. Over

a piece of leftover pie, she and her mother talked about the day and the weekend.

"I'm going to clean my room," Nicole said as she put her plate in the sink.

"Good idea."

It took a while to pick up her clothes. She put some things away and came across her flashlight, remembering that it died in the woods. Nicole went down to the pantry and got new batteries. *"Maybe Alice would like to see what's in the attic,"* she thought, arriving back at the second-floor landing. She went to her bedroom and slid the new batteries into the flashlight. She pulled on a sweater, returned to the back stairs and stepped up. At the top of the stairs, something touched her face. Nicole jumped, waving her arms in front of her. *It's just a string.* She pulled it. A dim bulb illuminated a circle on the floor and cast a bit of light around the attic. *Amazing. It works.*

Scanning the room, there were many things she hadn't noticed before. Cobwebby bookcases, rolled up rugs and some faded, cardboard signs that said "On strike! International Mercantile Marine Unfair to Seamen."

Nicole ran her hand across some old clothes hanging from a rack. *Maybe I could do the fashions of Elk River.* She shook her head. *I don't think so.*

She remembered a trunk, full of dolls and stuffed animals. Nicole went to it and lifted the rounded lid, running her fingers over the plush lining.

She examined the dolls, more carefully this time than the last. Some were worn but others looked like they had hardly been touched. One doll wore a dress that felt like silk. Its face was ceramic and the features appeared Asian. Another one looked African. She picked up a little stuffed elephant with a jewel-studded collar inscribed with strange letters. *These must have been Dolores Weber's when she was a little girl.* She stroked the fur of a cuddly tiger. Nicole took out every doll and stuffed animal. The last was a tattered clown that looked like it was made for a baby.

She shined her flashlight into the trunk. On the bottom there was a large black leather wallet and a packet of envelopes tied together with a ribbon. Nicole lifted the wallet out of the trunk and opened it. Inside, there was a stack of small green pieces of paper. She examined the one on top. On the left side, it said "United States Coast Guard Certificate of Discharge." The name "Henry Christopher Weber" was written where it said "Signature of Seaman." A different name was on a line for "Master of Vessel." On the right side of the paper, there was more information: "Date of Shipment: 4/29/46; Place of Shipment: Boston, Mass; Date of Discharge: 6/30/46; Place of Discharge: Boston, Mass; Name of Ship: S/S Atlantic Pride; Class of Vessel: Steam; Nature of Voyage: Foreign." Nicole looked briefly at a few more of the green papers. They were all the same except for the dates and the names of the cities, the names of the ships and the master.

Dolores Weber's father was a sailor. These were from his voyages.

She put the bundle back into the leather folder. There were more papers. One folded-up document was a "Seaman's Certificate of Identification." It had a little photograph of a bearded man. Next to the photo it said "Seaman's Thumb Print." Below was an inky smudge. In the middle of the paper, it said "The bearer, Henry Christopher Weber, whose home address is Cliff Road, Elk River, Maine, born in Maine on September 17, 1885, is a citizen of U.S.A."

Nicole carefully refolded the document and returned it to its place. There was a "Certificate of Service to Able Seaman," membership dues receipts, passes and papers in foreign languages and a tattered passport which on every page bore stamps from countries all over the world. *This stuff is cool.*

Maybe I could do my report on the famous Mr. Weber. Nicole put everything back where she found it and closed the wallet.

Next, she picked up the packet of envelopes. The top one was addressed to:

Miss Dolores Weber
Cliff Road
Elk River, Maine
USA.

Nicole looked at the postmark. It said "Deutschland." *I think that means Germany.* She untied the ribbon and looked at the next one: "France." Nicole couldn't read the postmark on the third envelope. Some of the letters looked backward or upside down. Some she didn't recognize at all. The stamp showed a picture of a man with a military hat and a bushy black mustache.

The envelopes had been opened. Reaching carefully inside the first one, Nicole pulled out a handwritten letter. Holding the pages carefully, she sat down on the floor and began to read.

> S.S. Abraham Lincoln
> The North Atlantic
> October 22, 1946
> 0015 hours

Dear Dolores,

It's dark here. It's just past midnight where I am so a new day has begun. Yesterday's storm is behind us and now, steaming toward Europe, the sea is calm. There's lots of fog, so we can't see where we're going but the ship's whistle is blowing every 30 seconds; we have lookouts posted on the bow and the bridge and there's a good sailor at the wheel so I believe we'll be all right. We're north of the 35th parallel and winter is not far off, so storms are always a possibility. We'll keep our fingers crossed for good weather ahead.

I just finished my watch. I'm on the eight to twelve. That means I work every day from eight in the morning until noon and from eight p.m. until midnight. Most people think that's the best watch because your eating and sleeping are almost normal. Right now, I'm in the crew mess. (On a ship, that's what they call the room where the crew eats. I can't imagine how it got that name.) I can't write in my room ("fo'c'sle," we call them) because some of my cabinmates are sleeping. A few decks below me, the engine is pounding and it's well over a hundred degrees down there. But up here, the vibration gets to be almost relaxing after a while and there's even some fresh ocean air coming in. It's a good time to write.

Back in Maine, you and your mother and your cat might be getting ready for bed. If you're already asleep, I hope you're having pleasant dreams. Before we sailed into this fog bank there was a beautiful moon overhead that made our wake sparkle. It reminded me of "Moonlight," my favorite piece that you used to play on your harp. And it makes your old man feel good to think that, before you went to bed, maybe you were looking at the moon too. Remember, when you were little, we used to say that even when we were far apart, both of us could still see the moon? We pretended that we could use it like a mirror to send our love back and forth across the oceans. I think you'll agree that we drifted apart sometimes even when I was home. Maybe especially then. I know you're not little anymore but I wonder if the old moon still relays messages. Want to try? Maybe it works best at a distance.

It was hard for me to leave Elk River but as you know, things have been kind of tough for seamen during the last year. After the war, lots of men on the waterfront lost their jobs and then, as you also know, we had to go on strike a few times. So, now that things have settled down a bit, I think taking this ship was the right thing to do. Maybe if we put extra fuel into the burners, we can get a few more knots out of Old Abe. I'll be back home before you know it.

As usual, I'm sailing with an interesting bunch. For starters, we've got a great cook aboard and many sailors say that's the most important ingredient for a good voyage. There are many people in the crew I don't know but a few are men I've sailed with before. Some of us were together during the war, on ships just like this one. Some of us walked picket lines together when one union or another was on strike.

We've got men of every color from all over the United States and even some from other countries. It didn't used to be like that. For a long time, colored sailors, especially, had a very hard time getting the jobs they wanted and it took some tough fights to change the rules. Even today, just about every ship's officer is white. We've got real problems but, in some ways, the 43 of us, or most of us anyway, get along better than a lot of people do on the beach.

Some of these guys have had pretty tough lives. They say that many seamen were orphans and maybe that's true. I've noticed that, especially around holidays like Thanksgiving and Christmas, fights sometimes break out. I guess that's because we all get lonely. Some of the men are battling the bottle—or as our electrician admits, "it hasn't been much of a fight." Some like to read, some have hobbies, some just walk the deck smoking their pipes. We even have a tough-talking kid, a deckhand with brand new tattoos, who keeps asking questions about you. (You don't have a boyfriend named Brian out here, do you?) But most of the guys keep to themselves. We've got a young Able Bodied Seaman (AB for short) named Casey that they call Scorpion. He wears a big knife on his hip and never says a word. The only person I've ever seen him talking to is the old man, the Captain, whom I don't like much. He seems to think that, apart from the officers, the crew is a bunch of bums. A lot of captains are like that. But most of us try to get along in our little floating world and we generally put up with each other's ways. The owners have let the Lincoln run down but I think the crew

THE WEBER HOUSE

will see us through.

Now for something pretty interesting. Just before I left, I found an object that was hidden a long, long time ago near where our house stands today. Guess what? The old legends may be true! Years ago, even before the American Revolution, something mysterious was stashed away and maybe you can find it!

What I found was a brass plaque. It seems that William Taggart, the man who built our house almost two hundred years ago, left behind something important. As you know, he was not a good person. The inscription on the plaque suggests that Taggart hid something but it doesn't say what or where it is. It may not be worth anything today but who knows? Trying to find it might be fun.

I could tell you where the plaque is but I have a better idea. Remember when we used to have treasure hunts? I'd hide clues around the house or the yard and you'd follow them to some "treasure" I'd hidden. I know we haven't done one for years but maybe this would be interesting. I'll give you a clue in this letter which I'll mail from our first port, Bremen. (You can look on the globe to see where that is.) I'll send the next clue from Marseilles and the final clue will come from Odessa, our last port before we sail for home. Don't think that you can just read the third letter and go straight to the mysterious plaque. The last clue won't make any sense unless you figure out the ones before it. Let's see how far you get before I'm back in Elk River. Even if you figure out all of the clues before I get home, I think you may have to wait a while to locate the "treasure." It might even end up being a four-day early Christmas present. Confused? That's great!

Here is your first clue.

Start from the red stone in the walkway in front of our house. That stone is one vertex of an invisible triangle. The second vertex is 125 feet away. The third vertex is 70 feet from the second corner and about 143 feet from the first one.

You must go to the third vertex of the triangle. When you get there, you have to think of a place where 0 equals 360. I think you know what that means. Walk toward 180 as far as you can. You will see a rock which has your initials carved into it. The next letter will tell you what to do from that point.

Good luck!

I'm getting pretty tired so I guess I should turn in. I miss you and Mom. I know that my leaving is hard on you both in some ways (maybe it's easier on you in some ways too) but I'm sure you'll both be fine without me for a little while. I'm already counting the days and the miles. I'll see you in Europe.

Love,
Dad

Nicole put the letter onto her lap. *This is unbelievable. There might really be a treasure around here someplace!* Nicole glanced at the other envelopes. *And I'll bet that these have the rest of the clues for finding it.*

Nicole looked at the first clue again. *But what does it mean? How am I supposed to find an invisible triangle? And where does 0 equal 360?* Setting the envelopes aside, she put the leather folder back into the trunk and then replaced the dolls and stuffed animals. Nicole picked up the envelopes, got to her feet and started for the stairs. *Wait 'til I tell Alice.*

An idea came to her. *We can do our research project together.* Nicole slapped the envelopes across her hand. *We'll solve the mystery of the Weber House!*

CHAPTER TWENTY-ONE

DECEMBER 7

Nicole was making her bed. At a few minutes past eleven, she looked out her front window and saw Alice and her father coming up the walk in front of the house. Six inches of fresh snow had fallen during the night. She tossed some shoes into her closet and closed the door. She picked up yesterday's clothes and pitched them into the laundry basket.

Nicole was coming down the stairs when she heard footsteps on the porch followed by the clunk of the knocker on the front door. Her father emerged from the sitting room with a mug of coffee.

"I'll get it!" Nicole said.

She pulled the door open and felt cold air. Alice and her father were wiping their feet on the mat. Alice was holding a foil-covered plate. Her father carried a small duffel bag with a pillow under his arm.

"Hi, Nicole," Alice said, smiling.

"Hi, come in."

Nicole pushed the door closed behind the guests.

"I'm sorry we didn't get the walk shoveled," Nicole's father said.

"We're used to snow," Alice's father said. "Should we take our shoes off?" He was a big man, Nicole noticed. Handsome, and he looked strong. She took the plate while her friend pulled off her hat and slipped out of her parka.

"No, don't bother. We don't." Nicole's father said, extending his hand. "I'm Paul."

"Louis Attean." The dads shook hands as Nicole's mother came out of the sitting room.

"I'm Mary," she said, offering her hand. It disappeared into Alice's father's. "Nicole's really been looking forward to this weekend."

"Alice has too," her father said. He looked around the hallway. "This is quite a house."

"Living here's been pretty interesting too," Nicole's father said.

Mr. Attean nodded. "My wife told me that Nicole had a scare in the woods the other night."

The girls glanced at each other.

"It sounded awful," Alice's father continued, shaking his head. "Imagine, trying to frighten somebody that way. But every December, people get interested in this house and the woods around here. I'm sure you know all the legends."

"*Now* we do," Nicole's mother said, with a sideways look toward her husband. "But don't worry, we'll keep a close eye on these two." She pointed at the plate that Nicole was holding. "What have you got there?"

"Alice brought it."

"My mom made some oatmeal cookies."

"That was so nice. Will you please thank your wife for us, Mr. Attean?"

"Call me Louis. Anne was glad to do it."

"Nicole, why don't you hang Alice's coat up and put the cookies in the kitchen? Then you can take her things upstairs."

"I just made some coffee," Nicole's father said. "Would you

like a cup?"

"No, thanks," Mr. Attean said. "I have to get going. We're driving down to Bangor this afternoon." He opened his arms to his daughter. "Bye, Alice. Have fun."

Alice gave her father a hug.

"Remember, your mother and I won't be home tonight. We're driving to your aunt's. We'll see you tomorrow around noon. Okay?"

"Okay," Alice said. She and Nicole and the cookies went up the stairs as their fathers talked about the snow on Route 9.

Nicole closed the door to her room as soon they were inside.

"Well," Nicole said, as she put the cookies on her dresser, "do you want to do some homework?"

"You're kidding, right?"

"Nope. Do you have a topic for your Elk River project yet?"

"Not really, do you?"

"We both do, if you want to. We can try to solve the mystery. You know, the treasure and everything."

"I have *no* idea what you're talking about."

"Check this out." Nicole went to her desk and pushed the cover up. She pulled out the packet of envelopes and held them up. "The secret of the Weber House."

"*That* is the secret of the Weber House? It looks like a bunch of old letters."

"These aren't just *any* old letters. I found them last night in the attic in an old trunk under some dolls and stuffed animals that must have belonged to Dolores Weber. There was some sailor stuff too, from her father."

"So far I'm not getting how this solves any mysteries."

"You gotta read the letters. Or the first one anyway. I read it last night. It's from Dolores' father to Dolores."

"And?"

"You know how some people think there's a treasure

buried around here someplace, right?"

"Yeah," Alice answered, reaching for the envelopes in her friend's hand. "A pirate's treasure. And those letters say where it is?"

Nicole pulled the envelopes back. "Maybe. The first one says that Dolores' father found a brass plaque and the plaque says that the pirate hid something someplace."

"'The pirate hid something someplace.' So, I guess you're rich now?"

"Nobody's rich yet. But maybe together we can figure it all out."

"Thanks. We'll *both* be rich."

"All I know is that some people think there's a treasure and this letter says . . . hold on . . . where is it?" Nicole opened the envelope and quickly scanned the pages. "Here it is. *'The old legends may be true!'* Read it yourself."

Nicole handed the first letter to her friend. She put the other two back into the desk and pulled down the top.

"Cool desk," Alice said.

"I keep my personal stuff in here. That's why I always roll the top down."

"You think that would keep a burglar out?"

"Parents, hopefully."

Alice sat on the bed and began reading. After a minute or two, she looked up. "It sounds like sometimes Dolores and her father didn't get along too well. Reminds me of my family."

"Yeah," Nicole agreed. "Mine too. Did you see the part about bouncing messages back and forth off the moon?"

"Yeah. How old do you think she was then?"

"Too old for stuff like that."

"This is kind of interesting," Alice noted, "about the guys on the ship and how they all used to be white."

"Yeah."

"Oh, here it is," Alice said. *'The old legends may be true . . .'*"

"Keep going."

"All right, all right. *'It seems that William Taggart, the man who built our house almost two hundred years ago, left behind something important.'* Oh my god, there really *is* a treasure!"

"Keep reading."

"Okay. The letter says Taggart was bad. We know that. Then it says *'The inscription on the plaque suggests that Taggart hid something but it doesn't say what or where it is either. It may not be worth anything today.'*" Alice looked up. "Yeah, right. He hid it because it was worthless."

"Keep reading."

"Okay," Alice said as she disappeared behind the letter.

Nicole waited. A minute later, Alice put the letter down.

"Unbelievable. The letters are going to tell us where the treasure is. All we have to do is follow the clues."

"That's what I thought at first, but there's just one problem."

"What?" Alice asked.

"If the letters say how to find the treasure, how come Dolores never found it?"

"Hmm," Alice said. "Good question." She got off the bed and went to the front window.

"Maybe," Nicole said, "she couldn't figure out the clues."

"But didn't Dolores' father *want* her to figure them out?"

"I guess so but whatever the reason was, we know Dolores didn't find the treasure or everyone would have heard about it. So, if there ever really *was* a treasure, it's still out there and, thanks to these letters, we have a better chance than anybody to find it."

"It should be easy enough to start," Alice held up the letter. "This says to start at a red stone in the walkway in front of the house. Do you know if there's one there?"

"Nope. Want to find out?"

"What do *you* think?"

The girls went into the hall and down the stairs. Nicole pulled the front door open.

"Are you two going outside?" Nicole's father had appeared in the hallway.

"Just for a minute."

"Put your coats on."

Nicole closed the door and looked at Alice. She shrugged. The girls went to the closet and put their coats on before hurrying outside. They stepped off the porch and crouched down. With bare hands the girls began brushing the snow away from the spot in front of the step. In a few seconds, enough was uncovered. The stone was black.

"Maybe it's the next one," Alice suggested.

In a few seconds, the next stone was visible. It was black too.

"My hands are getting cold," Nicole said.

"Mine too," Alice agreed. "Maybe we should get a shovel."

"We can use our feet," Nicole suggested.

"My feet are cold too."

"Let's just do a few more," Nicole said.

The girls kicked enough snow away to determine the color of several more stones. All were black.

Nicole looked at her friend and let out a disappointed breath.

"One more?" Alice said.

"Okay."

The first few kicks uncovered some grass.

"I think the walk turns toward the driveway around here someplace," Nicole said.

The girls shifted their position slightly and took a few more swipes at the snow.

"You should be good at this," Alice said. "You play soccer."

Nicole took aim at an imaginary ball and swung her foot. A cloud of snow flew into Alice's face. "Goal!"

"Nice shot," Alice said sarcastically, wiping her eyes.

"Sorry."

Alice was looking down.

"Are you okay?"

"It *was* a nice shot." Alice pointed at the ground. "Look."

The stone was red.

Nicole leaped into the air. "It's true!" She hugged Alice and they both fell into the snow.

"Get off!" Alice laughed. "The snow's going down my back."

The girls got to their feet. Alice scooped up a handful of snow and tossed it into Nicole's face.

"Ow! That stings," she said, laughing.

Alice crouched down and brushed away some snow in a new spot.

"What are you doing?"

"What if there are more red stones? What if *all* the rest are red?"

The girls went back to work. Five more walkway stones were uncovered. All were black.

"All right," Nicole said, "I'm satisfied. Are you?"

"Yup," Alice said. "Cold, too. Let's go in."

They turned toward the house. Nicole's father was standing in the doorway. "I was afraid you two were fighting."

"No," Nicole said, putting her arm around Alice. "We were, uh, shoveling the walk."

"It might be easier if you used a shovel. Not to mention gloves and boots."

"That's okay, Dad, we're finished."

"You're finished? You didn't even go halfway."

The girls stepped up onto the porch. Nicole grinned at her father. "That was enough."

CHAPTER TWENTY-TWO

The girls sat on Nicole's bed, a few slices of pizza and several crusts between them.

"Now all we have to do is find a giant triangle," Nicole said between bites.

"Yeah, an invisible one," Alice added. "*Start from the red stone in the walkway in front of our house,*" she said, reading from the old letter. "*That stone is one vertex of an invisible triangle. The second vertex is 125 feet away. The third vertex is 70 feet from the second corner and about 143 feet from the first one.*" Shaking her head, Alice put the letter on the bed.

"There's a good view of the yard from up here," Nicole said, picking up the letter and walking to her front window. "Maybe we can see some things that could be the other vertices."

Alice climbed off the bed and stood next to her friend. "If they're rocks or something like that, we'll never be able to see them under the snow. Maybe they're trees."

"We'd need a tree that's 143 feet from where the red stone is." Nicole pointed to some evergreens beyond the driveway and close to the cliff. "Like those over there, maybe."

"Can I see the letter?"

Nicole handed it over.

"And it has to be 70 feet from the second one which has to be 125 feet from the red stone. I don't see any trees that match up."

"I don't think it's a tree," Nicole said. "But like you said, Dolores' father *wanted* her to figure out the clues. Whatever it is, it might even be in plain sight."

Alice peered outside. "How about the tower?" That looks like it might be about 125 feet away."

"All right," Nicole said. "Let's say it's 125 feet from the red stone and it's the second vertex."

"Okay."

"So," Nicole continued, "the third vertex is only 70 feet from there but it's even *further* from the red stone than the tower is."

"Okay."

"Well, the tower is at the edge of the cliff, right?"

Alice nodded

Nicole took a bite of pizza. "So, to be further away would put the third vertex out over the water someplace."

The girls stared out the window.

"It's lying right out there in front of us. Why can't we see it?"

Alice didn't answer.

"Alice? Earth calling Alice."

Alice turned around slowly. "What if it isn't?"

"What if it isn't *what*?"

"You said 'it's lying right out there in front of us.' What if it isn't *lying* out there?"

"What?"

"What if the triangle is sticking up in the air?"

"Can I see the letter again?"

Alice handed it back and Nicole studied it before looking up. "We said the tower was probably 125 feet away, right?"

Alice smiled.

Nicole smiled back. "How high do you figure the tower is?"

Alice looked out the window. "It could be 70 feet."

"So, if it's 125 feet from the stone to the bottom of the tower and it's 70 feet from the bottom of the tower to the top, how far would it be from the top back to the red stone?"

"That would be a right triangle," Alice said, "so 'A' squared plus 'B' squared equals 'C' squared. Do you have a calculator?"

Nicole handed the letter back to Alice and went to her backpack. "Got it. What are the numbers again?"

"The base is 125."

"One twenty-five squared is 15,625. The height, if we're right, is 70, and 70 squared is . . ."

"Forty-nine hundred."

Nicole looked up. "Correct. And 4,900 plus 15,625 is . . ." She pecked at the keys. " . . . twenty thousand, five hundred twenty-five."

"And the square root of that is . . .?"

"One forty-three point 265. That's it, Alice! The third corner of the triangle is the top of the tower. That's where we've got to go next!"

"Have you mentioned to your parents yet that you've been up there?"

"Nope."

Alice smiled. "I'll bring the letter," she said, sliding the envelope into her back pocket.

Nicole picked up her flashlight. "We should wear sweaters." She got one from her bureau. Alice pulled one from her duffel bag.

"How about these?" Alice asked, holding up the binoculars that were on Nicole's desk

"Good idea."

Alice put the strap on her shoulder.

The girls hurried into the hall. Then Nicole stopped abruptly, causing Alice to bump into her.

"Sorry."

"Let's take the back stairs," Nicole explained. "If no one sees us we won't have to answer any questions."

"Lead the way."

They crept down the stairs. Nicole peeked into the kitchen and signaled that they could proceed. A moment later the girls stood in front of the heavy door that led to the basement. Nicole slid the bolt back and pulled the door open. "I think there're mice down here."

"Mice don't bother me," Alice said.

"Spiders, too."

"They don't bother me either."

Nicole started down the steps. "They bother me."

"Should I close the door?"

"Good idea."

The door thumped shut and they were shrouded in darkness. Nicole switched on her flashlight. When the girls reached the bottom, Nicole aimed her light across the cellar to the far corner. "That's where we've got to go."

"Okay," Alice said.

"Watch out for all the junk all over the place," Nicole said, pointing the light into the center of the cellar. "See, there's even a boat down here."

"That's a skiff. My dad has one."

In a moment the girls stood in front of the mirror.

"Is this how we get into the tunnel?" Alice asked.

"Watch."

Holding the light in one hand, Nicole pulled on the edge of the mirror with the other. It swung open. Nicole twisted the switch next to the opening. Far down in the tunnel, a dim light came on.

"Unbelievable," Alice whispered.

"Ready?"

"Ready."

Side by side, the girls stepped into the tunnel.

"I can't believe you came in here by yourself," Alice said.

"Me either. And I wouldn't have if I hadn't been chasing Ivy."

"This sure doesn't look like a natural tunnel," Alice said, as they approached the first light. She ran her hand over the wall of black rock. "Do you think the pirate did this?"

"Or his prisoners."

The girls rounded a bend and passed under a second light. Nicole pointed her flashlight into the opening on the right side of the tunnel. "Check out the chains in there."

"I see what you mean."

"The end is up here," Nicole said, pointing her light ahead.

In a few seconds they were under the tower. Alice peered at the stone stairway circling into the darkness above. "I'm not too crazy about heights."

"Want me to go first?" Nicole asked.

"Okay, but go slow, all right?"

Nicole nodded and took the first step. Alice stayed close. Before long, daylight was reflecting through the opening at the top of the stairs.

Nicole turned toward her friend. "Want to rest?"

"No, let's keep going."

They resumed climbing.

"Here we are," Nicole announced as they neared the top. The light shining through the trapdoor was dazzling. She climbed the final steps then turned to watch her friend emerge from the darkness. Alice blinked as she came into the light.

Securely on the floor, Alice looked outside. "Oh my god. This is incredible!" The sky was bright blue. The bay was covered with whitecaps and the wind whipped their crests into spray. Beyond was the vast, gray ocean.

"The height doesn't bother you?"

"It's okay when I'm indoors." Alice lifted the binoculars to her eyes. "I wonder if I can see my house from up here." She adjusted the focus. "Yup. There it is." She shifted her view to the left, toward the ocean. "I can see Puffin Island!"

"Which one is that?"

"The one with the lighthouse," Alice said. "Want to look?"

"Sure."

Alice handed over the binoculars and Nicole looked in the direction that her friend was pointing.

"Cool."

"It's kind of funny," Alice said.

"What?"

"This tower. It's like a lighthouse except for one thing."

"No light."

"Right," Alice agreed. "Usually, they build towers like this so people out on the water *will* see it. It's like the pirate built this one so *he* could see ships without being seen."

"Sort of an *anti*-lighthouse," Nicole said. She put the binoculars on a shelf and pointed to the woods on the right side of her house. "Can you see that little clearing down there?"

Alice nodded.

"That's where I saw the light on Wednesday night."

"And that's where you went the next day on your way to getting lost, and finding the cabin and falling down the hill and seeing the pirate's tombstone and everything?"

"Yeah, that's the place," Nicole said, smiling. "And now, let's see if we can figure out the rest of the clue."

Alice pulled the envelope from her back pocket. "Once we get to the third vertex of the triangle, we're supposed to *'think of a place where o equals 360.'* Then it says *'I think you know what that means. Walk toward 180 as far as you can. You will see a rock which has your initials carved into it.'*"

"All we have to do is figure out a place where o equals

360," Nicole said.

"That might not be too hard."

"Really?"

"In Mrs. Thorn's class," Alice said. "Explorers? Navigational instruments?"

Nicole stared at her friend.

"Binnacle?"

"A compass!"

"Mrs. Thorn would be *so* proud of you."

"On a compass 0 degrees is the same as 360 degrees. They both mean 'north.'"

Alice smiled.

"So, if 0, or 360, is north," Nicole continued, "180 has to be south."

Alice looked at the letter. "We're supposed to walk south as far as we can." She walked around to the right side of the tower. "Do you think 'as far as you can' means the cliff?"

"It must."

"I don't see any big rocks in that direction," Alice said. "The one with Dolores' initials must be under the snow. But we have to know *exactly* where south is. What we need now is a compass."

Nicole stepped beside the "ghost" in the center of the room and yanked off the sheet.

"Ta-da," she said with a flourish. "I saw this the first night I came up here but I forgot all about it—a giant compass! At least that's what I think it is."

Alice looked at the glass-covered instrument. "A binnacle! My father had something like this on his old boat, only smaller. The glass protects the compass from the weather. And see, the needle is pointing north, up the coast.

"East is exactly in front of the house," Nicole said. "That's where the sun comes up. If we look down the coast, that's south, more or less."

"I'll bet that's where we'll find the stone with the initials," Alice said. "At the edge of the cliff, where the yard ends and the woods start."

"Let's go look."

"I think one of us should stay here to keep an eye on the compass," Alice suggested. "If both of us go out, we won't know exactly where to look."

"Do you want to go or stay?"

"I'll go," Alice said. "You can watch and signal me to move one way or the other. When I'm at exactly the right spot, put both arms up and I'll look for the stone under the snow. You'll probably have to direct me from outside and I think I'd feel better down on the ground."

"Okay," Nicole said, "but be careful. You'll be close to the cliff."

"I will. What should I tell your parents if they ask me where you are?"

"Tell them I'm upstairs."

Alice smiled. "Okay. You should see me out in the yard in a few minutes."

"Take the light."

"Thanks." Alice handed the envelope to Nicole. "You better keep this. We don't want it to get wet."

Nicole slid the letter into her back pocket. She watched as her friend disappeared down the stairs but Nicole could still hear Alice's footsteps echoing off the tower's stone walls. She followed the flashlight's reflection as it spiraled into the darkness. Soon there was neither sound nor light from below.

Nicole waited a few minutes before stepping outside. The wind was stiff. She looked down, nearly straight down, at the water. Waves crashed into the cliff and white foam swirled around the rocks. Feeling slightly queasy, she gripped the icy railing and circled around to the side facing the yard. A minute or two later Alice appeared at the far side of the house. She was wearing her parka.

"I wonder if Mom or Dad saw her."

Alice waved. Nicole waved back. Then Alice turned right and walked toward the furthest point of the yard where the cliff met the woods. When she was a few feet from the spot, Alice stopped and faced Nicole. She held her hands up as if to say: "How's this?"

Nicole hurried back inside the tower. From the far side of the binnacle, she stood so she could see what point on the dial corresponded to Alice's position. Alice was at 182 degrees: too far to the right.

Nicole went outside and motioned for Alice to move to the left. Alice took several steps in the direction Nicole was pointing. Nicole went inside for another look. Now Alice was too far to the left. As Nicole came back outside, she noticed something moving among the trees behind Alice. A deer, probably. She pointed to the right and Alice moved a few steps in that direction.

Nicole went back to the compass. She squinted at the dial and looked up. Alice was exactly above the 180 on the compass. Nicole went outside and put her hands up. Alice dropped to her knees and began to brush away the snow. While Alice searched, Nicole looked back toward the woods. *There it is again.*

Nicole hurried inside, grabbed the binoculars and ran back into the cold. Alice, oblivious to everything else, was still sweeping the snow with her hands. Nicole stared at the trees to Alice's right, raised the binoculars and focused them.

A chill shot through her. A short distance from where Alice was kneeling in the snow, a dog—a big, black dog—was creeping through the trees toward Alice. Nicole could see the animal's breath coming out in blasts.

"Alice! Alice!" Nicole shouted, waving her arms.

Alice stopped digging in the snow. She stood up, turned toward the tower and pointed to the ground.

She must have found the stone but she doesn't see the dog. Nicole pointed and waved for her friend to go back to the house but she seemed to think it was a game. "Run, Alice! Run!" Nicole screamed but her voice was drowned out by the wind. Instead of running, Alice flopped on her back and started to make a snow angel. Trying not to panic, Nicole turned the binoculars toward the trees. The dog seemed to be looking right at her. Suddenly, the dog's ears perked up and it turned its head. It sprang deeper into the forest and veered toward the cliff, stopping abruptly at the edge. The beast turned back and looked up at the tower. Nicole felt like it was staring right into her eyes. Then the dog turned toward the water, crouched, and jumped off the cliff!

Shaken, Nicole tried to process what she had just seen. Down on the ground and across the yard, Alice got up from the snow, brushed herself off and waved. Nicole waved back weakly. Alice started toward the house. Nicole went back inside the tower and lowered herself through the trapdoor and into the darkness.

CHAPTER TWENTY-THREE

Despite not having a light, Nicole hurried as she circled down the steps, through the tunnel and basement and back up to the first floor. She pushed the heavy door shut and opened the one to the backyard. Alice was already there, stamping her feet and brushing the snow off her coat, a big smile on her face.

"We did it! We found the stone! It had 'DW' carved in it!"

Nicole reached around her friend's neck with both arms and hugged her tight.

"Stop," Alice laughed, "I can hardly breathe."

Nicole released her.

"God, I've only been gone for a few minutes." Alice said as she stepped inside the house. "Is that snow on your face? You look like you're crying. What's the matter? Did your parents catch you?"

"While you were looking for the stone, a gigantic dog was creeping up on you. It looked like a wolf. I thought it was going to attack you."

"What?" Alice said, her smile evaporating.

"When I was waving to you, I was trying to tell you to run."

"How close was it?"

Nicole shrugged. "I don't know, like fifty feet at first. But then it moved even closer. Then it looked like somebody called it. Then it jumped off the cliff."

"You're kidding."

"No, really. I swear."

"I can't believe I didn't see it," Alice said. "Are you sure it wasn't a deer?"

"You sound like my parents. I *saw* it with the binoculars."

"Sorry. I wonder if it was the same dog that chased *you*."

"It's gotta be!" Nicole shook her head. "Maybe this time, I *should* tell my parents."

Alice was silent.

"I guess we can at least read the next clue," Nicole said slowly. "There can't be any harm in that."

The girls went into the pantry and were about to go up the back stairs when Nicole's father came in from the hall. He looked at Alice and then at his daughter. "I'd say that one of you isn't dressed quite right."

Alice unzipped her parka. "I had to go outside for a minute, Mr. Kelly."

The girls went into the hallway and Alice hung up her coat.

"What have you girls been up to?" Nicole's mother asked as she came out of the sitting room. "I haven't heard a sound from upstairs."

Alice looked at Nicole.

"School stuff."

Her father came out of the pantry with a can of beer. "Boy stuff, more likely," he said with a smile.

Nicole sighed. "Right, Dad. We were talking about boys."

The girls went up the front stairs and soon were behind Nicole's closed door.

"And you think the dog was *watching* me?"

"That's sure what it looked like."

Alice went to the front window. "I guess it's possible that it was just wandering through the woods when I happened to be out there." She turned toward Nicole. "I mean, it didn't really *do* anything."

"Yeah right, and it didn't really *do* anything to me either when it followed me through the woods. Unless you count almost chasing me over the cliff."

"You said it looked like somebody called the dog. Maybe it was the same guy you saw on Thanksgiving."

"Who knows," Nicole said. "But *that* guy didn't have a dog. At least I didn't see one."

"So, should we tell your parents what happened?"

Nicole shook her head. "I don't know. I don't want to start another round of 'maybe you just *thought* you saw something, dear.' And after all, *you* didn't see anything either."

Alice shrugged. "Maybe you *are* making it all up."

"*What?*"

"Just kidding."

"You had me worried there for a second," Nicole said.

"Sorry."

"Do *you* have any theory about what's going on around here?"

"Not really," Alice replied. "I guess it *could* have something to do with the time of year when everybody starts thinking about the treasure and all that. But who knows? I think we should agree that neither of us should go outside alone anymore."

"Good idea."

"So, now what?" Alice asked.

"Want to read the next letter?"

"Have you read it yet?"

"No," Nicole said. "It'll be the first time for both of us."

Alice sat on the end of the bed. Nicole rolled up her desk's cover, pulled the envelope from her back pocket and put it inside. She took another envelope out of the desk and sat across from Alice. "It was mailed from France."

THE WEBER HOUSE

Alice nodded and Nicole started to read.

> The Pillars of Hercules
> November 6, 1946
> 0015 hours

Dear Dolores,

It's dark outside but we are in a very interesting place. Right now, the Atlantic Ocean is behind us, and the Mediterranean Sea is ahead. Europe is on our port side and Africa is to starboard. This spot is truly one of the crossroads of the world. Do you know where I am?

If you look on your globe, you will see that we are sailing through the Strait of Gibraltar. To the ancient Greeks, this strait was the gateway to the Infinite Ocean. It was the end of the known world. The ancient myths say that the mountains on either side of me were put here by Hercules, the son of Zeus himself!

In port, the crew is always very busy but we are back at sea now and this gives me time to think and to write. Once again, I'm in the crew mess. My watch is over but a few minutes ago, I was up on the bridge. I could just make out the silhouettes of the gigantic Rock of Gibraltar on one side of the ship and, less than eight miles away, the mountain known as Jebel Musa on the Moroccan side. But most important, the moon was out so I sent you a message our special way. I hope you got it. I miss you very much.

Nicole stopped reading and looked toward her friend. Alice shrugged and Nicole rolled her eyes before returning to the letter.

Someday, I hope that you will see for yourself how beautiful the ocean is. Tonight, it's glittering like a million jewels. As we approached the strait, I stood outside on the bridge wing just to feel the breeze and smell the salt air. Somehow at sea, the world seems a fresh and clean place. You'll see. It almost makes you forget the terrible things that happened ashore and at sea, too, during the last seven years.

We sailed from Germany a few days ago. In Bremen, the destruction from the war is terrible. Much of the city was bombed and burned. I saw young children, alone, picking through the rubble where houses and schools once stood. They were looking for food and I don't know what will become of them. Those poor children made me think of you. And it's not just Bremen, either. Near the end of the war, the city of Dresden was completely burned in a single night. Who knows how many died? Many, very many, innocent people were killed who were not even soldiers. And I think that many of the soldiers were victims too.

Of course, not everyone was innocent. In Germany, millions of people, <u>millions</u>, were killed by the government—the Nazis—and their helpers, only because they were Jews. This happened in many countries in Europe. A few of my shipmates lost relatives. Perhaps some of your classmates did too.

Some of the people who are responsible for this are dead or in jail but not all of them. Some of them are even walking around as free as you or I. Some are still wealthy and powerful. This seems impossible but it's true.

I wish you didn't have to learn about war. I wish we could live in a world where there were no wars. Maybe someday we will. But for now, I think we have to look at what happened and try to understand why it did and who is to blame so it never happens again. That's the least we can do in memory of all those innocent people who perished.

Somehow, we must all go on. Your mother must still take care of you and teach art at Chamberlain. You must still go to school and continue to learn. I have to do my part to help sail this ship. All of us must somehow try to do our work and make the world a better place but that's not all. We also have to laugh and play and even solve mysteries for fun.

THE WEBER HOUSE

I'm sorry to write about such terrible things. Your mother will try to help you understand and I hope you are learning about these horrible events in school. When I get home, we'll all have a lot of time to talk. Thinking about that day helps me do what I must do, hour by hour, watch by watch, day by day.

Meanwhile, I know you're working hard at school. What are you learning in math right now? How about geography? Those are the skills of a navigator and the lives of all of us on the Lincoln depend on them. Be sure to keep all your drawings and everything you write. Don't forget to practice your harp. Say hello to Kimberly for me and give your feathered friends outside an extra ration of chow, okay?

One final thing, Sweetheart. Did you think I forgot? Here is your second clue. Start from the stone that bears your initials. The old shipmate is on your port side. You will be standing on a line that is precisely 628 feet long and has neither beginning nor end. It's not straight and you can't see it but you must go to a point on the line exactly 157 feet away. When you reach the right spot, the old shipmate is neither closer nor further away but now she is pointing right at you. Face the cliff. Now jump off.

Welcome to the crow's nest.

Love,
Dad

Nicole looked at up Alice and then back at the last page. "'Face the cliff?' 'Jump off?' 'Welcome to the crow's nest?'" She put the letter on the bed. "What's all that supposed to mean?"

Alice shook her head as she reached for the letter. "This guy was really into invisible things."

"True."

"Let's see," Alice said as she looked at the letter. "We start on the stone we found in the snow."

"Actually, you found it."

"Whatever. When we stand on the stone," Alice continued,

"we're supposed to be on a very strange line. First the clue says how long the line is, and then it says the line has no beginning and no end. Then it says the line isn't straight and we can't see it but we have to stay on it. How are we supposed to do that?"

"One step at a time," Nicole said. "Like we said before, he wanted Dolores to figure it out."

Alice nodded.

"Maybe the part about the line isn't so hard," Nicole said. She went to her desk for a pad of paper and a pencil. Returning to the bed, she drew a pear-shaped squiggle. "See, you could say that any line that comes back to where it started has no beginning and no end."

"Okay," Alice said. "And we know we have to go, how far?" She looked at the letter again. "*Exactly 157 feet.*' But how do we know what direction to go in? And how do we know what shape the line is?"

"We don't," Nicole admitted. "But I'll bet he made it some regular shape like a square or . . ." She tore the top page off the pad and drew a round shape on the next one ". . . a circle!"

"I'll bet you're right," Alice said. "And we can find out for sure. The circumference of a circle is pi times diameter, right?"

"Correct."

"So," Alice continued, "if the shape is a circle, and it's 628 feet around, the diameter would be 628 divided by 3.14."

"Correct again." Nicole wrote 628 next to the circle.

"What's 628 divided by 3.14?" Alice said. "Where's the calculator?"

Nicole went back to her desk, reached for her calculator and entered the numbers. "Six hundred twenty-eight divided by 3.14 equals 200. If the shape is a circle, the diameter is 200." She climbed back onto the bed and wrote the number in the center of the circle. "Now what?"

Alice read the clue again. "Let's think about this 'old shipmate' thing," she said. "You think some old sailor's been standing in your yard for 50 years and nobody noticed?"

Nicole laughed. "Maybe it's a tree or a rock that's shaped like a man."

"The clue says 'she,'" Alice pointed out.

"Oops," Nicole said. "Well, anyway, how can *she* stay at the same distance as we walk around the circle?"

"Easy," Alice answered, "if *she's* at the center of the circle."

"I knew that." Nicole drew an "X" in the middle of the circle. "That means *she* is 100 feet from the stone."

"Exactly," Alice agreed. "We know how big the circle is and we know that the old shipmate is at the center. We just have to find *her*. That can't be too hard. When do you want to look?"

"Right now!" Nicole looked at the drawing. "If the circle is 628 feet around, how far is 157 feet? It's less than halfway."

"Right. Halfway would be, let's see, 314 feet," Alice said, picking up the calculator. "Maybe it's a quarter of the way around. Six twenty-eight divided by 4 is... one fifty-seven! We walk a quarter of the way around the circle and that's where you jump off the cliff!"

"I thought we were in this together."

"I'm afraid of heights."

Nicole erased the "X" and drew a stick figure wearing a dress. The figure pointed to the right. "Here's the center," she said. Then she wrote "DW" at the bottom. "And here is south. That's where the stone is." She drew two radii starting from the stick figure: one pointed down to the "DW," the other pointed to the right. She wrote "100" on each radius and "157" on the arc between them. At the upper end of the arc, she drew an "X." Okay," Nicole said. "When we reach the 'X,' the old shipmate is supposed to be pointing right at us."

"Sounds right."

"But what about the 'crow's nest' thing?" Nicole asked. "We're supposed to jump onto a bird's nest?"

"A crow's nest could be part of a ship."

"What a surprise."

"It's at the top of a mast," Alice continued, "where the lookout watches for ships and icebergs and stuff."

"That's even worse," Nicole said frowning. "Now you're saying we have to jump off the cliff onto the top of a ship."

"One step at a time."

"Okay," Nicole said, "you're right. We'll go outside and stand on the stone. Then we look for the old shipmate. If we can find *her*, we'll know where the center of the circle is, and it should be 100 feet away. But how are we going to stay on the invisible line for 157 feet?"

Both girls looked at the drawing.

"I've got it!" Alice said. "We don't need to stay on the circle."

Nicole looked doubtfully at her friend. "We don't?"

"Nope," Alice said. "The clue doesn't say how we get there." She pointed at the sketch. "Look, the old shipmate, whatever and wherever she is, is at the center of the circle, right?"

"Yeah?"

"Well," Alice explained, "the stone we found today and the place where you jump off the cliff are both on the circle. If we count our steps from the stone to the center, and then go the same distance in the direction the old shipmate is pointing, we'll be at the right spot, right?"

"Right. All we have to do is find her."

Alice pointed to the drawing. "We just have to find a stick figure person wearing a dress."

CHAPTER TWENTY-FOUR

"Alice and I are going outside for a little while," Nicole said to her father when they found him in the kitchen. "It's for our research project."

"Don't go too far, okay?"

In a few minutes, they were stepping off the front porch and into the snow. They walked to the corner of the house. "Do you have the drawing?" Alice asked.

Nicole patted her jacket pocket. "Right here."

"I wonder if anyone is going to be watching us?"

"I didn't want to tell my dad what we're doing, but I do sort of hope he can see us."

"I meant anyone *else*."

"Like the dog and whoever?"

"Yeah," Alice said. "Them."

Nicole frowned. She scanned an arc in front of the house from the tower on the left to the woods on the right. "How about if instead of walking straight to the stone, we kind of come at it from the left and stay away from the woods as much as we can."

"Okay," Alice agreed. The girls started to walk toward the cliff. "Where did you see it anyway?"

Nicole pointed to the right, toward the woods. "At first, it was over there. Then it moved even closer to where you were. That's when I was screaming but you were busy making your snow angel."

"Maybe my snow angel scared it away."

The girls trudged through the snow. Alice nodded toward the woods. "What if it's still back there?"

The girls stopped and looked at each other. "That would be bad," Nicole said.

"Very bad."

"Maybe if we go up close to the cliff, we can see the place where it jumped off. If we don't see anybody then it probably isn't around. If we do see it, we'll run back to the house."

"All right," Alice said.

The girls walked straight to the cliff. Then they followed the edge toward the woods. When they got close to the trees, Nicole knelt down and leaned forward slightly, looking down and to the right. Wind gusted up the cliff carrying the sound of crashing waves.

"See anything?" Alice said.

"Right here it's pretty steep down to the water. But over there"—Nicole pointed into the trees—"there *are* some rocks a few feet below the edge. That's probably where the dog jumped to. No sign of anything now." She got to her feet and brushed the snow off her pants.

Alice was staring into the woods. "I saw something moving over there."

Nicole immediately looked in the same direction. "Like what?"

"I don't know," Alice said slowly. "Something." She crouched down and made a snowball. She stood up, leaned back and lofted it into the trees.

Nicole heard rustling in the woods and saw a blur of brown and white.

"It's a deer!" Alice said.

Nicole let out a big breath. "That was scary."

"Yeah, but it shows that there aren't any dogs or people around."

"Yeah, you're right," Nicole agreed. "So, where's the stone?"

"Closer to the woods." Alice led the way, parallel to the cliff. After about twenty feet, she pointed.

The stone was gray and rough and two initials were carved into the center: "DW." Nicole pulled her mittens off and dropped them on the snow. She took the paper out of her jacket pocket and squinted as she looked at the drawing. "Okay, if we're right, we should be on the circumference of a circle that's 628 feet around and 200 feet across but we don't know where the center is."

"That's true," Alice said, "but wherever the center is, we should see 'the old shipmate,' unless she got tired of waiting for 50 years."

Nicole pointed to a large, snow-covered rock in the middle of the yard. "Do you think that could be her?'"

"Nah. I don't see how anyone could call that any kind of a shipmate. Besides, it's too close. The center of the circle has to be 100 feet from here."

The girls turned slowly, shielding their eyes with their hands. Nicole surveyed the area to the left of the house. Alice scanned the front yard. After less than 30 seconds: "Got it!"

"Where?" Nicole shouted. "Where is it?"

Alice pointed. "It's that statue sticking out from the top of your house. Now that I look at her, I think she *is* a she and she must have been a figurehead from an old ship. And she's pointing, too. She's *got* to be the old shipmate."

"And she must be about a hundred feet from here," Nicole said, high-fiving her friend. "That's definitely it."

"Okay," Alice said. "According to the clue, she's supposed

to be on our 'port' side."

"Is that left?" Nicole asked.

"That's right," Alice said.

"Port is right?"

"No, it's left," Alice said, smiling slightly. "You were right the first time when you said 'left.'"

The girls arranged themselves so the pointing figurehead was on their left. "Now," Nicole said, looking at the drawing, "if that's the center, the circle must curve in front of the house just like the cliff."

"Right," Alice said, "and now we have to count our steps from here to right under the figurehead. And then we pace the same number of steps in the direction she's pointing. We should be right back on the line or pretty close to it."

"Very good," Nicole said. "Now Ms. McDowell would be very proud of *you*."

Marching together as well as they could through the snow, the girls counted their steps toward the front of the house: ". . . eighty-five, eighty-six, eighty-seven, *eighty-eight*!" They were directly in front of the center of the house. Above them, the figurehead pointed her icicle-draped arm straight ahead, to the east, toward the ocean. The girls made a quarter turn to the right and looked toward the cliff.

"Ready?" Alice said.

"To the cliff!"

They started pacing again in the direction the figurehead was pointing. The closer they got to the cliff, the quieter the counting became: ". . .eighty-five, eighty-six, eighty-seven . . ." They were just one step from the edge, with nothing but air and sea in front of them. Straight ahead, high over the gray ocean, seagulls circled in the wind. Far below, the surf pounded the bottom of the cliff. Nicole and Alice looked at one another and took one more, little step.

"Eighty-eight," they said together. They looked down and

laughed. About four feet below the precipice, there was a ledge. It was about a yard wide with a rock wall at the front edge.

"The crow's nest!" Alice said.

"Let's check it out."

They sat on the edge and eased themselves down. "Well," Alice said, "we didn't exactly jump but here we are."

"Oh, great," Nicole said.

"What's the matter?"

"My butt's wet."

Alice laughed and looked back toward the house. The yard was at about eye-level. "I hope your dad wasn't watching us. From the house it would've looked pretty weird. By the way, how are we supposed to get back up?"

Nicole finished brushing off her pants and then examined the back wall of the "crow's nest." It was covered with vines, snow and ice. "Look," she said, pointing to some openings in the rock. "It's like a ladder." She cleared away some of the snow, climbed up a few "steps" and jumped back down. "I don't see anyone looking for us so I guess we're not in trouble."

"I'm sure glad this wall is here," Alice said as she peeked over the top of the wall facing the ocean. "From here it's almost straight down."

Nicole nodded. She ran her hand over the surface of the rock. "Somebody carved all this," she said. "It reminds me of the walls in the basement."

"Look," Alice said, pointing to the left. "There's a little ledge about fifteen feet below us. If you could climb down there somehow, maybe you could get the rest of the way to the beach."

"I think you're right," Nicole said, peering over the edge. "But I can't see how anyone could get from here to that ledge. And you wouldn't want to slip."

"I wonder if the next clue will tell us, I mean 'you,' to go down there," Alice said. "I hope not, for your sake."

"Maybe," Nicole answered, turning away from the ocean. "And maybe not. Look what I found."

Alice looked.

"Check out what's behind this stuff," Nicole said, pulling at the snow-covered vines at the back of the crow's nest. Behind the vegetation was an opening about waist-high and approximately two feet across. It was too dark to see more than a few feet inside.

"It looks like a cave," Alice said. "I think if we crouch down, we can go in."

"I don't know. Who knows what's in there?"

"I don't think anything's disturbed these vines," Alice replied. "Not for a long time, anyway. And the only footprints here are ours."

Nicole picked up a small stone and threw it into the opening. The girls listened as it bounced into the darkness. "Well, maybe just a little way. It's pretty dark in there and besides, we probably should get back to the house."

"Okay," Alice said. "Let's just take a peek to see if it goes anywhere."

Nicole stuck her head into the opening. She shrieked and pulled back.

"What is it?"

"Spiderwebs!"

"Want me to go first?" Alice offered.

"Be my guest."

Alice peered inside and waved an arm into the darkness. "I'm not exactly in love with spiders either." She braced herself against the sides of the entrance, leaned back and stuck one leg inside. "It feels like it gets bigger." Then she ducked her head inside and pulled her other leg in.

Nicole crouched down and stuck her head into the hole.

"See anything?"

Suddenly she was face to face with Alice. Both girls jumped backward and laughed.

"It's a lot bigger than the opening," Alice said. "Come on in."

"Any spiders?"

"They seem friendly."

Nicole climbed inside and crouched next to her friend. Together, they took a few steps forward. "We can stand up straight."

"Yeah," Alice agreed. "And it goes downhill."

The girls crept ahead for a few minutes. Outside, a cloud blocked the sun and the light dimmed.

"Maybe we should turn back," Alice suggested.

Nicole turned back toward the opening. "Okay."

Soon they were back in the crow's nest. They scrambled up the stone steps, brushed off their knees and gloves and started toward the house. "What if the next clue tells us to go back down *there*?" Alice said.

Nicole made a face. Just then the front door opened and her father came onto the porch. He watched as the girls crossed the yard. "You guys had me worried. One minute, I saw you marching around like two soldiers and the next minute I couldn't see you at all."

"We're fine, Dad."

The girls had some warm cider and then Nicole showed Alice around the house. They decided to read the next letter after dinner and spent most of the afternoon exploring the attic. They sat down to eat around seven.

"Are you girls interested in watching a movie?" Nicole's mother asked as everyone got up from the table a few minutes past eight.

"We're going to go up to my room."

"It's a mystery," her father said, holding up a cassette.

"You're not afraid of a little mystery, are you?"

The girls looked at each other. "We want to get started on our homework," Nicole said.

Her father looked at the girls over his glasses. "On a *Saturday night*?"

"We have a project."

"Maybe we should call the doctor."

Nicole rolled her eyes. "Come on, Alice."

"How about some hot chocolate?" her mother offered.

"Yes, please," Alice said.

"Can we have it in my room, Mom? We have to do some reading."

CHAPTER TWENTY-FIVE

"Sorry about all the questions," Nicole said between sips of hot chocolate.

"It was okay," Alice said. "Dinner at my house is usually over in about fifteen minutes."

"They always want to get so *involved* in everything. It's embarrassing."

"Anyway," Alice said, "this is so cool. We might solve a mystery that nobody's figured out in 200 years."

The girls kicked off their shoes and sat on the bed. "Here," Nicole said, as she handed the third envelope to Alice. "Why don't you read this one?"

Alice scanned the pages. "It looks like there's three different parts. The first one's from the Sea of Marmara."

"I have *no* idea where that is."

"Me either." Alice shrugged, leaned forward and started to read.

> The Sea of Marmara
> November 27, 1946
> 1900 hours

Dear Dolores,

    It must be around noon in Elk River so maybe right now you're having lunch. As for me, I'm once again in the crew mess. This time, it's just before my watch. I have to be up on the bridge to take the wheel in about 40 minutes. The moon is out so I'll be watching for a message sent our special way. But meanwhile, I'll send an old-fashioned letter that I'll mail from Odessa.

Alice looked up. Nicole slowly shook her head.

Soon we'll be sailing through the Bosporus, a narrow, 17-mile strait that leads to the Black Sea. According to Homer, the ancient Greek poet, Jason and the Argonauts sailed through here in search of the Golden Fleece. Beyond the eastern shore are the Caucasus Mountains. It was there that the Greek god Zeus tortured Prometheus for giving fire to mankind. I always liked that myth. When men gain knowledge, the gods get angry.

Our sturdy ship is once again steaming between two worlds. Most people say the Bosporus separates Europe and Asia. It flows right through Istanbul, the largest city in Turkey, a city that is more than 2,600 years old. From out on deck, you can see the lights on the towers, called minarets, on the mosques where Muslim worshippers pray.

Once I take the wheel, though, I won't do much sightseeing. Many regard the Bosporus as the most dangerous strait in the world. There are a dozen course changes between rocky shores (just a few hundred yards away in one spot) and believe it or not, we'll be sailing uphill! The slope is 20 degrees and in rough weather the current can be six or seven knots. Coming home, sailing downhill, will be like a sleigh ride.

It takes about two hours to get through the strait. By the time I'm off watch, we'll be in the Black Sea. We'll steam north northeast, past Bulgaria and Romania, toward the Soviet Union. I figure we'll arrive in Odessa during the 12 to 4 watch tomorrow afternoon.

"We ought to be able to find *that*," Nicole said.

The girls slid off the bed and went over to the globe that rested on a wooden stand next to Nicole's desk. "There's the Black Sea," Alice said, putting her finger on the globe after a short spin. "It's right on top of Turkey." She leaned a little closer. "And there's . . . Odessa."

Nicole nodded. "Just where he said it would be." The girls climbed back onto the bed and leaned against the pillows and headboard. Alice sat cross-legged with the letter before her and continued to read.

> There's a lot of ship traffic in the strait. In addition to the big tankers and freighters, there are countless fishing boats, ferries and private craft all in the same narrow passage. But once we're back in the open sea, it will be much less crowded. If we're not too far from the coast and the weather stays clear, I should see lights in the villages off to the west. I suppose that many of the people here are fishermen, just like in Elk River, and they'll be going to bed soon since fishermen, the world over, get up early.

Alice looked up and nodded.

> From the sea, the world ashore always looks peaceful. But less than two years ago, the war raged in this part of the globe—especially where we're headed. It's over now and the invading German army was defeated, but the people in the Soviet Union paid a terrible price for their victory. More than twenty million died. Not far from where we're going, the Nazis murdered tens of thousands of people, maybe more. Most were Jews. It was the Holocaust.
> While we're in port, I'm sure I will speak with some of the brave people who fought and survived the war and I will tell you what they say.
> We sailed from France, a week ago, where there is also terrible destruction from the war. I don't know how

to explain some of the other things I saw there but I guess I should try. First, though, I need to back up a little bit. In 1940, not long after the war started, Germany invaded France. Almost all of the French government gave up pretty quickly and the Nazis took over. Many of the French supported the invaders. They were called collaborators and they even helped the Nazis kill other French people, especially Jews.

But not everybody helped the Nazis. Some French people fought them the best they could. They called themselves the Resistance and they had to go underground, which means they went into hiding. It was very dangerous and many lost their lives in the struggle.

A year ago last May, when the Nazis were defeated and the war in Europe finally ended, there were plenty of people who didn't lift a finger against the Nazis who nevertheless claimed that they were in the Resistance. You would think that everyone who really was in the Resistance would be treated like heroes. But it isn't happening like that. Today, some of the men and women who fought against the Nazis are under attack again, this time by other Frenchmen, some of whom were collaborators! In Marseille, gangs of thugs have been beating up dockworkers who risked their lives by resisting the Nazis.

There is someone on our ship mixed up in all this: that young AB named Casey—the one they call Scorpion. I saw him in a bar talking to some of the local thugs. He seems plenty smart but he is one sailor I just don't trust. Some crew members say he is a fink, which means he is against the union. He has a big, jagged scar on his neck. I'm going to keep an eye on him.

I guess I'll have to finish this later, Sweetheart. It's time for me to go up to the bridge. If I'm too tired to write when I get off watch, I'll write some more after we're tied up at the dock. See you in the Soviet Union.

Love,
Dad

"Scorpion?" Nicole said. "That's a nice nickname."
"Yeah. Really. Want me to read the next one?"
"Sure," Nicole answered, nodding. "No new clues yet."
"Maybe it'll be in this one." Alice started to read again.

>Odessa
>November 28, 1946
>1500 hours

Dear Dolores,

 We tied up at the dock and "finished with engine" at about two o'clock in the afternoon around the time you were probably getting up. I lay down in my bunk at noon at the end of my watch but I had to get up again an hour later for docking. Now, however, I have a little time off. In port, we "break watches." That means that most of us work regular daytime hours until it's time to go back to sea. Later tonight I have gangway watch but that's pretty easy. Other than that, I don't have to "turn to" until tomorrow morning. Most of the other guys went ashore so after supper, alone for once, I went to my fo'c'sle. I'm now sitting on my bunk, with some time to write and much to write about.

 The Odessa dockworkers came aboard as soon as we tied up. Now I can hear them and what's left of our crew shouting and cursing in English and Russian as they open the hatches and attempt to get the winches and cranes to work.

 It's been more than four years since the last time I visited the Soviet Union. This city, Odessa, was occupied by the Germans at that time so we had to sail to the northern part of the country, to Murmansk, which is above the Arctic Circle, and Arkhangelsk which is just below it on the White Sea. Our greatest fear was that we would be spotted by German planes and the submarine fleet that sailors called the wolfpack. The voyage was very dangerous. We were carrying planes, tanks and fuel for the Soviet Army and we sailed in a convoy of 33 ships. Only 11 made it. Ships with friends of mine aboard exploded and sank before my eyes. Many brave men froze in the water or in their lifeboats. Hundreds of sailors were lost. I was lucky. Very scared, too.

Here, the signs of the war are everyplace. As we steamed into port this afternoon, I saw the twisted, blackened skeletons of factories, schools, hospitals and homes, bombed and burned during the war. And it's not just the wrecked buildings that stand as grim reminders of the war. Many of the dockworkers here are women. Their husbands and boyfriends, fathers, sons, brothers and sisters too, left to fight the Nazis. Many, very many, did not come back.

This is the biggest country in the world but in many ways, it is very poor, too. The people in this country have been trying to build a different kind of society but even before the war, life here was very hard. I'll never forget an old woman I met in Murmansk in '42. Her back was bent from a life of toil on a farm. Her hands were callused, her hair was gray and many of her teeth were gone. She lost her husband and two sons to the Nazi invaders. Her English was pretty good and I asked how she could endure such sorrow.

"We are like seedlings," she told me, "struggling to reach the light. Even if the old ones like me do not get to see the sun, we hope that our children or our grandchilddren will."

I've known many tough sailors in my years at sea. Good men in a storm or a fight. But I don't think I ever met anyone stronger than that old woman. People sometimes ask me why I took those voyages during the war. It was to help people like her.

It's been a long four years. I hope she made it.

Right now, your old man is starting to get pretty sleepy and my bunk feels mighty good. I think I'll lie down now while I have the chance. Before long, I'm sure someone will be banging on my door and telling me it's time to get out on deck.

See you soon,
Dad

THE WEBER HOUSE

There was a knock on the door and the girls jumped. "Hide the letters!" Nicole whispered.

Alice covered them with a pillow.

"What?" Nicole called out.

"It's me," her mother said from the other side of the door. "Do you want any more dessert?"

The girls looked at each other and shook their heads. "No, thank you," they answered together.

"Okay."

The girls listened as the steps receded.

"Is there much more?" Nicole asked her friend.

"A few more pages. And we still don't know what the clue is."

"Let's keep going."

Alice pulled the letter out from under the pillow.

> December 1, 1946
> 2200 hours
>
> Dear Dolores,
>
> Well, I was right about one thing. I didn't get much sleep. When I stopped writing the other day, I lay down in my bunk and had just started to dream when a deckhand woke me. Some problem with the cargo. Oh well, I can always use the overtime. I was pretty sleepy at first but once I had a cup of coffee in me, I felt okay. And then, after the cargo was straightened out, I had gangway watch. Usually, all I have to do is make sure the mooring lines don't get too tight or too loose when the tide moves the ship. Sometimes, I have to help crew members get back aboard when they've had too much to drink ashore, but otherwise, gangway watch is pretty easy.
>
> Yesterday, however, I had a little excitement. I was up forward, next to the number two hatch, when a winch cable slipped and a ton of steel came swinging toward me. I never saw it but, lucky for me, a Russian dockworker shoved me out of the way at the last second. When the

steel crashed onto the deck, the whole ship shook. That was close!

Then, last night, I was walking alone on deck just before midnight. I was near an open cargo hatch when I thought I heard something. I bent down to see if the noise was coming from the hold. As I did, a heavy hook from one of the ship's cranes swung past me. If I had been standing up, I'd have been knocked into the hold for sure and by now I'd be part of the cargo. I can't understand it. That hook should have been secured.

Maybe your cat loaned me a couple of her extra lives.

Thanks, Kimberly. I'm bringing you some Russian caviar.

Anyway, now I'm back in my fo'c'sle safe and sound. We'll be leaving Odessa at 10 tomorrow morning and I'll be at the wheel. It could be a rough ride. Sparks says a cold front is blowing in from the west and that means bad weather. I'll mail this just before we cast off.

Oh! I suppose you're wondering about the next clue. Okay, I've been working on it for quite a while. First of all, I'm pretty sure you've been in the "crow's nest" by now and I'll bet you've even explored the tunnel that starts there (even though, by yourself, you weren't supposed to). But I don't think you've ever been where you're going to go next. Ready?

This clue is different from the others in three ways. For starters, you are looking for someplace I've decided to call "the vault." You'll find out why when you get there. To help you, I'm sending directions which you must follow care-fully. I had to estimate the distances because the path is uneven—and mostly downhill—but I think they're pretty accurate. If I were reading this letter, I'd use the directions to make a map. That's up to you. Second, <u>do not try to find the "vault" by yourself</u>. Alone, it would be too dangerous. You can either go with Mom or else wait for me. I should be home in a few weeks. The trail is not especially rough but you must know where you are going. Obviously, you will need a flashlight or lantern. Third, even when you find the "vault," the mystery will not be

THE WEBER HOUSE

solved. You'll still have to figure out the meaning of the words on the plaque. I found the "vault" just before I left but I don't know what is hidden or where it is. I suspect that there is a particular date each year for solving the mystery and if I'm right, it's a few days before Christmas. If it isn't solved by then, I think you'll have to wait for a whole year to try again. Or, maybe you will be the one to figure it all out after all these years. That would be great.

Okay, here are the directions to the "vault."

It's not far from the crow's nest to the "vault." I estimate that it is only about 500 feet.

1. The first leg of your journey starts at the crow's nest and is one-fifth of the entire distance. Then you will come to an intersection. Turn right.

2. The second leg of your journey is half the length of the first. When you have traveled that distance, turn left.

3. The third leg is the same length as the second leg. When you have gone the correct distance, turn left again.

4. The fourth leg is half as long as the third leg. At the end, turn right.

5. The fifth leg is the same length as the fourth leg. At the correct distance, turn left. You are now halfway to the "vault."

6. The sixth leg is twice as long as the fifth. Turn left when you've traveled that distance.

7. On the seventh leg, walk straight for one-tenth of the entire distance from the crow's nest to the "vault." You will come to an underground stream. Cross it and keep walking in the same direction for another one-tenth of the entire journey. When you come to a "T," turn left.

8. Walk a distance equal to three-fourths of the first leg. Bear right at the fork.

9. Twenty-five feet away, hidden behind a stone, is an opening in the rock.

10. Crawl through that opening. Congratulations! You are now in the "vault."

Once you see what's there, you'll know as much about this mystery as anyone.

As for me and the rest of the Lincoln's crew, it's almost time to go. Tomorrow morning, the Russians will lift our mooring lines off the bollards on the dock. They'll drop them into the water and we'll winch them aboard. We'll be back at sea and heading for home. From then on, when the sun sets, it'll be over the bow, not the stern, and I'll be one day closer to Elk River. I can hardly wait.

Until then, keep an eye on the moon.

With love,
Dad

Alice put the letter down. "He never got home, did he?"

Nicole shook her head.

Alice swung her feet over the side of the bed. "It's sad."

Nicole climbed off her bed and looked out a side window. The moon barely shone through the cloudy sky. "Yeah," she said. "It really is."

Alice slid off the bed. She joined her friend at the window and looked up. "The moon."

"Yeah." Nicole walked over to the globe by her desk and spun it. "By the time Dolores got this letter, her father was dead."

Alice turned and leaned against the windowsill. "And just a week or two later, she found her mother out there in the water at the bottom of the cliff."

Nicole shook her head slowly. "Can you imagine what that would be like?"

"No."

Nicole walked back to her bed and sat on the edge. She picked up the letter and read silently for a few moments before looking up. "And now we're trying to solve a puzzle that Dolores' father wanted *her* to figure out."

"Are you thinking that we shouldn't do it?"

Nicole lay back on her side and propped her head up with one hand. "I never really thought about it before. It was just a cool mystery and a treasure hunt. But then you remember that Dolores' parents *died* and it doesn't seem the same."

"I know what you mean," Alice said. "All of a sudden, the game was over."

"Well, what do you think we should do?"

"I don't know."

"Me either," Nicole said. She rolled onto her back and looked at the ceiling. "Are there any cookies left?"

Alice walked over to Nicole's dresser and peeled back the tin foil. "Yup."

"Let's go downstairs and get some milk."

"Okay," Alice agreed.

"Want to go online?"

"I've never done it."

"You're kidding."

"We don't have a computer yet," Alice said. "My dad says we're getting one soon."

"It's fun. I'll show you."

"Okay."

Nicole put the letters inside her desk and the cover rattled down. The girls went downstairs and got two glasses of milk. They returned to the second floor, got the cookies and went into the study. Nicole dragged a second chair in front of the monitor. The modem chirped and the connection was made.

No one from Elk River was logged on. Of her New Jersey friends, only Alexandra was online.

"whats up?" Alexandra wrote.

"just hanging out at home with my friend."

"is that alice?"

Alice smiled. "Is she talking about me?"

"I guess so," Nicole said. "They must have heard about you down there."

"I wonder how."

"she's right here," Nicole typed. *"u want to say hi to her?"*

Alexandra's message came right back: *"hey alice whats up?"*

"What should I say?"

"Whatever you want."

Giggling, Alice put her hands on the keyboard. *"Hey, Alexandra. What's up?"*

"i never talked to anyone from maine before . . . nicole doesn't count . . . what r u guys doing up there?"

Alice turned to Nicole. "What should I say?"

Nicole shrugged.

Alice typed her response: *"We're thinking about our homework."*

"on saturday night?"

"Oh my god," Nicole laughed. "My reputation is ruined."

"we're thinking about not doing it."

"o that's better well i gotta go . . . some of us are going to the mall to see a movie say hi to the eskimos for us."

Nicole noticed that her friend stared at the monitor for a second and seemed to frown. Then Alice leaned back in her chair and sighed. "Think we should tell her we don't have a mall here?"

"She'd *never* believe that," Nicole said, reaching for the keyboard. *"have fun say hi for us."*

"ok I will talk to you later luv ya."

Alexandra was gone.

"She seems pretty nice," Alice said.

"Yeah, she's funny."

"Was she your best friend?"

"Yeah, I guess so," Nicole said, reaching for a cookie. "I'm surprised that no one from Elk River is online."

"Tonight is Michelle's party, remember?"

"Oh yeah, that's right."

Alice looked at her friend.

"What?"

"I was just wondering if you wished you were at the party."

"No, I'd rather be doing what we're doing."

"What *are* we doing?"

"Well, we can watch a movie if my parents aren't down there. I got a horror movie and we could make some popcorn."

The girls went downstairs. They popped popcorn, laughed at the horror movie and devoured almost a quart of cookie dough ice cream. It was 1:15 when they went back upstairs. The house was cold.

They changed into their pajamas, brushed their teeth and went back to Nicole's room. Alice climbed into bed. Nicole closed the door, walked around to the other side of the bed, closer to the window and joined her friend. She leaned over and turned off the light on her nightstand. Outside, the wind coming off the ocean was rising and the trees swished and creaked. It felt good to be under the thick down quilt. For what seemed like a long time, neither girl spoke and Nicole wondered if Alice was asleep. The ship's clock chimed three times in the hall downstairs.

"Are you still awake?" Alice whispered.

"Yeah."

Alice folded her arms behind her head. "You know how when you look at a star, you're really seeing light that left the star maybe millions of years ago?"

"Yeah, I know," Nicole said. "The star might not even be there anymore."

"Right. Well, those letters that Dolores' father wrote are kind of like that."

"Yeah, that's true I guess."

"I mean, he was writing about things that just happened but since then everything's changed, not just for him but for Dolores and the whole world. It's like somebody from 50 years ago just stepped out of a time machine."

"That's true," Nicole agreed, rolling onto her side. "It's not like reading about it in a book or a movie. He was really there and really scared and even saw some of his friends die."

"I think he wanted to tell his daughter what he saw and why he went there."

"You mean why he went on those boats with all the submarines around?"

"Yeah," Alice said.

"I can hardly believe all the terrible things that happened to the Jewish people back then. Just because they were Jewish."

"Yeah," Alice said softly. "People can do some really bad things."

The room was quiet except for the sound of the wind in the trees. Once again, Nicole thought that her friend might be asleep. A minute or more passed.

"Did you read *The Diary of Anne Frank*?" Alice asked.

"Yeah, we read it last year."

"We did too. I felt like I really knew her. She had problems with her parents and worried about school and boys and being popular and everything."

"She was thirteen, just like us," Nicole said.

"I cried when I read it, probably like a lot of people. I cried for Anne and everything that happened to her and her family but it also reminded me of what happened here, to my ancestors."

Nicole didn't know what to say.

"It wasn't exactly like in Germany," Alice continued, "but a lot of people died. Even here in Maine. Whole villages were wiped out."

The only sound was from the wind.

"A lot of it was from diseases," Alice said, "but there were wars and massacres too. My dad says that by the end of the war with the English, there were only about 1,000 Abenakis left in Maine. It was bad."

A fir tree brushed against the side of the house. "Has anyone ever, like, discriminated against you?"

"Nothing really bad has ever happened to me," Alice said. "But little things happen all the time, like in a store or a restaurant, or even at a party. Things that sort of remind you that you're different. Like Alexandra telling us to say 'hi' to the Eskimos."

"Oh," Nicole said. "I'm sure she didn't mean anything by it."

"Yeah, I know."

"It must really make you mad."

"Sometimes it does. Sometimes you want to scream or sometimes you just figure it's not worth it. People will be like 'Don't be so sensitive.' Sometimes you wonder if maybe you're imagining it when you think someone is looking at you funny." Alice was silent for a moment before she continued. "But I guess it's better now in some ways than it used to be."

"How do you mean?"

"Well, my parents always taught us to be proud of who we are. It wasn't always like that."

"What do you mean?"

"My parents told us that some Indians used to try to hide who they were. They might say they were French or something."

"That's really sad."

"But me, I'm an Indian," Alice said in the dark. "My dad has this book that says the Abenakis were fierce warriors."

"Really?"

"The English thought we were the worst." Alice chuckled. "Worst for them."

Nicole laughed too.

"So you better be nice to me."

"Believe me, I will."

"All right then." Alice pulled the quilt up to her chin.

"Anyway," she said, "what do you think we should do about this treasure hunt we're on?"

"Well, now that we've read the letter," Nicole said. "I'd like to see this 'vault' place. As long as we both go. I'm not going down there by myself."

Alice yawned. "The clue seemed easier this time. Easier to understand, anyway. Why don't we check it out in the morning?"

"Let's make a map like Dolores' father suggested."

"Okay," Alice said as she rolled onto her side with her back to Nicole. She pulled the quilt in her direction.

Nicole rolled over the other way, tugged the quilt back and listened to the wind.

CHAPTER TWENTY-SIX

DECEMBER 8

Nicole was terrified. She was falling. From above, a huge dog snarled, its breath like blasts of smoke. Gigantic waves crashed into the bottom of the cliff. White foam boiled in whirlpools around jagged rocks. Nicole plunged downward. A flickering light. Then it was gone.

Nicole was awake. She was breathing hard. *It was a dream.*

Alice was still asleep. Slowly, Nicole sat up. She smelled something. *What is that?*

Her eyes darted to the fireplace. "Ivy?" The cat was asleep at her feet. Nicole looked toward her side window. Something shadowy blocked the faint light from outside. "Mom? Is that you?"

The shadow hesitated then vanished. Nicole was too frightened to move. Despite the fear flooding over her, she slowly reached for the light next to her bed. As Nicole felt for the switch, something clicked on the other side of the room. Nicole found the switch and the light came on.

No one was there.

Nicole fell back against the headboard. Her hands were shaking.

Alice stirred and rolled over. "Is it time to get up?" she mumbled, eyes closed.

"No, it's the middle of the night. Did you hear something?"

"No," Alice said dreamily.

"I think somebody was in here."

"Your parents?"

"No. Somebody else."

Alice opened her eyes. "Who?"

"I don't know. I was dreaming. Then I woke up and I thought something moved by the window."

Alice sat up. "You mean like a person?"

"I don't know *what* it was. All I saw was a shadow."

"Maybe it *was* one of your parents?"

"They're supposed to knock." She pulled the covers off and went to the door. It creaked when she opened it. "I don't think anybody came in this way."

"I hate to sound like your parents," Alice said, "but maybe you *were* dreaming."

Nicole walked back toward her side of the bed. She stopped and turned toward the fireplace. Ivy had jumped down to the floor. She was sniffing and scratching at the wood molding on the right side of the fireplace. Nicole looked at her cat. Then she looked at the mantel. Bewilderment quickly turned to fear. "Oh my god!"

"What is it?"

Nicole stared at a wrinkled envelope propped up in the center of the mantel. Her hand shook as she reached for it. Nicole turned toward her friend. "Somebody *was* in here. This wasn't here before."

"He might *still* be here!" Alice almost shouted as she threw the covers off and scrambled next to Nicole. "He might be under the bed!"

Nicole saw the fear in her friend's face. "We have to look," she whispered. "If anyone's there, I'm gonna scream and we'll run for my parents' room."

Alice nodded, her eyes wide.

Slowly, the girls sank to their knees. The quilt blocked the view under the bed. With her heart pounding, Nicole yanked the quilt out of the way.

Nothing.

Nicole exhaled and sat on the cold floor next to Alice. "What about the closets?"

They got to their feet. Nicole picked up the flashlight from her desk. They went to the nearest closet. Alice reached for the doorknob. Nicole switched on the light. Their eyes met. Alice took a deep breath and pulled the door open.

Nicole's clothes appeared undisturbed but she swept them out of the way. Again, nobody. It was the same in the other closet.

Nicole picked up the wrinkled envelope from the floor and stared at the faded postmark.

"What is it?" Alice asked.

"It says 'España.' It was mailed from Spain. You need to see it."

"*Me*? What have *I* got to do with anything?"

"See for yourself. Maybe he or *she* wanted us to read this."

Alice took the envelope and stared at it before looking up, appearing astonished. "It's addressed to Louis Attean in Elk River, Maine. I think that's my great grandfather."

The clock downstairs chimed six times. It was 3:00 a.m.

"Go ahead," Nicole said softly. "Read it. Somebody wants us to."

Alice slid the letter out of the envelope and took a deep breath. "It says '*The Mediterranean, near Barcelona.*'"

She began to read.

December 8, 1946
1 a.m.

Dear sweet Dolores,

If you are reading this letter, it means I didn't come home. I am writing to try to explain.

Let me say first, that as I sit here on my bunk, my heart is breaking at the thought that I might not see you again. I hope you never read this, but if you do, there are some important things I must tell you.

In my last letter, I wrote that I almost had two bad accidents. I'm now certain that these were not accidents at all. Someone was trying to kill me. It all starts with the "treasure" that some people believe is hidden somewhere near our house. I always thought it was just a legend until I discovered that plaque underground. I thought we could make a game of finding whatever it is that the plaque hints at. But someone on this ship must believe that there is a real treasure because he is willing to kill to get it. This is no game.

A few nights after we left Odessa, I went for a walk on deck when I got off the wheel and went up to the bow like I usually do. The weather in the Mediterranean was pretty rough. As I gazed at the water, someone snuck out from the shadows and swung a steel bar at me. I must have heard something and luckily, just as my attacker was about to strike, a big wave struck the ship. I turned and the blow hit my shoulder instead of my head. We started to fight and with the help of another big wave, I got in a lucky punch, and my assailant went down. It was the tough, young deckhand who asked so many questions about you. Now I know why.

I wrestled him back to the house where we met the bo'sun and some other guys that I trust. We brought the deckhand to my fo'c'sle and demanded to know why he attacked me. He didn't seem so tough anymore. Mainly, he seemed like a scared kid in a whole lot of trouble and I couldn't imagine what would make him do something so crazy.

"Why? Why?" I kept yelling. Finally, near tears, he blurted it out.

"It was the letters to your daughter," he said. "With you out of the way, we were going to find the treasure when we got home and split it."

"*We*?" I said. "Who else is in on this with you?" But then he looked more scared than ever and wouldn't say another word. We finally let him go back to his fo'c'sle. We figured we'd get to the bottom of it eventually. We also assumed the kid couldn't disappear on a ship. That was a mistake. The next morning, the deckhand was gone. We searched the entire ship but we didn't find him and no one ever will. There's no doubt in my mind that he was murdered during the night and then thrown over the side. I believe that the killer was the other person the deckhand inadvertently revealed last night. If I'm right, and he was killed to keep him quiet, then the murderer might now come after me himself.

That's why I'm writing you this letter. I now realize that all along, someone has been reading my letters to you. We're stopping in Barcelona for fuel after daybreak. Spain is a dangerous place these days but I have friends near the port and I'll have this letter mailed secretly to our friend, Louis Attean. If I don't come home, Louis will deliver it to you and another one to your mother.

Dolores, I have just two things to tell you and they're both very important. First of all, <u>I want you to forget about solving the mystery or finding any "treasure."</u> This was supposed to be a game for us but now someone <u>very bad</u> is involved, and he is playing for keeps. I know your mother agrees. For your safety—please, <u>please</u>, forget about the clues, the "vault" and anything that someone may have left someplace a long time ago. <u>Please</u>!

The second thing is even more important. No matter what happens, I want you to know how much joy you have given me during the last fourteen years. They've been the happiest of my life. Even now, when you are far away, it makes me smile just to think of you. You always made me smile. I know we fought sometimes and I know that sometimes I drove you crazy but I hope you also know that a lot of those times it was just your old man trying to hang on to a little girl who wasn't little anymore. There's so much more to say that it's impossible to say it and maybe it's not even necessary.

I honestly don't know what is in store for me but I want you to know that, thanks to you, I consider myself a lucky, lucky man.

Right now, I'm going up to the bow where, high above the water, you can hear the waves and feel the cold spray coming off the sea. I've been in a few scrapes before so I'm not too scared and I don't want you to be afraid either. No one knows what lies ahead but if you have to be brave, I know you will be.

Tonight, the main deck is shrouded with a ghostly, low-lying fog but from high up on the bow, the sky will be clear. I'll see the stars but shining brightest of all will be the moon.

I love you, Dolores
Dad

Alice put the letter onto the bed and wiped her eyes. "That shadow you saw was Dolores Weber."

Nicole brushed her face with the sleeve of her pajamas. "*Now* what do we do?"

"Like you said, she *wanted* us to read it. Maybe that means she wants *us* to find the treasure."

"Or maybe," Nicole said. "She wants us to *stop* looking; like her father told her to."

"Or maybe *she* doesn't even know why she brought it. Maybe she's, you know . . ."

"Crazy?"

"I wasn't going to say that," Alice said. "But if she's poor and homeless and everything for all these years . . ."

"I've been thinking the same thing," Nicole said, "plus I'd like to know how she got in and out."

"Well, it was her house. Still is, really, I guess."

"Maybe Ivy can tell us."

Alice made a face. "Ivy? Your cat?"

"Remember when I got up and opened the door?"

Alice nodded.

"Well, just before I saw the envelope, I noticed Ivy sniffing and scratching around the fireplace."

"So?"

"She did the same thing in the library the night the thing with the mirror happened."

"Are you saying that Ivy was sniffing around a secret doorway in here someplace?"

"Well," Nicole said, "Dolores Weber, or whoever it was, got in and out of here somehow."

"So, she could be right behind the wall, right now."

"Oh," Nicole said. "Yeah, I guess she could be."

"And your plan is what? To open the secret door and say 'hello?'"

"I guess we could wake up my parents."

"They'd have to believe you this time since we have the letter."

"But then I'd have to tell them about the other letters and the treasure and everything."

"Yeah," Alice agreed. "I guess you would."

Nicole took a deep breath. "Let's think about this for a minute."

"Okay."

"Let's say it was Dolores Weber."

"Okay."

"Well, if it was, she's had a couple of chances to hurt me before tonight. Out by the cliff and when I got lost in the woods. Instead, she helped me. Twice. Tonight, she could have hurt both of us, killed us maybe. I'm not saying she's not crazy. All I'm saying is that tonight, all she did was deliver this letter, whatever the reason was."

"All right," Alice said. "Let's see if we can find the secret door and say 'hello.'"

"You sure?"

"Yeah," Alice said, not sounding entirely convinced. "Let's check it out. I just hope if we find the secret door, a giant dog doesn't jump out and eat us."

"Me too."

The girls went to the right side of the fireplace. Carved wood paneling surrounded the dark stones. Alice rapped on the wood with her knuckle. It sounded hollow.

"Let's see if we can find something loose," Nicole said.

The girls poked, prodded and pushed different parts of the wooden panel without success. But as Nicole ran her fingers along the edge of the panel, she said "I felt something move."

Alice looked closely and Nicole pushed on the corner. Something clicked and the whole panel swung inward. A doorway.

"Oh my god!" Alice said. "That's how Dolores got in and out."

Nicole got her flashlight and shined it into the darkness beyond the panel. "Thank god there's nobody there," she said with real relief.

"Look!" Alice said. "There's a stairway."

"Should we go in?"

"Okay," Alice whispered. "But just a little bit."

The girls stepped into the opening. There wasn't much room and they had to squeeze past the rough bricks and mortar on the back of the fireplace.

"What's that?" Alice said, pointing to a speck of light coming through the wall in front of them.

"It must be from the computer monitor," Nicole said. "I wonder if that room has a secret panel, too."

"That looks like some sort of handle," Alice said. "Let's try it."

Nicole lifted a metal latch and the panel in front of them swung toward them, revealing another room. A dim glow came from the computer.

Nicole pushed the door closed. "Let's see where the steps lead. She aimed the flashlight down into the darkness. "Maybe we should do this in the morning."

Alice peered into the blackness beyond the flashlight's beam. "Good idea."

The girls stepped back into the light and closed the wooden panel. "Now what?" Nicole said.

"I guess we should try to go back to sleep," Alice said.

"How are we supposed to sleep after all of this?"

"We should try to block that doorway somehow."

"Good idea," Nicole said. She put a chair in front of the wooden panel and her backpack on top of that.

Alice looked doubtfully at the barricade. "I don't think that's going to stop anybody especially since the panel swings *in*."

"If somebody tries to come in," Nicole said with a glance at the secret door, "maybe we'll at least hear him. Or *her*, I mean."

The girls climbed into bed. Alice pulled the covers up to her chin and yawned. "Or maybe we won't have any more visitors and we can get some sleep."

"That'd be nice," Nicole said as she turned off the light.

But just as she lay back, there was a knock on the door. Nicole sat bolt upright and turned the light back on. "It must be my parents," Nicole scrambled out of bed and opened the door.

Her father was standing there in his robe. "Is everything okay? I got up and saw the light under your door."

"We're fine, Dad."

"I'm sorry if I startled you."

"We were just talking," Nicole said. She turned toward Alice and saw the letter on the floor. Her father saw it too.

"Looks like you dropped something."

"Oh, it's just an old thing Alice was reading. We're going back to sleep now."

"I'm sorry if we woke you up, Mr. Kelly."

"You didn't," Nicole's father said. "I just wanted to make sure everything was okay. This is the Weber House, after all," he said with a smile.

Nicole put her hand on the doorknob. "We're fine, Dad."

"All right. I'll see you girls in the morning."

"Good night, Dad."

"Good night, Mr. Kelly."

"Good night, girls."

Nicole closed the door. She picked up the letter, put it on her desk and then climbed into bed.

"Do you think he suspected anything?" Alice whispered.

"I doubt it."

"I'm kind of glad that he checked on us."

"I guess so."

"He seems pretty nice."

Nicole looked at her friend. "You don't live with him." She turned off the light and wriggled under the covers. The room was silent. Nicole lay back and let out a deep breath.

"I'll bet you one thing," Alice whispered.

"What?"

"I'll bet they didn't have this much excitement at Michelle's party."

Though her eyes were closed, Nicole smiled.

Outside, the wind rose and the evergreens swayed, brushing against the house.

CHAPTER TWENTY-SEVEN

A knock on the door roused Nicole from her sleep.

"It's ten o'clock, girls," her mother said from the hall. "Breakfast is almost ready."

Nicole opened her eyes and saw Alice pull the covers over her head.

"Are you up?" Nicole's mother asked through the door.

"Yeah," Nicole said. "I guess so." She nudged the quilt-covered form lying next to her. "You awake, Alice?"

"No."

"I think we better get up."

"I hardly got any sleep," Alice said from her cocoon. "You were kicking me all night."

"*Me*? You kept trying to take all the covers."

Alice slowly sat up, brushed her long black hair away from her face and looked at Nicole. "You look terrible."

Nicole frowned. "Thanks. You look great too."

The girls crawled off the bed. Pulling robes over their pajamas, they went down to the dining room. Nicole's mother held a spatula and plate with a stack of pancakes. Her father lowered his newspaper as the girls sat down in front of two glasses of orange juice. "Good morning."

"Morning," Nicole growled.

"Good morning, Mr. Kelly," Alice said.

Nicole's mother put three pancakes on each girl's plate.

"Thank you, Mrs. Kelly."

"Thanks," Nicole mumbled.

"I hope you didn't stay up too late," Nicole's mother said as she put a bottle of syrup on the table.

"I think it was around three-thirty when I heard you talking," Nicole's father said.

Chewing a mouthful of pancakes, Nicole wondered what, if anything to say when a loud knock at the front door reprieved her.

"Who could *that* be." Nicole's mother said, looking at her watch. "I don't think Alice's parents should be here yet."

Nicole's father put down his coffee mug. "I'll see who it is."

Nicole listened as her father walked down the hall and opened the front door.

"Officer Baldwin. Come in. What can we do for you?"

"Sorry to bother you," Nicole heard the policeman say. "But last night, we received a report of a prowler in the area. We wondered if anyone here saw or heard anything."

Alice returned Nicole's wide-eyed stare. Nicole's mother pushed her chair back and went into the hall. The girls followed. Nicole's father turned toward them. "You remember my wife, Mary, and our daughter, Nicole. And this is Nicole's friend, Alice."

Officer Baldwin nodded.

"When was this prowler seen?" Nicole's mother asked.

"Between three and four this morning."

"You girls were up around that time," Nicole's father said. "Did you hear anything outside?"

"No," Nicole answered. "We were in bed."

Alice hesitated, then nodded.

"Well," Officer Baldwin said, "even if nobody was around

your house, it seems that old lady Weber may still be with us after all. I didn't say it last week since I wasn't sure but it must have been her that grabbed your daughter out by the cliff."

Nicole and Alice looked at each other but remained silent.

"But now that she's on our radar screen," the policeman continued, "we'll find her and bring her in."

"But she didn't do anything wrong!" Nicole blurted out. She noticed the surprised look on her parents' faces. "When that dog was chasing me out by the bridge, she's the one who *helped* me. *Twice* she did that."

Everyone was silent. Now Alice looked surprised too.

"*Twice?*" her father said. "When was the second time?"

Nicole realized her blunder and glanced at Alice. "It was Thursday after school. I went out in the woods and when it got dark, I got lost. That's why I was dirty and everything."

"And you saw her?" the policeman asked.

"I didn't really see her."

Officer Baldwin glanced at Nicole's parents. "Well, what *did* you see?"

"I saw a light and I followed it. I never would have found the way by myself."

Her mother was frowning. "You should have told us, Nicole."

"If you didn't *see* her," the policeman said, "how do you know who it was?"

"I heard her."

"And what did she say?"

"She didn't really *say* anything. But I heard her sort of moan. And cough. That's another thing. I think she's sick."

"A '*moan*' and a '*cough*,'" Officer Baldwin said with a hint of sarcasm as he jotted in his notepad. "Anything else I should know?"

Nicole didn't appreciate the policeman's tone and saw that Alice didn't seem pleased either.

"Maybe there is," Nicole's father said. "The very first night that we were all here, my daughter told us she heard someone playing the piano and then a few nights later, she told us she thought someone had been in the house again."

"At the time we thought it was her imagination," Nicole's mother said with a sympathetic smile toward her daughter, "but maybe we were wrong."

The policeman put on his gloves and reached for the door handle. "I'm going to look around outside," he said. "It snowed a little last night and I want to see if there are any fresh footprints."

"Nicole," her mother said when Officer Baldwin was gone, "have you had any *other* contact with that woman? It's important that you tell us."

Nicole glanced at Alice. "No. The only times I've seen her were out by the cliff and in the woods on Thursday."

"Why didn't you tell us about her leading you out of the woods?"

"I don't know," Nicole said, looking at the floor. "I guess I was afraid you would freak out or something and besides, nothing really happened. I mean, she didn't *hurt* me or anything."

Nicole's father shook his head.

A few minutes later Officer Baldwin reappeared on the front porch. Nicole's father opened the door. "There aren't any fresh tracks," the policeman said, stepping inside and closing the door, "but we'll be looking for her."

"I don't like prowlers," Nicole's mother said, "but if it's that poor woman, I think she needs help, not incarceration."

Cold air wafted into the room as the policeman opened the front door to leave. Then he stopped and turned around. "That's not up to me." He looked at Nicole and Alice and then at the adults. "But that woman has been connected with some serious complaints. She could be dangerous. My advice is to stay away from her. And if any of you . . ." he paused and looked at the girls again, ". . . *do* see her, I urge you to call us immediately."

"We will, Officer," Nicole's father said. "Thank you for coming." He closed the door then turned and looked at his daughter.

"What?"

"Nothing," he said, sighing as he walked down the hall.

"You girls should get dressed," Nicole's mother said. "Alice's parents will be here soon."

"Good idea," Nicole said immediately. "Let's go, Alice."

The girls hurried up the steps. As they walked around the balcony, they heard Nicole's mother say, "Paul, I think we'd better consider moving out of this house."

Nicole pushed her bedroom door shut.

"How are we ever going to solve this mystery," Alice said, "if you move?"

Nicole shook her head. "I don't know. But does that mean you still want to try to?"

"*Definitely!* But I'm sure your parents wouldn't want you getting mixed up in this. I know mine wouldn't."

"I'll bet they wouldn't mind if we found the treasure," Nicole said. "And if we do, maybe we can even *help* Dolores."

"I was thinking that, too," Alice said. "Maybe we could show everyone that she's not all those bad things that they say about her. A witch and everything."

Nicole walked to her desk and picked up the letter. "Do you think it could be dangerous?"

"Because of Dolores?"

"No, not because of her," Nicole answered. "Because of what it says in this letter. Dolores' father thought a *murderer* was after the treasure."

"That was fifty years ago."

"What about that dog that keeps showing up?"

"You think that *dog* is after the treasure?"

"Maybe that dog has a master and *he* wants the treasure."

"Or," Alice said, "maybe the dog's owner is a weirdo who likes scaring people. But that doesn't mean that he has anything to do with a treasure if there even *is* one."

"And speaking of weirdos," Nicole added, "who was the guy I saw on Thanksgiving, out by the cliff? He scared me to death too. And then *he* disappeared."

"But now we know that it must have been Dolores that wrote on the mirror since she can get in and out without anybody seeing her."

"Well," Nicole said, "whatever she's done, she's been living alone and maybe outside for a long time. She could sure use some help."

Alice turned toward her friend. "So even though we don't know if Dolores wants us to stop or keep going, we're going to stay on the case?"

"I will if you will."

Alice pointed to the secret panel. "Want to see where it goes?"

Nicole thought about it for a few seconds. "I think we should get dressed first."

CHAPTER TWENTY-EIGHT

Nicole went to the fireplace and lifted the backpack and chair out of the way.

"Great barricade," Alice said.

"Nobody came through it, did they?"

Alice laughed as they opened the panel.

Nicole switched on her flashlight and peered into the opening. "Anybody in here?" she whispered.

"That's not funny."

"I wasn't joking."

The girls stepped into the darkness and onto the steep stairway. They reached a landing and heard Nicole's parents talking.

"We must be in the wall between the sitting room and the dining room," Alice whispered.

Nicole nodded. She shined the light from side to side. Each wall had a latch like the one they had seen on the floor above. "We can go from room to room, and floor to floor and no one can see us. Like ghosts."

"And Dolores," Alice added.

The girls continued their descent. "Do you think we should keep going?" Nicole said, following the flashlight's beam into the void ahead.

"I'm not sure," Alice said. "Maybe if we go a little further, we'll see how Dolores got into the house."

"That's what I'm afraid of," Nicole said.

"Maybe just a little further."

Nicole wiped her forehead and squinted into the darkness below. Then she looked at her friend. Alice looked spooky in the flashlight's reflected glow. "Scared?"

"A little."

"Me too," Nicole admitted, peering further into the shadows. "How about if we just go to the bottom of the stairs and look around? Then we'll come back up."

"Okay."

Slowly, the girls continued, neither one speaking until Nicole's footstep felt different. She touched the chimney's rough bricks and the cool stone of an adjoining wall and shined the flashlight onto the wooden panel in front of them. "Here's another one of those handles." She lifted the latch and the door opened. Grimacing, Nicole brushed away the cobwebs and peeked past the door. On the other side were the shelves with old coffee cans full of rusty screws.

Nicole stepped through the opening. "We're in the basement." She recognized the heavy beams and floorboards overhead, the furnace, the workbench, the boat, the ladder.

"Can I see the light?" Alice said. She shined it at a cabinet on the opposite wall. "Do you think there's something behind that one too?"

"Anything's possible in this place."

The girls walked across the basement and examined the cabinet. Its shelves were filled with old cans of paint. They found a section of molding that felt loose. Nicole moved it and the shelves swung toward them. A stairway led upward.

"It must go up to the wall behind the library," Nicole said after following her friend into the opening. "But what is *that*?"

Alice pointed the flashlight straight ahead. The beam seemed to disappear. "Is it a cave?"

"I can't see the end," Nicole said, following the light. "Maybe it's another tunnel."

"Want to see where it goes?"

"You must be kidding. We don't know what might be in there."

"Just a few steps?"

Nicole frowned. "Just a few steps. I really don't like caves and tunnels that much."

"Me either," Alice admitted. "Besides, I think the batteries are getting weak."

Alice led the way with Nicole close behind. The floor was uneven and sloped downward. The walls and ceiling were rough. Everything was solid rock. Ahead, it was pitch black. They crept forward.

"I see the end," Alice whispered. 'It's just a cave."

But when they got to the back wall, about twenty-five feet away, there were tunnels leading to both the right and left. Alice shined the light into the darkness on the right. The underground path continued downward.

"Let's just go a little further," Alice said.

"Just a little."

They inched ahead. "Watch out for this rock sticking up over here," Alice said, aiming the light downward. It was covered with moss. "It looks like a big egg."

Nicole stepped around the stone. After another minute of slow, silent walking, she said, "I think we should go back."

Alice shined the light forward and then turned it around to examine the beam which had faded from white to yellow. "Hello down there," she called into the darkness. There was a faint echo. "Did you hear that?"

"Yeah. It was an echo."

"No," Alice said, turning. "Not that."

Nicole listened. "It sounds like squeaking. "Maybe it's mice. Or *rats*.

Come on, let's go."

"They're coming closer," Alice said, stumbling as she tried to hurry back up the slope. "Hurry, Nicole!"

In an instant the noise, flapping and squeaking, was right above them. "They're bats!" Nicole screamed, "Run, Alice!"

Nicole started running back up the tunnel. Alice was right behind her. The light bounced off the stone overhead and on both sides. Suddenly, Nicole tripped and fell and Alice landed on top of her. The bats flapped overhead. The girls stayed down, covering their heads with their arms.

When the noise stopped the girls looked up. The bats were gone. "Are you alright?" Alice said. "I didn't see that you fell until it was too late."

"It wasn't your fault," Nicole said. "I tripped."

Alice shined the light on the stone sticking up in the middle of the path.

"The egg," Nicole said, rubbing her knee. They got to their feet and brushed themselves off.

Alice tapped the stone with her slipper. "Stupid rock."

They made their way back up the rocky path, slipping a few times, but not stopping until they were back at the entrance to the basement. They stepped inside and pushed the shelves over the opening.

"We better get upstairs before my parents get here and everybody's looking for us," Alice said.

"Good idea."

They crossed the basement in silence and went upstairs the same way they had come down. As they passed the first floor, they could hear Nicole's parents talking. Soon the girls were back in Nicole's room.

Alice packed her duffel bag and the girls went downstairs and into the sitting room. Her mother was reading the newspaper. Her father was sipping coffee. "Any homework?"

"We have to tell Mrs. Thorn what our Elk River projects are going to be about."

"What's yours going to be?"

Nicole glanced at Alice. "It's going to be, this house. The treasure and everything."

Nicole's mother put the newspaper onto her lap. Her father put his coffee mug down. Neither looked pleased.

"We *live* in the oldest building in town and everybody's interested in it," Nicole said.

"*Too* interested," her father shot back.

"I'm sure there are plenty of other good topics," her mother said, closing the newspaper.

"Like what?"

"Let's see," her father said. "How about 'the architecture of Elk River?' There are lots of wonderful old buildings around here. That might be interesting."

Nicole looked at Alice and rolled her eyes. Alice shrugged. "You're kidding, right?"

"Or how about something about the history of the town?" her mother suggested.

"Why can't I choose my own topic? You're always saying I should think for myself."

"It's just that we don't know what's going on around here," Nicole's mother said, "and we don't want you involved in something that might be sort of, well, dangerous."

"It's just a stupid school report," Nicole said. "God!"

"It's not really the report we're concerned about," her father said. "It's what's been happening around here. Apparently, this treasure thing makes everyone go crazy and I don't want you to get caught up in it." He took a sip of coffee. "Don't get mad but I think you should remember that you girls are still in the eighth grade."

"What's *that* got to do with anything?"

"All I'm saying," Nicole's father said, "is that we're a little nervous about prowlers."

"So, when a policeman says somebody's been around here, you believe *him*. But not when *I* say it."

"We admit that we should have listened to you," Nicole's mother said, "and that Dolores Weber, or somebody else, might have been in the house but that only makes us more concerned."

"She didn't hurt anybody," Nicole said.

"It's true she didn't, thank goodness. But you can't blame us for being worried. I'm sure your parents will be very concerned as well, Alice."

Alice nodded. "Probably."

"Your father and I are wondering if we should find someplace else to live."

"No!" Nicole insisted. "I don't *want* to move again. Doesn't anybody care what *I* want? First you drag me up here, away from all of my friends." She looked at Alice. "Then, when I meet a good friend, you want to mess it all up again."

Her mother put her hand on her daughter's arm. Nicole pulled away.

"We have to be concerned about your safety. And ours, too."

For a few long seconds, the room was quiet.

"Anyway, Alice, what's your project going to be about?" Nicole's father asked.

"I was thinking of working with Nicole."

"Oh my god! Maybe you better check with your parents about that after we tell them everything that's happened." He checked his watch. "Speaking of your parents, Alice, do you have all your things together? They'll probably be here soon."

"Come on, Alice," Nicole said before her friend could answer. "Let's go upstairs and pack your bag."

"What's up?" Alice said as soon as they were in Nicole's

bedroom. She picked up her duffel bag. "You know I'm already packed."

"We're going to do this, right?"

"I want to."

"Good."

"But what about what your father said?"

"He said he wasn't really concerned about the report and that's all we're doing: a report."

Alice smiled.

"It makes sense for us to do it together. Whatever it is that we're doing, *both* of us are obviously already involved. Even your great grandfather was involved."

"Writing it should be the easy part," Alice said. "And I'm sure Mrs. Thorn will say it's okay. We'll definitely have the best project."

"Okay" Nicole said, "what do we do next?"

"Well, there's no way our parents are going to agree but I think we should figure out a way to get into the vault."

Nicole smiled. "They didn't say not to."

"How could they? They don't even know about it."

"What they don't know won't hurt them."

"I had no idea you were so devious," Alice said.

"Well, it makes me mad when they treat me like a little kid. '*You're just in the eighth grade,*'" Nicole said in a mocking voice. "But anyway, since your parents will be here pretty soon, why don't we copy the directions from the last clue? That way, we can both make a map."

"Let's both do it tonight," Alice said, "and we can compare them tomorrow in school."

"Okay."

Nicole heard the knocker clunk on the front door, followed, seconds later, by footsteps in the hallway and then a tap on her bedroom door.

"Girls," Nicole's mother said, "Alice's father is here."

"Okay," Nicole answered. "We'll be there in a minute." She pushed up her desktop and took out the rest of the Henry Weber's letters. She hurried into the study and copied the directions to the vault on the printer. Back in her bedroom, she handed the copy to Alice who put it into her bag. Then they went downstairs and peeked into the sitting room where Nicole's parents and Alice's father were speaking quietly.

"Look how serious they are," Alice whispered. "They must be talking about the police and Dolores and everything." Nicole nodded and the girls walked into the room. The room went silent as they entered.

"I hear the police wanted you for questioning," Alice's father said with a smile.

"Told you," Alice said to Nicole.

"Ready to go?" Alice's father asked.

"Please tell Anne that I'll call her soon," Nicole's mother said.

"I will."

"Thanks for letting me stay," Alice said as she got into her parka.

Nicole's mother smiled. "We were glad to have you, Alice. Come again soon."

"See you tomorrow," Nicole said, waving.

"See you," Alice answered.

Nicole watched as Alice and her father stepped off the porch and onto the partly cleared walk. Then her father closed the door. "Are you going to get started on your homework?"

"I'm going to do it right now," Nicole answered. "I have to draw a map."

CHAPTER TWENTY-NINE

DECEMBER 9

"Have you got it?" Nicole whispered to Alice on Monday morning when they met outside their homeroom.

"Yup. Got yours?"

"It's in my backpack." Nicole glanced around the hall. "Let's compare them inside."

But the girls had no chance to talk in homeroom and after three periods, they still hadn't spoken privately. They finally met up in social studies.

"Good morning, everyone," Mrs. Thorn said as the students took their seats in room 308. "Today we're all going to hear what each of you has chosen as the topic for your Elk River projects. Who wants to go first?"

No hands went up.

Mrs. Thorn scanned the classroom. "How about you, Billy? Are you still planning to report on local disasters?"

"Definitely."

"Any progress?"

"So far, I've found a big fire, a couple of hurricanes and a bunch of blizzards. I'm still hoping for an earthquake or something really huge like that."

"Good luck," Mrs. Thorn said.

Nicole heard a few chuckles around the room and saw Alice shaking her head.

"How about you, Simon? Will you be researching the man our school was named after?"

"Yes," Simon answered. "I've already started. Joshua Chamberlain was from Maine and he was a hero in the Civil War."

"Very good, Simon," Mrs. Thorn said. "I'm eager to hear it. How about you, Nick? Can we look forward to hearing about celebrities from Elk River?"

"Do criminals count?"

Everybody laughed.

"As long as they were Elk River criminals."

Jason planned to report on the history of the Elk River Fire Department. Michelle chose the mayors of Elk River. Margaret said she intended to find out what happened to the elk of Elk River. When Jerry said she would report on the Native Americans who originally lived in the area, Nicole saw that several students glanced at Alice but her friend gave no sign of noticing. Mrs. Thorn went from student to student until only two were left.

"Alice?" the teacher said. "Is your report still going to be about the sea?"

"Well, sort of," Alice said, looking at Nicole. "It has to do with a pirate. But Nicole and I want to do our project together, if that's okay."

"I think that would be all right," Mrs. Thorn said, looking at Nicole. "What topic did you girls select?"

"It was your idea, Nicole," Alice said. "Why don't you say what it is?"

"Our project," Nicole said quietly, "is going to be about the house I live in."

"The Weber House," Alice added.

"Whoa," someone in the back of the class said.

"You think *you're* going to find the treasure?" Nick said.

"They think they're gonna be rich!" somebody called out, to some laughter.

"Actually," Nicole said when the class quieted down, "we don't know if there *is* a treasure. But even if there isn't one, there are a lot of interesting stories about the house. That's what we're going to do our report on."

"That's very ambitious," Mrs. Thorn said. "Let's talk later about how you're planning to do your research, okay?"

The girls nodded.

At lunch, Nicole and Alice, as usual, sat together but their table was too crowded for them to compare their maps. Before long, however, the numbers in the cafeteria thinned out as students went outside or to the gym. When the girls were finally alone at their table, Nicole pulled a piece of paper out of her pocket. "Let's see if our maps are the same."

Alice opened her notebook and took out a sheet of paper. Nicole looked around for eavesdroppers.

The girls laid the papers side by side. Both drawings had "crow's nest" marked on the right side, then a series of zig-zagging lines and numbers which ended, on Alice's map, with a large "**X**." On Nicole's drawing, it said "the vault."

"They look pretty much the same," Nicole said. "See, we both think that, after all the twists and turns, the vault must be pretty close to the crow's nest."

"Let's see if we agree about the numbers," Alice said. "All that stuff about 'half the distance,' and 'twice the distance.'"

The girls studied their drawings, looking back and forth from one to the other, comparing their calculations as they traced the path with their fingers. When they reached the end, they looked at each other.

"They're the same." Nicole said. "But now what do we do? Between prowlers and Dolores Weber and the police and everything, no way our parents are going to let us go down into those tunnels."

"I guess another sleepover is out," Alice said.

"Maybe you could come back if your parents came too."

"A family thing?" Alice said. "To find the vault? Are you kidding?"

"What if my family invited your family over, for dinner or something? Maybe then we could find a way to do what we have to do."

The girls thought for a minute. "I've got it!" Nicole said. "Why don't we say we have to work together on our social studies project?"

"That might work."

"Okay," Nicole said. "I'll ask my mom to invite your family over for brunch. While they're eating and talking, we can say we have to work on our homework. We'll even be telling the truth."

"Sort of."

As the girls folded their maps, Nicole heard footsteps. It was Mrs. Thorn. She was spinning a soccer ball on her fingertip.

"The partners," their teacher said.

"I don't think you're allowed to use your hands in soccer, Mrs. Thorn," Alice said.

"You are if you're a goalie."

"Nicole plays soccer," Alice said, pointing to her friend.

"I joined the club," Nicole said, somewhat embarrassed.

"Working on your project?"

"Sort of," Nicole answered, glancing at Alice.

"Where do you plan to get your information?"

The girls looked at each other. "In my house?" Nicole suggested.

"That's one good place," Mrs. Thorn said. "But where else can you get information about things that happened a long time ago?"

"The library?" Alice said.

Mrs. Thorn nodded. "That's right. I'm not aware of any books on your subject but I'm sure that you can find some information in old issues of the *Elk River Tribune*. We don't keep them in the school library but the town library does. Maybe you should look there."

"Thanks," Nicole said.

"You're both very welcome. I'm really looking forward to seeing your report. Let me know if you need any help, okay?"

"We will," Alice answered.

Mrs. Thorn pointed to the gym. "Want to kick the soccer ball for a few minutes before you go back to class?"

"Sure," Alice said, glancing at her friend.

"Okay," Nicole added.

They left the cafeteria and walked to the gym. Nicole pulled the door open and the shouts and echoes of dozens of students rolled over them. Mrs. Thorn tossed the soccer ball to Alice who bounced it to Nicole. She trapped the ball and began to dribble across the gym. Then Mrs. Thorn stole it.

CHAPTER THIRTY

DECEMBER 10

After school on Tuesday, as Nicole rounded the corner on her way to the gym, she almost bumped into Alice. "Oh, hey," Nicole said.

"Hey."

"I forgot to ask you at lunch," Nicole said. "Are you and your family coming over for brunch on Sunday? My mother said she was going to call."

Alice nodded. "I think so. My mother said something about bringing something." She lowered her voice. "I just hope we have enough time to, you know, do our homework."

"Don't worry. They'll probably be so busy talking about how worried they are about us that they won't even notice that we're doing what they're worried about."

Alice laughed. "I hope so," she said. "Oh, I forgot to tell you. Tomorrow, I might have some stuff for our report. I'll call you later."

"I've got to get to soccer practice but I might have some new stuff too. I'll talk to you tonight."

"Okay," Alice said as she started down the hall. Nicole headed for the gym.

After soccer practice, Nicole changed her clothes and

hurried outside. The night was bitter cold and it took her a few seconds to adjust to the darkness. She walked along the side of the gym facing the water. A lone streetlight reflected dimly off the docks and fishing boats. Nicole turned right onto Atlantic and walked past the front of the school.

It was a short walk from Chamberlain to the library. Two blocks and then a right on Main Street for a few more blocks. On Main, there would be light from the stores and Christmas decorations, but on Atlantic, half the streetlights weren't working. Across the street, past the bandstand, and beyond the park, was the ocean. Waves pounded in the darkness and, a few seconds after each impact, Nicole heard the icy spray rain down onto the park. Summer was far away.

Nicole shivered and her breath came out in puffs. She looked at the starless sky and wondered if more snow was coming. The streets were pretty clear but the sidewalks were mostly covered by the piles of ice and snow left by the plows. As Nicole trudged past an unlit house, she heard a dog barking and picked up her pace. On Main Street, the going was a little easier. She passed a darkened church and was startled when something moved in the cemetery. A black crow, or some big bird, landed on a tilted tombstone. When Nicole finally arrived in front of the library, her fingers and toes were nearly numb.

The library was an old-fashioned brick building with a steep roof. A snow-covered clock tower loomed overhead. The windows on the upper floors were dark and for a moment, Nicole wasn't certain if the library was open. The clock said it was five but she wondered if it always said that. *What will I do until Mom picks me up?* Someone came out of the front door. She hurried up the icy steps and went inside.

The library's main room had a dozen large wooden reading tables but no one was sitting at any of them. The card catalog with its many wooden drawers stood at one end of the room and the checkout counter stood at the other but nobody was at either one. Nicole could see two floors of dimly lit bookshelves at the back of the building. The main desk was straight ahead. She walked across the uneven floor, dropped her backpack and looked around.

Where is everybody? Nicole wondered, turning back toward the reading room.

"May I help you?"

Startled, she spun around. No one was there.

"Up here."

Nicole looked up. An elderly woman peered down from the balcony of the floor above, a cart full of books in front of her. She removed her glasses. "I'm Mrs. Alexander, the librarian. What can I do for you?"

"I need some help," Nicole said softly.

"If I can help you from up here, it will save me a trip down the steps."

Nicole nodded. "I need to look at some old newspapers."

"Which ones?"

"Some old *Elk River Tribunes*."

Mrs. Alexander put her glasses back on and slid a book onto its shelf. "What dates?"

"Um, I'm not sure."

Mrs. Alexander put another book on a shelf. "Well, what are you working on?" Once again, she took off her glasses. "A school project perhaps?" She stepped to the balcony and placed her hands on the railing. Her glasses dangled from her neck by a cord.

"I'm trying to find out about an old house in Elk River called the Weber House," Nicole said. "I live there."

"Hmm," the librarian said.

"My teacher said I should look here to help me write a report about it."

"You must be in Mrs. Thorn's class."

"How did you know that?"

"I'm the librarian," Mrs. Alexander said. "I'm supposed to know things. It must have been one of your classmates who inquired yesterday about local earthquakes. He seemed quite anxious to find one. Or at least a tsunami."

Nicole smiled.

"I'll be right down," the librarian said.

Mrs. Alexander disappeared into the stacks of books and Nicole heard her shoes tapping on the metal stairs. Soon the librarian stood behind the information desk. "That's better," she said. "Now, I've told you my name. What's yours?"

"Nicole Kelly."

"Well, Nicole, if you live in the notorious Weber House, I guess you don't believe in ghosts."

"Not really. But it is a pretty weird house and some strange things *do* happen there."

"I believe it." Mrs. Alexander said. "Now, what is it that you want to know?"

"I want to know how all the strange rumors got started. I thought I would start with Henry Weber."

"He was a brave man, in my opinion," Mrs. Alexander said.

"You mean during the war?"

"Exactly."

"But he didn't die in the war, did he?" Nicole asked.

"No, he didn't. And I see that you already know some of the history."

"Well, so far I've just heard stories. I thought if I could find some things to read, maybe it would start to make sense."

"You really should talk to Mr. Clovewood. He's the reference librarian and our resident expert on the subject of the mysterious Weber House." She scanned the reading room. "He's around here someplace, although I have no idea where."

"I'd like to talk to him," Nicole said.

"I'm sure you'll bump into him eventually."

Nicole nodded.

"Now," Mrs. Alexander said, "where do you want to start?"

"If it was in the paper, I'd like to read what it said after Mr. and Mrs. Weber died, and also if there's anything about their daughter."

"It was definitely in the paper. I've read the articles myself. As a matter of fact, it was Mr. Clovewood who showed them to me. Both Henry Weber and his wife died in 1946, the year after World War II ended. It was right around this time of year." Mrs. Alexander took a little pencil out of a drawer and wrote something on a small pad. "As for Dolores, I think the fire in the woods was in 1992, also in December. That's the last article about her that I recall." She tore the top sheet off the pad and handed it to Nicole. The dates were written on it.

"Thanks."

"You'll find the bound volumes of the *Tribune* downstairs. They're on shelves arranged alphabetically starting near the bottom of the stairs. The 'E' shelves are way down the aisle at the very back of the basement. You won't have any trouble finding them." Mrs. Alexander pointed into the darkened shelves at the rear of the library. "The stairs to the morgue are over there."

"The morgue?"

The librarian laughed. "That's what Mr. Clovewood calls the stacks where we keep old newspapers."

"Okay," Nicole said.

She found the steep circular stairway and looked back toward the information desk. Mrs. Alexander was gone and Nicole listened to the echoes of her footsteps tapping slowly back up to the second floor.

Nicole gripped the thin metal railing and started down the steps. At the bottom, the floor was stone. It reminded her of the basement of her own house. A string hung from an overhead fluorescent light and a narrow aisle led into the darkness. On either side were row after row of metal bookshelves reaching from floor to ceiling. On the right side, the first row was marked with the letter "A." Nicole walked slowly down the main aisle. At the far end of the rows, there were small desks.

An overhead steam pipe banged loudly. Momentarily startled, Nicole continued past the "B" shelves. She noticed that a light was on at a small, unoccupied desk at the end of the row marked "C." Nicole proceeded down the main aisle toward the back of the basement until she came to the "E's." Still wearing her backpack, she squeezed into the narrow space between the shelves. The bound volumes of the *Elk River Tribune* were at the end of the shelf. "Naturally," Nicole said out loud, "but at least there's a light." She reached up and pulled the string. The light didn't work.

Squinting in the dim light from the aisle, Nicole followed the volumes from year to year until she found 1946, the first date on Mrs. Alexander's note. Thankful that it wasn't on the top shelf, she slid the cloth-covered, newspaper-sized book out and laid it on the floor. Turning back to the shelves, she quickly found 1991. The next volume was missing. Nicole looked to see if it was just out of place. It wasn't. After 1991 there was a space and then 1993. *Who else could be interested in these old newspapers besides me?* The name "Scorpion" flashed into her mind.

Nicole picked up the volume she had put on the floor, lugged it down to the end of the shelves, turned right and started back toward the stairs. When she reached the "C" shelves and the desk with the light, her eyes widened. There was a large cloth-covered book on the desk. Nicole turned it so she could see the binding: *Elk River Tribune 1992*.

Nicole looked around for some sign of another researcher. There was none. She listened. Nothing. *Whoever it was is gone*, Nicole assured herself. She put the two volumes together on the desk, took off her backpack and coat and sat down. She began paging through the issues of the 1946 *Tribune* until she came to December.

There was no mention of the Webers in the issues dated December 3 or December 10. But on the front page of the issue dated December 17, Nicole saw a picture of a bearded man wearing a dark, double-breasted coat and a stocking cap like sailors wear. Next to the picture was the headline:

Henry Weber, Local Seaman, Lost in Atlantic Gale

The story said:

> As we go to press, the *Tribune* has learned that longtime local resident Henry Weber, a veteran sailor aboard the steamship *Abraham Lincoln*, has been lost at sea.
>
> The *Lincoln* sailed from Barcelona, Spain, on December 9. According to a statement released by the Great Circle Shipping Co. in New York, Weber was lost overboard during a storm in the north Atlantic that struck the *Lincoln* on December 12. The initial report of Weber's death was sent via ship's wireless and the details are incomplete.
>
> Weber was 61. He is survived by his wife, Anna, 46, and a daughter, Dolores, 14.
>
> Further information will be available when the *Lincoln* arrives in the U.S. The ship is due in Boston on December 19.

There was nothing else. Nicole turned the pages slowly already knowing what the "news" in the December 24 issue would be. *Christmas Eve*, Nicole thought, shaking her head, *exactly 50 years ago*. And there it was, with a picture of the same man, standing behind a seated woman and a smiling little girl who held a kitten. It was the same photograph she had seen in the cabin in the woods. Nicole started to read.

THE WEBER HOUSE

Anna Weber Dies in Fall from Cliff
Death Comes Nine Days after Husband Lost at Sea.

December 23—In a shocking sequel to a tragedy on the high seas which occurred only nine days ago, local schoolteacher Anna Weber was found dead in the early-morning hours of December 21 when she fell from a cliff near her home. The dead woman's daughter, fourteen-year-old Dolores, discovered her body shortly after sunrise.

The death of Anna Weber follows the December 12 announcement of the passing of her husband, Able Bodied Seaman Henry Christopher Weber, who was lost overboard when a violent storm struck his ship, the *SS Abraham Lincoln*.

Local residents expressed sorrow and shock as news of the latest tragedy became known. "I taught school with Anna for years," said Mrs. Beatrice King. "She was a wonderful mother, a great teacher and a dear friend. My heart goes out to poor Dolores."

Chief William Jenkins, of the Elk River Police Department, was at a loss to explain why, in the dark and during a heavy snowfall, Mrs. Weber was walking near the cliff in front of her home when she fell. A neighbor, Mr. John Morgan, Sr., suggested that Mrs. Weber, mourning her husband, might have wanted to be near the sea. "Now, we'll never know," Morgan said. "First Henry and now this. God works in mysterious ways."

The death of Henry Weber was reported by ship's radio on December 12 while the *Lincoln* was still at sea. When the vessel docked in Boston a week later, Captain E.V. Johnson stated that Weber was lost overboard shortly before midnight, while checking the ship's on-deck cargo during one of the fierce storms for which the North Atlantic is known in December. It was the second fatality of the voyage. On December 1, a 20-year-old deckhand, Brian McCarthy of Boston, disappeared and is presumed dead. Johnson wouldn't comment on the incidents except to say that the authorities are investigating both deaths, which officials say are not related.

Weber, 61, was returning from a voyage that took the *Lincoln* to Germany, France and the U.S.S.R. The ship left Odessa on December 1 and, after stopping for fuel in Barcelona, Spain, on December 8, departed for Boston the same day.

Weber first went to sea at the turn of the century aboard the last of the sail-carrying ships. During World War II he made many voyages to northern Russia through waters infested with German submarines. It is ironic that his last trip took him to the same country. Weber survived the war at sea only to perish little more than a year into the peace.

In 1931, Weber married Anna Monroy and a year later Dolores was born. The family lived in a formerly abandoned house on Cliff Rd. According to local legends, the house was built in the 18th century by a pirate whose ghost still haunts it. The recent tragedies are sure to give new life to the legends.

For the last four years, Anna Weber taught art and music at the Joshua Chamberlain Junior High School in Elk River, where her daughter is currently an eighth-grade student. A relative will care for the orphaned child.

No funeral arrangements have been announced.

Nicole closed the big book with a thump. For a few moments, she just sat there, thinking. Then she pushed the book away. Reaching for the volume labeled "1992," Nicole quickly paged through it to the December issues. The article she wanted was on the bottom of the second to last page of the *Tribune* dated December 23, 1992:

THE WEBER HOUSE

Homeless Woman Missing after Fire

December 22--Fire swept a cabin in the woods north of town yesterday morning, destroying the last known dwelling of Dolores Weber, a troubled, homeless woman whom many area residents feared.

A neighbor reported the fire at 3 a.m. and the Elk River Fire Department arrived at approximately 3:45 after struggling through the dense forest with portable equipment.

There were no injuries and no one was found at the scene, although Chief William Bierney of the ERFD said "someone was living here recently." Bierney attributed the fire to a flammable liquid, most likely kerosene, probably from a lantern.

For years, Dolores Weber has been a shadowy figure in the woods. Several area residents blamed her for the disappearance of their pets and were careful to keep their children from playing in that part of the forest. Midnight fires have been reported previously, Chief Bierney said.

The cabin, now little more than blackened, stone walls and scorched timbers, was built as an artist's studio for Dolores' mother, Anna. In 1946, Anna Weber fell to her death from the cliff in front of the family's home just nine days after her husband, Henry, a merchant seaman, perished in an accident at sea.

For a time, the Webers' orphaned daughter lived in the main house with a relative. But by the mid-sixties, the house was abandoned and Dolores reportedly lived alone in her mother's studio.

Following the fire, Elk River Police Chief Thomas Felts conducted a thorough search of the Webers' abandoned home in hopes of locating Dolores. Chief Felts was accompanied by a neighbor, John Morgan, III. "We searched high and low," Chief Felts said, "We even went up into the stone tower in front of the house. There wasn't a sign of her.

Hmm, Nicole thought, closing the book with another thump, *that's strange*. Then she heard something. A step. Then another. Coming down the circular staircase from the main floor. *It's probably the librarian. Must be time to go.*

The footsteps were coming closer.

"I'm over here, Mrs. Alexander." Nicole said softly.

There was no answer but the steps were louder. It sounded like they were coming from the next aisle of shelves.

"Mrs. Alexander?"

Still no answer. "Scorpion" flashed into Nicole's mind again.

"Mrs. Alexander? It's me, Nicole Kelly. Is that you?"

No answer and now, no time to run or hide. Nicole froze.

"Hey. What are you doing here?"

It was Alice.

Nicole started breathing again.

"I thought you were at soccer practice."

"I was. Then I came here. You almost scared me to death. I thought you were Scorpion. Didn't you hear me calling?"

"Sure," Alice answered. "But I'm not Mrs. Alexander and I'm not Scorpion either. See?" She held up her hands as if they were claws. "Don't you know you're supposed to be quiet in a library?"

"You're not supposed to scare people either."

Alice shrugged.

Nicole pointed to the newspaper volume in front of her. "I've been reading some old *Elk River Tribunes* about Dolores' family like Mrs. Thorn suggested."

"I read them too," Alice said.

"*You* left this book here?"

"Sure. Who else would be reading something like that?"

"Besides me? Nobody, I guess," Nicole admitted. "Did you find this stuff yourself?"

"The librarian showed me. He was very interested in what

I was doing."

"*He*?" Nicole said. "The librarian I talked to was a she."

"The guy I talked to was a guy," Alice said, glancing around. "Kind of weird too. One second he was there and then he disappeared."

"This whole place is kind of weird," Nicole said as she got into her coat and picked up her backpack. "Ready to go?"

"Yeah, I guess so."

"How come you came back down here? You already had all your stuff with you."

"I had to go to the girls' room," Alice said. "And I was afraid to leave my stuff lying around because I was afraid some weirdo might show up." She squinted at Nicole. "It looks like I was right. Anyway, I came back to get these newspapers. They have a copying machine upstairs."

"Good idea." Nicole picked up one of the volumes. "We can each take one."

The girls started toward the stairs. As they reached the main aisle, Nicole looked back toward the desk where she had just been working. The light at the desk had already been turned off. "Somebody else is down here."

"Mr. Clovewood, probably," Alice said as she stepped onto the stairs.

Nicole hurried after her. "I didn't know Dolores went to Chamberlain," she said as they reached the main floor. She glanced down the steps. The library basement was now completely dark. "She was a lot like us."

Alice nodded. "There's Mrs. Alexander. Maybe she'll help us copy the articles."

A few minutes later, the girls had their photocopies and were walking through the reading room toward the front door.

Nicole looked at her watch. "It's almost six so my mom is probably here by now. Do you need a ride home?"

"No, thanks, I have to stop at the grocery store."

The girls walked across the reading room as, one by one, the lights behind them began to go out. When Nicole reached the exit, she thought she saw the reflection of a man facing them from somewhere behind. She whirled around but no one was there.

"Forget something?" Alice said.

"I thought I saw someone in back of us, but I guess I imagined it." Nicole pushed the door open. The girls stepped outside and into the cold air. "There was something I was going to tell you," she said, "but now I forget."

"You'll think of it," Alice said, her breath looking like a puff of smoke. She pointed to a car on Main Street. "There's your mom."

Nicole was quiet on the way home as she reflected on the newspaper articles she had read. Once inside her house, and after a brief stop in the kitchen, she went up the back stairs.

"We'll be eating in about half an hour," Nicole's mother called after her.

"Okay," Nicole answered. Sitting on her bed, she paged through a magazine and put it aside when she noticed her journal. She opened it to the last entry, sat at her desk and picked up a pen.

Tuesday, December 10

I read old newspapers in the library today. How lame does that sound? But I found some stuff about the Webers. I keep thinking about Dolores seeing her mother in the water. That's so horrible. I can't even imagine what it must have been like. And it was right after her father died. She was just a girl. Almost the same age as me.

Nicole sat back in her chair. She looked up at the portrait of the young girl and her kitten and then to her window and the darkness outside. It was only after the clock chimed downstairs that she turned back to her open notebook. Nicole looked at the pages for a while before she continued.

> And now we're talking about going into some underground vault that her father didn't want her to go into by herself. Underground. Just Alice and me. It's one thing to *say* you're going to do something. It's another thing to really do it. Maybe we should think about it some more.

Nicole put her pen down and closed the notebook. She put it on a shelf inside her desk and pulled down the top. She pushed her chair away from the desk, stood up, and went downstairs for dinner.

CHAPTER THIRTY-ONE

DECEMBER 15

Sunday morning, Nicole climbed out of bed and went to her front window. It looked cold outside. The trees were swaying and the clouds moved swiftly to the east across a bright blue sky. Nicole pushed her desk cover up and looked at her map. She traced the path from the crow's nest to the vault. Five hundred feet, a big number.

The clock next to her bed said nine. *It'll be hours until Alice gets here and we'll still have to eat with our parents before we can sneak out to the crow's nest.*

Nicole picked up her backpack from the floor and dumped everything onto her bed. She slid fresh batteries into the flashlight and put it, along with her map, some paper and a pencil, into the backpack. She put on jeans, a warm shirt and hiking boots and went downstairs with a glance at the rainbow on the wall.

Nicole's mother stood at the dining room table, already set for brunch. Her father put some wood into the fireplace. "Good morning," he said, looking up.

"Morning."

"Did you have a good sleep?" Nicole's mother inquired. Nicole nodded.

"How about some breakfast to tide you over until Alice and her family arrive?"

"I'll just have some toast."

"All right," Nicole's mother said. "How about some tea?"

"Yes, please." She followed her into the kitchen. The kettle was whistling. Nicole got the bread out of the refrigerator. "When are they getting here?"

"Around eleven-thirty."

"What are we having?"

"Lox and bagels," Nicole's mother said. "Pasta with shrimp. I hope they like seafood."

"Alice's dad is a fisherman, Mom. I'm pretty sure they like fish."

Nicole's mother smiled. She handed her daughter a steaming mug. "Maybe you should work on your homework until they arrive."

"I'm going to do that with Alice."

"Want to help me? You could slice some onions."

Nicole took a sip of tea and considered the options. "I probably *should* review my math."

After finishing her toast and tea, Nicole went back to her room. She looked at her math book for a few minutes, and then settled onto her bed with a book, a mystery. It was hard to concentrate, so she put on her earphones and listened to a CD. She closed her eyes and pictured the tunnel she and Alice were going to explore. *It's going to be dark, obviously, with spiders and webs. Maybe bats.*

She frowned and wriggled a bit to get more comfortable. *But figuring out a real mystery, maybe even finding a treasure . . . that would be something. Everyone at school would know about it. Maybe even in New Jersey. We could be on TV and Mom and Dad won't be able say anything.* Nicole smiled. *But still, 500 feet. In the dark. Dolores; the dog; the old man on Thanksgiving.* She was nervous, almost nauseous. *Thank goodness for Alice. I could never, ever, do this alone.*

Nicole took a deep breath and listened to the music. Eventually, she dozed off.

There were footsteps and voices on the front porch. Nicole looked at her clock. It was 11:35. *They're here.* She sat up on the edge of her bed and heard the knocker. She hurried into the bathroom and splashed water on her face. By the time Nicole was on the stairs, Alice and her parents were in the hallway. Alice's backpack was slung over one shoulder. Nicole's father was shaking hands with Alice's dad.

"This is Anne," Alice's father said.

"I'm Paul."

"It's very nice to meet you," Alice's mother said.

She's really pretty, like Alice, Nicole thought, noticing her long black hair with some wisps of gray.

"And I'm Mary," Nicole's mother said as she came into the hall, wiping her hands on a dishtowel. "Let me take your coats."

Nicole went to the bottom of the stairs and waved to Alice.

"Hello, Nicole," Alice's mother said. "It's nice to meet you. Alice has told me so much about you."

"Good or bad?" Nicole's father said.

The parents laughed. *They all seem nervous*, Nicole thought.

"It was all good," Alice's mother said.

The girls looked at each other. Alice rolled her eyes. Nicole smiled.

"Hey," Alice said.

"Hey."

"Your son isn't with you?" Nicole's mother asked.

"No," Alice's mother replied. "Larry had a sleepover last night at a friend's and he's spending the day there."

"What a shame," Alice said.

Alice's mother held out a plate wrapped in foil. "I brought this for dessert."

Nicole's mother took the plate and peeked under the foil. "It's a blueberry pie! It's still warm and it smells wonderful. Thank you, Anne."

"I hope you like it."

"I'm sure we will," Nicole's mother said. "Is everybody hungry?"

"I am," Alice's father said.

"Can I help you in the kitchen?" Alice's mother asked.

"I think we're all set, thanks," Nicole's mother answered, "but why don't we put the pie on the stove to keep it warm."

Alice's mother followed Nicole's down the hall and into the pantry.

"Nicole," her father said, "maybe you could help set the table?"

"It's already set, Dad. Besides, Alice and I have to go upstairs to start our homework."

"You're going to start your homework *now*? *Before* we eat? That's a first."

"We have a lot of work to do. Right, Alice?"

Alice agreed.

"You girls are almost twins," Alice's father observed. His daughter was also wearing jeans, a sweatshirt and hiking boots. "You two must be planning to work awfully hard on that project."

"Yes. The *project*," Nicole's father said. "Maybe we should *all* talk about that."

"Come on, Alice," Nicole interjected. Alice grabbed her backpack and the girls headed for the stairs.

"I better go check on my fire," Nicole's father said, pointing toward the sitting room. "You like football?" Nicole heard her father say as the girls hurried up the steps.

"Sometimes," Alice's father answered.

"Dallas and Washington are playing at one."

"Did you bring a flashlight?" Nicole asked when they were safely in her room.

Alice reached into her bag and pulled out a big yellow flashlight.

"Whoa, that's huge. Did you bring your map?"

"Yup," Alice said, displaying a neatly-creased piece of paper, "but I've got a question. Weber's instructions say to go 100 feet, 50 feet or whatever. How are we going to know when we've gone the right distance?"

"I was thinking about that too," Nicole said. "If we measure how long our steps are, then we just have to count how many steps we take."

"Okay," Alice said. "I'll measure you. Have you got a tape measure or a ruler or something?"

Nicole got a ruler from her desk. "We'll be probably be taking smaller steps than usual since it'll be dark." She took a step and stopped.

Alice crouched down and measured from the front of Nicole's left foot to the front of her right. "One foot," she said, smiling. "Get it? Your step is one foot. If we go 50 steps that will be about 50 feet. That should be close enough. Do you have any chalk?"

"I think so. What for?"

"We can use it to mark our trail so we can find our way back."

Nicole went to her closet and rummaged through a few boxes. "Here it is." She held up a big piece of pink chalk.

"Perfect!" Alice said.

Nicole put the chalk into her pocket.

"Girls!" Nicole's mother called from the bottom of the stairs. "It's time to eat."

Nicole opened her door. "Coming."

"We should eat fast so we can get going while our parents are talking," Alice said.

Nicole nodded. "Right. And get back before they know we're missing."

The girls went downstairs, stashed their backpacks in the hall closet and went into the dining room. They gobbled down their lox and bagels as planned.

Nicole pushed herself away from the table and stood up. "We have to get back to work."

"No pie?" her mother said.

"Save us some."

"All right, but put your dishes in the sink, please."

From the kitchen, Nicole and Alice went through the pantry and into the hallway. Without speaking, they pulled on coats, hats and gloves and then their backpacks. As they snuck past the door to the sitting room the girls heard their mothers talking about school and their fathers talking about boats.

"Does your dad have a boat?"

"Nah. He just likes talking about them."

"My dad does too. You'd think he'd be sick of the ocean but he even reads books about it. They'll be at it for hours."

Nicole opened the front door as quietly as she could and the girls crept outside. Looking over their shoulders a few times, they headed for the cliff. The wind stung.

"Are you ready?" Nicole asked when they reached the edge.

"I guess so," Alice answered. "Are you scared?"

"A little." Nicole looked out at the waves advancing toward the rocks below them. She turned to her friend. "Actually, more than a little. But not as much as I'd be by myself."

The girls glanced back toward the house. Alice took a deep breath. "Okay, let's go."

They climbed down into the crow's nest. Nicole pulled the

vines and branches away from the opening. Alice shined her light inside. "See any bats?" Nicole asked.

Alice threw a stone into the tunnel. "All clear."

The girls took their maps out of their backpacks. Nicole pulled the chalk out of her pocket. "We're supposed to go 100 feet and then turn right. How about if you lead since your light is better? I'll count our steps."

"Let's use both lights," Alice said. She switched hers on and stepped into the tunnel with Nicole crouching close behind. The circles of light danced on the stone floor and walls.

Past the entrance, there was no need to stoop. The floor was uneven but it was wide enough that the girls could walk side by side. The tunnel sloped down steeply.

"I think this is how far we got before," Alice said after a minute or so. "I remember the light from the outside looked like that."

Nicole looked back. "We've only come about 50 feet," Nicole said. "We're about halfway to the first turn."

"Are you sure?" Alice asked, "because there's another tunnel coming up and it's on the right."

"This can't be it," Nicole said when they were even with the black opening. "We've only come 60 steps. I think we should keep going."

They continued forward.

"This must be it," Alice said, after what seemed like a long time. Alice's light revealed tunnels to the right, to the left and straight ahead.

"I counted ninety-eight steps," Nicole said, "It's got to be! Let's look at our maps." The girls held their drawings side-by-side in the light.

"We're supposed to turn right here then go 50 feet and turn left," Alice said.

Nicole marked the wall with a pink arrow and looked back. The entrance to the tunnel, 100 feet away, was barely a speck of light.

"Be careful," Alice said. "It's steeper here."

"At least it's not too cold."

They reached another crossroad. Nicole marked the wall and the girls turned left. "Fifty feet to the next turn." They crept ahead.

"It looks like this tunnel ends here," Alice said a few minutes later. "We have to turn."

"The map says go left," Nicole answered. "Only 25 feet this time and then we turn right." They came to another intersection. "Here it is, right on schedule." They veered sharply to the right. The path ahead sloped down even more steeply.

". . . Twenty-three, twenty-four, twenty-*five*," Nicole announced as the girls reached yet another crossroad. "According to Henry Weber, we're halfway there."

"We turn left here, right?" Alice said.

"Correct."

Alice shined her light down the tunnel which continued straight ahead. "I wonder where all these other ones go."

"Who knows? But I'd sure hate to get lost down here." She marked the wall with her chalk. "This place is like a maze. I wish we'd see something that would show us we're on the right track."

"We're supposed to cross a stream someplace."

Nicole looked at her map. "Right. Fifty feet from here we turn left and go fifty more steps. That's where the stream is supposed to be."

The girls picked up their pace. At the next intersection, they turned left, barely slowing down for the chalk mark. Moments later, Alice stopped and pointed. Just ahead, the light reflected off a crystal-clear stream flowing across their path.

"We're almost there," Nicole said. The stream was narrow and, using rocks as steppingstones, the girls crossed without getting wet. They continued until the end of the tunnel, fifty feet away, and turned left. Seventy-five paces further, the tunnel forked.

"Just like it's supposed to!" Alice said, almost shouting.

"We turn right here," Nicole said, just as excited.

"The letter said the opening would be hidden by a stone."

"Right," Nicole agreed.

They slowed down as they reached the end of the tunnel. "It sure *looks* like a dead end," Alice said, shining her light at the blank wall that faced them. The rock walls were damp and glistened in the light.

Nicole crept forward and aimed her light at the base of the wall. "How about that rock?" she said. "It looks like it might be loose."

"Let's try it."

The girls put their lights down after training them on the rock. They ran their hands over the edges, feeling for someplace to grip.

"Ready?" Alice said.

"Ready," Nicole answered. "One, two . . ."

"Three!" they shouted together and pulled.

The stone rolled easily and revealed an opening in the wall.

"That wasn't too hard," Alice said.

"Especially considering it's been sitting there for 50 years."

They crouched down and peered into the low opening of a tunnel that appeared to be just a few feet long.

"You go first," Alice said, pointing with her light.

"Okay. Here goes."

"Oh my god!" Nicole said as she emerged from the tunnel. "It really *is* a vault. It's huge!"

Alice quickly joined her and together they gaped at the sight. "I'll bet my whole house would fit in here," she said, pointing her light upward. The vault's ceiling soared overhead and was covered by shapes that looked like stony icicles.

"What do they call those things?" Alice asked. "I always get them mixed up."

"I think the ones that hang down are called stalactites and the ones that stick up are stalagmites," Nicole said. "Look! Sometimes they meet and make a column."

"It looks like giants made them."

Nicole shined her light onto a nearby wall. "And look," she said as the beam seemed to disappear into an opening in the rock. "A cave."

Alice pointed her light into another black hole. "That's not the only one," she said. "There are lots of them."

"This place is like a maze inside a maze."

Suddenly, Alice shut off her light. "What are you doing?" Nicole said.

"Shut yours off too."

Nicole pressed the button on her light and the darkness covered them.

"I thought so," Alice said.

"What?"

"There's light in here," Alice said from somewhere in the dark.

Nicole saw it. On the other side of the vault, near the bottom of the wall, there was a small spot of light. "Do you hear that?"

"I hear an echo. Is that what you mean?"

"Not that," Alice said. "The pounding. Don't you hear it?"

Nicole listened. "Yeah, I do. It sounds like waves crashing."

"I think you're right," Alice said, switching her light back on. "We must be near the bottom of the cliff."

"I don't see any treasure around anywhere," Nicole said, turning her light back on. "How are we supposed to find something in a place this big."

"I have no idea," Alice said, shining her light onto the floor. She stopped when the beam came to a large stalagmite in the center of the vault. "But check *that* out."

"Whoa!" Nicole said, walking up to the stone. "This thing is big. It's taller than we are."

"Hey," Alice said as Nicole disappeared behind the far side of the stalagmite, "this looks weird."

Nicole quickly reappeared. "What looks weird?"

Alice pointed to a blackened rectangle that was fastened to the front of the stalagmite. "That," she said, pointing. "I don't think a giant made *that*."

Nicole picked up a stone and scratched the edge of the blackened rectangle. The mark glistened. "It's metal!" she said. "I think it's brass." She looked at her friend. "This must be the plaque Henry Weber wrote to Dolores about!"

Alice ran her fingers over the dark metal. "I think there's some kind of inscription here. Maybe we can read it!"

With their faces and flashlights just inches from the massive stone, the girls squinted at the metal. "It's tarnished," Nicole said. "It feels like there might be letters but I can't read them."

Alice climbed onto a small ledge a few feet above the stalagmite's base and shined her light downward. "This is weird too," she said. "It's flat up here like somebody chopped off the point. Except in the middle, there's like a little pedestal thing sticking up. It's smooth and the top is shaped like a stop sign."

"Very weird," Nicole said.

Alice shifted her light. "Maybe if I shine this from up here you can make out the letters better." She pointed her light down onto the plaque. "Now try it."

"I can see the words, Alice!"

"What does it say?"

Nicole moved close to the carving and slowly began to read:

The Age of Reason
The world made bright
Yet cannons speak loudest
And say might makes right

What you seek is now mine
Seized and locked tight
Violet to red
The keystone clearly in sight

Soon I cast off
For endless night
But on the day when darkness triumphs
I'll shatter the first light
– December 1769

Nicole was silent.

"That's it?" Alice finally said.

"That's it."

Alice climbed down from the ledge and examined the plaque. "I can't believe it."

"Me either, but that's all there is. What are we going to do now?"

Alice shined her light at the mysterious poem and shook her head. "I guess we should go back."

Nicole squinted at her watch. "Yeah, you're right. We've been gone 45 minutes. I hope they're not looking for us yet."

"Let's copy the poem," Alice said, "We'll have to figure it out later."

"Good idea," Nicole fished a pencil and a piece of paper out of her backpack. As Alice aimed the light and read the lines out loud, Nicole wrote them down.

The girls hardly spoke on the way back. Following the map in reverse, they traveled quickly. Before each turn, Alice shined her light on the chalk mark Nicole made on the way down. "I'm sure glad you did that."

"Me too. All these tunnels look the same."

After the final left turn, they saw daylight. The crow's nest was 100 feet straight ahead and the girls hurried toward it.

When they first emerged from the tunnel it took a few seconds to adjust to the bright sunlight. The wind was cold. The girls scrambled up over the top of the cliff and walked quickly through the snow toward the house.

"What are we going to do if they're looking for us?" Alice said as the girls approached the house.

"Maybe we should go inside and listen. If they're still in the dining room, we'll just go upstairs and everything will be fine."

Alice nodded. "And if they're upstairs wondering what happened to us? What do we do then?"

"We'll sneak into the basement. We'll either pretend we were there all along or else we'll go up the secret stairs."

Alice looked doubtful.

"Don't worry. They're probably still talking about school and boats." Nicole opened the big front door just far enough to peek in. She motioned to Alice that the coast was clear and they went inside.

"There you are!" It was Alice's mother. Nicole realized that she must have been behind the door.

"Great plan," Alice said.

Alice's father and Nicole's parents appeared in the hallway. "Where *were* you two?" Nicole's mother said. "You said you were going to work on your homework."

"You haven't been outside all this time, have you?" Nicole's father said.

"No, we were hardly outside at all," Nicole said, glancing at Alice.

"And we *were* working on our project," Alice added. "We just wanted to see something."

All four parents looked at the girls and then at each other.

Nicole smiled and took off her coat. Alice started to do likewise.

"Don't bother taking that off," her father said. "It's time for us to go."

Alice rebuttoned her coat.

"And the next time," he continued, "let us know if you're going off somewhere by yourselves, okay? You have to admit that some strange things *have* happened around here, if you know what I mean."

The girls nodded.

"No harm done," Nicole's mother said. "We only went to look for you a few minutes ago."

Alice and Nicole smiled at each other.

"How's the project going, anyway?" Alice's mother said.

"We started out great," Nicole said.

"But right now, we're sort of stuck," Alice added.

"Need any help?" Alice's father said, as he pulled on his jacket.

The girls looked at each other. "We'd rather try to figure it out ourselves first," Alice answered.

"Good for you," her father said. "Did you say thank you for the nice brunch?"

"Thank you, Mr. and Mrs. Kelly."

"We didn't get any pie," Nicole said.

The families exchanged thanks for the brunch and the pie and then everyone said good-bye.

"See you at school, Nicole," Alice said from the front porch.

When the Atteans were gone, Nicole's father asked, "So what's next on your mysterious project?"

Nicole shook her head. "I'm not really sure."

CHAPTER THIRTY-TWO

DECEMBER 17

During the next few days, concentrating on schoolwork was difficult. The cryptic verses in the vault kept coming into Nicole's mind. *What do they mean?*

She knew that Alice was having the same problem. On Tuesday morning in social studies Nicole was thinking about the inscription on the plaque when she realized that everyone was looking at her. And her teacher was speaking to her.

"Oh, I'm sorry, Mrs. Thorn, I didn't hear what you said."

"Space cadet," Billy offered.

Nicole knew she was blushing.

Mrs. Thorn frowned. "How about *you*, Alice. Do *you* know what happens this weekend? Something special? Something to do with the earth and the sun?"

Alice was staring into space and it looked like she *still* didn't hear a word.

"Earth to space, cadet number two," Billy called out, and everybody laughed.

"Alice, did you hear me?"

Finally, Alice snapped out of it and saw that everyone was staring at her. "Excuse me, Mrs. Thorn, did you ask me something?"

"As a matter of fact, I did. Michelle, can you tell Nicole and Alice what happens this weekend?"

"I think Saturday is the first day of winter," Michelle said, smiling at Nicole.

"That's right," Mrs. Thorn said. "This year, in the northern hemisphere, December 21 is the shortest day and the longest night of the year. Know what it's called, Michelle?"

I know that, Nicole thought: *the winter solstice.*

"The winter solstice?" Michelle said.

"Very good," Mrs. Thorn said.

Nicole frowned. She could see that Alice was annoyed too.

"The solstices have been a big event in civilizations all over the world for a very long time. Anybody ever hear of Stonehenge?"

A few hands went up. Mrs. Thorn pointed to Simon.

"It's in England. I think it's an ancient temple or something."

"Good," the teacher said. "You're right. It's a prehistoric monument in England made of huge stones. Most scholars say it was probably used in religious rituals. And some believe it was also a sort of astronomical calculator."

"A prehistoric calculator," Nick said. "Right."

"Maybe it's true." Turning to the blackboard, Mrs. Thorn picked up a piece of chalk and drew several thick vertical bars with a horizontal bar on top. "They built rough arches like these and linked them together in concentric circles." Then she drew a small trapezoid under the middle arch and a little sun right over it. "For example, on June 20, the summer solstice, the sun rises right over this stone." She put the chalk down. "Other stones mark different astronomical events on the calendar, such as sunrise on the morning of the *winter* solstice."

"Is this going to be on the test?" Nick asked.

Mrs. Thorn shook her head and sighed. "Possibly. But it will cover the entire Age of Discovery that we've been studying."

Nicole groaned along with the rest of the class.

"So, on that note of enthusiasm, let's continue our review."

The day dragged on but two forty-five finally arrived and Nicole went to her locker. After loading her backpack and getting her coat, she trudged past the classroom door. Alice was a step behind. Mrs. Thorn suddenly appeared in the doorway and Nicole hoped she wouldn't have to talk to her teacher. Nicole kept her eyes on the floor.

"Excuse me, Nicole," Mrs. Thorn said.

Nicole froze.

"You too, Alice. May I speak with you girls for a second?"

Nicole looked at Alice. Together they turned to face their teacher.

"You've seemed a bit distracted this week. Is anything wrong?"

Nicole looked at her friend. "I guess we've been thinking about our Elk River project."

"Ah, the mystery of the Weber House," Mrs. Thorn said, looking from one student to the other. "Are you having a problem?"

Alice glanced at Nicole. "We were doing great, but now we're kind of stuck."

"Can I help?"

"We found something that might be important but we don't know what it means."

"It's sort of a poem," Nicole added.

"That sounds interesting."

"The poem says something about 'the day when darkness triumphs,'" Alice said. "We're trying to figure out what that means."

"Do you know anything about the context of the poem? What was on the author's mind or even when or where it was written?"

"It was written around here," Nicole said, "a long time ago."

"In 1769," Alice said.

"That *is* a long time ago."

"We don't know what was on his mind," Nicole continued. "That's sort of what we're trying to figure out."

"Do you think the writer might have been talking about death?"

"He might have been, I guess," Nicole said.

"Will you two keep me posted about your progress? It sounds very intriguing."

"Okay," Alice said.

"Sure," Nicole agreed.

"But right now, girls, I'm afraid I have to go to a meeting."

"I've got to go, too," Nicole said. "I've got soccer."

Alice frowned. "You're both lucky. I've got to babysit."

CHAPTER THIRTY-THREE

DECEMBER 19

"That wasn't too bad, was it?" Mrs. Thorn said when Nicole handed in her social studies test on Thursday morning. Nicole glanced at the clock. There were still fifteen minutes before the end of the period. Most of her classmates were still writing.

"I think I did okay."

"Maybe you and Alice can do me a favor."

Alice looked up. She was finished too.

"Would you girls take these boxes down to Mrs. Petersen's office?"

"Sure," Nicole said. Alice nodded and came up to Mrs. Thorn's desk. Each girl picked up a small box.

"Mrs. Petersen is in a big hurry to get them, so don't stop in the girls' room or anyplace, okay?"

The girls nodded.

"How'd you do?" Alice asked, as they started down the third-floor hallway.

"Okay, I think. How about you?"

"It was all right." Alice balanced the box with one hand and pulled the stairway door open. "But I was kind of distracted."

"Me too. I can't stop thinking about the pirate's poem."

"Same here. That's about *all* I've been thinking about." They went down half a flight and stopped on the landing. Alice put her box on a windowsill and pulled a piece of paper out of her pocket. It was the verses from the vault.

Nicole put her box on top of Alice's. "Come up with anything?"

"Just something pretty obvious."

"What?"

Alice looked at her paper. "The thing in the vault said 'What you seek is now mine.' That must mean the treasure. And I'll bet that's what Dolores' father thought too. The rest of it, who knows?"

"I agree with you about the treasure," Nicole said. "And I thought of something else."

"What?"

"I think Mrs. Thorn might be right."

"That the poem is talking about death?"

"Yeah," Nicole said. "Remember when I got lost in the woods after I found that cabin?"

"Sure. Then Dolores, or somebody, led you back home, right?"

"Right. But before that, I fell and stumbled onto Taggart's tombstone."

"I remember."

"It didn't hit me until last night. I was looking out my window toward the woods where I got lost. Then I remembered that the date on the tombstone is 1769."

Alice pointed to her paper. "Same as the thing in the vault."

"Yeah," Nicole said, "but the thing in the vault says *December* 1769, so if the pirate put it down there in December, he must have been still alive, right?"

"Gee, do you think so?"

"Well, that means that when he put the plaque down there,

he had less than a month to live."

"And he must have known it, too," Alice said. "That's why he said 'Soon I cast off for endless night.' He *was* talking about dying."

"Right," Nicole said. "What I don't get is why he left any message at all."

"What do you mean?"

"Well," Nicole said, pulling her copy of the verses out of her pocket, "first, Taggart admitted that he 'seized' whatever it is that we're trying to find. That means he stole it, right?"

"Probably. He was a pirate. Stealing stuff was his job."

Nicole laughed. "Okay. So, he knows he's about to die but he doesn't give the treasure back or say where it is. He hides it."

"Well, like I said, he was a pirate."

"Okay," Nicole said, "I agree. He was a pirate. But if he was going to bury the treasure just to be mean and selfish, why did he leave any message at all."

"Hmm. Maybe he did it for spite. Sort of like dissing everybody on his way to the grave."

"But he didn't just say 'I've got the treasure and you don't.' He says 'violet to red, the keystone clearly in sight.' It sounds like he's giving a clue."

"Just what we need," Alice frowned. "Another clue. But I think you're right. It *does* sound like that. It's like he's *daring* us to find the treasure. Like he doesn't think anyone can do it."

"So far, he's right," Nicole stared at her copy of the verses. "Maybe it would help if we knew what Taggart meant by 'the Age of Reason.'"

"*There* you two are!" Mrs. Thorn was at the top of the stairs. "Mrs. Petersen just called on the intercom to ask where the boxes are. What's taking so long?"

"Let's ask Mrs. Thorn," Alice suggested. "She'll know."

The girls ran up the stairs.

"You're coming back *up?*" Mrs. Thorn said, with her hands on her hips and shaking her head.

"This is *really* important," Alice said.

"I hope so," their teacher said, suppressing a smile.

"Go ahead," Nicole said, nudging her friend. "Ask her."

"Mrs. Thorn," Alice said, "what is the Age of Reason?"

Mrs. Thorn didn't say anything. Then she smiled. "It's about seven years old. By that time, you're old enough to know that you're supposed to take things straight to the principal's office when she's waiting for them."

"Sorry," Alice said.

"I'm just teasing. The 'Age of Reason' was a period of European history when many people began to think that a lot of the world's problems and many of nature's mysteries could be solved and figured out with science and logic. It's also known as the Enlightenment."

"When was it?" Nicole asked.

"This is a strange place for a history lesson," their teacher said, squinting at the girls. "But the Enlightenment was in the seventeenth and eighteenth centuries, the sixteen and seventeen hundreds."

"So, 1769 would be in the Age of Reason?" Alice asked.

"I'd say so."

"I still don't know what it means," Alice whispered.

"Thanks, Mrs. Thorn," Nicole said, starting back down the steps. When the girls got to the landing, Alice took one box and handed it to Nicole. Then she picked up her own. "We'll be right back," Alice said, as the girls continued down the stairs.

"You better be, or you two are going to be living in the age of detention."

After delivering the boxes, the girls took a circuitous route back to room 308. When they finally got to the third floor, Alice stopped abruptly at the top of the stairs. "Wait a minute," she said, once again producing her copy of the verses. First, he writes 'The Age of Reason, The world made bright.'"

"Yeah?" Nicole said.

"Well, doesn't that mean he thinks the age of reason is a good thing?"

"I guess so."

"But the next line is 'cannons speak loudest and say might makes right.'"

"So?"

"Well," Alice said, "Was this guy for reason or for cannons?"

Nicole shook her head. "I don't know. Both maybe."

"Let's look at the poem again," Alice said. "If there really is a treasure, it's our only clue."

Nicole looked at Alice's paper. "Okay, the first part says he thought that reason was good but cannons are better."

"Right," Alice said. "Then the second part says: 'What you seek is now mine, seized and locked tight.' That's the treasure."

Nicole nodded. "But what about the 'keystone'? It says it's 'violet to red' and 'clearly in sight.' Did you see any purplish reddish keystone-shaped rocks down there?"

"How about a key made out of a giant ruby wedged in the ceiling?"

"That would be nice."

"Because if that's what the treasure is," Alice said, and it's clearly in sight, then why didn't Taggart just leave it on top of the stalagmite and say 'Here it is. You found it'?"

Nicole threw up her hands. "I don't know." She stared at the paper. "And then the last part. He knows he's about to die and he predicts—or brags—that on that very day, the day he's going to die, he's going to shatter the first light, whatever that means."

"'First light' sounds like sunrise," Alice said.

"Okay. On the day that he's going to die, he's planning to

shatter the *sunrise*. What does *that* mean? He was planning to blow up the sun?"

"It means we shouldn't spend our money yet."

Nicole laughed.

"What else do we know about this guy?" Alice asked.

"According to my neighbor, for a while he was the captain of a *slave* ship."

"God," Alice said. "I didn't know that."

"He was also really good at navigation and all that stuff but he was really cruel even to his own crew."

Alice looked at her paper and shook her head. "If this last stanza is about the pirate's death, maybe we need to know exactly when he died. Not just the year and the month but the exact day. Then maybe we could figure out what he meant by 'shatter the first light.'"

"Maybe we should go back to the library."

"I think we should. Maybe there's some book about Taggart or pirates or something that would tell us the date he died or give us some hint about what this poem means." Alice held the paper up. "These verses are still our best clue."

"I haven't got any better ideas," Nicole said.

The girls got back to class just as the bell rang. Mrs. Thorn was collecting the last of the social studies exams.

"I had no idea the principal's office was so far away."

"We were talking about our project," Alice said.

Mrs. Thorn looked dubious.

CHAPTER THIRTY-FOUR

After lunch, both girls called home and got permission to go to the library. At 3:15, they were on their way. They stopped for slices of pizza and by a quarter of four they were walking into the library.

Mrs. Alexander was at the main desk.

"Hello, ladies. Looking for more information on the Weber House?"

"Yes," Alice answered. "We want to learn about the man who built it."

"Oh, Mr. Taggart," Mrs. Alexander said. "You should speak with Mr. Clovewood. I just saw him a minute ago." Peering over her glasses, the librarian looked around. "I'll tell him you'd like to speak with him."

"Thanks, Mrs. Alexander," Alice said. She put her hat and backpack on a nearby table and her coat on the back of a chair. Nicole did likewise. "I'm going to the bathroom," Alice said. "I'll be right back."

Nicole walked to the card catalog and opened a long drawer labeled "Tab-Tran" and began flicking through the cards. Out of the corner of her eye, Nicole saw someone at the back of the library moving between the dimly lit bookshelves.

He was gone when she turned.

Nicole returned to the file cards. There were no entries for "Taggart." She pushed the drawer shut and walked back to her seat. Someone had left a teen magazine on the next table. Nicole sat down and paged through it. "Love Quiz," "Stylin' Swimsuits," "Making Him Want You." She came to the last page and looked up. *Where is Alice?* Nicole twisted around to see the clock and was startled to see a man looking at her. He was halfway down a narrow aisle between rows of bookshelves. He was old, with silver hair, a gray beard and glasses. Nicole turned back to the magazine and stared at an ad for lip gloss.

I've seen him before. Then it hit her: *Thanksgiving. The old guy with binoculars.* Nicole peeked up from the pictures of smiling girls. He was gone.

Nicole spotted Alice. She was in the periodicals section leafing through a magazine. Nicole pushed her chair back and hurried to her friend. "There's a weird guy in here watching me!"

Alice looked up. "Where?"

Nicole pointed toward the bookshelves. "He disappeared when he saw that I saw him."

"Maybe he wasn't really looking at you. Maybe he was just looking for a book or something."

"No," Nicole insisted. "And I've seen him watching me before."

"Really?"

"Yeah. On Thanksgiving. On Cliff Road. He had binoculars and he was limping. I was by myself and he freaked me out. Then he disappeared. I told you about him."

"*That* guy? You saw *him* in *here*?"

Nicole pointed. "Yeah, right over there."

"Maybe we should tell Mrs. Alexander."

"Fine with me," Nicole said.

The girls went to the information desk.

"What can I do for you ladies?" Mrs. Alexander said, looking over her glasses.

Nicole looked at Alice before she answered. "There's a man in here who keeps staring at me."

"Really?" Mrs. Alexander said. "Where is he?"

Nicole pointed toward the shelves. "I don't know where he is now but he was over there before."

The librarian walked around to the front of the information desk. "What does he look like?

"He has a beard and glasses," Nicole said. "And he's kind of, you know, old."

Mrs. Alexander smiled and gestured toward the shelves. "Is that he?"

Nicole spun around. The same man was standing in another aisle, once again looking straight at her. "Yes," she whispered, not wanting to draw attention. "That's him."

Alice pointed. "*That's* the guy you're talking about?"

Nicole pushed her friend's arm down. "Yes. That's him. And it's the same guy I saw staring at me on Thanksgiving."

"That's Mr. Clovewood," Alice said.

"Mr. Clovewood is the reference librarian," Mrs. Alexander said, "and the man to whom you should speak about your project."

"And here he comes," Alice said.

"Oh my god."

"And he's not limping either."

Nicole turned. The gray-haired, bearded man emerged from the bookshelves and walked toward the information desk. When he stood in front of the girls, he extended his hand. "Ms. Kelly?"

Nicole looked at Alice and then limply shook the librarian's hand. "You know my name?"

The old man nodded toward Alice. "Your friend told me

last week about your project and Mrs. Alexander mentioned it as well. I'm Mr. Clovewood. I too, am quite interested in the subject."

"Nicole thinks you've been spying on her," Alice said with a grin.

"*Alice!*"

"That's what you said. With binoculars and everything."

"I'm afraid I don't understand," Mr. Clovewood said with a glance at Mrs. Alexander, who had removed her glasses and now seemed quite interested herself. "I did notice you sitting near the card catalog and since I saw you and Alice enter the library together, I did wonder if you were, well, you. I'm sorry if I made you uncomfortable." Mr. Clovewood took off *his* glasses. "As for these, while the lenses *are* somewhat thick, I don't think anyone would consider them to be binoculars."

Everyone was looking at Nicole. "Well," she said, after directing a scowl at Alice. "I'm pretty sure I saw you near my house on Thanksgiving."

"Thanksgiving," Mr. Clovewood said, "Let me think," he said, glancing at Mrs. Alexander. "Oh yes, now I remember. I *was* out by Cliff Road that day. Around noon, I think."

Nicole smiled triumphantly at Alice.

"I was birding."

Alice smiled back at Nicole.

"It was a lovely day but I almost didn't go because my knee was hurting me. I saw an osprey but I'm afraid I don't recall seeing you."

"It looked like you were staring right at me."

"I guess you didn't make much of an impression," Alice said.

"Perhaps I was looking at a bird in your direction."

There was an awkward silence before Mrs. Alexander came to the rescue. "Why don't you see if Mr. Clovewood can help you with your research?"

The girls nodded.

"Shall we sit?" Mr. Clovewood suggested, pointing to the table with backpacks on it. The girls sat down across from the librarian with "Making Him Want You" in between. Nicole closed the magazine and pulled a pad and pen out of her backpack.

"How can I help you?" the librarian asked.

"Okay," Alice said. "You know we're doing a research project on the Weber House."

"Yes," Mr. Clovewood said.

"Nicole lives there."

The librarian looked at Nicole and nodded. "So I've heard."

"We'd like to find out whatever we can about the man who built it," Alice said.

"Taggart," Mr. Clovewood said.

"Right," Alice replied. "Taggart. The pirate."

"I looked in the card catalog," Nicole offered, "but I didn't see any books about him."

"There aren't any." He is mentioned in a few maritime histories but they're not particularly informative."

"I don't understand," Nicole said. "My neighbor told my parents and me that Taggart was a captain of a slave ship and this great sailor that nobody could catch when he was a pirate. Is that true?"

"Your neighbor is right," Mr. Clovewood said. "In England, there are both official documents and contemporary newspaper accounts which describe Taggart as simultaneously a murderous pirate, a brutal captain and a brilliant seaman. In South Carolina, records attest to Taggart's role in the slave trade. During the Seven Years' War, as it's called in Britain, or the French and Indian War, as it's known here, Taggart was particularly vicious to the Native Americans who lived in this area. We are not talking about a charming rascal. Captain Hook, if you will. Taggart was a bloody killer."

Nicole remembered the chains in the tunnel.

"One interesting thing about Taggart is the fact that he sailed after 'the golden age' of piracy had ended."

"How did he do that?" Nicole asked.

"Well, for a few years he preyed on French and Spanish ships and that was fine with the British. The Royal Navy only came after Taggart when he started attacking English vessels, starting around 1763. They never caught him. *That*, I believe, can only be explained by Taggart's incredible seamanship and perhaps also by his apparent fascination with science."

"Our teacher told us he lived in the Age of Reason," Alice said.

"The Enlightenment," Nicole added.

Mr. Clovewood smiled. "That's true. Scientists, or natural philosophers as they were called at the time, were making important discoveries in many areas including mathematics, chemistry, physics and astronomy."

"Astronomy," Alice said. "That would have helped him navigate, right?"

The librarian nodded. "Absolutely. Math, chemistry and physics would also have been useful to a man in Taggart's line of work."

"How?" Nicole asked.

"The accurate firing of cannons is a matter of science."

"Oh," Nicole said. "I see what you mean."

"In addition," Mr. Clovewood continued, "Taggart was evidently particularly intrigued by the science of optics."

"You mean, like in a telescope?" Alice asked.

"Precisely. But perhaps also for illumination. Before ships had electricity, some vessels had prisms set into their decks to spread sunlight into the darkness below."

"Pretty smart," Alice said.

"That's so weird," Nicole added. "Taggart was so smart and everything but such a bad person at the same time."

"That's very true, Nicole. Smart isn't the same as good. And the discoveries of the Enlightenment were often used for terrible purposes. Bad men can look at the stars too."

"How do you know all this stuff, Mr. Clovewood?" Alice asked.

"Primary sources."

The girls looked at each other. "What does that mean?" Alice asked.

"Documents that were written at the time that Taggart lived. I read them in London."

"You went to England to study about him?"

The librarian smiled. "No, I was on vacation but I did some research while I was there. If you like, you may copy some of these materials for your report."

"Thanks," the girls said simultaneously.

"You're quite welcome. But you needn't go all the way to England. There is one primary source on the subject right here in Elk River. It appears to have been written by William Taggart himself. Evidently, he fancied himself as something of a poet."

"Really?" Nicole said, with a glance toward her friend.

"Yes," Mr. Clovewood said. "Written in 1769. I'd say it was just about the last thing Taggart wrote. I read it myself."

Alice looked stunned.

"Yes. I was birding then too, as a matter of fact."

"You were bird watching *down there*?" Alice said.

"Absolutely. I gather you have been there as well."

"We both were," Nicole said, "but we sure didn't see any birds."

"We didn't think anyone else had been there," Alice said.

"It was at the bottom of a steep hill near a small brook. I remember the inscription quite clearly. It said:

> **The lords called me a pyrate**
> **Newgate's press, 'tis true, I did cheat**
> **But worse there are who ne'er fired a gun**
> **Their lair is Threadneedle Street.**

It was written in 1769."

It took Nicole a moment to recognize the words. "The tombstone!"

"Exactly."

"I thought you were talking about something else," Nicole said. "But I saw Taggart's tombstone too. Out in the woods."

"She was lost," Alice said.

Nicole frowned at her friend. "Thanks."

"Don't mention it," Alice said. "Speaking of the tombstone," she asked, turning back to the librarian, "do you happen to know *exactly* what day Taggart died?"

"No, I'm afraid I don't. I doubt that anyone does. This area was a virtual wilderness at the time, to Europeans anyway, and no records exist. The death wasn't reported in England until many months later. Is the precise day important to your project?"

"We don't know," Alice answered. "Maybe."

"What do you suppose the epitaph means?" Mr. Clovewood asked.

"I have no idea," Nicole said.

"Alice?"

"Me either."

"May I." Mr. Clovewood said as he reached for Nicole's pad and pen. Nicole watched as, from memory, he neatly wrote the lines from the tombstone. He looked up when he was finished. "The first line is pretty obvious, right?"

The girls nodded.

"What do you think the second line means?"

The girls looked at each other and shrugged.

"Well, Newgate Prison was one of the places where pirates were incarcerated in London during the eighteenth century. The press was one of the ways that pirates were executed. I'm afraid it's rather gruesome. Weights were piled onto the prisoners' chests until they were crushed to death. It sometimes took several days."

"Oh my god," Alice said. "That's horrible."

"Quite true," Mr. Clovewood agreed, shaking his head.

Nicole spun her notebook around so that she could read the verses. "So," she said after studying the lines for a few seconds, "Taggart is admitting that he was a pirate and is kind of bragging that he wasn't caught."

"Exactly," Mr. Clovewood said. "How about the last two lines, Alice?"

"I guess he's saying that, even if he was bad, there were other people who were worse even if they didn't kill people. I guess someplace called Threadneedle Street was their hiding place."

"I completely agree." Mr. Clovewood said. "In case you're interested, Threadneedle Street is where you will find the headquarters of the Bank of England. In Taggart's day, it was one of the most powerful financial institutions in the world. It still is, actually."

"I guess Taggart didn't like banks," Alice said.

The librarian smiled. "Oh, I don't know. But they definitely didn't like *him*. Banks took exception to the withdrawals he made from the ships they owned or financed."

Nicole closed her notebook and glanced at Alice before turning toward the librarian. "Thanks, Mr. Clovewood, for all the information. I can't think of any more questions right now, can you Alice?"

"No, not really."

"I hope that I've been of some assistance."

"Well, everything helps," Alice said.

THE WEBER HOUSE

"There's one thing you haven't asked me."

"What?" Alice said.

"People usually ask me if I think there's a treasure. Perhaps you ladies already have an opinion on the subject. Or perhaps . . ." he said with a nod toward Nicole, ". . . since one of you *lives* in the Weber House, you have *inside* information, so to speak."

"We haven't found anything yet," Nicole said. "No treasure, anyway."

"But if we do, we'll make sure you get some gold or jewels," Alice added.

"That's very kind of you," the librarian said. "And if *I* find the treasure first, I'll be sure to remember *you*."

Alice smiled. "Deal."

Mr. Clovewood extended his hand and each girl shook it. "And now," he said as he stood up, "I have some other research to do. Something to do with notorious local criminals."

"Nick," Alice said, laughing.

"Thank you, Mr. Clovewood," Nicole said.

"Yeah," Alice added. "Thanks a lot."

Mr. Clovewood disappeared between the bookshelves. "Well, that was all very interesting," Alice said, "but I don't see how it's going to help us find the treasure."

"Me either. And I still don't see why Taggart went to so much trouble to put his little poem in the vault where nobody might ever find it. If he wanted to mock everyone, or even leave a clue, he could have left the same message on his tombstone."

"Maybe," Alice said slowly, "he left that message there because there's something special about *that spot!*"

"And maybe," Nicole added, "there's something special about being there at the *right time* too—at first light. Sunrise, like you said. We have to go back down there!"

Suddenly the excitement in Alice's face melted away.

"What's the matter?" Nicole asked.

"If we want to be there at sunrise on the same day that Taggart died, there's just one problem."

"We don't know when that is."

"Right. All we know is that it was in December. We can't just camp out down there. We might have already missed it. We might have to wait for next year."

"Don't even say that, Alice, not after all we've been through. I might not even be living here a year from now."

They stared at each other, frowning.

"Wait a minute," Alice said. "Maybe we *didn't* miss it. In Dolores' father's first letter, didn't he write that the treasure or whatever might be a Christmas present?"

"And he thought he might be home in time too, didn't he?" Nicole added hopefully.

"I think so. But how would Dolores' father know what day Taggart died? Even Mr. Clovewood doesn't know. And he went to England."

"Dolores' father was a sailor," Nicole said. "He probably went there too. Maybe he found something."

"Yeah, right," Alice said. "Maybe he met a 200-year-old sailor that knew Taggart."

"Maybe that's what *we* should do."

"Except now he'd be 250 years old."

Nicole laughed. "But really, what if we went there, the vault, I mean, not England, for *some* sunrise? Maybe we'd learn something. Maybe we'd even get lucky and be there on the right day."

"The sun comes up around seven o'clock at this time of year. How are we going to explain to our parents that we want to go cave exploring at that hour?"

"I have no idea," Nicole admitted.

"And we still don't even know what we're looking for," Alice continued "other than maybe a purplish, reddish keystone-shaped ruby that's stuck in the ceiling."

"Maybe the ruby really *is* a keystone, like in an arch," Nicole said. "And when we pull it out of the ceiling, it's a booby trap and the whole cave will collapse like in a movie."

"*What?*"

"*Or,*" Nicole said, "maybe the keystone is really a key that's made out of stone. Taggart said that the treasure is 'locked tight.'"

"Aren't keys usually made of metal?"

"Usually, yes."

"Well, whatever it is," Alice said, "we don't have it."

"But it's supposed to be in plain sight."

"Yeah, it was," Alice said, "two hundred years ago."

Nicole glanced at the library clock. It was almost five. "I better get going, my mother's picking me up and she freaks out if she has to wait." The girls put on their coats and hats and picked up their backpacks. "Want a ride?"

"No thanks. I can walk from here."

The girls started across the reading room.

"Here's something so that you never get lost again."

Nicole and Alice turned around in time to see Mr. Clovewood emerging from the bookshelves. When the librarian got closer, he handed something shiny to Nicole. At first, she thought it was a silver dollar but then she saw that it was a compass. The librarian gave another one to Alice.

"Thanks," the girls said in unison.

Mr. Clovewood smiled. "My pleasure."

The girls turned to go.

"Knowledge . . ." Mr. Clovewood said softly . . .

The girls turned back toward the old man.

". . . is something you still possess even after you give it away."

"That's true," Alice said with a smile. "But you don't have your compasses anymore."

"On the contrary," the librarian replied, "I have a whole drawerful of them. The problem isn't that I don't have any more compasses. The problem is that I can't find people to give them to."

Nicole put her compass into her coat pocket. Alice slid hers into her backpack.

"Good luck," the old man said. "And be careful."

CHAPTER THIRTY-FIVE

DECEMBER 20

The clock just chimed downstairs. It's midnight. Mom and Dad went to bed a while ago. I did too but I couldn't sleep. The wind is blowing pretty hard and it's cold in here. It must be horrible outside.

The cold always makes me think of Dolores. I wonder where she is right now and if she's keeping warm somehow.

It's like Dolores is two different people. Sometimes I think of her like a girl, like she is in the painting. Almost the same age as me. Same house. Same school. I know she fought with her dad sometimes. I wonder if she went to parties or had a boyfriend. I know lots of things were different back then but not everything.

But sometimes I think of her like she is now. I feel bad about all the terrible things that happened to her and I wish we could help her somehow but she scares me too. That night she came into the house I don't know what I would have done if Alice hadn't been here.

Lots of things would be different without Alice. I never would have gone to the vault without her the first time and I wouldn't be going back now either. I think she's brave. She isn't *afraid to be herself even if it means being by herself.*

Tonight, if we can figure out a way to talk our parents into letting us have a sleepover, we'll be making plans to go back down to the vault. What if, after more than 200 years, we're the ones who find the treasure that everyone's been looking for? Maybe my parents would stop treating me like a little kid. I know I'm only 13 but I'm not a baby.

I can't believe we went down there by ourselves. I guess we were so excited we didn't think about what we were doing. But now that I've had time to think about it, we must have been crazy. Tunnels, spiders, bats. I don't believe that there are any pirates or witches around but, like that cook said on our first day in Elk River, people have died here. Even Mr. Clovewood said to be careful.

We'll talk it over again at school today but, even if it's crazy, I think we're going to do it. I don't know how, or even when exactly but we're going back to the vault.

On Friday afternoon, the entire school attended a holiday assembly in the auditorium. The band, the orchestra and two different choruses played or sang. During a spirited rendition of "Rudolph, the Red-Nosed Reindeer" performed by sixth graders, Nicole felt a tap on her shoulder. Nicole twisted around. "This is so lame," Alice whispered.

"Yeah, but we've got to talk. How about after school?"

"I have to go right home to babysit. And this isn't going to end before school's out."

Nicole nodded toward the stage. "We'll be lucky if this ends before New Year."

"Let's meet in the girls' room."

"Okay," Nicole said. The girls stood up and went in opposite directions.

"What a coincidence," Mrs. Thorn said with a smile when

Nicole whispered to her teacher. "Alice seems to be asking Mrs. Deagan for permission to go someplace, too."

Nicole grinned.

"Go ahead," Mrs. Thorn said. "Say hello for me. But don't take all day."

A sixth-grader was coming out of the girls' room as Nicole entered. Alice was washing her hands. "Well," she said, when they were alone, "did you figure out a way to get down into the vault at sunrise sometime before Christmas? By the way, the sun comes up at 6:56 tomorrow."

"I have an idea."

"What?" Alice said.

"I think our best chance is to try to go down there this weekend, tomorrow if we can. If we can't do it, or if we go and we don't find anything, we'll still have another chance next week."

"Okay. But that doesn't explain how we're going to get down there."

"Well," Nicole said. "You're gonna have to stay at my house tonight. We'll get up at six. My parents will be asleep. We'll have plenty of time to get out to the crow's nest and down to the vault. This time, we know exactly where we're going. When the sun comes up, we'll see what happens."

"It's worth a try."

"We'll tell our parents that we need a sleepover for our Elk River project." Nicole chuckled. "And that's actually true."

"I thought of something else that's kind of interesting," Alice said.

"What?"

Two seventh-grade girls came in and whispered to each other. Nicole and Alice waited for them to leave.

"Okay," Alice said. "All this stuff about darkness and light. What difference does it make? Who cares what day it is or what time it is? It's underground. There isn't any light down there."

"Well," Nicole said. "There was a little light."

"Exactly! When we shut off the flashlights, there was a little spot of light shining in from somewhere."

"Yeah," Nicole said slowly. "So?"

"Well," Alice said, "We heard the waves but the walls of the vault must still be pretty thick."

"I guess so, or else the ocean would've come in and we'd be dead."

"Anyway," Alice continued, "where the light comes through can't just be a hole. It has to be like a tube or a tiny tunnel through the rock."

"Is this headed someplace?"

"Maybe," Alice said. "Remember when Mrs. Thorn was talking about that Stonehenge place in England?"

"Yeah, I remember."

"What if that spot, where the light comes in, is like that? What if, on the date that Taggart died, and only on that date, when the sun comes up, it shines straight through that little tunnel?"

Nicole stared at her friend. "Oh my god," she finally said. "The sunlight might show exactly where the treasure is."

"That's just what I was thinking."

"I'll bet anything that you're right," Nicole said, clenching her fists. "You're a genius!"

"What can I say?"

"Wait a minute," Nicole said.

"What?"

"Wait a *minute*."

"*What*?"

"Do you know where the sun is going to come up on the day you die?"

"*What*?"

"Well, *do* you?"

"No, but I'm not dying. At least not soon, I hope. But Taggart *was* dying and we already agreed that he knew it."

"But how did he know *exactly* what day that was going to be?"

"Oh," Alice said slowly. "You're right." She reached into her pocket and pulled out her wrinkled copy of the verses from the vault. "We've been assuming that 'on the day when darkness triumphs,' is about the day when Taggart was going to die. But it can't be."

"Right," Nicole said. "Maybe it's a day that Taggart *could* have and *would* have known about—the day when the rising sun shines straight through that little tunnel."

"And shows where the treasure is!"

"And that day is coming up, isn't it?" Nicole said. "They even said it in class, that day we weren't listening."

"The solstice!" they exclaimed together.

"It's got to be!" Alice said. "'When darkness triumphs' must mean the longest night of the year. My dad was talking about it last night. The sun never rises further south than where it comes up tomorrow morning. It must shine straight through the opening where we saw that spot of light. Oh my god, this is so exciting!"

"Now we *definitely* have to get down there tomorrow," Nicole said.

"Uh-oh."

"*Now* what?"

Alice frowned. "We want a clear sunrise tomorrow, right? Or else the sun might not shine into the vault."

"Absolutely."

"My dad said that there's a storm coming."

"Great," Nicole said. "*Now* what are we going to do?"

"Go back to the assembly?"

When Nicole and Alice returned to the auditorium, a seventh-grade class was finishing a comical version of "Santa

Claus Is Coming to Town." Mrs. Thorn looked at her watch and shook her head before she let Nicole squeeze past.

The assembly ended and Nicole's class went back to room 308. Mrs. Thorn told everyone to have a great vacation but she reminded her social studies students not to forget the Elk River projects which would be due right after the holidays. Then, amid whoops and shouts of "Merry Christmas!" and "See you next year!" the class was dismissed.

When the final bell rang, all of Chamberlain, even the staff and teachers, seemed to be milling in front of the school. Light snow was falling and the cold air felt good. Nicole saw Alice coming toward her. "I thought you went out the back."

"Seems like this is the place to be," Alice said. "Plus, I wanted to tell you that I'll call you."

"Okay," Nicole said. "I'll be home." She waved, climbed aboard the bus and took a window seat near the back.

With a cloud of blue smoke, the bus pulled out of Chamberlain's driveway onto Atlantic Avenue before turning right a few blocks later onto Main Street. As the bus made the turn, Nicole saw the "Homemade Doughnuts and Biscuits" sign in the diner where she and her mother stopped on their first morning in Elk River.

As the bus headed through town, Nicole leaned close to the window. The church, the cemetery, the library, the bank, the stores, even the streetlights and benches all seemed familiar now. The bus clunked over the railroad tracks at the edge of town. Nicole's eyes followed the rails toward the abandoned cannery, its silhouette shrouding the waterfront.

As the bus labored back and forth up the hill, Nicole gazed down at Elk River. *When I first came here,* she thought, *I didn't know a single person. Now I know lots of people. I even have a friend, a good friend . . . .*

The bus turned onto Mountain Highway and continued to climb. Boats rested on the dark water of the Elk River Bay.

Plus, we're up to our ears in maybe the biggest mystery ever around here with a real pirate and a real treasure. She looked up. *Alice's father said a winter storm is coming.* Dark clouds pressed forward above the peaks.

And what about Dolores? Twice she was there when I really needed her and this whole mystery centers on her house but what do I really know about her? I don't believe she's dangerous like people say but what if I'm wrong?

The bus whirred over the blackened bridge that spanned Elk River just before it flowed into the bay. On the other side, Mountain Highway continued upward. The sky was darkening. Nicole wondered where Dolores would go in the storm.

They were on a straight section of the highway close to the cliff on the right. Far below, waves advanced in uneven white lines toward the rocks. *Maybe we'll be the ones to solve the mystery.* Nicole smiled. *What will everybody say then?* she thought, glancing at Michelle. She put her forehead against the cold window. *But there's still so much that we don't know.*

The bus slowed down as it approached Cliff Road and Nicole gazed at the gray ocean. Out to sea, the lighthouse kept its lonely vigil, the beacon sweeping past every few seconds. The bus squeaked to a stop. Nicole walked to the front and climbed down the steps. *"The keystone clearly in sight,"* she remembered, shaking her head.

The bus pulled away. Nicole started down Cliff Road and was soon surrounded by the trees. The woods darkened as the storm clouds rolled over the mountaintops and blotted out the descending sun. Snow was falling. Nicole dropped her backpack, made a snowball and aimed for a dead tree. It missed but something moved in the woods. She froze until she saw a red blur darting from a little fir tree nearby. *The cardinal.* Nicole smiled. *Looks like I'm on my own today.*

She trudged through the snow, trying to keep in the tire tracks. Crossing the bridge, Nicole heard a car approaching from behind. Headlight beams, illuminating the falling snow, swung into view and Nicole's mother's car appeared. It crunched to a stop where Mr. Morgan's driveway split off. The driver's window went down. "Happy vacation!" Nicole's mother called out.

Nicole walked to the passenger side and climbed in.

"Sorry I'm late. I drove to town after I finished cleaning. I planned to meet your bus but I guess I didn't quite make it."

"That's okay."

"I still need a few things and have to go back to the supermarket. Want to come?"

"Not really."

"Oh, come on. It'll be fun. We can get some hot chocolate. Since you're on vacation, you don't have to do any homework, right?"

"Nope. No homework. Not tonight, anyway. But I do have to go home for something pretty important."

"What?" her mother asked.

"I have to go to the bathroom."

"*Now*? Can't you wait until we get into town?"

"No bathroom, no Elk River."

Nicole's mother smiled. "All right. We'll go back to the house."

"Can Alice sleep over tonight?"

"I don't know," Nicole's mother said slowly. "We have lots of stuff to do and Alice's family probably does too."

"If her parents say it's okay, then can we? It's really important for our school project."

The car came to a stop at the end of the driveway. "I really don't know," Nicole's mother said. "I'll think about it. But for now, hurry inside. I'll wait for you here."

Nicole opened the car door and jumped out.

"And take your boots off."

Nicole shut the car door. She hurried up the walk, past the

black cannons and onto the porch. She reached under the doormat for the key, unlocked the door and pushed it open. Inside, Nicole sat down on the floor and pulled her boots off.

Nicole went up the stairs in her stocking feet. As she came out of the bathroom, she heard her mother come in the front door. She noticed something on the floor and picked it up. It was a little glob of gray mud. *Guess she missed a spot.*

"It's a good thing we came back," Nicole's mother called from the hallway, "because I forgot my shopping list. Are you ready?"

"Hold on," Nicole answered as she hurried toward her room. "I just want to drop my backpack off."

As Nicole came back out of her room, she saw her mother on the other side of the balcony. "I thought I told you to take off your boots," she said, sounding annoyed. "You tracked mud on my clean floor."

Nicole turned around and saw her mother going into the bathroom. She came back out with a towel. "Want to help me wipe up this stuff?"

"I *did* take my boots off. You walked right past them downstairs. And I never went over there. I went into the bathroom and then right into my room. There was dirt in there, too. Maybe it's from *your* shoes."

Nicole's mother suddenly looked very serious and walked quickly into her daughter's room. She crouched down and picked up another little piece of mud. "This was *not* here when I finished cleaning. And I didn't go outside until I left for town."

Ivy strolled into the room. She went to the fireplace and sniffed at the woodwork.

Nicole glanced at her desk and froze. The desktop was halfway open!

"Were you in my desk?" she said, glancing again at Ivy who was now scratching at the wood around the fireplace.

"No," her mother answered. "Why?"

"Because *somebody* was. Look. It's open."

"Maybe you left it open."

Nicole shook her head. "No. I keep my journal in there. I *never* leave it open."

"Put on your coat," Nicole's mother said calmly. "We're leaving the house right now."

"Do you think someone's been in here?"

"Put your coat on *right now*," Nicole's mother said. Her voice sounded strained. "We're leaving the house *this instant!*"

Suddenly, Nicole was alarmed, too. *Dolores.* She grabbed her coat and hurried down the stairs a step in front of her mother. At the front door, she picked up her boots.

"Hurry, Nicole."

They rushed outside and into the car. Her mother locked the doors and started the engine. The car roared down the driveway, kicking up a spray of snow and gravel.

"Where are we going?" Nicole asked as they sped into the woods.

"To Mr. Morgan's. We'll call your father from there."

In a minute, they were in front of Mr. Morgan's house. His car was in the driveway.

"Good, he's home," Nicole's mother said. They hurried to the front door. Her mother rang the bell. "Come on, *come on.*"

Mr. Morgan opened the door. He was holding a cordless phone to his ear and Nicole thought he looked surprised. "I'll call you back," their neighbor said into the phone. "Come in, Mary. Come in, Nicole. Is something wrong?"

"Someone was in our house," Nicole's mother said as they stepped into the warm hallway. "He might still be there. I need to call the police."

"Certainly." Mr. Morgan handed her the receiver. "Do you want to call Paul?"

Nicole's mother nodded as she started to press the keys.

THE WEBER HOUSE

"I'd like to speak to Officer Baldwin," she said. "When will he be in?"

Nicole heard the tension in her mother's voice.

"Then I'll speak to you. My name is Mary Kelly. Someone has broken into my house. He might still be there."

"No, my daughter and I are at a neighbor's house. How soon will someone come to investigate?"

"I'll wait here. I think that will be all right with my neighbor."

Mr. Morgan nodded.

"I'm in the home of Mr. John Morgan."

"That's right, the president of the bank. It's the first house on the left past the covered bridge on Cliff Road. My house is the second house."

"That's right. The Weber House. I'll be waiting." Nicole's mother immediately tried another number. "I'd like to speak to Professor Kelly, please. This is his wife. It's urgent."

"Then, please have him call this number." She looked at the phone. "It's 322-7735. Thank you."

Nicole's mother handed the phone back to Mr. Morgan. "The police should be here right away. They said there's a car nearby. Paul's in class. The secretary said she'd have him call here. I hope that's all right."

"Of course," Mr. Morgan said. "Is there anything I can do? Would you like something to drink? A glass of wine or a cup of tea? Would you like something, Nicole? And let me take your coats."

Nicole and her mother took off their hats and coats. "Some tea would be wonderful, John, thanks," Nicole's mother said, pushing her hair back. "Nicole, would you like some tea?"

"Yes, please."

Nicole and her mother sat on a couch in the living room. Mr. Morgan went into the kitchen. A minute later, Nicole heard a siren. Their neighbor returned with the tea and a plate of cookies. "They'll get to the bottom of this," he said. "Did you see anyone?"

Nicole's mother shook her head as she sipped some tea. "No, thank goodness, but we may have surprised him. I had just come back from town to meet Nicole. When we went in the house, there was mud on the floor where I had just cleaned." She shook her head. "My god. Nicole went inside first, alone. What if he was still there?"

"It might not have been a 'he,'" Mr. Morgan said. "I'm thinking it was Dolores." He walked to a front window. "But it could have been kids. They sometimes come around this time of the year."

"So we've heard."

Mr. Morgan turned to Nicole's mother. "It was exactly fifty years ago tomorrow morning, that Dolores found her mother in the water below the cliff."

They sipped their tea. Nicole noticed how nice Mr. Morgan's home and furniture were. In a few minutes, she heard chimes and Mr. Morgan went to the door. It was Officer Baldwin.

"Hello, Mr. Morgan."

"Hello, Bob. Mrs. Kelly and her daughter are in the living room."

"Hello, Mrs. Kelly," Officer Baldwin said, taking his pad and pen out of his pocket.

"Hello, officer," Nicole's mother said as she stood up. "Did you find anyone?"

"No ma'am, I didn't. And I didn't find any sign of forcible entry, either. Did you actually *see* an intruder?"

"No," Nicole's mother said. She told the policeman about finding mud on the floor when she returned from town. "Also, my daughter's desk was open. She is certain she left it closed this morning."

Officer Baldwin closed his notebook. "It's not very much

to go on. If there *was* someone in your house, I'd have to suspect Dolores Weber. If she's alive, I'd assume that this is a hard time of year for her." The policeman clicked his pen and slid it back into his pocket. "Will you be going back to the house, ma'am?"

"Definitely *not!* I have to talk to my husband, but I think we'll be staying in town tonight."

Nicole thought of the plan for a sleepover with Alice.

"If it's not too much trouble," Officer Baldwin said, pulling his gloves on, "could you stop at the station and fill out a report?"

"Yes, we can do that if you think it might help."

Officer Baldwin left and Nicole's mother picked up her coat. "I think we should be going, too."

"Do we *have* to stay somewhere else, Mom?"

"I don't know where we'll be staying, Nicole. One thing at a time." Turning to Mr. Morgan, she said "John, when Paul calls, would you ask him to meet us at the police station. Please tell him what happened and tell him not to worry. He'll probably come back later to feed Ivy and pick up some clothes."

"I'd be glad to. You're welcome to stay here, you know. We have plenty of room. And Nicole, if your mom or dad gives me a key, I can always feed Ivy until you come back home."

"Thanks, Mr. Morgan."

"And I appreciate the offer to stay," her mother said, "but right now I just want to talk to Paul."

Mr. Morgan smiled. "Well, you're always welcome. I feel terrible about all of this but I'm sure everything will be all right. Elk River really is a great place to live."

"Can you recommend somewhere in town to stay?"

"There's a nice inn facing the water at the corner of Atlantic and Third," Mr. Morgan said. "And the food is good. Would you like me to call for you?"

"No, thanks. I doubt we'll need reservations. But can you tell me where the police station is?"

"It's on Granite Street, just off Main."

"Thanks again, John," Nicole's mother said, opening the front door. "Thanks for everything."

Mr. Morgan did his best to smile. "Don't mention it."

Nicole's mother was quiet as they drove down the driveway, crossed the covered bridge and continued onto Cliff Road.

"Do you think the police will arrest Dolores?" Nicole asked.

"I suppose so, if they find her. But who knows if that policeman even believed me? He might think I'm just a hysterical female."

The snow was beginning to stick on Mountain Highway. Neither Nicole nor her mother spoke. From high above the water, Nicole looked out over the blurry bay and town. As they approached the Elk River Bridge, she turned toward her mother. "I don't think we have to stay at a motel, Mom."

"We can't stay in a place where people can just come in whenever they want to. What if we had been home? Or sleeping?"

Nicole remembered her fright on the night of the sleepover with Alice. "That scares me too," she admitted. "But I don't think Dolores would hurt us. Maybe we could just talk to her. Maybe we could even help her. *You* even said that she needs help."

"She *definitely* needs help," Nicole's mother said, glancing at her daughter. "But we can't assume that she's not capable of harming someone."

Nicole slumped down in her seat. "Alice and I wanted to have a sleepover tonight to work on our project."

"That's not a bad idea. Who knows what kind of running around your father and I might have to do? I'll call Alice's mother from the police station."

"Okay," Nicole said, surprised at her mother's agreement.

Five minutes later they were on Main Street. The sidewalks were, by Elk River standards, full of shoppers and students now on vacation. Snow was falling in big, fluffy flakes.

They turned left on Granite and saw the Elk River Police Headquarters which stood directly behind the bank. Compared to all the old-looking buildings in town, the police station looked new. Instead of dark brick, the building was made of shiny yellow stone. Nicole followed her mother inside and a policewoman, speaking into a microphone from behind a thick window, asked if she could help.

"Officer Baldwin said I should fill out a report on a house break-in."

The policewoman slid a paper under the glass and Nicole's mother sat down at a desk to fill it out. When she was finished, she asked Nicole for Alice's number and then went into a phone booth. A few minutes later, just as her mother was getting off the phone, Nicole looked out the window and saw her father hurrying into the station.

"Are you alright?" he said, sounding worried. "John told me what happened."

"We're fine. We were a little frightened before, though, weren't we, honey?"

"Dad," Nicole pleaded, "the police are going to arrest Dolores. We've got to help her."

"Let's let the police do what they have to do to get this cleared up. Nobody wants to hurt Dolores."

"She's not a burglar, Dad."

"We have to find someplace to stay," her mother said. "We are *not* staying in that house. I just called Alice's mother and Nicole can stay there tonight. John recommended a nice inn here in town."

"*Alice's*? house," Nicole interrupted. "I thought we were

staying at our house?"

"Not tonight," her father said. "Why don't you take Nicole over to Alice's and then get us a room. I'll go up to the house and get some clothes."

"Okay," Nicole's mother said. "I'll meet you at the inn. It's at Atlantic and Third."

Nicole's father turned to his daughter. "I'm really sorry about all of this. But we're going to get it all cleared up. I promise."

"Can't we stay at *our* house tonight?" Nicole pleaded. "Dolores isn't going to hurt anybody."

"I don't think staying at our house is a good idea, Sweetheart. I really don't know what Dolores might do."

"I know she didn't hurt me when she had the chance," Nicole snapped. "Twice."

"We don't have time to discuss this right now, Nicole." He pulled on his gloves and started toward the door.

Nicole stepped in front of her father. She felt her legs shaking. "Dad. This is *real* important. Alice and I might be able to *help* Dolores but we have to stay at our house tonight. *Please*."

For several seconds, he didn't answer. Father and daughter looked straight into each other's eyes, neither one giving way. Finally, Nicole's father took a deep breath. "No, I'm afraid that's out of the question." He stepped past her and pushed the door open. "I'll see you tomorrow. Say 'hello' to Alice and her parents for me."

"Be careful at the house," Nicole's mother said.

Nicole felt the cold air as her father went outside. The falling snow swirled around him.

CHAPTER THIRTY-SIX

"Ready to go?"

Nicole nodded and pulled her hat on.

"Alice's mom said to turn left off Granite onto Bayview," Nicole's mother said as she started the car. "We follow that past the cannery and take the third right after we cross the railroad tracks. Then it's two blocks to North Street. Alice lives in a white house on the corner. It's number five, across from the dock."

After traveling just a few blocks, and despite being only a short distance from Chamberlain, Nicole was in a part of Elk River she hadn't seen before. Abandoned warehouses lined both sides of a street paved with bumpy stones. A weedy railroad track ran up the middle. The area near the cannery was dark. Almost all the streetlights were broken. Under one that did work, the falling snow appeared in an inverted funnel of light. Across the street from the cannery, there were more dark structures, some with their windows boarded up. In one building, it looked like there had been a fire. Above the broken windows, the bricks were scorched black.

Through the swirling snow, the car's headlights startled some stray dogs sniffing at an overturned garbage can. Otherwise, the street was deserted. Nicole and her mother passed a broken-down, snow-covered old truck, bounced over some railroad tracks and drove for three more blocks before turning right. Here the streets were lined with small wooden houses, some with Christmas decorations in the windows.

Nicole's mother parked in front of a small grocery store. Across the street, in the window of a place with a neon sign that said "Bar," the lights on a little Christmas tree blinked on and off. Alice's house was around the corner. Nicole and her mother crossed the small yard and stepped up to the porch of number five. Nicole rang the doorbell, then turned around. Alice's house wasn't far from the Elk River bridge, its blackened beams arching high above the water. She saw the reflections of headlights as a truck crossed the bridge. At the dock across the street, lobstermen's and fishermen's boats rocked gently in the water. Out to sea, the Puffin Island light swung in and out of view.

Nicole turned around to see Alice's mother opening the door.

"Come in," she said, wiping her hands on a dishtowel. "Is the snow getting deep?"

"It's not too bad yet," Nicole's mother said as the visitors stepped inside. The living room was small, the walls lined with bookshelves. "But they say we're in for a storm."

"I don't think Alice knows you're here yet," Alice's mother said to Nicole. "Why don't you surprise her? Her room is upstairs. It says 'Keep out' on the door."

Nicole's mother gave her daughter a little hug. "We'll see you in the morning. Have fun with Alice."

"I'll be fine, Mom."

Walking up the steps to Alice's room, Nicole heard her mother say, "Thank you so much, Anne, I don't know what we're going to do but we just *can't* stay in that house tonight."

Nicole stopped at the top of the stairs.

"I don't blame you," Alice's mother said. "You and Paul can stay here too. Louis just went to the store for some groceries. We're just having stew but there'd be plenty for everyone."

"That's very kind of you, but I think it might be better for us to stay at the inn. We'll probably have to talk to the police again and I'm hoping Nicole doesn't have to be involved. This whole thing is so upsetting."

"I can imagine. But don't worry about Nicole. She can stay here as long as you like. We're glad to have her."

"Thanks again, Anne. I guess I'd better get going. If you need to reach us, the place where we're staying is at Atlantic and Third. I don't know the name."

"It's called the Ocean View. It looks very nice. We'll find the number if we need it. But don't worry. We'll be fine. And if you need *us*, don't be afraid to call."

"Thank you again," Nicole's mother said, opening the door.

"We're happy to help, Mary. We'll see you tomorrow."

Nicole found the door with the "Keep out" sign. She knocked but there was no answer. She knocked again, louder. Still no answer. Nicole opened the door and stuck her head in. It was dark. Alice had her back to the door. She had headphones on and was looking out the front window. Alice finally turned around when she noticed the light from the hall.

"Oh, hi," she said, pulling her headphones off. "I didn't know you were here."

"Here I am."

"I was just thinking about tomorrow morning."

Nicole closed the door. While her eyes adjusted to the darkness, she took off her coat and laid it on the bed. "What's the use?"

"Well, we got our sleepover," Alice chuckled. "We're just in the wrong house."

Nicole joined her friend at the window. Except for a distant flash when the lighthouse beacon swept past, it was hard to see anything through the snow and blackness outside.

"I don't know about that," Nicole said. "I wish I could move in here permanently."

"What's the matter?"

"They make me so mad. Him especially."

"Who? Your dad?"

"After all that's happened. After all those times when they wouldn't believe me. Like the piano music or the writing on the mirror or the light in the tower. Then, after Dolores was there for me *twice, and they know it*, I tell them that we might be able to *help* her if we can stay at our house tonight. But then he's like 'No, that's out of the question. Let the police handle it.' Even though that means they're probably going to arrest her and put her in jail. That's *really* going to help."

"Nicole?" Alice said softly.

"He's always telling me something: 'don't be satisfied with an A minus.' 'Don't be a quitter.' 'Don't back down in soccer.' 'Make some new friends.' 'Don't be such a follower.' Then, when I actually have a chance to help somebody it's like 'you're only thirteen.'"

"Nicole?"

"The way they treat me is so totally not fair."

"Nicole?"

"What?"

Alice took her time answering. "We can still get there if we really want to."

"I don't see how," Nicole answered. "Our parents aren't going to take us, that's for sure. Not after what happened today and definitely not at seven in the morning. And I hope you're not going to say we can walk. There's like a blizzard out there. The roads will probably be buried."

"My dad says the storm should pass a couple of hours past midnight," Alice said, once again staring into the darkness, "but we wouldn't be going on the roads."

"Then how *are* we going to get there? Have you noticed that there's about five miles of ocean between here and my house?"

Alice turned toward her friend. "It's less than three miles, and that's exactly how we *could* get there. By water."

Nicole stared at her friend's silhouette. "You've *got* to be kidding."

"Nope. That's the only way. For the reasons you just said."

"I don't get it."

"My dad doesn't keep his fishing boat at the dock," Alice explained. "He keeps it moored out in the water and he gets to it in his skiff. The skiff has a motor and I can run it. My dad's not going out tomorrow. If we get up early enough, and we're quiet, my parents will still be asleep."

Nicole sat on Alice's bed and shook her head. "Your parents will kill you."

"They'll be mad," Alice said, sitting down beside Nicole. "So will yours. But like you said, maybe we can help Dolores. And what if we really *do* find a treasure? I'll bet they won't be mad then."

"Do you really think we can do it?"

"I'm not saying there's no danger. There is. But I've crossed the bay plenty of times in the summer," Alice said. "With my dad, I mean. But if the weather is good, I'm sure I can do it with you, too. We'll dress warm and there are life jackets in the boat. Just in case."

"In case what?"

"In case we go into the water."

"Great," Nicole said, shaking her head. "We won't drown. We'll just freeze to death."

"We can always turn around. If the water is too rough, we'll come back."

"If we do it," Nicole said, walking over to the window

again, "what time would we have to get up?"

"About four-thirty. It'll take about half an hour to cross the bay and we'll need some time to get to the vault."

"And we have to get up the cliff somehow too."

"I know," Alice said. "I've heard other kids say that they climbed it."

"Kids *our* age? In the winter? And in the dark?"

Alice shrugged. "Like I said, I know it's not going to be easy. But maybe there's a path or something. Or maybe we *won't* be able to do it. I don't know. But I think it's worth trying."

Nicole looked out Alice's window. "Okay," she said slowly. "Let's say we do it. But *if* the weather's good, and *if* we make it across the bay, and *if* we find a way up the cliff and *if* we get into the vault in time . . ."

"We still don't really know what we're looking for."

"Right," Nicole said. "We still don't know what Taggart meant by the keystone."

Alice nodded.

"But," Nicole continued, "*if* we're in the right place at the right time and the sunlight comes through the little tunnel, maybe it'll shine on a treasure chest or something. Then, even if we don't have a key, we might still be able to open it. With a tool or something."

"It makes sense to me," Alice said. Then she laughed. "Well, sort of, anyway. But who knows what Taggart was thinking? Or what he has in store for us?"

Nicole glanced out the window again as the beacon on Puffin Island swept past. "That little eight-sided pedestal thing you found sticking up from the top of the stone. I wonder what that's all about."

Alice was silent for a moment. "It wasn't eight-sided," she said. "It was six-sided."

"You said it was shaped like a stop sign."

"Right. A stop sign has six sides."

"No it doesn't. It has eight sides."

"We ought to ask my brother. He knows all kinds of useless information like that."

The girls turned toward the window and stared into the darkness until someone banged on the door.

"Dinner's ready," a boy's voice called.

"Speak of the devil," Alice said. "Are you hungry?"

"Starving. I haven't eaten since lunch."

Alice turned the light on and opened her door. Her brother had a fist raised, ready to pound again. "We heard you the first time."

"I'm Nicole."

"You live in the Weber House?"

"I'm afraid so."

"Larry," Alice said to her brother, "how many sides does a stop sign have? Six or eight?"

"Eight. It's an octagon. Any idiot knows that."

"He just called you an idiot," Alice said to Nicole.

"*I'm* the idiot?"

Larry started down the stairs. "Your turn to set the table."

"Well, anyway," Alice said. "Even if it's *not* shaped like a stop sign, I still don't know what it means."

"Maybe it's some kind of superstitious thing. You know, hexagonal, six-sided, 666, the devil's number, something like that."

"And you people say *we're* crazy."

"Who's '*you people*'?" Nicole asked with a smile.

"*You* people," Alice said. "White people. Europeans."

"I'm not European. I'm from New Jersey."

"That's probably worse."

After dinner, the girls went into the living room and put a tape in the VCR. Alice's father made a fire and then disappeared behind his newspaper. The phone rang a few minutes later and he answered it in the kitchen.

"Hi, Paul," Nicole heard Alice's father say. "How are you folks doing?"

Nicole tried to listen. Alice picked up the remote and lowered the volume on the TV.

"Did you go up to your house?"

. . . .

"Everything seem alright?"

. . . .

"That's good. Maybe it was just kids. It's still a shame, though."

. . . .

"She's right here. They're watching a movie. Hold on."

Nicole twisted around and saw Alice's father signaling for her to come into the kitchen. "It's your dad."

"Thank you," Nicole said as she took the phone and held it up to her ear. "Hi."

"Hi," her father said. "Are you okay?"

"I'm fine. Why wouldn't I be?"

"Well, you know. With everything that's happened and all."

Nicole listened.

"Did you have dinner?" her father said.

"Yeah." She glanced at Alice's father, who was sitting at the kitchen table. "We had stew and biscuits. It was really good."

"I'm sorry if I seemed abrupt at the police station. It just didn't seem like a good time to talk. Mom was real upset."

"Me too."

"Yeah, that must have been pretty scary when you and Mom went in the house."

"That's not what I mean. I was saying that maybe Alice and I could help Dolores, since she helped me, instead of her getting arrested."

She heard her father's sigh. "Let's not talk about this now, Nicole. Maybe when all this gets straightened out, if Alice's parents say it's all right, you girls can have another sleepover at our house."

"Yeah, okay, Dad. But it might be too late by then."

"I'm sorry, Nicole. I'm just trying to do what I think is best."

Nicole waited.

"I'll see you tomorrow, okay?"

"Okay."

"Let me talk to Alice's dad, okay?"

"Okay," she sighed. "My dad wants to talk to you again, Mr. Attean."

Alice's father came to the phone. "Thanks, Nicole."

She handed him the phone and started for the living room.

"Hi," Alice's father said. And then, a few seconds later, "Don't mention it. We're glad to have her."

Nicole plopped down on the couch next to her friend. The picture on the TV screen was frozen. Alice was eavesdropping too.

"I know the feeling," Mr. Attean said. "Alice is mad at me half the time too. But until you know what's going on over there, I think you're doing the right thing."

. . . .

"Well, you don't have to worry about *that*. There's no way they could get there. We'll keep an eye on them."

. . . .

"Okay. We'll talk to you tomorrow."

. . . .

"Don't mention it. Say 'hi' to Mary."

Alice's father came back into the living room and disappeared once again behind the newspaper. The girls watched the rest of the movie without saying much. When it was over, Alice announced that she and Nicole were going upstairs and would soon be going to bed.

Alice's father looked at his watch. Her mother met them at the bottom of the stairs.

"So early?" she said, looking surprised. "I'll bring Nicole a nightgown in a few minutes. It's still in the dryer."

As Alice's father put another log on the fire, Nicole noticed a gun mounted above the fireplace mantel. He walked to the stairway and kissed Alice on her cheek. Alice returned the kiss.

"Good night, Sweetheart. And good night to you too, Nicole."

"Good night Mr. Attean," Nicole said. "Thanks for letting me stay."

"Don't mention it. Tomorrow morning we'll sleep late and then have a big breakfast. After that, we'll call your mom and dad. Okay?"

"Okay," Nicole said, feeling slightly guilty. The girls started up the stairs. Nicole stopped after a few steps. "Is this going to be a big storm, Mr. Attean? Alice told me you think it might not last all night?"

Alice's father turned and glanced out the window. "I think it'll be clear by three or four. The barometer's already rising. There could be some fog, though."

Nicole hurried to catch up with Alice. At the top of the stairs, she whispered, "Is that a real rifle?"

"It's a shotgun."

"Does your dad hunt?"

"Him? Hardly ever."

Nicole followed her friend into her bedroom and closed the door. In the light, Nicole saw that there were lots of books and some posters of women basketball players on the wall. Some clothes on the floor, too.

"Well," Alice said, "are we doing it?"

Nicole looked into her friend's dark eyes. "Yes."

"Okay," Alice said. She went to her closet, pulled out her

backpack and put it on her bed "I've already packed my map, two flashlights, extra batteries and a pair of binoculars."

"I guess you want to do it, too."

Alice chuckled. "I've got long underwear for both of us and we'll need it. Warm socks too." She held up a thermos. "I even made some hot chocolate. It'll still be warm in the morning. Plus, we've got some fry bread and two bottles of juice."

"What's fry bread?"

"Here, try a piece," Alice answered, handing her friend what looked like a crispy piece of dough. "My mom made it."

Nicole tore off a corner and took a small bite. "This is good," she said, helping herself to another piece. "It looks like you've thought of everything." She sat on the bed. "Are you nervous?"

Alice put the backpack next to her dresser. "Yes. Are you?"

"Yeah. In fact, I'm kind of scared. Are you *sure* you want to do it?"

"If you do," Alice said slowly. "*Do* you?"

Nicole took another look out the window and then turned to face her friend. "Yes. Let's do it. We'll show everybody."

There was a knock at the door. It was Alice's mother with a folded nightgown. She handed it to Nicole. It was still warm.

"Good night, girls," she said. "Sleep tight." She kissed Alice and pulled the door shut.

The girls changed, climbed into Alice's bed and pulled up the covers.

"Good night, Nicole," Alice said. "See you in a few hours."

"Good night, Alice."

Lying on her back, Alice set the alarm on her watch. Then she turned out the light and rolled over onto her side. In a few minutes Nicole knew that her friend was asleep and turned the other way. Through the window she could see the light from Puffin Island sweeping past every ten seconds or so. As it came around, it reflected for an instant off a thick icicle that hung outside.

Once again, Nicole thought about all that had happened since arriving in Elk River: the piano, the mirror, the dog, the old woman, the letters, the woods, the cabin, the grave, the tunnels and the vault.

The beacon from Puffin Island swung around. Nicole noticed that, as the light hit the icicle, there was a glimmer of color.

She thought of Dolores and her father's plea to forget about looking for a treasure. She thought of the message in the vault and remembered once again that they still didn't have the key.

The light struck the icicle once more, igniting instantaneous sparks of purple, blue, green, yellow, orange and red. Nicole felt her pulse quicken. She was wide awake.

"*Violet to red.*"

She sat up. *"I'll shatter the first light,"* Nicole whispered. The beacon swept past once more and the colors looked like fireworks. Smiling, she fell back onto the bed. It was a long time until she closed her eyes. But before Nicole finally nodded off, she whispered to her sleeping friend: "I know what the keystone is."

CHAPTER THIRTY-SEVEN

DECEMBER 21

Nicole peered into a long black tunnel, a pinpoint of light barely visible in the distance. She was afraid. A voice said, "Do you dare?"

An old woman smiled and Nicole struggled to understand. "What should I do?"

"You should wake up. It's four-thirty."

Alice was holding a tiny flashlight.

Nicole tried to focus in a dark room. "I was dreaming." She sat up and rubbed her eyes.

"Shhh," Alice whispered. "We have to be very quiet."

Nicole swung her feet onto the icy wooden floor. Alice reached for a suit of long underwear and slowly pulled the pants on. Nicole did likewise. As she looked out the window, the Puffin Island light swept past and, for an instant, an icicle glimmered. "Alice, I know what the keystone is," Nicole whispered after the beacon swung around again.

Alice's head popped out of the thermal shirt she was wriggling into. "You do?"

Nicole nodded. "We have to go into the house, my house, to get it. But I know exactly where it is."

The radiator clanked and startled the girls. They listened for sounds from Alice's parents' room. There were none.

"We better talk outside," Alice said in a hushed voice.

The girls finished dressing. Alice picked up her backpack and a bigger light, switched it on and led the way out of the room, an illuminated circle showing the way. They crept past a closed bedroom door and started down the stairs. When they were halfway, the door opened. Nicole froze. Alice pointed the light.

It was Larry. In pajamas. He held up his hand to shield his eyes.

"Go back to bed," Alice hissed.

"Where are you going?"

"Don't worry about it. Just mind your own business and go back to bed."

"I bet Mom and Dad don't know you're going out." He had a big smile on his face.

"Will you please be quiet, Larry?"

Alice's brother held his hand out with his palm upward. Nicole heard her friend sigh. "What do you want?"

Larry held his hand up, his fingers spread apart.

"All right, you little crook. Five bucks. Now go back to bed."

Larry smiled again. He stepped back and closed the door.

The girls waited. Hearing nothing, they continued down the stairs. Silently, they put on their shoes, boots, coats and hats. Alice took a look at Nicole's beret and frowned. She pulled a scarf and a heavy woolen cap off a coat rack and handed them to her friend. Nicole put on her gloves and held them up for inspection. Alice frowned again. She opened a closet door and rummaged in a box on the floor. She came up with a pair of heavy, lined, leather gloves. Then Alice pulled a similar pair out of her own coat pockets. With a final look upstairs, Alice picked up the backpack, opened the door and the girls were outside.

The cold air stung. Following Alice's light, Nicole stepped off the porch and the fresh snow, maybe six inches deep, crunched beneath their feet. The sky was clear. An almost full moon and thousands of stars shone above them. *I never saw a sky like this in New Jersey.*

They crossed the street and, with muffled footsteps, stepped onto the dock. The snow on top of the round, dark pilings reminded Nicole of baker's hats. Two seagulls lumbered into the air.

"The skiff's down at the end."

A moment later Alice pulled off her gloves and dropped them. She handed the flashlight to Nicole, put her backpack on the dock and scrambled down a battered ladder. Hanging on with one hand, with the other she yanked a canvas cover halfway off a small boat. Fresh snow flew into the air, fell into the water and disappeared. Alice climbed into the boat, seeming unconcerned as it rocked back and forth. "Hand me my gloves, the backpack and the light. Then untie that line, that rope, up there and climb in."

Nicole handed Alice her gloves, backpack and flashlight and fumbled with the frozen rope that was tied around one of the pilings. She finally stuffed her gloves into her pockets and worked the rope loose with her bare hands. By the time it was free, her fingers were numb. Nicole tossed the rope to Alice and then climbed carefully down the ladder while her friend held the boat steady. She put her gloves back on.

"Take a seat in the back," Alice said, as she sat down in the middle of the boat facing Nicole. "I'll row out a little way before I start the motor. Use the light to see if we're about to bump into anything."

Nicole sat down, took Alice's light and looked into the backpack. She pulled out the thermos. "Want some hot chocolate?"

Alice had the oars in place and started to row. "Sure. Why don't you pour a cup and we'll share it?"

The skiff began to glide through the black water as Nicole unscrewed the top of the thermos. The steaming cocoa felt good. She held the cup out for Alice, who stopped pulling on the oars to take a sip and then handed the cup back. Nicole looked over her friend's shoulder to make sure the way was clear.

"The sky is really beautiful. All those stars."

Alice resumed rowing. "Well, we might have something to worry about," she said, motioning toward the closed end of the bay and the mountains looming above. "Fog."

Nicole looked toward the mountains. Even in the darkness to the west, it was possible to see something ghostly advancing toward the water. One minute Nicole could see lights on the Elk River Bridge, and the next minute, they were fading.

"If it would just stay clear, I'm sure we could find our way to the beach below the crow's nest," Alice said. "But if that fog keeps coming…" She twisted around and looked out over the front of the boat. "What the…" Alice turned back toward Nicole and reached into her backpack. She pulled out the binoculars, twisted around again, and raised the glasses to her eyes.

"What is it?" Nicole said.

"I don't believe it, but I swear I can see a light on top of the tower."

"The tower in front of my house?"

"See for yourself."

Nicole took the binoculars from her friend. It took a few seconds to find the tower but a white light was definitely shining from the top. "It's like somebody is trying to show us the way."

"It might not help us for long," Alice said. "If the fog keeps coming, we could get lost, light or no light." She shook her head. "When the radio said the snowstorm would blow over

by morning, I thought that meant it would be clear. I should have brought a compass."

Nicole looked to her left. The fog had reached the water and was starting to engulf the boats. One by one, they disappeared. She glanced around the skiff. "Maybe there's one here someplace."

"No. My dad takes everything in at night."

"Wait a minute," Nicole said, "I *did* bring a compass." She reached into her coat pocket and pulled out a round, shiny object. "From Mr. Clovewood, remember?"

"Great!" Alice said. "Take a sighting on the tower."

"Maybe you should do it."

"I think I better keep rowing."

"Okay," Nicole said, "Tell me what to do."

"Hold the compass flat in your hand."

"Okay."

"Now rotate the compass around until the needle is right over the "N.""

Nicole pulled her gloves off. Holding the flashlight in one hand, she manipulated the compass with the other. "Got it."

"Good," Alice said, "Keep the needle on the 'N' and try to see what number on the compass lines up with the light on the tower."

Alice kept rowing. The skiff rolled gently from side to side. "Can't you keep this thing steady?" Nicole said, as she tried to read the number on the compass corresponding to the tower's position.

"This *is* steady. And the swells are going to get bigger as we get farther out."

"All right," Nicole said, "I think I got it. The tower is halfway between 300 and 330 on the compass."

"Three-fifteen. That's where we want to keep the front of the skiff. Then we'll be headed straight for the tower even if we can't see it."

"Okay," Nicole said. "Right now, we're aimed at about 290 on the compass. We need to go a little bit to the right."

"To starboard."

"Oh yeah, 'starboard.'"

"Let's change seats," Alice said. "I'm going to start the motor. You can sit here and be the navigator and the lookout at the same time."

"I guess you're the captain?"

"I'll try not to be too bossy."

The girls moved carefully, Alice to the back of the skiff; Nicole to the middle seat. Then Alice fiddled with something on the engine and yanked a handle on a rope a few times. The motor sputtered and came to life and the skiff began to move. Nicole heard the water slapping against the front. As Alice predicted, the swells got bigger. Now, in addition to the side-to-side rocking, the boat was pitching from front to back. Nicole looked toward the open end of the bay. The sky was still dark but, on the horizon, there was a faint pink light. Alice followed Nicole's gaze toward the east.

"Red sky," she chuckled. "You know what that means?"

"The sun is coming up?"

"It's an old saying. 'Red sky at night, sailor's delight; red sky in morning, sailors take warning.'"

"Great," Nicole said with a frown. She twisted around to take another look at the tower but it had vanished in the fog. The front of the skiff, however, was almost perfectly lined up with 315 on the compass.

"Full speed ahead, Captain," Nicole said, turning back to face her friend.

"This is full speed."

But the fog was soon upon them too, and except for a cold breeze and the rocking, there was hardly any sensation of movement. There was simply nothing to see.

"We'd really be in trouble without that compass," Alice

said. "Too far to the west and we'd be on the rocks to the left of the beach. Too far to the east and we'd be headed for open water."

"I think I'll turn around and be a full-time navigator," Nicole said, swinging around in her seat. "I'm not ready to visit Europe yet."

"Good idea."

Engulfed by the eerie white cloud, the skiff plowed ahead, its passengers mainly silent. Aside from the water and the motor, the sounds were of unseen gulls and, in the distance, a foghorn. At one point, a dark shape loomed nearby. Nicole swung her flashlight to the right and saw something black. It was a yacht, its stern facing the girls. Nicole aimed her light and saw gold letters:

Corsair
Elk River, Maine

It faded in the fog.

A few minutes later, Nicole heard a sound like a cowbell and a moment after that, she saw something red appear in the mist, rocking with the swells. It startled her and she turned to Alice.

"Channel marker. It means we're halfway there. We'll be getting even bigger swells soon, coming straight off the ocean. Bigger waves at the beach, too."

Nicole focused on the compass, occasionally turning toward her friend to say "steer to the left" or "more to the right."

"Port," Alice would say, shaking her head. "Starboard."

The skiff stayed on course even as it rose and fell on the larger swells. Squinting into the fog, Nicole wondered how long it would be before they saw another sign of daylight.

"It's kind of funny that the sunrise is so important to us

right now," Alice said.

Nicole turned and saw that her friend was also looking at the sky. "What do you mean?"

"The Abenakis are known as the people of the dawn."

The girls' eyes met. Alice smiled and glanced at the sky. "What time is it?"

"Five after five."

"We should be there soon."

Nicole peered into the fog and saw nothing. She glanced at the compass and lined up the front of the skiff with the dial.

"315 degrees," Nicole shouted over her shoulder. "Right on course."

"As soon as you see any land, let me know," Alice shouted back, "and I'll kill the motor."

Nicole heard the tension in her friend's voice and twisted around on her seat.

"Let's hope the waves aren't too bad," Alice said. "If one catches us the wrong way, we could go into the water."

Nicole shuddered. She was already cold. The motor slowed and she shined her light straight ahead. Nothing but fog. But there was a new sound: waves breaking on the shore. There were rocks ahead. And close.

"I see rocks, Alice," Nicole yelled. "Big ones!" They were huge. Hulking and jagged with white water hissing around them.

The motor stopped. "Move up to the front, Nicole. I'm going to start rowing again."

Nicole did as she was told. She twisted around and saw Alice, already facing backward in the skiff's middle seat, putting the oars into their locks. "Look for the beach," Alice said. "If we hit the rocks, we're in big trouble."

Nicole felt her heart pounding. She peered ahead but the fog shrouded the shore. The waves' roar was deafening. With both hands, Nicole gripped the top edges of the skiff and leaned forward, willing the beach to appear.

"There it is, Alice!" Nicole shouted over her shoulder. "I see the beach. It's just to the right or port or whatever you call it!"

"Okay," Alice answered crisply. "The waves aren't too bad. We'll ride the next one in. There's a little anchor right in front of you under the canvas. As soon as we hit land, throw it onto the beach and jump out."

"What about you?" She yanked at the canvas and spotted the anchor.

"I'll be right behind you."

The front of the skiff dipped. Stinging water splashed over Nicole and she tasted salt.

"Ready?" Alice shouted.

"Ready," Nicole yelled back, tightening her grip.

"Here we go!"

Another wave, just starting to crest, lifted the skiff. Nicole looked back. Alice pulled hard on the oars and the boat shot forward. More cold spray. The rocks on either side were gigantic and almost close enough to touch. The beach was coming up fast. With a thunderous crash, the wave broke on both sides of the skiff and a moment later Nicole felt a thump as the bottom of the boat hit sand, nearly pitching her into the water. Regaining her balance, she swung the anchor as far as she could.

"Jump!" Alice yelled as she pulled the oars inside the skiff. "Before the next wave hits!"

Nicole jumped and landed on the black sand. Foamy water splashed over her feet as it rushed down the beach, back to the sea. Alice scrambled to the front of the skiff and jumped. A moment later, another wave hit and the skiff lurched sideways.

"We've got to drag it farther up the beach, past the high-water mark," Alice yelled over the roar of the surf. "The tide is rising. If we leave it where it is, the waves will wreck it."

The girls dragged and pushed the boat until it was past a line of seaweed and driftwood.

"It ought to be okay here," Alice said, slumping against the side of the skiff.

"You were amazing. It's a good thing that you were the captain."

Alice smiled. "The navigator did a good job too. And remind me to thank Mr. Clovewood the next time we're in the library."

Nicole ran her hand over her sleeve and looked at her glove. It glistened with water. "Are you wet?"

"Just on the outside. What time is it?"

Nicole glanced at her watch. "It's about a quarter after five. What time did you say the sun comes up?"

"Six fifty-six."

"Okay," Nicole said. "We've got an hour and three quarters to climb the cliff, go in the house, get the keystone, and then get back down to the vault. Think we can do it?"

"I guess so. Anyway, we have to. How about some more hot chocolate first?"

Nicole went back to the skiff and got the backpack. She pulled out the other light and the thermos and then tossed the backpack toward Alice. It landed on a rock and Nicole heard glass breaking. "Uh-oh."

Alice opened the backpack and shined her light inside. Nicole looked too. "I'm sorry, Alice," she said. "I forgot about the bottles."

"It was just juice. Don't worry about it."

They passed the steaming cup of hot chocolate back and forth while gazing up at the dark cliff looming above them.

"We'll use our lights," Nicole said. "And we'll be careful." She switched her flashlight on and shined it at Alice. "And we'll go slow, okay."

Alice stood up and exhaled a big cloud into the light. "Ready?"

"Ready," Nicole said.

They walked to the base of the cliff and shined their lights upward.

"How far do you think it is to the top?" Alice said.

"I don't know. A hundred feet, a hundred-fifty?"

Alice pointed her light toward a jumble of boulders at the base of the cliff. "Why don't we start there? It looks like we could climb them pretty easily."

"Okay," Nicole agreed. "Let's go."

With their lights flashing crazily against the cliff, they climbed from rock to rock and soon were twenty feet above the beach.

"Now what?" Alice asked.

"It gets steeper," Nicole said, following her flashlight's beam upward. She pointed it to the right. "But it looks like there might be a trail."

"I think you're right," Alice agreed. "Let's try it."

The narrow, snow-covered path was steep and slippery. With each step, the girls checked their footing and gripped every available rock or branch.

"I think we're halfway there," Nicole said, breathing hard, after a few more minutes of climbing.

"I stopped looking down," Alice said. "Did I mention that I'm not too crazy about heights?"

Nicole looked. They were no longer over the beach. Below them now were jagged rocks and pounding surf. "You're doing fine. Just keep your eyes on the path."

The path, however, soon came to an end. Nicole shined her light just ahead of her friend. Alice inched forward, staying as close as possible to the face of the cliff. When they were side by side, Nicole switched off her light and saw that they had climbed above the fog. Most of the horizon was now orange.

But in one spot, it was almost golden. *East.* Above them, the sky again showed stars in a canopy of purple and black. Across the bay, a few lights from Elk River flickered over the ghostly whiteness. More than fifty feet below, the waves pounded the base of the cliff. *So beautiful. So dangerous.*

"Now what?" Alice said. "It looks like the path ends here."

Nicole turned away from the water, switched on her flashlight and looked up. "It gets a little steeper, but the first part doesn't look too hard."

"I'm glad *you* think so," Alice said, shaking her head. "And if you think this *next* part doesn't look too hard, what about the last part?"

"I think it'll be okay, but one thing at a time. There are plenty of good steps and hand holds and we can rest when we get to that ledge that's sticking out." She pointed with the flashlight. "By the time we're there, we'll only have about 10 feet to go to get to the crow's nest."

"Maybe some crows will help us," Alice muttered.

Nicole stayed close to Alice as they worked their way upward. The cliff was steep but still not vertical. In a few minutes, the girls were on the ledge. "That's the crow's nest," she said, pointing "Just a few feet to go."

Alice shined her light where Nicole was looking. It was straight up. "I can't do it," she said. "I just can't. You go ahead. I'll climb back down to the beach."

"You *can* do it, Alice. I know you can. Besides, it's probably more dangerous to climb back down and I definitely can't go on by myself."

Alice was shivering. She looked at the ledge ten feet above them and rested her forehead against the cold stone.

Nicole squeezed past Alice and examined the rock face they would have to climb. She reached into a small opening and scooped out some snow. She reached up a foot higher and scooped more snow out of a similar opening. She shined her light up the face of the cliff.

"Alice! Check this out. It's a stone ladder, just like the one that goes up to the yard from the crow's nest. There's a little ridge on top of the stone and you can get a good grip. We can do it!"

Alice felt the top of the first step. "Maybe," she said. "*Maybe* we can." She looked down at the beach. Nicole looked too. The skiff looked like a toy. The tide had almost reached it.

Nicole glanced at her watch. "It's about twenty to six," she said. "At least we don't need the flashlights anymore. There's enough daylight to see."

"That's good," Alice said. "'cause I'm going to need both hands." She put the flashlights into the backpack and handed it to Nicole.

"Me too," Nicole said, as she slipped her arms into the straps of the backpack. "Do you want to go first? That way I'll be underneath you just in case . . . ."

"No, you go first. I'll be all right."

"Okay," Nicole said. "See that little sapling growing out from the rocks at the top of the steps?"

Alice nodded.

"I'll get a good hold on it," Nicole said, "and I'll wait for you there. Then we'll just step sideways right into the crow's nest."

"Okay," Alice said, looking over her shoulder to the rocks and surf below. "Be careful."

Nicole climbed up the first few steps, clearing out the snow as she ascended. She counted the steps as she climbed. The last one was number fifteen. She felt for the ridge. When she gripped it, the stone wobbled, but held. Nicole reached to her right and grabbed the sapling. It felt firm.

"It's not too bad, Alice," Nicole called down to her friend. "I cleaned the snow out of the steps pretty well. Just be careful when you get to the last step. It's kind of loose."

Alice started climbing. As she got closer, Nicole could see her face was white. She looked scared but she kept going. As Alice neared the top, Nicole saw that, despite the cold, her friend's forehead was covered with sweat. Nicole watched Alice's handholds as she climbed.

"Just one more," Nicole said, extending her hand.

Alice reached into the last step and started to pull herself up. Then Nicole saw the stone move and her friend's hand came free. Alice started to fall back. She screamed.

Nicole's arm shot out. She reached for Alice's arm and got it. She clamped her hand around her friend's bare wrist and Alice did likewise, splicing the two girls together, come what may.

With her arms extended, Nicole tightened her grip on the sapling. "I've got you," she said, locked into Alice's wide eyes. "Reach over and grab the wall of the crow's nest."

With her left hand, Alice reached for the rock wall. When she had a good grip the girls released their holds on each other and Alice climbed over the wall to safety. Nicole followed a moment later and the girls embraced. Both were near tears.

"The stupid rock came loose," Alice said, looking away.

Nicole wiped her eyes. "You might have been really hurt or even . . ." She looked down at the waves breaking on the rocks far below, ". . . and it would have been my fault. You didn't want to climb the cliff and *I* talked you into doing it."

Alice brushed her cheek with her glove. "But I *wasn't* hurt," she said, looking straight into Nicole's eyes. "Thanks to you. Besides, it was *my* idea to come this way." Alice smiled at her friend. "*Nothing's* going to stop us now. Not after all we've been through."

Nicole breathed deeply.

"We better get going," Alice said. "What time is it, anyway?"

Nicole looked at her watch. "About ten of six. Just over an

hour to sunrise."

"Okay. Let's go."

Nicole started to climb the steps up to the yard.

"Uh, Nicole . . ."

"What?"

"What if somebody is up there? Like somebody with a dog?"

Nicole stepped back down. The girls looked at each other. "I've got an idea."

"I'm listening."

"No one followed us up this cliff, that's for sure."

Alice nodded.

"As soon as we climb up to the yard, we'll look for footprints. This is fresh snow. If anyone has come near the house, we'll see their tracks and we won't go in."

"And we'll just forget about getting the keystone?"

"I think it would be too dangerous," Nicole answered. "Don't you?"

"Yes."

Nicole climbed up two steps so that she could see the yard.

"See any footprints?"

"Nope. All clear. You ready?"

"Ready."

Nicole scrambled up the stone ladder and scanned the yard and house as her friend joined her. "Let's go," Alice said.

The girls hurried through the snow toward the house. They arrived at the front porch without seeing any tracks.

"Maybe we should check all around the house," Alice whispered. "Somebody could have gone in some other way."

"Good idea."

They circled the house as quickly as the snow allowed but saw no footprints other than their own.

"Is the house locked?" Alice asked when they stood before the front door.

"Should be," Nicole said, stooping down "but there's a key under the mat."

"Great hiding place."

Nicole stood up with the key and slid it into the lock. After a little fumbling, the key turned and Nicole pushed the door open. They stepped into the darkened house and pulled off their gloves, hats and scarves.

"Nice and warm in here," Alice said.

"We've got to go down to the basement."

"Is that where the keystone is?"

"No, that's where a ladder is and we'll need our flashlights." Nicole led the way through the hall, the pantry and down a few steps. They stopped at the door to the cellar.

"Are you telling me that I need to climb again in order to finally see the keystone?"

Nicole pushed the door open and turned on her flashlight. "I'll do the climbing. And you've already seen it."

They moved carefully down the stairs until they felt the solid rock floor.

"There it is," Nicole said, her light shining on the ladder that lay next to the skiff.

"What's that noise?"

Nicole heard a faint squeaking. "Mice, I think."

"As long as it's not bats." Alice shined her flashlight onto the paint cabinet in the corner. "I'm glad we don't have to go in there again."

"Me too." Nicole shined her flashlight onto her watch. "It's almost six. We better hurry."

The girls picked up the ladder, Nicole at one end, Alice at the other. They banged their way up the steps, through the pantry, and into the front hall until they were at the bottom of the front stairs.

"Now where?"

"Up," Nicole said, pointing.

Alice groaned.

"Just a few more steps. We're going to the front of the upstairs hallway."

Clunking the ladder from side to side, the girls hurried up the steps to the second floor and around the balcony to the front of the house.

Nicole pointed to the stained glass. "That," she said, pointing upward, "is where the keystone is. At least I hope so."

Alice looked. A faint glow dimly illuminated the entire glass seascape but in one spot the light sparkled with color.

"The sun," Alice said. "It's a prism."

"It's *got* to be it!"

"'*Clearly in sight* . . . .' How'd you think of it?"

"It was in your room last night. I was thinking about Taggart's poem. Then I saw the light on Puffin Island shining on an icicle outside your window. I saw colors. Then it clicked."

Alice laughed. "That's just how I planned it." Nicole laughed too. "Come on," Alice said, "let's put the ladder up."

They leaned the ladder against the wall and Nicole climbed up to the top. She ran her fingers around the edge of the crystal. "It's like, cemented in," Nicole said. "But maybe I can move it." Gripping the protruding stone as tightly as she could, she pushed, pulled and tried to wiggle it.

Alice held the ladder steady. "Be careful."

The crystal moved. Suddenly it was loose. "I've got it!" Nicole shouted. "It's free!" She slid the glass sun out of the surrounding sky and held it up for Alice to see.

"Cool."

Nicole climbed down and they examined the stone. It was six-sided and only about an inch long. "Look, there's a tiny sun carved into one of the sides. I wonder what that's about."

"Who knows? Let's wrap it up and put it in the backpack."

"Good idea."

"How much time do we have?"

Nicole glanced at her watch. "It's ten after six. We should have just enough time."

The girls hurried back down to the first floor. At the front door, they wrapped the prism in Nicole's borrowed scarf and placed it in the backpack. When their hats and gloves were back on, Nicole pulled the door open. The sky was now much brighter.

They jumped off the porch and hurried across the yard. When they reached the edge of the cliff, they stopped. Above them, the still-dark sky was showing signs of blue as a backdrop for the wisps of clouds. The horizon was a strip of orange, with one rapidly brightening spot of gold. The fog was mostly gone and the ocean was silver.

The girls looked back toward the house. Nicole noticed the snow-covered, icicle-clad figurehead hanging just below the roof. She was pointing straight at them.

"Ready?" Alice said.

Nicole took her friend's hand. "Ready," she said.

The girls jumped together.

CHAPTER THIRTY-EIGHT

They landed with a thump. The girls went straight to the tunnel entrance and pulled the vines aside. Alice put the backpack on the ground and pulled out her map and the flashlights. She handed one to Nicole. "One hundred feet to the first turn, right?"

"A hundred feet."

They climbed through the opening, switched on their lights and walked quickly down the slope. They arrived at the first turn and Nicole pointed her light at the wall. "There's the mark. We turn right."

Alice didn't hesitate. Nicole paused to take a final look at the light from the crow's nest. Fifty feet to the next turn. Glancing at the chalk mark, they went left. Another 50 feet and another left. Twenty-five feet more and a sharp turn to the right. They hurried down the rocky slope following their map and the chalk marks.

"Halfway," Alice said as they reached the next mark.

Nicole shined her light onto her map. "Right," she said. Then she pointed it at her watch. "Six thirty-three."

A left turn, 50 feet, then another left. They came to the underground stream and barely slowed down. Fifty feet further and left again. The way was nearly level here and the girls walked quickly. The tunnel forked and they bore to the right. Twenty-five feet ahead the tunnel came to a dead end and the girls stopped. Two lights focused on the same spot, an opening in the rock wall.

"Go ahead," Nicole said. "I'll hand you the backpack when you're inside."

Alice disappeared and Nicole checked her watch.

"Hand me the backpack," Alice's muffled voice said. Nicole crouched down and crawled into the opening. Alice pulled the bag forward. In a moment, the girls stood together inside the vault.

"What time is it?" Alice said.

"Almost six fifty-four. We just made it."

"Look, Nicole," Alice shouted, "the light!"

She knew where to look. A bright spot shined out of the darkness at the back of the vault. "We better hurry. I'll get the prism."

While Alice held the light, Nicole dropped to her knees, reached into the backpack and pulled out the scarf. She unwrapped the little bundle and held up the crystal. Colors flashed as Alice's light shined on the prism. Nicole stood up and saw that the spot of light was now much brighter. "You know where it goes," she said. "I'll hand it up to you."

They hurried to the stalagmite. Alice stepped up onto the stone ledge. Nicole handed the prism to her friend.

"I don't know which way it goes!"

"Does the prism match up with the six-sided pedestal?" Nicole said, trying to remain calm.

"Yeah, but the prism could stand on either end and I don't know which side is supposed to face the light. It could go twelve different ways!"

"The light's getting brighter!"

"I know! We've only got a few seconds!"

"Wait a minute," Nicole said, nearly shouting. "Do you see the little sun that's on one side?"

"Yeah, I see it!"

"Try making it face the light. Then there's only two ways!"

Alice stood the crystal on one end. The light shined on the prism but nothing else happened. "Try the other way!"

Alice flipped the prism over and stood back as the beam of sunlight illuminated the entire stone. "It's glowing!"

Nicole looked at her watch. "It's six fifty-six! The sun is up! We have to shut off our lights!"

The vault went dark except for the radiant crystal.

Nicole reached for Alice's hand and held her breath. The waves thumped outside the vault and her heart pounded just as hard inside her chest.

Something flashed across the blackness and a band of bright colors shone high on the wall.

Nicole felt her jaw drop as she stared up at the brilliant rainbow of purple, blue, green, yellow, orange and red.

Suddenly the colors faded and, in another moment, they were gone. The vault was dark again except for the dimming spot of light from outside.

"We have to look there," Alice said, turning her flashlight back on and shining it where the colors had been. "Right where that jagged rock is."

Trying to stay calm, Nicole aimed her flashlight on the rock. "I think we can get there." She took a deep breath. "It looks like a ledge runs right up to it." They scrambled to the bottom of the ledge and Nicole pointed her light up the slope. "It's easy, Alice. It's not even steep. I'll do all the work. All you have to do is shine your light."

Nicole heard her friend sigh and Alice's light moved forward.

"All right but this is the last climbing I'm doing."

The girls worked their way up the ledge until they reached

the jagged rock. Alice's light reflected off the black stone. It was about as high as their shoulders. Nicole steadied herself and grabbed the rock with both hands. "Here goes," she said as she started to alternately push and pull on the stone.

"Feel anything?"

"I think it's moving!"

"You're kidding."

"No, really. I can feel it moving."

"Let me help," Alice placed her light so it shone on the jagged rock then put her hands next to Nicole's. The girls pushed and pulled together.

"You're right, it *is* loose," Alice shouted.

"It's going to come out!"

With another good tug, the rock sagged and fell free. The girls jumped back as it fell onto the ledge and tumbled down to the floor of the vault. The crash echoed off the walls. Alice grabbed her light and pointed it into the hole. "There's something in there, Nicole, I think it's a strap!"

"If we clear away a little more dirt, I think we can pull it out."

Reaching over each other's arms, the girls clawed at the dirt until the end of a small, dark-colored chest was visible. Side by side, Nicole and Alice gripped the leather strap and pulled the chest free. Together, they lowered it to the ground.

"Let's get it down from the ledge," Alice said, "and then figure out what to do."

"It's not very heavy. Why don't you go first with the light? I think I can carry it."

A minute later, the chest was on the floor of the vault.

"I'm so excited, I can't stand it," Alice said.

"Let's try to open it!"

"Why don't you let *me* take over from here?"

Nicole felt her blood run cold. She spun around and saw another light coming toward them. She looked at Alice. There was just enough light to see the shock and fear in her eyes.

The light came closer. There was a man and next to him, another shape. A dog. A big one. The man shined the light in Nicole's face. Blinded, she tried to shield her eyes with her hand.

"I finally get to meet the great detectives," the voice said from behind the light.

The girls were too frightened to speak.

"And I must say, it's very nice to meet you, Nicole. You too, Alice."

Nicole felt a glimmer of hope. "You know our names?"

"I know all sorts of things about you. After all, I've been waiting for you for 50 years."

The man lowered his light and the girls faced a shadow. It bent down and a moment later, the cave brightened. Nicole saw that the illumination was coming from an electric lantern hidden behind rocks.

"That's better," the man said. "I thought we might need a little more light."

As Nicole's eyes adjusted, she saw that the man facing her wore dark clothes and gloves. He was old and when he turned, Nicole saw a long, purple scar on his face and neck.

In an instant, fear replaced hope. Nicole was barely able to move. She looked at the dog. It stood still as a statue and stared right into her eyes. Its ears lay back and Nicole thought she heard a low growl.

"You're here for the treasure," Alice said softly.

"Correct," the old man said with a smile. "And on behalf of my associate and myself, I'd like to say 'thank you' for finding it for us. It is no exaggeration to say that we couldn't have done it without you."

"Was it you that chased me by the cliff?" Nicole managed to say.

"Good heavens, no," the old man said. "That was my

THE WEBER HOUSE

associate. He and this animal were also watching *you,* Alice, when you discovered the stone with Dolores Weber's initials." He shook his head slightly. "I warned him about letting himself be seen but I'm afraid he *likes* to scare people. That's why he keeps this dog."

"Were you in my house yesterday?"

The old man held up his hands. "Leave mud on the floor? I would never be so careless. I will say, however, that it was fortunate, for you, Nicole, that you didn't meet him then because I'm afraid my associate also likes to *hurt* people. We would have blamed it on the old witch of course."

"Dolores?" Alice said.

"Obviously. If there were any justice in the world, she should get a share of the treasure. She made our work a lot easier. The ridiculous legends are enough to keep most people away and that crazy old woman does the rest. Sneaking into your house in the middle of the night. We should have been paying her."

The old man laughed. "But you girls didn't scare so easily. And when it was obvious that you had found Weber's letters and were following the clues, I had a feeling that you might actually end up here. So, since it was getting close to December 21, we thought we might as well see if you could do what nobody else has been able to accomplish: figure out Taggart's puzzle." He pointed to the chest. "And my trust in you is about to be rewarded."

Turning slightly, the old man grabbed one of the straps on the chest and began to drag it across the ground. "The light is better over here."

"If he gets distracted," Alice whispered, "maybe we can get away."

"Maybe if he tries to open it."

"In case you girls are thinking of running," the old man said with his back still turned, "I think the dog would be *very* unhappy." He faced the girls and snapped his fingers.

Instantly, the dog leaned forward, growling and baring fangs.

Nicole heard a noise from behind the light and the girls squinted to see. Someone else was coming into the vault. The old man didn't look up as the newcomer emerged from the shadows.

Nicole recognized him as he came into the light. "Mr. Morgan!"

"Did they find it?"

"Yes, they did. What took you so long?"

"I wanted to be sure nobody saw me."

Nicole stared at Alice in disbelief.

"How'd they do it?"

"The keystone was a prism," the old man said. "I have no idea where they got it but they put it on the stalagmite. When the sun came up, a rainbow appeared up on the wall. That's where they found this chest just a few minutes ago."

For an instant, Nicole's anger overcame her fear. "*You pretended to be my friend!*"

Mr. Morgan turned slightly and glanced at the girls. He looked annoyed. "What are you going to do with Nancy Drew and Pocahontas?"

"What am *I* going to do with them?" the old man said. "Suddenly they're *my* problem?"

"That's what I hired you for, Casey or whatever your name is," Mr. Morgan snapped back. "It's what my family has *always* used you for: to take care of problems. I warned you that if they found the treasure, you'd have to get rid of them."

Nicole saw the horror on Alice's face.

"After all, you're the *Scorpion,* aren't you?" Mr. Morgan said sarcastically. "But let me remind you, *I* am the boss here. It was *my* grandfather that told you about this treasure when you were just a thug on a boat."

THE WEBER HOUSE

"And let *me* remind *you*," the old man said, stepping toward Mr. Morgan, "that *I* am the one who did everything your family didn't have the guts to do. Let's not forget who took care of Weber and his wife on your kind, old grandfather's orders."

Mr. Morgan stepped back. "I don't want to know the details. Just do what you have to do and then disappear like always. You'll get your money."

"I better," the old man hissed.

"*Murderer!*"

It was *another* voice, weak but somehow familiar and the girls saw a shadow moving toward them. The shadow became a black silhouette as it stepped in front of the light.

"*Murderer!*" the silhouette rasped again.

"Dolores!" Nicole and Alice whispered together as they stepped toward her.

"Stay where you are!" the old man commanded. He snapped his fingers and the dog snarled.

The girls froze but Dolores continued walking slowly toward them with the growling animal watching every step. As the old woman neared the dog, she extended her hand and the beast sniffed. Dolores put her hand on the dog's head. The huge animal's ears stood up and its tail moved slightly.

Nicole and Alice looked at one another, amazed. Dolores continued walking, stopping behind the girls. She rested her hands on their shoulders.

"How did you get in here?" Mr. Morgan demanded.

The old woman coughed but otherwise remained silent.

"I guess we're not the only ones that know their way around down here," the old man said.

"I suppose you think you're going to walk out of here with this," Mr. Morgan said, putting his foot on the chest. "But you're wrong."

Dolores coughed again, more violently than before. She

stared at Mr. Morgan.

"What do you want?" he said. "Money?"

Dolores seemed to chuckle. Then her scoff turned into another cough. She spat on the ground. Her saliva was red.

"You would have avoided a lot of trouble if you got off this land when we wanted it 50 years ago," Mr. Morgan said. "Cutting off your money; all the stories about you; the fires. *You* forced us to do all that."

"Don't take all the credit," the old man said.

The old woman glared at him then turned back toward Morgan. "Murderers," she repeated hoarsely. Nicole felt Dolores squeeze her shoulder. "But no more."

"Well," the old man said, smiling, "if you're referring to your parents, I plead guilty." Then he whipped a long, thin knife from inside his coat. The blade glinted. "But my work is not quite finished."

Nicole felt a shiver run down her spine at the same time as another firm squeeze on her shoulder.

"This is such a useful tool," the old man said as he examined his knife. He glared at Dolores. "It's not only perfect for opening letters undetected," he said, slowly drawing the blade past his throat, "but it can also be used to dispose of annoying sailors."

Nicole felt Dolores' hand tighten.

"*Now* what are you going to do?" Mr. Morgan said.

"Relax, Morgan," the old man said, touching the point of his knife with his fingertip. "This old hag that you're so concerned about is actually going to help us."

"*Help*? How?"

"I can see the headline in the *Tribune* now. 'Local Girls Found Dead in Cave—Murdered by Dolores Weber.' The sad story will say that the brave little girls went looking for Elk River's legendary pirate treasure. But all they found was the crazy homeless woman who's been scaring everyone around here for years. The old woman killed the dear girls, and then took her own life by hurling herself off the cliff at the same spot that her mother perished exactly fifty years ago." The old man gestured toward the chest. "The imaginary treasure, of course, was never found. It's brilliant, don't you think?"

Mr. Morgan smiled. "It's perfect."

The old man pointed the knife at the girls. "This would be just the thing for an old witch to use. Don't you agree, Dolores?"

"I guess I can get the chest out of here," Mr. Morgan said. "You can do what you have to do without me."

"Don't you want to see what's inside?"

"Definitely." Mr. Morgan gestured toward the girls. "But I also want to get out of here before someone comes looking for them."

"Don't worry," the old man said. "We'll have this out of here in a few minutes. I just want to know what we've got here before you carry it off." He leaned toward Mr. Morgan and smiled. "It's not that I don't trust you. You being the president of a bank and all."

"Let's just see what's inside," Mr. Morgan said. He nodded toward Dolores and the girls. "Then we can each do what we have to do." He pointed at the chest. "You should be able to cut those straps with your knife."

As the men crouched over the chest, Nicole felt Dolores' breath close to her ear. "Run when I say." She coughed into her sleeve. "After the stream, go straight. Don't turn. And don't stop."

"I'll have it open in a second," the old man said.

"Hurry," Mr. Morgan said.

"What about you?" Nicole whispered over her shoulder.

Dolores coughed and squeezed Nicole's shoulder again. "Do what I say," she hissed. "Be brave."

Mr. Morgan looked up. "Hey!" he yelled over his shoulder.

"Shut up! And stop coughing. You're making me sick." He turned back to the chest.

Nicole heard Dolores stifle a cough and felt her bony hand squeeze her shoulder. "Go!"

Nicole turned and looked up at the old woman.

"*Go!*"

Stumbling at first, the girls started to run.

"Hey," Mr. Morgan shouted, "They're getting away!"

"Stop them!" the old man yelled.

Nicole was at the tunnel. Alice grabbed her backpack and was right behind her. "You go first," Nicole said. As Alice got to her knees, Nicole looked back. Mr. Morgan was running across the vault toward Dolores. As he got close to her, he drew back his fist.

"Don't hit her!" Nicole screamed.

Dolores didn't flinch. Her face was contorted, nearly unrecognizable. Her eyes blazed. "*Lucy!*" she shouted.

Nicole saw the dog look at the old woman and tilt its head. Mr. Morgan was only a few steps away from Dolores but the dog was in his path.

"*Lucifer!*" Dolores commanded.

The dog suddenly turned on Mr. Morgan and bared her fangs.

He stopped.

"God, you're helpless," the old man yelled.

Nicole saw Scorpion's knife. She looked at the old woman who had slumped back against a rock and was coughing uncontrollably. But despite her distress, Dolores gestured angrily for her to go.

Scared and confused, Nicole got to her knees and crawled into the tunnel. She heard a terrible cry. It sounded like an animal.

"Kill them!" Morgan screamed. "They know *everything!*"

"When I get them," Nicole heard the old man yell, "I'll cut

their throats!"

"Hurry!" Alice yelled from the other end of the tunnel.

Nicole emerged and got to her feet. "We've got to help Dolores!"

"We've got to *get* help!" Alice shouted. "But we've got to get away first!"

Nicole heard stones rattling in the tunnel. "He's right behind us."

Alice fumbled with her backpack. She turned the bag upside-down and shook it. The broken glass from the juice bottles tinkled onto the stones at the mouth of the tunnel. "Let's go!"

The girls started running. They hurried to the first turn, 25 feet away. As they veered left, they heard a voice behind them yelling and cursing.

"My hands!" the old man screamed.

The girls ran to the next turn, 75 feet away. Alice slowed, pointed her light at the chalk mark and made the turn. Nicole looked back and saw a beam of light come into view. It swung around and pointed in their direction.

"Let's go," Alice said. "We don't have much of a lead."

Nicole stared into the darkness of the tunnel straight ahead, which slanted downhill. She looked at her light and heaved it down the dark slope. "I hope it doesn't break." The light bounced once in the darkness and came to rest behind a rock, casting an eerie glow off the tunnel wall.

"Why'd you do *that*?"

"We don't need both of them. Maybe he'll follow my light down the wrong tunnel."

"Let's hope so," Alice said. They started running again.

When they reached the stream, Alice crossed first, then turned back to light the way for her friend. As Nicole splashed out of the cold water, Alice shut off her flashlight. "Look!"

A light appeared at the spot where Nicole had thrown her

light. It slowed down. Then it continued, straight ahead and disappeared.

"Yes!" the girls whispered together.

"The next chalk mark should be coming soon," Alice said. She was breathing hard.

"That's where Dolores said to keep going straight."

When they came to the chalk mark, the girls stopped. They were both out of breath. They looked back and, 100 feet away, a light re-appeared, shining in their direction.

"He's back on our trail," Nicole said.

"Let's go."

"We don't know where this tunnel leads."

"I think we should do what she said," Alice answered.

With just one flashlight, the girls went as quickly as they could up the steep, unfamiliar path.

Nicole slipped and fell. Alice helped her friend up. Nicole's pants were torn and her hand was bleeding. Looking back down the tunnel, she saw the light was getting closer. "Shut off your light."

The tunnel went black. "I think he crossed the stream," Nicole said. "Maybe he'll see the chalk mark and turn right."

The girls watched as the light, now only 50 feet away, came to a stop. For a moment, it reflected off the wall of the tunnel, then it swung back and started moving toward them again.

"You went the wrong way. Come back. I won't hurt you."

"What are we gonna do?" Nicole whispered. "We don't even know where we're going."

"Let's cover our light. Maybe he'll think *he* made a wrong turn."

"Okay."

Alice used her jacket to shield the light's beam as they moved forward. But, just after rounding a bend in the tunnel, she stumbled and fell. Nicole tripped over her friend and fell on top of her. In an instant, the tunnel was pitch dark. Stones rattled down the tunnel.

"I've got you now, you little punks!"

"Are you okay?" Nicole whispered.

"I hurt my ankle. I tripped over something."

Nicole got to her feet. "Can you walk?"

"I think so."

"What happened to the light?"

"It went out when I dropped it," Alice answered. "It's here someplace."

On her hands and knees, Nicole groped blindly for the light. Her hand bumped into something hard. And furry. She yanked her hand back.

"Here it is," Alice said, turning the flashlight back on. She pointed it at a large, moss-covered rock sticking up from the floor of the tunnel. "This is what I tripped on."

Both girls stared at the rock.

"It looks like a giant egg," Nicole said. "A moss-covered egg."

"Are you thinking what I'm thinking?"

"Oh, girls, where *are* you?" He was just around the bend in the tunnel.

"It's *got* to be the same one," Nicole whispered. "This is where we got scared by the bats. This tunnel leads to the cellar of *my house*!"

"That's why Dolores wanted us to go this way."

"Shhh, do you hear something?"

Alice listened. "Yeah. And it's getting closer."

"Bats!"

Light reflected off the wall of the tunnel behind them. "There's no use trying to escape," the old man's voice said from just around the bend, "I'm going to get you anyway."

The squeaking got louder. Alice squatted down and shut off her flashlight. "Maybe they'll scare him."

Nicole ducked down. The flapping and squeaking was right above them. Nicole fought the urge to scream. But the bats kept going and in a few seconds had rounded the bend in the tunnel.

"Ahhh! Ahhh!" the man's voice shrieked as the beam of light disappeared. "Get off me!"

Alice's light came back on. "Let's go," she shouted. "We've got to make it to the cellar!"

Limping and bleeding, the girls hobbled ahead as quickly as they could.

"Look," Alice said as they rounded another slight bend. She pointed her flashlight fifty feet ahead. "There's a left turn up there. I think it's the one that leads to your cellar!"

"We're gonna make it!" But Nicole's excitement turned to terror when she saw light reflecting off the rocks just behind them. "He's right behind us! Run, Alice! Run!"

Ignoring their pain, they ran and tripped and stumbled and helped each other when they fell. They reached the turn and Nicole had a glimpse of a doorway twenty-five feet away. But at that same instant, she felt a painful grip at the back of her neck. Alice's flashlight clattered to the ground and went out. Screams echoed in the darkness. Nicole was yanked backward and felt herself flying through the air. She hit something hard and slumped to the ground.

Dazed, she tried to focus. Nicole was staring into a light.

"Did you think some *bats* were going to stop me?" the old man snarled. He turned and pointed his light at the ground. "Where's my knife?" he growled. "Damn bats."

Nicole sat up and saw that Alice was a few feet away. "Are you okay?"

"Yeah," Alice said weakly. "You?"

"I hit my head, but I'll be all right."

Slowly, both girls struggled to their feet. "We've got to make it to the door," Alice whispered.

THE WEBER HOUSE

"Shut up, you two! And don't try anything."

Alice showed Nicole the small stone in her hand. She pretended to rub her head. When the old man looked away for a second, Alice threw the stone and it rattled into the darkness.

The old man spun around. "Is that you, Morgan?" He aimed his light back into the tunnel. "I got them right here." He took a few steps forward. "Ah, there it is."

When the old man crouched down, the girls started to run but, without a light, they didn't get far. After just a few steps, they both were on the ground again. The old man stood over them. For a second, his light reflected off the door to the cellar. It was just ten feet away.

"I've had it with you two." He stepped forward, brandishing the knife, the light reflecting off the blade.

The girls screamed and tried to get up but they slipped and fell against one another. The old man stood over them, pointing the knife. Frantic, Nicole tried to crawl but slipped onto her stomach. Twisting around, the last thing she saw before her eyes closed was that blade. The girls screamed again.

Then . . .

. . . nothing happened.

There was no sound. The next few seconds were an eternity. Finally, Nicole opened her eyes.

She saw boots.

"Put it down," a voice said. "Real slow. I know how to use this."

Still dazed, Nicole looked up. Light was coming from the open cellar door. A big man stood at her head and he was pointing something over her. Nicole struggled to focus. It was a shotgun. It was aimed at the old man who slowly crouched down and put the knife and his light on the ground. When he stood up, he raised his hands over his head.

"Dad!" Alice yelled.

Nicole realized that she was breathing again.

"Alice!"

The voice was Alice's mother.

"Nicole!"

Her mom.

"Can you crawl over here behind us?" It was Nicole's father. He had a light and shined it from one girl to the other.

Nicole looked at Alice. Her friend's face was streaked with sweat, dirt and tears. Her hair was matted with mud. Her clothes were torn and her hands and knees were bleeding.

Through nearly crying, Alice looked at Nicole and started to laugh. "You look terrible."

Nicole smiled through her own tears. They crawled past Alice's father who remained still, his shotgun pointing at the old man's chest. The girls got to their feet and were immediately embraced by their mothers. Nicole saw that both her mother and Alice's were crying.

"Alice, Alice," her mother said, hugging her daughter tight. "Are you allright?"

"You might have been killed," Nicole's mother said as she squeezed her daughter.

"If we hadn't heard the screaming..." Alice's mother said, shaking her head and stopping in mid-sentence.

The girls wriggled free.

"How *did* you hear us?" Alice asked.

"We were in the cellar looking for you," her mother said. "We searched all over the house and then came downstairs. We heard screams coming from behind the cabinet. Your father broke it open." She hugged Alice again.

"We're fine, Mom," Alice said, prying herself free once again. "But we've got to get back to the vault. Dolores needs help!"

"*Dolores?*" Nicole's mother said.

"Mr. Morgan might kill her!" Alice interrupted.

"*Mr. Morgan?*" Nicole's father said. "*He's* down here?"

"He wants the treasure," Nicole said. "It's been him all along."

"What's the *vault*?" her mother said.

"It's where the treasure is," Alice said.

"This is all about that crazy treasure?" Nicole's father said.

"It's not crazy. We *saw* the treasure chest. It was buried down there. But that guy"—Alice pointed at the old man—"was waiting for us. Then Mr. Morgan came in and he's the boss of the whole thing. We tried to get away but . . ." Alice was out of breath.

For a long moment, no one said anything. The parents stared at the girls and then looked at each other.

"What about you?" Alice's father finally said to the old man. "What have *you* got to say about all this? And who *are* you?"

The old man glared at Alice's father. "I've got nothing to say."

"We can explain it all later," Nicole pleaded, "but we've got to help Dolores!"

"The police must be here by now," Alice's mother said.

"The police?" Alice asked.

"We saw that you were gone," her mother said, "Larry told us you went out and then we saw that the skiff was missing. We knew you must have come here so we called Nicole's parents. When we got here, we called the police."

"They're probably upstairs looking for us," Alice's father said. Then he gestured toward the old man. "I'll take him up there and hand him over. Then I'll lead the cops back down to where you're going."

"I think you should call an ambulance," Alice said. "Dolores is *real* sick."

"Okay, I will."

"What if you get lost?" Alice's mother said.

"Just turn right when this tunnel ends, Dad," Alice said,

pointing into the darkness. "Then keep going straight until you cross a stream. By that time, you'll see the chalk marks we left on the rocks. They'll lead you right to the vault. It looks like a dead end but there's an opening."

"I'll find you," Alice's father said. He handed the shotgun to his wife. "Take this, okay? Just in case." He motioned to the old man. "Let's go."

"Hurry, Dad," Alice begged. "Please."

The old man glared at Nicole and Alice as he walked past. The girls drew back.

"I'll be free as soon as we're above ground," he smirked. "I've committed no crime."

"Right," Alice's father said. "You were just showing them your knife." He put his hand on the old man's back and pushed him forward. "Get going."

"Hey! Here's my light," Alice said, stooping down. She pushed the switch. "It still works!"

Nicole's father handed his light to his daughter. "I'll use the old man's."

The girls led the way. Turning right at the first corner, they hurried ahead and the parents struggled to keep up. When they passed a chalk mark, the girls picked up the pace.

"Be careful," Alice called over her shoulder as they neared the stream, "it's slippery up here." The girls splashed through the water.

"Are we almost there?" Nicole's mother called.

"Not much further," Nicole yelled back.

They turned left. The girls were practically running. They slowed down only at the last fork and finally stopped where the tunnel seemed to end. The girls turned to wait for their parents.

"Now what?" Nicole's father asked, breathing hard.

Alice shined her light at the entrance to the tunnel that led into the vault. "You have to crawl here," she said. "Watch out for the glass."

"Paul," Nicole's mother said, "you better go first."

But Alice was already gone and Nicole was right behind her. She scrambled through the tunnel.

"Where's Dolores?" Nicole said as she got to her feet.

"There!" Alice shouted.

Nicole saw the old woman in the light the old man left behind. The girls hurried to her. She looked tiny and frail and hadn't moved, except that she had slumped to the ground and was sitting on the floor of the vault, her back against a stone wall. The old woman's eyes were closed and she was very still. The huge black dog was lying next to Dolores. Her hand, streaked with red, rested motionless on the dog's back. Nicole saw a shiny red blotch matting the fur on the dog's shoulder.

The girls knelt by Dolores' side and Nicole heard a faint growl from the dog. Coughing faintly, her red-stained fingers weakly stroked the black fur and the growling stopped.

The three parents hurried to the girls' side. Alice's mother crouched down, set the gun on the ground, and felt Dolores' wrist. "You're with friends," she said softly, wiping the old woman's forehead.

"Is she bleeding?" Nicole's father asked.

"I think that's the dog's blood," Alice's mother said, glancing at the animal. "I think the dog will be okay but . . ."

"What about Dolores?" Alice said.

Her mother hesitated. "She's very sick."

Nicole watched as her mother and Alice's spread their coats on the ground and gently moved Dolores onto them. Nicole's father used his jacket to make a pillow. Nicole and Alice took their coats off, too and lay them on her.

Alice's mother stood up. "We've got to get her to a hospital."

"What do you think is wrong?" Nicole's father asked quietly.

"She's burning up," Alice's mother whispered. "I'm no doctor but I've seen a few cases and I'd say she has pneumonia." She crouched down and felt Dolores' wrist again before looking up. "*Advanced* pneumonia."

"It's amazing that she was able to make it down here at all," Nicole's mother said. "I wonder what made her do it."

"To save *us* from Mr. Morgan," Alice said, her voice breaking.

Nicole's father scanned the vault. "Where *is* he?"

"He must have gotten out when the girls escaped," Nicole's mother said.

"Dolores will be all right, won't she?" Nicole asked softly.

Alice's mother looked at Nicole's parents before she answered. "We're going to get her to a hospital as fast as we can."

"Thank god you're here," a voice called out. "That wild animal had me trapped. It might have killed someone."

Nicole whirled around. The voice was coming from one of the caves that opened into the vault. She recognized Mr. Morgan's voice.

Alice picked up her flashlight and shined it into the mouth of the cave. Morgan's face appeared in the darkness. He held up his hands to block the light.

The dog struggled to her feet and snarled.

"See what I mean?" Mr. Morgan took a step forward but when the dog bared her teeth, he stopped.

"I was out walking early this morning." Mr. Morgan pointed toward Dolores. "I had a feeling that she might be up to something, this being the anniversary of her mother's suicide. I don't know what's wrong with her now. *I* certainly didn't touch her. When I saw the girls, I got worried, so I followed them here. As you can see, it's a good thing I did."

"That man was pointing a knife at them!" Nicole's father yelled.

"I don't know who you're talking about," Mr. Morgan said

calmly. "The girls were obviously terrified . . . of *her*. When they ran off, I tried to follow them but that animal wouldn't let me pass."

"That's a lie," Nicole shouted. "The old man is his partner!"

"We *saw* him!" Nicole's mother shouted. "He might have *killed* them!"

Mr. Morgan shrugged his shoulders. Then his eyes narrowed and he took a step forward.

Alice's mother picked up the shotgun, stood, and pointed the weapon at Mr. Morgan.

"Someone could get hurt with that," he said in a low voice, still walking and staring into Alice's mother's eyes.

She didn't blink. "That's right, so you better stay where you are."

Mr. Morgan took another step forward and Nicole stopped breathing.

Something clicked on the gun.

Mr. Morgan stopped and then backed up.

Nicole exhaled.

"Way to go, *Mom*," Alice whispered.

Voices echoed out of the tunnel. It was Alice's father, followed by two policemen. Nicole recognized Officer Baldwin.

"Bob," Mr. Morgan said, "thank god you're here." Then, stepping forward and extending his hand to Alice's father, he said, "I'm glad to see you, too, Louis."

The dog snarled again.

"There seems to be some misunderstanding," Mr. Morgan said as he stepped back without a handshake. He pointed toward Alice's mother. "Louis, perhaps you could take the gun away from your wife."

"Nah," Alice's father said. "She's a better shot."

"Put the gun down, ma'am," Officer Baldwin said, gripping the handle of his holstered pistol. "*I'll* take charge now."

Alice's mother hesitated. Then, very slowly, she lowered

the shotgun and knelt down next to Dolores. "This woman needs to get to a hospital immediately."

"There's an ambulance coming," Alice's father said. "We left flares to mark the way." He crouched next to Dolores. "How's she doing?"

Alice's mother shook her head. "Her breathing is very shallow. I don't think there's much time."

"You better go back and meet them," Officer Baldwin said to the other policeman.

The policeman nodded and started for the tunnel.

"Now, Mr. Morgan," Officer Baldwin continued, "please tell me exactly what's going on here."

"You're asking *him*?" Nicole said.

"*We'll* tell you what happened," Alice added. "That old man was going to kill us. He was going to cut our throats! And he *admitted* that he killed Dolores' parents!"

Nicole pointed at Mr. Morgan. "And when we started to run out of here, he yelled 'kill them!'"

"It's obvious that the children are hysterical," Mr. Morgan said. "Look at them. They've been through a terrible ordeal thanks to that woman. Perhaps the medical people can give them something when they get here."

"My daughter doesn't make up stories," Nicole's mother said angrily.

"And don't try to blame Lucy," Nicole said, cautiously petting the dog. "Dolores must have taken care of her. There's even a drawing of her in the cabin in the woods." She glared at Mr. Morgan. "Then *you* or your friend took her and made her vicious. It was *him*, Scorpion or Casey or whatever his name is, not Dolores, that brought Lucy down here."

"Bob," Mr. Morgan said to Officer Baldwin, "obviously, that's absurd."

"Go ahead, sir," the policeman said. "What happened?"

"This is the thanks I get," Mr. Morgan said, "I followed the girls down here out of concern for their safety."

"That's a lie!" Nicole shouted, surprising even herself. "The old man was waiting for us when Alice and I got here. Mr. Morgan came later. They wanted us to show them where the treasure was and we did."

Alice crossed the vault and stood by the old chest. "And here it is!"

"Hold on!" Officer Baldwin. "We'll find out what's in that box eventually. But right now, there are a lot of serious charges being thrown around here and I want to get to the bottom of it." He looked right at Alice and then at Nicole. "Somebody's lying and I'm going to find out who."

No one spoke. Then, one by one, everyone turned toward Dolores. With seeming great effort, she had raised her head, opened her eyes and pointed a bony finger directly at Mr. Morgan. Then her hand dropped and her head sank back onto her makeshift pillow.

"Dolores was pointing at *you*, Mr. Morgan!" Nicole cried. "*You* are the liar."

"I think Dolores is trying to say something," Alice's mother said. Nicole saw the old woman's cracked lips move slightly so she leaned down and put her ear close to Dolores' mouth.

"She said 'open it.' Do you want us to open the box, Dolores?"

The old woman nodded slightly.

"I guess that wouldn't hurt," Officer Baldwin decided.

"Quickly," Nicole's mother said.

Nicole's and Alice's fathers started toward the chest but they stopped as Alice picked it up. Two leather straps dangled from the bottom. She carried it across the vault, carefully placed it next to Dolores and Nicole and then knelt beside them.

"It looks like you almost got it open," Alice's father said to Mr. Morgan. "I thought you said your only concern was the girls' safety."

The two dads examined the chest. "I don't see any locking mechanism, do you?" Nicole's father said.

"Maybe there isn't one," Alice's father replied. "Maybe the pirate figured burying it down here was enough."

"It was," Nicole's father said, glancing at the girls, "until today."

Alice's father gripped the top of the chest. "I think it's loose."

Nicole held her breath as she saw the top of the chest swing open. Alice's father tilted the chest so everyone could see inside. Nicole squinted and saw that it was filled with something that looked like black jelly. "I think it's sailcloth," he said. "Covered in grease. Taggart must have wanted to protect whatever's inside." Alice's father reached into a corner of the chest and pulled out the slippery cloth bundle which he laid on the ground. "Who's going to open it?"

"Go ahead, Nicole," Alice said.

"We did everything else together. We should do this together too."

The girls looked at the grease-covered cloth and then up at their parents.

"It's okay, girls," Nicole's mother said. "Dolores wants you to."

Nicole felt so many things all at once she couldn't sort them out. "Ready?" she said to her friend.

"Ready," Alice said.

They felt for the edges of the cloth and slowly unwrapped it. Inside were two wooden boxes. Nicole picked up the larger one, which was curved on one side, and offered it to her friend. Alice looked at her mother.

"Go ahead, Sweetheart."

She gently laid the box down and lifted the lid. Nicole stared at the object inside. It looked like brass and was about

15 inches long. The bottom piece was curved, like part of a circle, and had numbers on it. Two slender arms rose up from the ends of the curved piece and met at a center point like spokes of a wheel. On one arm there was a small eyepiece and a mirror. On the other, there was a little telescope. There was a third arm in the middle that looked like it slid back and forth over the curved piece and pointed to the numbers. Alice lifted it carefully off its plush velvet pillow.

Nicole thought the device looked vaguely familiar.

"It's a sextant," Alice's father said. "In the eighteenth century, navigators used them to find their latitude—how far north or south they were."

"We learned about them in school." Nicole said.

"See what's in the other one," Alice said.

Nicole opened the box and saw a beautifully engraved silver object, about five inches across. It too, lay on a velvet pillow. Nicole thought it might be a jewelry case. She picked it up and lifted the cover. Bordered by lovely etchings of vines and leaves was the face of a clock. Twelve Roman numerals marking the hours surrounded by Arabic numbers representing the minutes and seconds. The three dark metal hands were motionless. Nicole looked up at Alice and her parents.

"It's just a clock."

At first, no one spoke.

"What would I want with an antique like that?" Mr. Morgan said after a few seconds. He pointed at the sextant Alice still held in her hands. "I have more accurate equipment than that on my yacht. Or in my car for that matter." Then he pointed at the silver timepiece Nicole held. "And as for that, I have something much better right here on my wrist. It's probably worth ten times as much as that overgrown pocket watch."

"May I see it, Nicole?" Alice's father said.

Carefully, she handed it to him. Everyone watched while

Alice's father examined the front of the timepiece. He reached into his pocket and took out his glasses. He put them on, then opened a cover on the back of the device and examined its underside. The only sound in the vault was the crashing surf, heard through the rock as dull thumps.

Finally, Alice's father smiled and looked at Mr. Morgan. He held the timepiece up for everyone to see. "Do you see the inscription here?" Alice's father asked, pointing to the back of the watch that shone like gold.

Nicole saw it and nodded. She noticed that her parents, Alice and her mother all nodded too. "It looks like a man's name and a date," she said.

"Is it important, Dad?" Alice asked.

Her father smiled. "Yes, Sweetheart," he said. "It's important." He paused and examined the timepiece once more, as if he were making sure of something. "And you're right, Nicole. The inscription says 'James Harrison & Son, A.D. 1759.'"

"So?" Mr. Morgan said, sounding bored.

"*So,*" Alice's father continued, "In 1759, an Englishman, a former carpenter named John Harrison, completed his fourth marine chronometer, a clock designed for sailing ships." He pointed to the timepiece. "It was just like this one. For the first time, navigators could determine their exact longitude—how far east or west they had traveled. Today, Harrison's clocks are in a museum in Greenwich, England. But there's always been a rumor that Harrison actually made *five* timepieces and that one was missing." Alice's father held the instrument up. The silver case gleamed in the light. "And here it is."

"And as for the sextant," he continued. "It was invented in 1757, just two years earlier. Taggart must have stolen both of these devices from British ships. He had the best navigational instruments in the world."

"No wonder no one could ever catch him," Nicole's father said. "It wasn't magic, it was science."

"Are you saying this stuff is valuable?" Mr. Morgan said.

Alice's father laughed. "Nicole," he said, "Your neighbor might know a lot about money but he doesn't know a real treasure when it's right in front of him. These instruments are priceless."

Nicole touched the back of one of Dolores' cold, bony hands which lay still on her lap. Then she held the timepiece close to the old woman. Alice did the same with the sextant. "Look, Dolores," Nicole said softly. "It's the treasure your father wanted you to find." Stifling a sob, she added, "and you did."

Dolores' eyes didn't open. Then Nicole felt something touch her fingers. It was Dolores. She was touching Nicole's hand, Alice's too. Old fingers brushed against young ones. Alice's eyes glistened. Nicole's cheeks were already wet.

"That homeless bum doesn't know what you're talking about," Mr. Morgan said.

"Shut up," Alice's father snapped angrily.

"None of this matters," Mr. Morgan said nonchalantly. "None of *you* matter. You're all a bunch of losers." The banker looked at the old woman lying on the ground and scoffed. "Especially *her*."

Nicole heard someone crawling through the tunnel into the vault. It was the policeman who had gone back to the house.

"The EMS crew is right behind me," he said to Officer Baldwin. "They're bringing a stretcher. And there's a reporter from the *Tribune* up there that wants to talk to you girls."

"Now everyone's going to know what kind of person you are," Nicole's mother said to Mr. Morgan.

"The *Tribune's* publisher is a friend of mine," he said, smiling. "I think he'll see things my way."

"Just get him out of here," Nicole's father said.

"If you'll come with me, Mr. Morgan," Officer Baldwin

said, "I'll take your statement."

"*Statement?*" Alice's mother demanded. "Aren't you going to arrest him?"

"Right now, it's Mr. Morgan's word against theirs. I'll be wanting *all* of you to come down to the station." He glanced at the girls. "If *anybody's* lying, they'll be in a lot of trouble."

Nicole's and Alice's parents just stared at each other.

"Are you ready, Mr. Morgan?" Officer Baldwin said.

"Yeah. Get me out of here, Bob."

Officer Baldwin pointed toward the tunnel from which two men with a stretcher had just emerged. A moment later, Mr. Morgan and both policemen were gone.

Nicole's and Alice's mothers knelt beside their daughters. Alice's mother felt Dolores' wrist. "She's getting weaker."

"Hurry," Nicole's mother called to the men with the stretcher.

"Dolores is trying to say something," Alice said.

Nicole and Alice bent close to hear Dolores. Her lips moved slightly and Nicole felt another touch, soft as a breeze, on her fingers. Then it stopped. Dolores' chest rose once more, then sank, and then was still. Her face seemed to relax.

The rescue workers hurried to Dolores' side, crowding the others away. They listened for breath and felt for a pulse, but after a few moments, they stopped. "I'm sorry," one of the men said. "She's gone."

Nicole's mother was crying. When Nicole looked to her father, he seemed to be trying to speak, but no words came. Alice buried her face in her mother's chest and sobbed. Her father stroked her hair.

Slowly, Nicole stood and felt her parents holding her.

The rescue workers put Dolores on the stretcher. Nicole gazed at the old woman one last time before she was covered. Though her face was etched from a lifetime of pain, she almost seemed to be smiling.

THE WEBER HOUSE

The long, sad procession up to the house was made in silence. Numb with exhaustion and grief, Nicole followed the lurid pink light of the policemen's flares without thinking. When she sloshed through the icy stream, she felt nothing.

When they reached the house, Nicole followed Dolores up the stairs and then outside into the daylight, standing mute as the stretcher was put into the ambulance and the doors slammed shut. Leaving a trail of swirling snow, the van drove down the driveway and disappeared into the woods.

"Good-bye, Dolores," Nicole whispered.

Nicole and Alice embraced and soon Alice and her parents were gone too.

Someone with a microphone asked Nicole something but she barely heard her own words. In a daze, she walked slowly through the snow until she stood at the edge of the cliff. Far below, the waves crashed ceaselessly onto the rocks. Out on the gray ocean, the wind snapped off the tops of the whitecaps. The light on Puffin Island swung in and out of view. Out to sea, a freighter labored in the gale. Gulls soared overhead, calling in the wind.

Nicole felt a hand on her shoulder.

"I'm sorry, Nicole," her mother said softly. "I wish I could say something else."

The sun was now high in the sky but it was little more than a bright spot behind thick gray clouds.

"She's gone, Mom," Nicole said evenly as she looked into her mother's moist eyes. "She never hurt anybody. They took her family and everything else and now she's dead."

More waves pounded the base of the cliff.

"She saved your life," Nicole's mother said softly. "And Alice's. I think that was her plan from the beginning."

Nicole turned back toward the ocean. "But we couldn't save her."

"You tried to. You girls couldn't have done more."

Nicole stared at the sea and the sky.

"What did Dolores say to you?" her mother whispered. "They were her last words."

Nicole closed her eyes, trying to shut out the pain she felt. When she finally opened them, the light, enduring, was breaking through the clouds.

"She said, 'We won.'"

ELK RIVER TRIBUNE

Homeless Woman Leaves Fortune: Dolores Weber's Will Found By Police

December 31—Elk River police announced yesterday that they had found the last will and testament of Dolores Weber.

Weber, 64, expired shortly after sunrise on December 21 in a cave underneath her former home on Cliff Road. A spokesman for the county coroner's office stated that the cause of death was pneumonia. The dead woman's scrawled, single-page will, dated and signed the day before she died, was found in what was apparently her residence—a partially-burned cabin in the woods less than a mile from her childhood home.

As reported last week in the *Tribune*, Weber's death occurred in the same place and just minutes after the discovery of two priceless navigational instruments buried more than two hundred years ago by the legendary pirate William Taggart. The devices were found by two 13-year-olds: Nicole Kelly and Alice Attean, classmates at Chamberlain Junior High School.

In the dark and dangerous cavern, the girls' encounter with the dying homeless woman must have been frightening. Fortunately, a neighbor, John Morgan III, was also at the scene. Mr. Morgan told police of his concern that Weber had been reported prowling in the vicinity recently. He stated that he followed the girls on the morning of December 21 out of fear for their safety. Another man, identified only as "Casey," was also seen underground that morning. His presence at the scene has yet to be explained. Morgan denied any association with Mr. Casey.

By the time parents and police arrived, the exhausted girls were reportedly nearly hysterical and claimed that Morgan and Casey had intended to harm them. "The girls' confusion is certainly understandable," Morgan told reporters. "We'll never know what Dolores was planning to do. I'm just glad I was there to help."

Mr. Casey was briefly questioned at the scene by police but was not detained. The girls' parents said the elderly man had threatened their children with a knife but this allegation remains unconfirmed. Mr. Casey's current whereabouts are unknown.

Although Weber died homeless and apparently penniless, she in fact leaves a considerable estate. She was the legal owner of the house and property on Cliff Road. In addition, her estate may have a claim to the treasure or at least to a reward that experts predict would be sizable.

The surprisingly lucid document states that the old residence known locally as the Weber House is to become a home for the homeless and that the grounds are to be used as a permanent shelter for injured and unwanted animals.

In a final, inexplicable gesture, Weber's will provides that "Nicole and Alice" should have "money for their education." Local attorneys say that Weber's handwritten document should stand up in court as an authentic will and testament.

Weber's last wish was to be cremated with her ashes spread at sea so that she will "rest with her family."

Elk River Project
Social Studies
Mrs. Thorn's Class
January 2

The Mystery of the Weber House
by Alice Attean and Nicole Kelly

By now, probably just about everyone has heard what happened recently at the old house on Cliff Road, the Weber House. It was even on TV and on the front page of the newspaper. But a lot of what's been written and said just isn't true. We told the police and all the reporters what happened but they didn't believe us. Maybe some people don't want to believe us. There are a couple of people though, who know exactly what happened—just as well as we do. After all, they were there with us—but they lied about it. We're writing this report so that, at least once, the truth will be told. That's the least we can do for Dolores Weber, the real hero of the story.

So much has happened since we decided to try to solve the mystery, it's hard to know where to start. But one thing is for sure: we did have a lot of luck. Six weeks ago, we didn't even know each other. Then we got to be friends. That was the first lucky thing. Neither of us could have solved the mystery alone. And it was sure lucky that our parents showed up when they did or else, we might not even be here to tell the story.

Speaking of our parents, you might be wondering if we got in any trouble for getting mixed up in something that turned out to be so dangerous. The answer is: "yes." When it was all over, after our parents said how glad they were that we were safe, that's when they really got mad. We'll probably both be grounded for about ten years.

But when it all started, we didn't know that it was going to be dangerous. We figured that if there was a treasure, any bad people who wanted it must have died a long time ago. We were wrong about that. We also thought that if we could find the treasure, maybe somehow, we could help Dolores, who really needed some help. We were wrong about that too.

Why didn't we ask somebody to help *us*?

We were afraid that if we said what we were planning to do, our parents would stop us, and people would laugh at us. We were probably right about that. We wanted to show everyone that we could do it by ourselves. That turned out to be a big mistake and, to tell the truth, our parents are right: it could have cost us our lives.

How we actually found the treasure has already been in the newspapers. In 1946, Henry Weber, who used to live in the house on Cliff Road, went to sea and sent three letters to his daughter, Dolores, who was in the eighth grade at Chamberlain. The letters contained clues that led to a cave where a real pirate named William Taggart had hidden a chest more than 225 years ago. For Henry Weber and his daughter, finding Taggart's treasure was supposed to be a game. When we read the letters, we thought we could play too.

But when Mr. Weber discovered that someone on his ship, someone very bad, had also read the letters and wanted to steal the treasure, he sent one last message. He begged Dolores to forget all about the game. Then, before he got home, Henry Weber was murdered. The killer's name was Casey and he was known as "Scorpion." Just two days after Mr. Weber's ship arrived back in the United States, the murderer struck again. "Scorpion" killed Anna Weber, the sailor's wife, and Dolores' mother who was a teacher at our school.

Dolores had lost her whole family.

Fifty years passed. Dolores was very poor. The people who could have easily helped her were the ones who hurt her the most. Her only friends were the animals she shared the woods with. She fed them and helped them when they were hurt or sick and when they died, she buried them. But people were afraid of Dolores and called her names. Some people said she was dangerous. Some people even said she was a witch.

During all this time, the treasure remained hidden. Dolores obeyed her father's last wish and never looked for it. But some people never stopped looking for the treasure and Dolores knew that at least one of them, Scorpion, would kill for it. When we read the letters and started figuring out the clues, Dolores tried to warn us but we didn't listen.

THE WEBER HOUSE

So we followed the clues into the tunnels and caves underneath the Weber House on the morning of December 21. We didn't know it then, but Dolores was watching us the whole time. She knew that other people were watching us too and that we were in danger.

We made it into a big underground cave just before sunrise. Like the newspaper said, a ray of sunlight shined into the cave onto a prism and showed where the treasure was hidden. It wasn't gold and jewels like everybody thought. It was two old instruments for navigating that we had learned about in school. The real treasure we found was knowledge.

But we weren't alone.

Scorpion was there waiting for us and, a few minutes later, someone even worse came into the vault. It was Mr. John Morgan, somebody who all along pretended to be a friend. He told Scorpion to "get rid" of us and he didn't care how Scorpion did it. That would have been the end of the story and the end of us, too but there was another person down there with us, and it was only because of her that we are alive today.

That person was Dolores Weber. She was homeless and dying but she stood in the way of the richest man in Elk River and she saved our lives. Some say that Dolores was mentally ill. Maybe she was and maybe she wasn't. But if she was sick, why? What, or who caused it?

One thing's for sure: Dolores Weber was the bravest person we ever met, and we will never forget her. We also won't forget the people who murdered her entire family. They killed Henry Weber with a knife, his wife, Anna, with a shove off the cliff and Dolores with the freezing cold. They think they can do anything they want to get what they want.

Maybe we can't prove it, but we know the truth.

On the pirate's tombstone out in the woods it says that there are worse people in the world than him.

Taggart was right.

ACKNOWLEDGMENTS

The Weber House began as a gift for our daughter, Alissa, based on vacations in Maine, treasure hunts, and many shared experiences. She was the inspiration for Nicole, and helped in countless other ways, including translating 13-year-old speak, demonstrating instant messaging, and recounting the world of middle school in the '90s.

My wife, Irma, was my first and constant editor whose reading of each iteration of the manuscript yielded countless improvements.

Among the first readers were long-time friends Charlie Brover and Denise Deagan and eventually their granddaughter, Sophie Andrews. Sophie's dad, the late Jim Andrews, an editor at *Poets and Writers* was extremely generous with knowledgeable suggestions. Likewise, my siblings, Anne Blanchard, Tim and his wife Anne Lance, Chris Lance, and his late wife Ann, all made contributions.

Lynn McGee and Jane Tarica, whom I know through teaching, read early versions of the manuscript. I incorporated many of their suggestions.

Two of my daughter's middle-school friends and soccer teammates, Zoe Greene and Rebecca Brady, kindly read the manuscript, spotted errors, and offered encouragement from the demographic I most wanted to reach: strong, young readers, especially girls.

Other early readers were our former neighbors Maria and Jonathan Glasser and Diane Michael and Larry Katz. The drawing of the mysterious house was done by another friend from the middle school soccer family, Kevin O'Connell. The remainder of the artwork was done by Abdelhak Nadif.

I belong to The Write Group in Montclair, NJ. Week after week, members listened patiently to reports on the progress (or lack thereof) of all aspects of my manuscript's never-ending story. Josie Zeman and Nancy Taini, especially, have my enduring gratitude for their chapter-by-chapter observations and suggestions.

It was by way of The Write Group that I met Lorraine Ash who offered invaluable advice. Thanks to her insightful (if painful) editing suggestions, I cut 13,000 words. It was due to Lorraine's vast knowledge of the publishing industry that I was introduced to Atmosphere Press where I met Content Manager Alex Kale; Editor Bryce Wilson; Art Director Ronaldo Alves; Book Publicity Director Cameron Finch; and Production Manager Erin Larson-Burnett. The cover design was done by Kevin Stone and Kevin O'Connell.

Serendipity played a part. Our in-law, Sue Byrne, read the manuscript and passed it on it to her sister-in-law, Cathy Nasenbeny. Cathy was teaching middle schoolers in a Chicago suburb. Through her good graces, Cathy's 7th-grade book club, The Lunch Bunch, read the story and offered comments and criticisms. This was incredibly valuable to me but is not recommended for the thin-skinned.

On April 28, 2003, *The New York Times* ran a piece in their *Writers on Writing* series headlined *Novels with the Power to Change Young Lives* by Robert Lipsyte. It said he lived in lower Manhattan. I called the *Times* and left a message asking if Mr. Lipsyte would be interested in coming to my class where we would be discussing the subsequent history of the characters in his young adult novel, *The Contender*. He was and he did. Bob kindly read my manuscript and offered advice. We've stayed in touch, off and on, over the years and I'm very grateful for his friendship.

In trying to ensure cultural sensitivity regarding one of the story's main characters, I contacted Chief Richard Menard from the Missisquoi Abenaki Nation. Without knowing me whatsoever, Chief Menard not only read the story but offered it to others in his family and the Abenaki community in Swanton, Vermont. Words cannot convey my gratitude for his, and their, generosity and support.

ABOUT ATMOSPHERE PRESS

Atmosphere Press is an independent, full-service publisher for excellent books in all genres and for all audiences. Learn more about what we do at atmospherepress.com.

We encourage you to check out some of Atmosphere's latest releases, which are available at Amazon.com and via order from your local bookstore:

Dancing with David, a novel by Siegfried Johnson

The Friendship Quilts, a novel by June Calender

My Significant Nobody, a novel by Stevie D. Parker

Nine Days, a novel by Judy Lannon

Shining New Testament: The Cloning of Jay Christ, a novel by Cliff Williamson

Shadows of Robyst, a novel by K. E. Maroudas

Home Within a Landscape, a novel by Alexey L. Kovalev

Motherhood, a novel by Siamak Vakili

Death, The Pharmacist, a novel by D. Ike Horst

Mystery of the Lost Years, a novel by Bobby J. Bixler

Bone Deep Bonds, a novel by B. G. Arnold

Terriers in the Jungle, a novel by Georja Umano

Into the Emerald Dream, a novel by Autumn Allen

His Name Was Ellis, a novel by Joseph Libonati

The Cup, a novel by D. P. Hardwick

The Empathy Academy, a novel by Dustin Grinnell

Tholocco's Wake, a novel by W. W. VanOverbeke

Dying to Live, a novel by Barbara Macpherson Reyelts

Looking for Lawson, a novel by Mark Kirby

ABOUT THE AUTHOR

For many years, Mark Lance was a labor reporter for socialist newspapers, filing highly partisan stories from picket lines across the country. *The Weber House* is his first book. He is currently working on a historical novel about the year 1877.

For decades, Lance was an autoworker in Detroit, refinery worker in Texas, and merchant seaman sailing from Great Lakes and East Coast Ports. In between were stints driving a cab in Boston, bartending in Greenwich Village, and as the world's worst waiter in various cities. He retired from industry as an electrician in New Jersey and currently teaches math in a GED program in New York City.

Made in the USA
Middletown, DE
13 November 2022